TYMP

EXOSK

Shane Stadler

A Division of New Street Communications, LLC

Wickford, RI

Published 2015

Dark Hall Press
A Division of New Street Communications, LLC
Wickford, RI

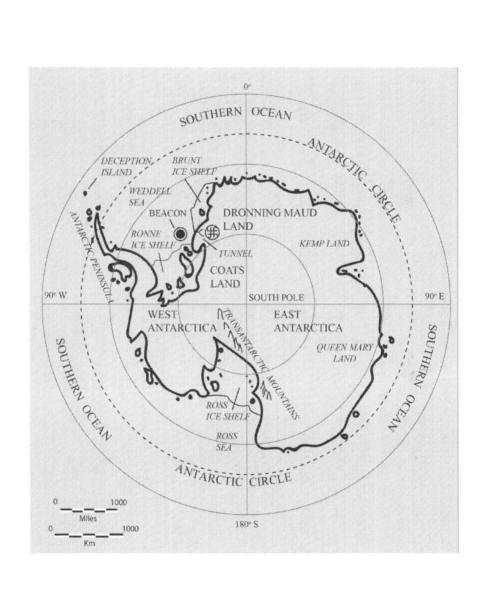

SOUTHERN OCEAN

0°

ANTARCTIC CIRCLE

DECEPTION
ISLAND

BRUNT
ICE SHELF

WEDDELL
SEA

BEACON

DRONNING MAUD
LAND

RONNE
ICE SHELF

KEMP LAND

ANTARCTIC PENINSULA

TUNNEL

COATS
LAND

90° W

SOUTH POLE

90° E

WEST
ANTARCTICA

EAST
ANTARCTICA

TRANSANTARCTIC MOUNTAINS

QUEEN MARY
LAND

SOUTHERN OCEAN

SOUTHERN OCEAN

ROSS
ICE SHELF

ROSS
SEA

ANTARCTIC CIRCLE

0   1000
        Miles

0   1000
        Km

180° S

CHAPTER I

~ 1 ~

He was going to end the world.

William Thompson didn't know where the thought came from, but he wiped it from his mind.

Black smoke from burning electronics and flesh billowed to the high ceiling of the treatment room and rolled back to the floor. Noxious soot coated his throat and mixed with the sweat on his naked body. He coughed, making him jerk violently against the tight frame of the Exoskeleton.

Sparks discharged in all directions from the blue-metallic extremities of his Exoskeleton while arcs of white-hot electricity cracked like whips as they struck the room's surfaces and the people who were scurrying about. The unfortunate ones were burned alive, from the inside out. Will was unmoved by their screams.

His concentration sharpened to a level of enlightened perception, as if viewing a maze from above while everyone else was lost below its walls. He focused on a man making his way closer to him, weaving to avoid the whirlwind of debris. He was carrying a gun in his right hand.

Barely avoiding a falling ceiling tile that might have killed him, the man dashed to the wall opposite Will, faced him, and extended his arm. An instant later, the muzzle of the gun flashed.

Time stopped. Silence.

Like a taught rope in the empty space between his body and the gun's muzzle, the trajectory of the bullet was clear – he could *see* it. It threaded through the titanium bars of his head cage, terminating just above his right eye. It was going to kill him. *The man was trying to kill him.*

Anger welled in Will's mind – his *soul* – and boiled to an uncontainable pressure. He focused on the man and released his rage with a scream.

1

White light saturated his vision, and a high-pitched ringing made his ears itch in pain. His sight returned seconds later, shrouded in darkness interrupted by intermittent flashes of white light, like lightning in a fog. Freezing air rushed through the Exoskeleton and over his body, clearing the area of smoke and powdered concrete. There was a gaping hole in the outer wall of the building, extending to the floors above and below. Sunlight illuminated the red brick wall of an adjacent building. The man and the bullet were gone.

The ceiling groaned above him, and his Exoskeleton tipped sharply to the right, barely hanging from its support on the ceiling. After a moment of awkward calm, the floor rushed toward him.

~ 2 ~
Saturday, 14 February
(6:55 a.m. Central Standard Time – Chicago, Illinois)

An orange-pink hue warmed Will's mind. The morning sun beamed on his closed eyes through the window of the hospital room. As he savored the warmth, he struggled to accept that the recurring nightmare from which he'd awakened was a perfectly accurate account of events that had occurred two weeks prior.

He'd come to realize many things since his release from the facility. The world had changed. And it wasn't just that he viewed it differently. It was different. *He* was different.

He'd seen elements of reality that had been concealed from humanity. They were facets of existence that, he believed, were purposely hidden, although he didn't know why, or by whom. His most profound discovery was that *he existed beyond the physical world.* And so did everyone else.

This knowledge had been obtained at great cost – to him and others – and the question now was what he was going to do with it, and the accompanying abilities. Thinking about it always led him to feelings of

2

predetermination, not unlike those he'd had before being incarcerated. Considering what he'd just gone though, it was absurd that his future now seemed even darker than before. He couldn't explain why – it was just a feeling.

He dozed off for a few more minutes and then opened his eyes against the brightness. Carts rattled past his closed door, and the odors of antiseptic and static-charged hospital blankets reminded him of where he'd been for the past ten days.

They had operated on his broken right femur the day he was brought to Chicago from the crumbling detention facility in Detroit. He had no recollection of the trip to Chicago, or of the first two days in the hospital. His leg still throbbed in the cast, but it was minor compared to the pain in the rest of his body. The treatments in the Red Box had taken their toll. But he was checking out today – no matter what.

He gently patted his forehead with his fingers to see if the bandages had remained intact over the night. Two days earlier, plastic surgeons had repaired holes from two bolts that had been screwed into his skull during his incarceration, one above each eye, on his forehead near the hairline. Only minor repairs had been made to two similar wounds on the back of his head. They'd told him the scars from those would be concealed when his hair grew back.

He turned his head in the direction of a soft knocking to his right.

A young woman with long, dark hair stood in the doorway with a black duffle bag slung over her shoulder. She was as much a reminder of his new freedom as was the morning sun. It was Denise Walker, one of the lawyers who had helped to free him from the Compressed Punishment facility.

"Clothes," she said, smiling.

She peeled the bag from her shoulder and set it on a chair next to the bed. A light sweat gleamed on her brow as she pulled her hair back into a ponytail and wrapped it in a green elastic band. She wasn't tall, perhaps 5' 4", but was willowy strong. She was 34, about seven years younger than Will, but looked to be in her mid-twenties.

"An entire wardrobe?" Will jibed.

Denise raised an eyebrow, walked to his side, and put her hand on his. "Ready to get out of here?"

He flinched at her touch.

She seemed to notice his reaction, but didn't remove her hand.

"You and Mr. McDougal have done enough for me already," he said.

"I told you not to worry about it," she said and walked back to the duffle and unzipped it. "And you can call him Jonathan now." She pulled out a pair of khaki shorts, a white cotton shirt, tube socks, a pair of sneakers, and blue boxer shorts. "Hope these fit."

"I think they're one-size-fits-all," he said, pointing to the underwear.

She laughed. "I meant the khakis. They're oversized to get over that cast. And so are the boxers."

"Good thing it's not cold out," he said and nodded towards the snow on the sill outside his window.

"It's already the middle of February," she said. "When your cast is removed it will be warmer, and shorts will be perfect. Besides, you'll be in a nice place on the north side. Completely self-contained – you won't have to go outside very often."

He shook his head. He knew that apartments in that suburb of Chicago were expensive. "I could've stayed with my parents."

"We've been through this," she said. "They're two hours away. We need you around for the investigation. Besides, the Foundation is paying for everything."

Headed by Denise's mentor, Jonathan McDougal, the DNA Foundation used biological evidence to overturn false convictions. Will had been fortunate that they'd chosen his case two months earlier. Other than freeing him, their investigation led to the shutdown of the entire program. It had been touted as an experiment in corrections called Compressed Punishment – a conspiracy-riddled government project that subjected inmates to horrific physical and psychological treatments. DNA Foundation investigators were now trying to uncover the hidden objectives of the program, but had so far made little progress.

"You should remain inaccessible for a while," Denise added. "For the reasons we've talked about." She raised her eyebrows, waiting for a response.

He nodded and put up his hands. "Okay." She was right. People were going to search for him. The FBI agents who had dropped in on him during his first conscious night in the hospital – just a week ago – had told him the same thing.

"Breakfast?" he asked.

"*Here?*" she responded with an expression of mild disgust.

He shook his head and laughed. "Don't like hospital food?" he asked and swung his legs off the bed and down to the tile floor. "Let's see if I can dress myself without falling down."

As Denise walked out and closed the door, he hobbled over to the chair and sorted through the clothes she'd put out for him. He examined his image in the mirror on the wall above a chest of drawers. He looked like shit: scars on his forehead, pale, unshaven, and generally unhealthy. His blue eyes stared from bruised, discolored sockets. His light brown hair was a few millimeters long now, but was patchy because of the closely shaved areas from the surgery. His body was thickly muscled and lean, but the weeks in the Red Box had aged him well beyond his 40 years.

As he dressed, he thought about what Denise and Jonathan had done for him. It was a debt that would be impossible to repay, but he'd try. He just wasn't sure there was enough time.

~ 3 ~
Wednesday, 18 February
(7:44 a.m. CST – Baton Rouge, Louisiana)

Zhichao Cho's black shoes clacked on the damp concrete as he made his way across the parking lot to the office building. The breeze that flapped his suit coat like a loose sail was brisk on his face, but not uncomfortable. He'd try to enjoy the cool spring in Baton Rouge before the Louisiana summer arrived.

He stopped at the entrance of the ten-story building and checked his reflection in the glass. Convinced he looked the part, he tugged the handle of a tall glass door and swung it open. Warm air infused with the aromas of coffee and bagels rushed through his short hair and fogged his glasses.

He strode through a short hallway, stopped in a tile-floored foyer, and squinted at a large chandelier in the central atrium as he cleaned his glasses. It was the first thing he'd remove, he thought.

Cho took a deep breath and got his mind set for the meeting. He didn't want to overplay his position, but he knew his offer beat those of his competitors, and exceeded the worth of the company's physical holdings by more than 10 percent. The physical assets were important, but not the priority. He wanted the company's priceless intellectual properties. Their value was something the current holders didn't seem to appreciate.

This morning he was meeting with the Chief Executive Officer of Syncorp, Inc. The massive biotech company had been a U.S. defense contractor until just weeks ago, when it suffered a severe security breakdown. Within days, everyone involved had scurried like rats. A week later, the company was on the market. And now Zhichao Cho, a so-called entrepreneur, would take over. He knew countries other than his beloved China used similar tactics to acquire sensitive technologies. He wondered how many were vying to collect Syncorp.

Ever since Syncorp had been exposed, its upper management distanced themselves from it and its government partners. According to Chinese intelligence, it was the most important U.S. defense contractor of them all. It developed technologies that were more sensitive than missiles, computer networks, and even nuclear weapons.

A male receptionist met Cho at a coffee kiosk in the lobby and led him through security to a top-floor conference room. The room's shape paralleled that of the oval conference table it housed, and floor-to-ceiling windows lined its outer walls. The morning sun glinted off the polished wood table and into his eyes, blinding him for an instant as he walked.

A woman he recognized as Marigold Reddington, the Syncorp

CEO, sat with three men whom he assumed to be Syncorp lawyers. His own lawyers had arrived earlier to hash out the final details of the contract.

Reddington stood and walked to him with her hand extended. "Mr. Cho," she said and seemed to force a smile.

They exchanged niceties for a minute, and then took their seats at the table with Syncorp on one side, and Cho and his two lawyers on the other.

"Your supervisory board approved our offer," Cho said, getting to business.

"Yes," Reddington said. "But I don't think we can fulfill your requirement regarding the information transfer in the time allotted."

He knew this would be a problem. The large volumes of classified electronic and physical files were stored at satellite companies scattered about the country. Their massive relocation could draw attention that Cho couldn't afford. It would arouse less suspicion if the current management handled the task. "What's a reasonable time?"

"Six weeks," Reddington replied.

"We'll give you four," Cho said, "with penalties if there are further delays."

"Agreed," Reddington said.

Cho nodded in approval. He knew Reddington could deliver them in less than three weeks, but he didn't want the conditions to threaten the deal. He couldn't have the Syncorp management bail out, but he couldn't seem too compliant, either – it would draw suspicion. It shouldn't appear to the other side that the files were important to him. After all, he was supposed to be developing a nutrition and medical technologies conglomerate – nothing to do with defense research. "Work up an amendment to our contract reflecting these new details," he said to his lawyers and then turned to Reddington. "We'll meet this afternoon to execute the deal."

After agreeing on a meeting time of 2:00 p.m., Cho excused himself and drove to a coffeehouse ten minutes away, on Bluebonnet Boulevard. He ordered a green tea, sat at a table, and gazed at the foot traffic through a window.

His official business plan for the takeover was to centralize all of the resources – including information – from Syncorp's satellite companies, and then shut them down. To the current Syncorp management, and the U.S. Government, it would look like a prudent restructuring.

His real objective was to gather all of the Syncorp files and get them to China. The physical files would be digitized at the Syncorp site, and then transferred electronically. The originals would be shipped later, or destroyed.

Syncorp's technologies could be reverse engineered – and this process was already happening in China – but technical plans would accelerate their progress. He'd make sure the company kept producing the most important parts, which was carried out at the Baton Rouge site, and delivering them to the homeland. That would persist until he ultimately burned the place to the ground.

When he had what China needed, he'd destroy all of the remaining technical and intellectual materials. This meant files, computers, and *people* instrumental to the American efforts. He'd leave the United States with nothing.

A flaw of the American government was that it disowned anything that threatened its politicians. They were trying to bury something that had been taking place since the end of World War II, when the Red Wraith project had begun. They were discarding priceless information that had been collected over a half of a century. Such stupidity didn't occur in China; the government had control of everything and wasn't afraid to keep its creations, regardless of who found out about them.

Over a year ago, when he'd learned about Red Wraith, Cho had used every contact he had to get appointed to the head of the Chinese equivalent. He recalled first hearing the details of the American project and thinking it was a ruse – science fiction. Then Chinese intelligence had informed him that the Americans had scaled up research and were already operating large-scale facilities. To this day he didn't know if he'd been trembling in fear or excitement when he'd learned that the rumors had been confirmed. Even more disturbing, or exciting, was the rumor that the

Americans had observed a successful conversion. He shuddered.

He smiled to himself as he thought about signing the final papers to take over Syncorp. Now China would have its own program. His Red Dragon project would be the only active one of its sort in the world.

His objectives were clear: copy, steal, buy, or reverse engineer everything developed in the American Red Wraith program. Remove or destroy any information that could be useful to the Americans. Finally, identify the man who was the Americans' lone conversion and either acquire him, or kill him.

~ 4 ~
Thursday, 19 February
(3:34 p.m. Eastern Standard Time – Antarctic Circle)

Tanya Beck threw the microphone and buoy over the railing of the science vessel, *Yonkers Belle.* They splashed into the dark Antarctic sea and the orange Styrofoam spheroid bobbed in the waves.

It was their final observation. They'd start the long trip back to Deception Island the next day, and fly out of Buenos Aires for the States a few days after that. Once she was back home in the northern hemisphere, it would be a semester of writing her dissertation, and then coasting through one more term that would conclude with her Ph.D. defense.

One thing she'd learned in the past three months was that she'd never again travel to Antarctica – at least not willingly. The idea of studying whales and other creatures that inhabited the frigid waters was fascinating. The practice of actually *doing* such a thing, however, was more uncomfortable and fatiguing than she'd ever imagined.

A door slammed behind her, and she turned.

Professor Amelia Gomez stood at the bridge entrance and yelled into the wind, "All clear?"

Tanya gave her a thumbs-up and walked to the stairs, careful not to lose her balance as the small boat swayed in the waves. She grasped the rails tightly and took the stairs one at a time as to not slip on the ice that had formed on the corrugated metal. She opened the door to the bridge, walked in, and fought the wind to close it behind her.

Her runny nose was greeted by warm air mixed with the ever-present smell of diesel exhaust and stale coffee. "How does anything live out there?" she said under her breath as she lowering her hood and pulled off her gloves. "Final stop, right?"

A large bearded man in a baseball cap rolled his eyes and nodded to Tanya from his position at the helm, behind and out of view of Professor Gomez. Tanya struggled not to smile.

"Yes," Gomez replied. "Just wanted to check this area on our way out. Another vessel spotted whales here. It would be nice to identify a few more before heading home."

Tanya had had about enough of her advisor's intellectual curiosity. She hadn't been warm in three months, and was sure her life had been shortened by a decade. It would take weeks to erase the taste of the brine and diesel that coated her throat day after day. They'd made some interesting discoveries about Sei whales, which were thought to be rare in Antarctic waters, and she'd accomplished enough to earn a doctoral degree in marine biology, but she wondered whether it was worth it.

"Turn on the microphones," Gomez instructed.

Tanya sat behind a small consul and flipped open a laptop that controlled the sound equipment. She booted up the system and donned a pair of headphones. Professor Gomez sat next to her and did the same.

"Volume," Gomez said and twirled her finger.

Tanya guided the cursor on the screen to a button labeled *Amplifier A*, and increased its setting from two to six.

They sat still and listened.

A strange noise filled Tanya's ears. It sounded like someone was striking a high-tension cable with a hammer, about once per second. "Are the motors off?" she asked.

Captain Tom nodded and shrugged his shoulders. "Everything's off," he said.

Gomez tilted her head. "Then what the hell is this?" She pulled off

10

the headphones and gestured to the captain to come listen.

Captain Tom walked over and slipped on the headphones. He crinkled his brow as he listened. "It's not from the boat," he confirmed.

"Any other vessels on radar?" Gomez asked.

"Nothing for 25 miles," Tom replied.

He walked back to the pilot station, pulled a walkie-talkie from its holster on the wall, and spoke. A response came back as a voice-static mix, and he put the walkie-talkie back. "Jules says everything is off," he said. "The sound is not from us."

For the next half hour, they listened intently and recorded everything. Tanya knew they could do some filtering later if they got good data. But the frequency spectrum of the mechanical noise confused her: it was more complex than the usual knocks and ticks of a boat.

Her head jerked in response to a blast of high-intensity static, and she pulled her headphones away from her ears. Professor Gomez did the same, and Tanya readjusted the amplifier to bring down the volume.

Gomez tapped her on the arm and pointed towards the door. The sound of rushing water came from the boat's starboard.

"Whales?" Professor Gomez said with hopeful eyes.

Tanya followed Gomez as she rushed up to the helm. They stopped at a large window and looked out over the water.

Tom, who had gone to the head, joined them and looked out the window. His face went blank, as if he saw something he recognized but didn't expect.

The shadowy image of a submarine loomed in the dark, barely visible. It was impervious to the waves, like a boulder in a lake, about 100 feet to starboard and aft of the *Yonkers Belle*. It was enormous.

An amplified voice emanated from the direction of the submarine, but Tanya couldn't understand it. When she turned to Captain Tom, he'd already grabbed a megaphone and made his way out to the upper deck. Tanya and Gomez followed.

The voice came again, louder this time, but still incomprehensible.

"English," Tom yelled into the megaphone.

A blinding light blasted from the submarine's conning tower, and

Tanya shielded her eyes with her hands. The voice rang out again.

"You are in a restricted area," it said, this time in English.

Tanya thought the accent was Russian.

Tom hesitated for a few seconds, and then replied, "Why is it restricted?"

"We are conducting military exercises. You are in danger."

In her peripheral vision, Tanya detected movement near the lower deck. A rubber raft rammed the side of the boat and a rope flew over the rail. "Tom!" she yelled, and grabbed his arm.

His startled eyes met hers, and then turned to where she pointed. His face turned white, even in the bright light.

Four men climbed over the rail, two came toward them, toward the upper deck, and two disappeared down the stairs that led to the engine room.

The masked men rushed up the ladder and confronted them. One pointed a pistol at Tom, while the other went into the bridge. Tanya watched through a window as the man grabbed computers and audio equipment and put them in a bag. He searched through everything – drawers, cabinets, and clothing.

Professor Gomez moved towards the entrance in a rage, but stopped in her tracks when the man shoved the gun in her face. She moved to Tanya's side.

As the man inside exited the bridge, the two that had gone to the lower deck returned with the boat's engineer, Jules, at gunpoint. Everyone was now on the upper deck: four masked men, Tanya, Gomez, Jules, and Captain Tom.

"What are you doing here?" asked the leader.

"We're a science vessel," Tom replied.

"We're listening for whales," Professor Gomez added.

"You are listening right now?" the man asked. "Recording?"

"Yes," Gomez replied and pointed in the direction of the buoy and the line hanging over the rail of the lower deck.

The man nodded to one of his men who then went the lower deck, reeled in the buoy and microphone, cut the cable, and put the microphone in a bag.

The boss then blurted orders in Russian, and two of the men went back to the bridge. One smashed the radio on the floor and other hammered the navigation equipment with the butt of his gun. The GPS, sonar, and radar electronics were all destroyed.

While the other two worked inside, the boss said something to the man who had returned from the lower deck. The two Russians approached Gomez and Tanya. Gomez screamed as one grabbed her waist. Tanya went limp as the other man did the same to her. He dug at her pants – into her pockets. He pulled something out and handed it to his superior. It was her data storage device.

The boss examined the small storage drive, and then threw it overboard along with the two he'd found on Gomez.

Tanya was tempted to jump into the sea after them, but remained still. Her heart sank with the data on the drives. They were going to take or destroy everything. Months of work in the hellish cold would be lost. Her Ph.D. research was gone.

The men then searched Jules and Tom, but found nothing.

The other two men exited the bridge and joined them on the upper deck.

The boss directed his words to Captain Tom. "You have 30 minutes to get out of the area. I hope you understand the consequences of us finding you here again."

Professor Gomez confronted the man. "Are you threatening us?"

Tom grabbed her arm and pulled her behind him.

The Russian boss ignored her. "I hope you can navigate the old-fashioned way," the boss said to Tom and gestured towards the destroyed navigation instruments.

Tom nodded.

The four men climbed down to the lower deck. Tanya watched in silence as they disappeared over the rail. A moment later their rubber boat sped towards the sub.

Everyone remained silent as they filed into cabin. Tom started the *Yonkers Belle's* engine, and Tanya braced herself as the big diesel

13

grumbled and accelerated the boat. She walked around the mess of smashed electronics to the back of the bridge. She peered out the aft window just as the black silhouette of the submarine sank back into the deep.

~ 5 ~
Saturday, 21 February
(9:52 p.m. CST – St. Louis, Missouri)

Lenny Butrolsky stared at the two police officers crammed into the small hospital bathroom. They remained still and in unnatural positions, with limbs at awkward angles. They were dead. The eyes of one remained open, and the legs of the other twitched sporadically. The latter had released his bowels, and the stench diffused through the room.

None of it shocked him. On the contrary, he'd seen, and done, much worse. But this wasn't his work. His attention turned to the man kneeling on the floor below him, tying his shoes.

"These are size 15 and your feet barely fit," the man said. He was dressed as a doctor. "Can you pull the coat over your arm by yourself?"

Lenny nodded. It would be painful, but he'd manage. He slipped his right arm out of the sling and gingerly passed his hand through the sleeve of the coat. He then squeezed his shoulder blades together and fed his left arm through the other sleeve.

"I got the largest one I could find," the man said. "Looks long."

"Fits well enough," Lenny replied. It was wide. If it were tight on the shoulders, the pain might be intolerable.

The man pulled a second gun out of his white coat and handed it to Lenny. He then reached into his inner breast pocket and handed him identification documents, an envelope, and a set of keys. "I'm connected with friends of the late Heinrich Bergman."

Lenny flinched at the sound of the name. He was supposed to deny any connection to his former boss. He suspected that everyone involved in

14

the program had fled, never to resurface. It now seemed that the network might attempt a recovery.

"There's twenty grand in that envelope," the man said. "Ten to get you reestablished. The rest is down payment for your first job. We'll contact you in a couple of months. Should be enough time for you to recover."

The man handed him a phone. "Use this for everything. It's secure."

Lenny pocketed it, and then grabbed a small duffle bag from a shelf. He forced open a locked cabinet, splintering the edge of the particleboard door, and filled the duffle with antibiotics and bandages. When he turned around the mysterious doctor was gone.

He had little time. If a nurse made a random visit, he'd have to kill her. The gun wasn't equipped with a silencer so he'd have to use other means – and that would be difficult with one arm.

He walked to the door and peered out. He stepped back and into the bathroom, pulled a black knit hat from the head of one of the corpses, and put it on his own. He pushed on the bathroom door to close it, but a leg of one of the dead cops jammed between the edge of the door and the bathtub. He kicked the man's shin and pushed the door closed. The body settled and thumped against the other side.

Lenny backed away and straightened his jacket. He started for the door, but then went to a tray near the bed and slurped down a few cubes of lime Jell-O, followed by a cup of lukewarm coffee. He didn't know when he'd eat again, especially if there was a chase.

He exited the hospital room, walked down a freshly waxed corridor, and passed the nurses' station on the left. He caught up to a man pushing an old woman in a wheel chair, and followed them into an open elevator.

As the elevator descended, he wondered about the man who'd just freed him. Was he CIA, or a part of an international network? All he knew was that he was again connected to the project.

The real question was whether they were going to try to *revive* it, or eliminate every trace. It could go either way. In light of them seeking *his* services, it was more likely the latter. Whatever they had in mind, it required the services of an assassin.

CHAPTER II

~ 1 ~

Tuesday, 31 March (7:23 a.m. CST – Chicago)

Will started the coffeemaker and began emptying the dishwasher. With the cast removed and two weeks of rehab, he could walk with only a minor limp and moderate pain. The soreness in his hips and lower back diminished daily, and the doctors had cleared him to start a walking routine. The apartment complex had a gym with a treadmill, and he planned to start immediately.

A knock on the door startled him out of his morning stupor. He set a dish on the counter and padded barefoot over the cold, hardwood floor. He looked through the peephole and his stomach twisted. How had they found him so quickly? He then realized he'd been out of the Red Box for eight weeks.

He'd been mostly confined to the apartment since his release from the hospital, and it wasn't in his name. Denise did all the outside work – groceries and running errands. They still found him.

He recognized the men. Both were in their mid-thirties and wore dark suits. The taller of the two, with blonde hair and a millimeter of beard on his face, held a briefcase. The other, shorter and broad shouldered, wore a black knit cap.

Will opened the door and looked at the men.

"Do you remember us, Dr. Thompson?" the taller man asked.

"You're Scott," Will replied and then nodded to the shorter one, "and Carver." The two FBI agents had made an unannounced, late-night visit to Will's hospital room his first conscious night out of the Red Box.

"We've known your whereabouts for a while now, but gave you some time to heal," Scott said, "and spend some time with your girlfriend."

Girlfriend? Will thought.

17

Will led them into the apartment. The odor of cigarette residue followed one of them. They sat at a small square table in the kitchen. Scott sat directly across from Will, opened his briefcase, pulled out a file, and put it on the table. Carver sat to Will's left.

"You know why we're here," Scott said.

Will responded with a shrug even though he remembered their conversation in the hospital.

"First," Scott continued, "we need to get you into protection."

"Am I in danger?" Will asked, not hiding his skepticism.

"We found you easily," Carver explained.

"Am I in danger right now?" Will asked.

Carver coughed lightly and looked down at the table. "There's been a leak – records, files, and video footage from your time in the facility," he explained. "It doesn't mean anyone has located you yet, but it's possible."

Will wasn't surprised that the videos had been preserved after the collapse of the Red Box facility. Most likely all of the electronic information collected up to that instant was safely stored on another part of the planet. "What am I supposed to do?"

"We'll relocate you," Carver said, "but first you'll go through some training. You'll need to learn some habits of self-preservation. Once that's completed, and you're relocated with a new identity, we'll integrate you into service."

"Back up," Will said and held up his hands. "I hadn't planned on changing my identity and relocating. And I haven't agreed to work for the FBI."

"Regarding relocation," Carver said, "you're not the only one at risk. Those around you are also in danger."

Will thought of Denise and he realized the quandary. If she or Jonathan were in danger because of him, then he'd leave. His parents could also be at risk. "When would all of this start?"

"Training starts next Monday," Carver replied. "It takes six weeks or so, depending on how fast you learn."

Scott pulled out a sheet of paper and handed it to Will. "Here are the details," he said. "Firearms training, communications security, survival, driving, surveillance and avoidance, and self-defense training."

"A lot for six weeks," Will said.

"Enough to keep you safe," Carver said as he closed his briefcase. "The address on that form is your rendezvous point with a contact who will bring you to the facility. Be there at 6:30 a.m."

Will walked the men to the door. As they stepped out, Scott turned to him "Take the training seriously," he said. "My feeling is that you'll be needing it."

Will nodded and closed the door.

One lesson he'd learned during the past two years was that life could change in an instant. Now he had to abandon everything and live somewhere else as someone else.

Although the Red Box had changed him in the most profound way, he'd decided to try to live a normal life. He understood now that that was not possible. He'd always be looking over his shoulder. Someone would always be searching for him.

In the short term, he'd have to trust the FBI. After all, they'd helped free him from the Red Box and shut down the horrific program. His trust was limited, however. The FBI had internal problems: leaks and factions with their own motives.

He poured a cup of coffee and sat at the kitchen counter. The effects of the morning's events would ripple through the future and produce a wake of uncontrollable consequences. He felt as if he were being forced down a path that had the appearance of free will but was actually constrained. It was like floating on a raft on a slowly flowing river: you had some local control of where you were going, but the river determined your final destination. His river, it seemed, was heading for a waterfall.

~ 2 ~

Monday, 20 April (7:20 a.m. EST – Washington, DC)

19

Daniel Parsons cringed as he pressed his hand on the wall-mounted scanner pad, yellowed with the oils of thousands of hands. He nearly gagged at the thought of the germs passed to him during this daily operation.

A green light illuminated above the pad and a door slid open. He passed through a narrow entrance into a load-lock, and the door closed behind him. The stale air in the tube always reminded him of his flights between the U.S. and Pakistan when he was a CIA operative. It was amazing how olfactory-induced memories could compress time: the Pakistan assignment had ended twenty years ago.

He walked to the center of the tubular corridor and stood on a pair of worn orange footprints. Seconds later, a door opened on the far side, and he walked out of the load-lock and into a large, marble-floored atrium teaming with people. The clacking of hundreds of shoes resounded from the surfaces of the structure. The southeast wall of the grand foyer was constructed entirely of windows, through which sunlight illuminated lush plants distributed amongst benches that lined the center of the floor. With all of the bustling, one sound was conspicuously absent: voices. Talking of any sort was forbidden in this part of the building, and that included phones.

Daniel weaved his way through the hurried crowd of well-dressed pedestrians to an elevator, and rode it up to the eleventh floor. He emerged in a large reception area, and approached a graying woman dressed in a dark suit-jacket. She was seated behind a long counter.

"Good morning," she said and glanced at the ID badge clipped to the lapel of his jacket.

"Good morning, Sandy," he replied. "Weekend went too quickly." It was nonsensical small talk. The day of the week was irrelevant – they worked every day – and "Sandy" wasn't her real name.

The woman stood and walked over to a bank of locked drawers embedded in the wall behind the desk. She entered a code on the number pad on Drawer No. 7 and removed a package labeled in red print: *Eyes Only.* She handed it to Daniel along with a receipt.

He signed the receipt and gave it back, put the package under his arm, and started walking down the hall to his office. After just a few steps he found himself practically running.

He arrived at his office door, shifted the package tightly under his left arm, punched in the access code on the electronic lock, and entered.

Morning light shone through the southeast-facing window, illuminating the mess that was his work area. Stacks of files of various heights littered every flat surface like the stumps of a harvested forest. Musty classified documents, and books dating back to the 1920's, lay open on the chairs, coffee table, and windowsill. Sticky-notes of all colors were stuck to everything and fluttered like leaves in the air that flowed through the vent in the ceiling. It was cluttered, but every page strewn about the large office was crucial to his current project. He knew exactly where everything was.

He put the package on the table, sat as his desk, and logged onto the computer. He scanned his email – nothing important – and returned his attention to the package. He cleared some space on the large couch against the wall on the far end of the office and sat.

Using wire cutters, he snipped the steel wires that bound the cardboard package, and then sliced through the excessive packing tape with a utility knife. He opened the box, removed the contents, and placed them on the coffee table.

He reached for the top of the pile, but then sighed and withdrew his hand. He recounted the events that had brought him to this point. He'd been approaching the final stages of another research project, but was then ordered to stop his work and start his current one. It was highly unusual for someone in his position to get a change of orders under a priority directive. It had never happened to him.

His type of research couldn't be accomplished without access to the most sensitive information. To this end, he and others in his special group had been given the ultimate clearance. It was a type of access that only a few people even knew about: Omniscient Clearance. It meant he had unlimited access to everything possessed by every government agency – NSA, FBI, CIA – everything. Even the President didn't have such clearance, and wasn't even supposed to know about it. The only people who had it were the Director of CIA and the Omniscients, or Omnis, like Daniel.

The Omnis were under the auspices of the CIA. They wrote in anonymity on sensitive intelligence issues, and their works were, of course, not published in the traditional sense. Daniel had been recruited in part for his performance as a CIA reports officer, a job that had required him to collect information from multiple intelligence sources, identify connections, and formulate the "big picture" for complex intelligence-gathering environments.

Being a single man in his mid-twenties at the time, he hadn't hesitated to commit to the Omniscients. Now, in his late forties, he knew he'd made the right choice. Every day was filled with intrigue and excitement sans the danger that came with being a CIA operative.

Since the inception of their secretive organization at the end of World War II, there had always been 8 to 12 active Omnis, where active meant alive. Omnis didn't know each other's identities. Their finished works, referred to as monographs, were identified on their covers by a title, the date of completion of the project, and the date of induction of the particular Omni who had authored it. The names of the Omnis were omitted to maintain anonymity. The oldest induction date of an Omni that Daniel had come across was 5-12-1945.

Omnis were well-compensated, but the job came with drawbacks, the most difficult of which for Daniel was being forbidden to travel outside the contiguous 48 states. As a former CIA operative, this limitation was stifling. But the excitement the job made up for it. The information to which he had access was better than traveling anywhere in the world. But that same information sometimes had negative effects. He'd had many sleepless nights in the past twenty years; in some cases it was a thrilling conundrum that had kept him awake. Other times he'd learned something so deeply disturbing that he'd been afraid to close his eyes.

Before his recent reassignment, he'd been researching a project called Red Wraith that was classified as black top-secret – meaning it was a crime to admit that it existed. It was the most frightening of all of the 18 assignments he'd had during his employ as an Omni. It made his dreams so unsettling that any sleep he was able to manage during those nine months had been ineffective. At the end, he'd been so sleep deprived that he'd become physically ill. One morning he'd dozed off at the wheel on the drive to work and ended up in a ditch.

Red Wraith was a continuation by the American government of an ancient Nazi project called Red Falcon. The Nazis had started the sinister program sometime before World War II. The timing, in relation to the Holocaust, had made him prickle with suspicion.

The Holocaust had been the perfect landscape for Red Falcon. Too perfect. The nature of the hideous actions carried out as part of the operation weaved seamlessly with those that had occurred in the concentration camps under the guise of medical experiments. Red Falcon and the Holocaust were connected, and Daniel was unable to determine which had started first. His gut told him that Red Falcon was the origin – it was the *reason* for the Holocaust. But he had no proof.

The horrible tortures inflicted upon concentration camp prisoners in Auschwitz, Treblinka, and others had been well known to the public for decades. However, the motives for these experiments had been written off as medical research for the benefit of the Nazi war effort. There was an enormous volume of documentation on the experiments themselves, as well as written communications between the scientists, the SS, and Hitler himself. But there were informational voids and inconsistencies that made the whole picture just not sit right with him.

The Red Falcon files were riddled with references to an undefined term: separation. Phrases such as "we've seen marginal evidence of separation" or "progress towards our goal of achieving separation" had appeared sporadically in the documents without explanation. The Nazis had not succeeded in obtaining separation, whatever it was, but that was the underlying objective, and, by extension, the goal of the American Red Wraith project.

The documents he'd collected on Red Wraith had been incomplete, and he'd often hit a wall when he requested information that could fill the gaps. Sometimes he was told certain files didn't exist. Other times he got no response whatsoever. Nonetheless, he'd been able to establish a direct link between Red Falcon and Red Wraith. It was this connection, and the insidious details of Red Wraith, that had brought on the nightmares. But the meaning of the term *separation* had eluded him, and it antagonized his mind continuously.

The timing of his reassignment was also suspect. He believed that some event related to Red Wraith had led to the removal of the former CIA Director two months earlier. The possibility that the project might still be active disturbed him.

Two unique events had occurred in the past three weeks. First, his research on Red Wraith had been put on hold. Second, he'd been reassigned to a new project that was deemed urgent. The subjects of all of his previous research had been old and dormant; the new project was undoubtedly active in the present. *That* was unusual.

His attention went back to the new pile of documents. He'd been given only two words to start his new research: Operation Tabarin. He grabbed the first folder on the top of the pile and started reading.

~ 3 ~

Thursday, 7 May (6:30 a.m. CST – Chicago)

William Thompson glanced back just as the hooded figure turned the corner a block behind him. His nose burned from breathing the exhaust of the morning traffic for two hours.

Convinced the man was following him, Will climbed the three concrete steps to his right, and moved out of the cold Chicago air and into the busy café. The thick aroma of freshly ground coffee filled his nostrils, and voices and espresso machines produced a drone that gave him a sense of anonymity.

His eyes adjusted to the dim lighting as he crossed a line of people placing orders. He spotted a sign for the restrooms and headed toward the rear of the establishment. He weaved around a cart with a tub of bussed dishes, and entered a narrow hallway. He passed the restrooms on his left and a door labeled "utilities" on the right. The hallway then turned 90° to the left and terminated at a large metal door. He extended his hand to actuate the press-bar handle but stopped an instant before he made contact; at eye level was a red sign that read "Emergency Exit Only – Alarm Will Sound."

Damn. He had a minute at most. His pursuer had been only 100 yards behind him and would have picked up pace as soon as Will entered the café. He concentrated on what he'd learned during the past weeks. Every operation had elements of improvisation. His attention turned to the smell of food.

He took off his jacket and retraced his path past the utility closet and restrooms. He picked up a half-full cup of cold coffee from the tub of dishes on the cart at the mouth of the hallway and poured it on his left arm, soaking his left sleeve. He walked into the main room and approached the end of the drinks counter, near a set of double doors that led to the kitchen. He caught the eye of one of the baristas and waved her over.

The young woman approached and looked at his coffee stained sleeve with an expression of concern.

"I think I burned myself," Will said, wincing. He cradled his left arm. "Someone's in the restroom; can I get a wet towel from the back – maybe with some ice?" He nodded towards the kitchen.

The woman seemed to read the desperation in his face, nodded, and walked into the kitchen. She didn't object when he followed.

She led him past two women in white aprons preparing food to a stainless steel utility sink against the far wall. He rolled up his sleeve and rinsed his arm with cold water as the barista disappeared into a nearby room. He heard her scoop ice, and a few seconds later she emerged with a plastic cup and a thin towel. She placed the towel over the mouth of the cup and turned it upside down, filling the towel with ice. She finished by twisting it to form a makeshift icepack.

"This should do it," she said and handed it to him.

Will put it on his arm and thanked her as she exited the kitchen. The busy cooks seemed to hardly notice him as he looked for an exit. He walked into the small room from which the barista had retrieved the ice, and discovered an ice machine and a door with an illuminated exit sign above it. This one had the same warning sign as the first one he'd encountered, but a sliver of light shone between the door and its frame. It was propped open.

He pushed it open and peered out. It led to a narrow alley between the café and the adjacent building. He set the icepack on the ice machine, put on his jacket, and stepped out, onto a small concrete porch. His nose alerted him to a bucket of sand mixed with hundreds of cigarette butts located just off the stoop, next to the building. To his left, the alley terminated with a red brick building: a dead end. In the direction of the storefront, a dingy green dumpster partially blocked the view of the street. The sweet-sour stench of its leaking contents nearly overwhelmed him as he stepped off the porch and crouched behind it, keeping his eye in the direction of the street.

A clicking sound alerted him that the door had closed behind him. Big mistake. He should've made sure it remained propped. Now he was trapped.

He pulled out his targeting device and started the "snapping" program. At that instant, his stalker stepped into view and looked down the alley. Well concealed, Will remained perfectly still and held his breath. He hoped his pursuer wouldn't decide to check out the dead end.

To his relief, the hooded figure continued toward the store entrance and was soon out of view. When Will was confident that the man wouldn't double back, he stood and walked quickly toward the street, stopping at the edge of the building. He peered around the corner to the right just as the man removed his hood and peered into the window of the café.

Will held the device around the corner and, through its view-screen, centered cross hairs on the side of the man's head. He pushed a button, withdrew the device, and looked at the screen – a perfect headshot. He waited for a few seconds and then looked around the corner just as the man entered the café. *Perfect,* he thought. Got him without being seen.

Will turned left out of the alley, and walked quickly. At the next block he turned right, crossed the street, and entered a small public park. He sat on a bench and used his phone to send the picture to his instructor.

A minute later, he got a call.

"Well done, Thompson," the gruff-voiced man said with a tone of approval. "Now I've got one for you."

Will's phone vibrated, indicating that a message had arrived. He pushed a button and opened the incoming file. His heart sank. It was a picture of *him* with cross hairs superimposed on his head.

"What the hell?" Will asked, annoyed.

The man chuckled. "There were *two* this time," the man explained. "We'll be there in a few minutes."

Will hung up. He slapped his knee and cursed under his breath.

Five minutes later, a gray SUV pulled up. Its brakes squeaked as it stopped.

Will climbed into the back seat and sat next to the man he recognized as Renaldo, his pursuer from the café. *One of his pursuers.* Someone he didn't recognize, a fit man in his mid fifties with short gray hair and sunglasses, sat in the passenger seat.

The man turned around and extended his hand behind the seat. "Nice to meet you, Dr. Thompson. I'm Roy," he said. "I got you at the art building on the corner of Milwaukee and Kimball."

Will remembered the six-way intersection. "Call me Will," he said and shook the man's hand.

"This was an important exercise," Will's instructor, Perry Dunlap, said from the driver's seat. "Never overlook the possibility of there being more than one pursuer."

"It also illustrates the effectiveness of a coordinated team," Roy added. "Losing two people is tough. Surveillance and pursuit is often done in teams of two, or more – up to a dozen."

"We'll analyze the exercise in detail later," Perry informed. "Your psychiatric evaluation isn't until 10 a.m., so we have time for breakfast. Anyone object?"

Ten minutes later they were in the café, sitting in a booth next to the front window – the same one through which Renaldo had peered 15 minutes earlier.

"Your limp made you easy to track," Roy explained as he took a sip of coffee. "That permanent?"

Will thought the limp had gone away, but he'd been working it pretty hard. He rubbed his right thigh even though the aching was in the bone and therefore unreachable. "No, a fractured femur," Will replied. "Healing quickly."

"How'd it happen?" Roy asked.

"Motorcycle accident," Will lied. "Four months ago."

Roy nodded.

He could tell Roy didn't buy it.

Renaldo shook his head. "How did you double back on me?" he asked.

Perry put up his hand indicating that he'd answer that question for everyone. He took a laptop out of the leather knapsack that never left his person and started it. A minute later a map of the area appeared on the screen along with three moving, colored dots. "The green one is Thompson, and the red is Roy," Perry explained. "You're the yellow one, Renaldo."

Perry fast-forwarded to the point where Roy snapped Will, and then stopped it. "You should never expose yourself on a corner like this – you're extremely vulnerable here," Perry said as he traced an area on the screen with his finger. "This is why you were snapped."

Will nodded. Watching it all unfold from above was revealing.

Perry forwarded to the point where Will ducked into the café. He switched to a display mode that exposed a rough layout of the building's interior so they could see Will's movements.

"How did you get into the kitchen?" Perry asked.

Will described his coffee trick.

"Not bad," Renaldo said.

"And he followed the rules," Roy added. "We do exercises here often, and I know this place well. You could've bolted out the back door, but that would have set off the alarm."

"Then it would've become a foot race – something you always

want to avoid," Perry chimed in.

Roy huffed. "Especially since you're currently lame."

Will nodded. "I need practice."

Perry shook his head. "This was your last exercise. You're as ready as you need to be for relocation."

For an instant, Roy's face distorted in an expression that Will interpreted as panic. The instructors had been informed that he was a relocation case, but even he didn't know exactly when that would happen. There was something about Roy that alarmed him. Will shrugged it off. It didn't matter; he'd soon be somewhere else.

~ 4 ~

Thursday, 7 May (9:32 a.m. EST – Antarctic Circle)

Captain Chuck McHenry weaved his way through the narrow corridors from his quarters to the sonar station where three young sailors, pressed shoulder-to-shoulder, stared at a computer monitor. A handful of others craned their necks to observe from their respective stations.

McHenry cleared his throat and all but the man seated at the sonar station scattered and returned to their posts. "Hear it, Finley?" he asked.

The young sonar technician nodded as he tweaked some controls. A mess of multicolored curves appeared on the computer screen.

"The signal is there, sir, loud and clear," Finley explained as he pointed to various locations on the screen. "About one pulse per second."

"Can you locate it?" McHenry asked.

"It's strange," Finley explained, "the frequency spectrum of the signal makes it difficult pinpoint its source – even with filtering – and we're getting too many reflections from the ice. All I can say is that it's deep."

"How far?"

"A thousand meters, maybe more."

It was surprising. McHenry knew that that was beyond the crush depth of most vessels, although specialized vehicles could certainly go that deep. "On the floor?"

Finley shook his head. "Floor's at 4,000 meters. The source is at 1,200 at the most." He turned away from the screen and faced McHenry. "If we switched to active mode – "

"No," McHenry cut him off. He wouldn't ping the area and reveal their location to every vessel in the vicinity. They were an attack sub, not a science vessel. "Anyone else in the area?"

"A few small boats on the surface. That's all," Finley responded. "Unless there are sleepers – running quiet like us."

McHenry was certain the Russians were in the area. They had ears, too. "Get a good recording, and mark our spot."

"Sir, an absolute location might be difficult. We're close to magnetic south, and these currents – "

"Give me your best estimate," McHenry responded.

In the nine years he'd served as commander of an attack sub, he'd never been given such odd orders. Antarctica as the location was certainly out of the ordinary, but even more so was the objective. They'd been sent to investigate a signal that had been detected by a science vessel. That had occurred more than two months earlier, and the captain of that vessel claimed that a Russian submarine had threatened to sink them. Why hadn't the incident been investigated earlier? It was unusual for a submarine to surface and scare away little boats. "I'm sure you'll be getting another shot at this, Finley," he said.

It was time to leave the area and get to radio depth. He needed to report their findings to Naval Command.

~ 5 ~

Thursday, 7 May (11:50 a.m. EST – Washington, DC)

Daniel Parsons paced in front of his large office window and gazed into the horizon over the evergreen forest. It calmed his mind, although he knew his brain was always working in the background, making connections his conscious mind was too distracted to find. His stomach grumbled. *Lunchtime.*

Spending most of his waking hours there, he appreciated the aesthetically pleasing Space Systems building. The name was a front for a deep-cover CIA complex. The many hundreds of Space Systems personnel were "identity sensitive," and could not be seen anywhere near the CIA headquarters. It was well known that foreign operatives catalogued everyone going near the Langley facility. This wasn't a problem for public officials or intelligence analysts who never left the country. However, it was a grave threat to operatives who traveled abroad, especially in the age of face recognition software. It wasn't a concern for Daniel since he was no longer allowed to leave the country, but he had to remain in deep cover for a different reason – for what was in his brain.

But it wasn't just his knowledge of dark secrets that made him unique; it was that he knew *truths*. Truths had deeper implications than secrets. A truth could be used as a foundation from which to extrapolate conclusions, or *origins*, with the highest degree of certainty. The things he'd discovered as an Omniscient had profoundly changed his life. The world looked different to him now. More correctly, the world *was* different from what he had thought it was. Now, even the shadows of clouds passing slowly over the dark green forest carried a different meaning to him. And his questions about the world ran much deeper than those he'd had during the earlier part of his life. There were new truths to be unveiled.

His research that morning had only whetted his appetite. He'd started more than two weeks ago with what he'd been given: Operation Tabarin. As he'd suspected, it was only the tip of the iceberg. As with every other project he'd been assigned, he was sure that Tabarin would lead to some complicated mess of things that eventually converged to a fundamental objective. If he'd learned anything in the past two decades, it was that actions and their consequences were difficult to conceal. Objectives and motives, however, could lie dormant like spores in frozen soil, maybe never to see light. It was these causal motives that he sought.

Antarctica. *What on earth did they want in Antarctica?* He'd dug up much information on Operation Tabarin in declassified sources. It was a secret British mission to the southern continent initiated in the midst of World War II, during the southern summer, November, 1944. They'd constructed outposts along the way: one on Deception Island in the South Shetland Islands, another in Port Lockroy in the Palmer Archipelago, west of the Antarctic Peninsula, and finally set up shop at Hope Bay, on Antarctica's Trinity Peninsula in 1945.

Daniel understood the scientific interest in Antarctica. In the current day, scientists of all types, from physicists to biologists, frequented the bottom of the world to study everything from the unique animal life to particle physics. In the 1940's, however, science was scarce in that part of the world, not to mention it was wartime. Research not related to the war effort, of the Axis or the Allies, would have been the last thing on anyone's minds.

His heart beat in his chest like a bass drum. *Something was there.*

~ 6 ~

Thursday, 7 May (2:22 p.m. EST – Antarctic Circle)

Captain McHenry fidgeted near the radio receiver. He folded his hands behind his back, took a deep breath, and blew it back out with force. "How long have we been at radio depth?" he asked.

"Twenty-three minutes, sir," a sailor replied.

"What are those DC bureaucrats doing?" McHenry asked.

"Golfing, skipper. It's 2:30 in the afternoon," the sailor quipped.

McHenry chuckled. *And putting down a few beers,* he was about to add when the receiver beeped, indicating an incoming message. *Finally,* he thought as he punched in a passcode. The printer hummed and a minute later he had pages in hand and shut down communications.

"Get to depth and get us the hell out of here," McHenry ordered.

The command echoed through the chain as he exited the control room. He stopped at the mess hall to refill his coffee mug, and then weaved his way to his quarters. He sat at a small desk and read the orders.

The instructions were diametrically opposed to his instincts. It was not how an attack sub was supposed to operate. Its effectiveness and safety depended on secrecy, stealth, deception, and surprise. The message indicated that other, unspecified subs and surface ships were on their way to the area. His neck muscles tightened. It implied something was afoot. *What was down there – a vessel? A weapon? A trap?*

His orders were to keep the operation under wraps until it was initiated. However, without revealing details, he'd bounce some ideas off of his first officer, Gerald Diggs.

Something big was happening, and it had something to do with whatever was making that noise in the deep.

~ 7 ~
Thursday, 7 May (3:37 p.m. CST – Baton Rouge)

Zhichao Cho gazed through the large southwest windows of his new office. Even though the air was cool, the intense sun hurt his face, and he moved into the shade. At his home in China, the sun was never as intense as in Louisiana. It was a good thing he'd only be in Baton Rouge for as long as it took to get what he needed.

He was still dumbfounded at how easy it had been for him to acquire Syncorp. His lawyers had been creative by working through a food engineering company owned by a Chinese-American citizen. On paper, it was that company that had purchased Syncorp. Were the Americans really that stupid? He knew they wanted to bury all the evil things Syncorp had done, but it seemed irresponsible to allow all of the information – the technology – to get into the hands of a foe. And Cho was no idiot; although they were not overtly at war with each other, the United States and China were *not* friends.

He was satisfied with his progress on two fronts. The first task was to send functional parts to the processing facility in China, where they had

33

already started assembling the technical innards of the first building. That was the difference between the two countries: the Americans had referred to their own research complexes as Compressed Punishment facilities in an attempt to disguise them as something with a more acceptable purpose. In China, there was no need to conjure such an elaborate ruse. They'd never advertise the real purpose of the complex, of course, but they'd create no facades.

The collection and processing of the information from Syncorp and its satellite companies was going well. The previous CEO had succeeded in delivering everything by the contractual deadline, and Cho's people immediately began digitizing and organizing the files. Every few days, he would oversee a massive data dump to a server in China. In the end, he'd ship the paper files, and then destroy the U.S.-based servers, leaving them with nothing. He thought it was an interesting concept: stealing information and then destroying the original source was much more devastating than simply stealing it. It was one step forward for the thief, and one step backwards for the victim – a net of two steps of separation. He smiled. Every successful operation against the U. S. brought China closer to its rightful place in the world.

The historical progression of the technology was entertaining, especially now that he was part of it. The evolution went from Red Falcon to Red Wraith and, now, to his Red Dragon project. He'd earn a special place in history.

In terms of the high-tech facilities, Red Dragon was well underway. But there was another objective that he had to pursue. He had to acquire data on the subjects treated at the two formerly active American facilities. One was in Detroit and the other on Long Island. Syncorp didn't have access to that information, but Chinese intelligence was working on it. The most crucial information was that connected to the Americans' successful conversion – if that was really true. At some level, he hoped it was. It meant that what they were trying to accomplish was possible.

A secret war was in progress, one to which the United States was oblivious. It was a race to duplicate and enhance what the Americans had done, and to acquire, or destroy, the fruit of their creation. It was a war that

34

Cho was going to win for his country, and himself.

~ 8 ~

Thursday, 7 May (8:21 p.m. CST – Chicago)

Will pulled open the heavy glass door and entered the restaurant. His stomach grumbled in response to the aroma of charbroiled steak. The warm air felt good, offsetting the chill that had invaded his body during the long walk in the cool Chicago night.

He passed by the host station and searched until he spotted Denise sitting at a table beside a large window, sipping a glass of wine.

The FBI agent had been right that morning six weeks ago when he'd suggested that Denise was his girlfriend. It was going to be difficult to leave her.

She looked up as he approached and smiled when she recognized him.

He made his way around a waiter and went to her.

She stood from her chair, tippy-toed in her high heels, and planted a kiss on his cheek. "Right on time," she said.

"Hungry?" he asked as they sat.

"I've been waiting for this all week. And I missed lunch today." She reached across the table and caressed his hand. "Are you happy it's over?"

Will nodded, but his feelings were mixed. He was happy that his training was completed, but he didn't know what was coming next. His neck twitched. All that was left was his final meeting the next morning, when he'd learn the details of his new life.

"Bad dreams again last night?" Denise asked.

He nodded. She read him better than anyone, but it was an easy guess: he had nightmares almost every night. His brain had much to exploit – his conviction, the destruction of his life and career, weeks of torture in the Red Box. It all seemed like it happened in another lifetime.

35

"How's the investigation coming along?" he asked, changing the subject.

She gave him a look acknowledging the deliberate redirection, and then answered, "Slowly." She shook her head. "Evidence is disappearing. Crucial files from the Red Box facility and DARPA have been stolen. And it's even more difficult finding the people who were involved."

Will found it unacceptable that files could be stolen from the Defense Advanced Research Project Agency. The only explanation was that DARPA itself was involved in their disappearance. The slower the investigation moved, the more difficult it would be to retrieve the evidence. The FBI was conducting an investigation into DARPA, but that gave him no solace – he suspected that the two organizations were colluding at some level. As with the CIA, the FBI probably had factions that were involved in Red Wrath.

Evidence connected to the CIA was also proving difficult to find, despite the enormous amount of funds and human resources that had been funneled into the Red Wraith project through CIA front organizations. Usually money could be tracked, but it wasn't straightforward in this case.

"Regarding *your* case," Denise continued, "the state is close to settling. You'll be getting pre-settlement funds for your house and belongings by the end of the week."

Will nodded. Recovering the things they'd taken from him when he was incarcerated gave him some satisfaction, but it was just the start. "Who have you tracked down from the Red Box?"

She shifted in her seat. "A few low-level employees—the dental assistant and a doctor—both still in the hospital, although the doctor is about to be released. We've located a few of the inmates, but haven't been able to question them – they're still in state custody."

Will had intended to visit the dental assistant, Kelly Hatley, but it looked like he'd be leaving before he got the chance. She'd been in a Detroit hospital since the collapse of the Red Box. His sympathy for her was shallow. She'd caused him much pain and many nightmares. He thought that seeing her in such a vulnerable state might get him past some of the horror.

Will had a T-bone steak with a baked potato, and Denise the

salmon special with pasta. Their dinner conversation was lighter.

"Desert?" she asked when they'd finished their entrees, and pointed to 'green tea ice cream' listed on the menu.

He was stuffed. "I'll take a bite of yours," he replied. He searched the room for a waiter and noticed a man turn his back as Will's gaze turned towards him. The man had moved casually, but deliberately. He turned back to Denise. "See the guy behind me in the brown coat? About six feet tall, fifties, dark hair and complexion."

Denise glanced quickly and nodded.

"He's following me. He was on the subway on my way here. This might be part of my training," he explained. "I'm supposed to call my instructor and identify the man."

Will thought about "snapping" him with his phone, but instead just made the call. A moment later a man answered.

"Perry here."

"I see your man," Will said.

"Thompson?" Perry said after a delay. "What are you talking about?"

"I've spotted the tail—fifties, tall, dark, brown coat, black handkerchief in the front pocket ... should I snap him?" A few seconds passed. "Perry?"

"Listen carefully, Thompson," Perry finally responded. "I did not send anyone after you tonight – the course is over. And do *not* snap him. You're sure he's following you?"

A chill slithered up Will's spine to the back of his head. He tried to recall all parts of his trip from downtown Chicago to the suburban restaurant. The man was definitely on the subway, but he couldn't remember seeing him on the street. "Fairly sure," he finally answered.

"I taught you what to do in this situation, right?"

"Yes."

"I'm going to call you back in ten minutes. If I don't get an answer, I'm sending help," Perry said and hung up.

He put the phone in his pocket and looked to Denise. "Desert will have to wait."

She looked confused.

"Give me a minute," he said. He stood and walked towards the man.

~ 9 ~

Thursday, 7 May (10:27 p.m. EST – Washington)

Daniel Parsons stood by his office window as he steeped tea. Thursday was about over, and a nearly full, red moon loomed on the southeastern horizon. He was pleased with his progress for the day.

He'd learned that the Brits' Operation Tabarin had been a response to something. Tabarin, in turn, had been followed by an American operation, codenamed Highjump, which started in the southern summer of 1946. Official reports indicated that Highjump had lasted less than two years. However, he'd found evidence that it had carried on much longer – perhaps a decade. Although the documents weren't consistent, they all agreed that the focus of both operations had been on a part of Antarctica called Dronning Maud Land, near the Weddell Sea.

The reason for their interest in the area was elusive. Every time a report converged on a crucial piece of information it was blacked out. And some documents were missing pages. Both were extremely unusual, and he was concerned that the missing information might be irretrievable; there were no documents with a higher order of secrecy. He didn't know who had the authority to redact such information. Maybe the CIA director could do such a thing, but he dismissed it – it was irrational. Information was power.

Daniel twitched in reaction to a sound coming from his desk and spilled tea on his hand. It was his office phone. It almost never rang – only the CIA director had the number. And it was late. He answered.

"Parsons?" a man said.

"Yes, sir," Daniel replied. He recognized the voice as that of CIA Director James Thackett.

His heart raced. He'd never spoken with the man.

"Your current project has become high priority, so we're going to have to do something somewhat unusual," Thackett explained. "Report to Room 713 tomorrow morning at eight o'clock."

"Okay," Daniel said. The phone went dead, and Daniel hung up.

It was more than just somewhat unusual. Other than Sandy, and the receptionist that had preceded her, Daniel had not met in person with *any* CIA personnel in over 20 years. He worried that the new director, being relatively new to the position, didn't grasp the importance of Omniscients' anonymity.

Now that his concentration was blown, he decided to go home. He packed his things and prepared for the thorough search he was about to endure before his departure from the Space Systems building.

~ 10 ~

Thursday, 7 May (9:44 p.m. CST   – Chicago)

Will maneuvered around a desert cart and approached his stalker. The man maintained direct eye contact with him. Will stopped squarely in front of him.

"Do we know each other?" Will asked. He tried to place the dark complexioned man, but couldn't. He was slightly taller than Will, slender but not skinny, and had black hair with occasional strands of white.

"Most definitely not, Dr. Thompson," the man replied.

Will flinched at mention of his name. He detected an accent. *Israeli?* "Who are you?"

"A friend," the man replied. The man reached out and touched Will's shoulder to turn him towards the door. "Can we talk?"

Will backed away, and the man put his arm down.

"Please, Dr. Thompson, there's a bench just outside," the man said. "I just need a few minutes and then you can get back to dinner with your lady friend. It will be worth your while."

Will looked across the dining room and made contact with a wide-eyed Denise. He lifted his finger to indicate that he'd be back shortly.

He followed the man outside to a bench that faced the street. It was a bus stop bracketed by a garbage can on one side and a newspaper dispenser on the other. The man sat first and, with his left hand, patted the seat next to him.

Will looked to check the area for others, and then sat.

"My country is taking a risk by approaching you," the man explained.

"What *is* your country?"

"Israel," the man said. "Call me Avi."

"What's this about?"

"You're in danger," Avi said with an expression that amplified the gravity of the statement.

Will shuddered as the cold Chicago air seeped into his flesh. "Explain."

"Your secret is out," Avi said. "Your files have been leaked. The videos, in particular, are quite revealing."

The FBI had warned him that he'd be exposed eventually, but he didn't expect things to be set into motion so quickly. Despite his training, he suddenly felt ill prepared for life on the run.

Avi continued, "We have known about you since your rather spectacular release from the Red Box, and we'd hoped the American government could keep a lid on it. A month ago, the Collections arm of our Mossad obtained documents indicating that Russia is now aware of your existence. Two weeks ago the same was discovered about China. And, yesterday, Iran."

Will was convinced that the man had some information, but he was aware of how one could bluff with limited knowledge in order to obtain more. "Tell me, why am I in danger?" Will asked.

Avi's expression revealed frustration. "You know why, and I know why, and now the rest of the world knows why," he said. "They will kidnap you. Or kill you."

"Why?" Will was aware of his value, but couldn't understand the

40

reason for such urgency.

Avi's expression changed as if he'd just realized something. "There are the obvious reasons – your use as an intelligence asset, for instance. But you already know that."

Will shrugged.

"But perhaps you are unaware of the other reasons," Avi said.

The man seemed to be looking for recognition in Will's eyes. He had no idea what Avi was talking about. "Other reasons?"

"Things that run deeper than geopolitical motivations," Avi replied.

"I don't know you mean."

"We believe that there is some other purpose for you – for the program – other than espionage and war."

"What is it?"

Avi shook his head. "We don't know."

Will's phone rang. It was Agent Perry calling back, as promised. Will turned to the Israeli. "I have to take this."

"Take precautions," Avi said, and then stood and disappeared around the corner.

Will answered the phone. "Agent Perry, everything's okay." Will quickly explained what had just happened, but omitted the details that Perry wasn't supposed to know.

"I'll inform the agent heading your case," Perry said. "In the meantime, get off the streets, and don't stay in your apartment for a few days."

Will ended the call and sat motionless in the cold. What the hell did the Israeli mean by things that "run deeper than geopolitical motivations"? What else was there?

He stood from the bench and went back into the restaurant. He'd explain it all to Denise over desert. She was in danger just by being involved with him. But he knew it would be okay – he'd be gone soon.

~ 11 ~

EXOSKELETON II: Tympanum

Thursday, 7 May (10:52 p.m. EST – Detroit, Michigan)

Lenny Butrolsky pulled his baseball cap down low on his forehead, lifted his collar, and directed his face away from the camera in the elevator. He caught himself rubbing his right shoulder, a reaction he figured that was triggered by the sterile odor that permeated the hospital. For weeks, he'd been wearing antiseptic as if it were cologne. That phase was over now that the bullet wound in his shooting arm was mostly healed. He wouldn't need it tonight anyway. This one had to look like natural causes.

He'd made three hits in the Detroit area in the past month. This would be the fourth. The latest target had been a psychiatrist: a Dr. Herbert Cole. Lenny had taken him down in the man's own driveway – double-tap to the head. Coles's car was still running when Lenny had vacated the scene. Even though a few extra murders in Detroit would hardly be noticed, he had to mix up his methods so the kills wouldn't be connected.

He got out on the eleventh floor, walked past a nurses' station, and headed for Room 907. The door was propped open and he glanced in as he walked by. A female nurse was inside the room, picking up dishes and cleaning.

He walked into a small waiting room at the end of the hall, pulled out his phone, and pretended to check his messages as he kept an eye on 907.

After a few minutes, the nurse exited the room with a cart and headed his way. He put his phone to his ear, walked towards the woman, and passed by without making eye contact. He turned left into 907, and closed the door quietly.

The woman was in bad shape. Her blonde hair was short – quarter inch at the most. It made it easy to see the jagged scars that patterned her skull like tectonic plates. He looked at her chart and confirmed the name: *Kelly Hatley.* She was on a large dose of intravenous pain meds and barely awake, which was good. He had no sympathy for the woman, but he wasn't interested in causing suffering for no reason. He was a professional

42

– it was only business.

He pulled a syringe out of his coat and uncapped it. He pierced the top of the IV bag with the needle and injected the clear contents of the syringe. He pulled out the needle, shook the bag gently, and then capped the empty syringe and put it in his pocket.

He started towards the exit but then turned back and looked at his victim. Shooting was so much easier – pull the trigger and it was over. Using a slow method always gave one time to change his mind, and hesitation could be fatal in this business. The woman was young and had obviously struggled hard to recover from her hellacious injuries. It looked to him like she might have survived them. But not now. She was the latest on what he knew was going to be a long list.

Lenny exited the room and headed for the elevators. This one was over. The next ones wouldn't be so easy.

~ 12 ~
Friday, 8 May (7:56 a.m. EST – Washington)

Daniel was still groggy from the restless night. Sleep was intermittent at best, and his eyes burned.

He dropped off his lunch in his office and then rode the elevator down to the seventh floor. The reception desk was identical to that on his floor, and he approached the man behind the desk whose eyes focused in on the ID clipped to his breast pocket.

The man pointed to Daniel's right and said, "713."

He walked down a carpeted corridor and knocked on the last door on the right. It creaked open, and a man he recognized as CIA Director James Thackett appeared.

"Come in, Daniel," Thackett instructed as he removed Daniel's security badge and handed it to him. "Put this in your pocket for now."

Daniel pocketed the I.D. and entered. The room was larger than he'd anticipated, and the scents of leather, light perfume, and what he guessed was pipe tobacco gave it a comfortable ambience. On the left side of the room was a large wooden table, well illuminated with inset lights mounted in the high, coffered ceiling. Ceiling-to-floor windows lined the entire wall opposite the entrance, providing a view of the pine forest similar to that from his office, but wider and not as elevated.

Sunlight illuminated the textured, beige tiles that covered the entire floor of the enormous room. A compact collection of furniture was arranged on a large, square-patterned area rug 50 feet to his right. At the center of the rug was a round coffee table, surrounded by a leather couch on the side nearest the windows, and two matching chairs on the other. A man occupied the far chair, and a woman the far end of the couch.

"Let's join them," Thackett said, leading the way. He pointed Daniel to the couch.

Daniel took a seat next to the woman. He sat on the edge of the couch and leaned forward with his hands on his knees. He wasn't sure if he was supposed to introduce himself or remain quiet. He did the latter.

The woman to his left had reddish-black hair and looked to be in her mid to late thirties. She wore square, black-rimmed glasses. In the chair across from her was a tall, bald man that he thought might be 100.

Thackett, still standing, grabbed one of two ceramic mugs from the middle of the table, placed it in front of Daniel, and then did the same for himself. "Thank you all for coming," he said as he poured coffee for Daniel and himself, and then topped off the cups of the others. "I realize this is highly unusual. Certainly it's a breach of our security protocols, but the situation calls for it."

It was an irreversible breach, Daniel thought. He was to avoid contact with all CIA personnel.

"Please introduce yourselves – first names only – and state the topic of your current projects," Thackett instructed, and gestured to Daniel to start.

Daniel cleared his throat. After a few seconds he managed to say, "I'm Daniel." After an awkward ten more seconds he continued, "I'm researching a mission carried out in Antarctica by the British during World War II called Operation Tabarin." His shoulders twitched upward, tensing his neck muscles and making his head tilt backward for an instant. He made an effort to relax and grabbed the coffee mug from the table. His hand trembled as he took a sip.

Thackett nodded and motioned to the woman.

She shifted in her seat, making the leather couch squeak, and pulled a red strand of her mostly dark hair out of her face. She looked as awkward as Daniel felt.

"I'm Sylvia," she finally said as she pushed her glasses closer to her eyes. "I'm currently investigating the escape of Nazi war criminals from Europe to Latin America, and the underground network they'd set up which remained active until the 1980's."

The old man set his mug down on the table with a shaky hand. He closed his eyes for a second and then spoke. "My name is Horace," he said in a nearly undetectable British accent. His voice was strikingly clear, and did not seem to fit his aged appearance. "I am the most senior Omniscient."

Daniel believed he *had* to be.

"I do not have a specific project," Horace continued, "And haven't for the past 20 years. However, you both have seen some of my reports. For instance, the Japanese atomic bomb monograph is mine."

"You're 5-12-1945?" Daniel asked. He recalled the "signature" from that particular monograph. It was the oldest signature that he'd seen.

Horace nodded. "Now I study the work of the other Omniscients and assess the big picture."

"Horace is our most valuable intelligence resource," Thackett interjected.

"I started in the Office of Strategic Services, or the OSS, during World War II," Horace continued. "Of course, the OSS became the CIA after the war, and I continued on as a case officer – collecting human intelligence in Eastern Europe during the Cold War. I then became a reports officer."

Thackett chimed in, "Like you, Daniel, he'd managed a dozen case officers, directed their efforts, and collected and analyzed their intelligence products. He's a big picture person – he can see connections between seemingly unrelated bits of intelligence."

"What I do now is similar to the work of a reports officer, but on a grander scale," Horace explained, "I manage the Omnis. I assign your projects, study your results, and look for connections."

Daniel wiped the corner of his mouth with his sleeve: it was the ultimate of all intelligence jobs. Although he had access to everything Horace did, he didn't have the *time* to read it all; his hours were spent creating new material – creating levels of the intelligence pyramid. Horace was on the top of that pyramid.

"Now, the reason why you are all here," Thackett said, directing his words to Daniel and Sylvia. "As you know, it's highly unusual – *forbidden* – for Omnis to ever meet each other. And, more so, to meet Horace, or to even know that he exists."

Daniel set his coffee mug on the table and leaned toward Thackett.

Thackett, sensing Daniel's anxiety, raised a finger to him and then nodded back to Horace.

"My brain is nearly 100 years old," Horace explained, the corners of his mouth turning up slightly in either a grin, or a wince. "It has made associations that depended on decades of experience and vast knowledge. Revealing these connections has been of great benefit to the intelligence community, national defense, and so on."

Horace halted and reached again for his coffee cup. Daniel could tell that, like himself, the old man didn't want to divulge information. It wasn't natural.

"Please, tell them, Horace," Thackett prodded in a gentle voice.

Daniel twisted in his seat, laced his fingers together and tightened them until they hurt.

"You see," Horace finally continued, "I've recently made the most disturbing connection. And your reassigned projects reflect this."

Daniel glanced down at his white knuckles and released them.

"Omnis' projects are usually focused on events of the past – mostly the far past," Horace said and looked at Daniel and then to Sylvia. "Your current projects both have origins in the far past, but they're linked to events of the present, and are connected to each other."

46

"Are they important enough to bring us together like this?" Daniel asked spontaneously. His face heated as he flushed with embarrassment for blurting out the question.

Horace answered without hesitation. "There are existential implications."

~ 13 ~
Friday, 8 May (7:15 a.m. CST – Chicago)

The final meeting started with a debriefing that seemed more like an interrogation. The room layout reflected the same, as did the stench of years of cigarette residue infused into the scant furniture. Until now, Will had been pleased with his treatment by the FBI. He turned his gaze back to the older man sitting across the table from him, the fluorescent light glinting off his hairless head.

"I'm not saying you're lying, Dr. Thompson," Agent Hank Fordham explained as he twisted a tuft of his thick gray mustache between his thumb and forefinger. "It's just that all of these things can be described by less uh … *magical* … means."

Will flinched. *Magical? What were they trying to do – make him look crazy?* He squirmed in his seat as the prickly sensation of annoyance tingled in his fingertips. The man was supposed to have been briefed on what had actually happened to him – the actual *transformation*. He'd supposedly seen all of the information – written, audio, and video. Will had been under the impression that the FBI believed his account of events; it was the reason they had trained him for relocation. It seemed now that they were trying to debunk his story.

"Then explain how thousands of flies can spontaneously ignite into flames in mid-flight," Will argued, referring to one of the more spectacular events that had occurred during his treatment. "You have that on *video*."

Fordham opened his mouth to respond, but instead he sighed,

47

opened a thick manila folder, and flicked through its contents. He slid out a document and quickly scanned it with his eyes. "Here we go," he said. "The burning of the flies, and hornets, was caused by an electrical discharge. Says here it was attributed to a problem with the wiring of the equipment."

Will recalled no electrical arcs during those events, but he made a quick estimate of the voltage required to produce a discharge that spanned the distances involved – up to a few feet.

"It's preposterous." Will said. "There's no way the Exoskeleton was energized to *thousands* of volts." The seed of distrust for the FBI, which up to this point had been dormant, sprouted in his mind.

"Our engineers say otherwise."

"Are you forgetting that I'm a physicist?" Without waiting for a response, Will continued. "There's a higher probability that magic was the cause."

Fordham looked down and didn't respond.

"How do you explain the numbers? The probability of doing that was literally one in a *trillion*," Will argued, referring to a daily "guess-the-number" exercise he was forced to carry out during his incarceration. "Magic again?"

Fordham responded by fingering through the folder and pulling out a report. "Says here you only guessed correctly once—the *first* time. After that, the room controllers were so shaken that they'd forgotten to turn off the microphone. You heard them speaking."

Will remembered *seeing* the numbers, not hearing them. He'd read a three-digit number between 0 and a 999 on a digital display, well out of his physical sight. He did it four times in a row, and could have continued indefinitely. "Are you suggesting that I'm lying?" Will asked. His temples pounded.

Fordham didn't respond, but just rolled his mustache and looked blankly at him.

Will had no doubt that it was to the government's advantage to prove him either insane, or a liar. Although it was inconceivable that they could eliminate the thousands of people involved in the colossal

Compressed Punishment program – including over 1200 inmates, and two giant facilities – he knew they'd try. If government leaders hadn't been aware of the secret program before, they certainly were now, and had probably concluded that it's in their best interest to bury it all. If the truth got out, there'd be serious problems – political and otherwise.

Although elements within the FBI had been partially responsible for bringing down the Red Wraith project and extracting him from the horrible Red Box facility, other elements seemed to be turning on him. He thought it strange, the FBI being fractured in such a way, but now he imagined a similar disjointedness in other entities – such as the CIA. It was disconcerting.

Fordham collected the documents, put them back in the file-folders, and pushed them to the side. He sat up straighter, put his elbows on the table, and interlaced his fingers in a ball in front of him. His voice indicating that he guessed what Will was thinking, he said, "I understand that you've gone through some horrific things, both physically and mentally. Without a doubt, such things could trick you into believing that certain events had actually occurred, even hearing voices."

"All of that really happened," Will responded. *And it was only one voice,* he didn't add.

"I believe that *you* believe that," Fordham replied. "But the only way I could ever believe it is to see it for myself. And my colleagues feel the same way. We were a little surprised at the clean bill of health reported by our psychiatrists. Our psych evaluations have become less stringent with time."

Will rubbed his eyes. Maybe a demonstration would convince him. He closed his eyes and concentrated on a specific pain experience from the Red Box – oral surgery, no anesthetics. His perspective began to move upward from his body.

He stopped. If he'd learned anything from the witch trial where he'd been convicted on no physical evidence, it was to control his urge to prove himself to people. He'd failed proving his innocence during the trial, and there was nothing that was as high stakes as that.

He collected himself and opened his eyes. "If you want to see it for yourself, Agent Fordham, perhaps you could ask them to restart the program and fit you for an Exoskeleton," he suggested with unveiled sarcasm. "Just make sure they record everything. Otherwise people have a tendency to not believe you."

Fordham's face flushed, but he grinned and spoke towards the window at Will's back. "I think that's enough."

A tinny voice emanated from a speaker behind Will. "Okay."

Fordham then looked to Will, smiling but still reddened. "I *do* believe you. So do the other members of our group. My job was to try to get you to do something to reveal your uh … *talents*."

Will understood and immediately cooled down. He had to be more careful. They'd almost succeeded in getting him to reveal himself.

"I'm an experienced interrogator," Fordham continued, "but it was unpleasant pissing you off like that – you having gone through so much. I feel ashamed." He reached an open hand across the table.

Will shook his hand and said, "You did a good job."

A door opened and two men and a woman entered. Will recognized two of them: the leader of his relocation case, Terrence Bolden, and the man who had snapped him during the surveillance exercise, Roy, who winked and nodded to him. He didn't recognize the woman.

They all took chairs around the table and introduced themselves. Bolden was the youngest of the group, early thirties, tall, short brown hair, and wore small wire-framed glasses. He handed a sealed envelope to Will and flopped a large leather pouch on the table, making a sound like that of a big purse with keys concealed somewhere in its bowels.

Bolden started, directing his message to the whole group, "The people in this room, and one or two FBI contacts in your relocation area, are the only ones who will know your whereabouts. These are the only people you can trust."

Will didn't trust any of them.

Bolden handed him some documents. "Your cover name is William Tasker, and you'll live in Baton Rouge, Louisiana for at least six months."

"Baton Rouge?" Will asked, surprised.

50

"There's some activity there," Bolden explained. "We were going to wait on this, but after what happened last night with the Israeli, we want you out of Chicago as soon as possible. It should work well since you're familiar with the place."

Will nodded. He'd left Baton Rouge over a decade ago, but it was where he'd attended graduate school.

Bolden handed him a Social Security card, a Louisiana driver's license, two credit cards, a mobile phone, a laptop computer, and a ring of keys. "A car is registered under your alias. The keys are for your new apartment. Nice place."

Will looked at the pile of stuff in front of him. His stomach seemed to close in on itself. "When do I leave?" he asked.

"Collect your things tonight and head out early tomorrow morning," Bolden replied as he handed Will the phone. "This has excellent security features, and it's the only phone you should use. Don't answer blocked calls or calls from unknown numbers." Bolden raised an eyebrow. "If you're going to continue to communicate with Ms. Walker, she needs to use a burner phone."

Will nodded. He knew she was savvy about such things.

"If we need to contact you," Bolden continued, "we'll first send a text message with the code *523*."

Will flinched at the number.

"We thought you'd remember it," Bolden said.

It had been Will's inmate number at the Red Box.

~ 14 ~
Friday, 8 May (8:38 a.m. EST – Washington)

Daniel listened intently. Horace's voice was commanding for his age, and his face projected calmness even though his eyes seemed to show something else.

"This story starts with the early quest for *Terra Australis*

51

Incognita, known now as Antarctica, of course," Horace explained. "James Cook, better known as the famous *Captain Cook* of the storybooks, crossed the Antarctic Circle in the late 1700's, but never found his way to the Antarctic mainland." He stopped and addressed Daniel. "Undoubtedly your early research on Operation Tabarin has taken you to Cook's voyages."

Daniel shook his head. "Not yet."

"It will, eventually," Horace explained, "and you'll then find that some of the details of Cook's Antarctic adventures have been overlooked."

"*You* wrote the monograph on the Cook expeditions," Sylvia blurted. "I've seen it."

"Yes, I published it in 1964," Horace said. "In December of '63, I'd discovered something in Cook's captain's log that didn't have much meaning to me at the time, more than a half-century ago." Horace smiled and rubbed the white stubble on his chin. "My, the time has passed."

"Does it mean something now?" Daniel asked, leaning forward in his seat.

"Patience, Daniel," Horace said as he smiled and raised his hand. "Cook's ship hit something, probably ice, and was damaged. They were dead in the water for two days while conducting repairs. They were fortunate to have calm seas at the time, since they had to get under the hull – an extremely dangerous operation in the icy waters."

"They had to go *into* the water?" Sylvia asked, and seemed to shiver.

"They'd devised means for handling such a situation, but a person could only stay in the frigid water for a minute at a time," Horace explained. "But it's fortunate that this incident occurred. You see, while the men were under water, they heard a noise."

"What do you mean, like an animal?" Daniel asked.

Horace shook his head. "Mechanical, like a knocking sound," he replied. "The sailors who'd worked in the water described it as a repeating pattern of sharp noises – painful to the ears."

Daniel wrung his hands. "Could it have been someone on the ship making the noise?"

"The crew was spooked, so Cook ordered everyone to the deck to make sure no one could do such a thing," Horace replied. "It would only take some prankster with hammer, although it might be hard to mimic the noise as it was described. Once everyone reported on deck, the repairmen were lowered into the water one-by-one to see if the noise persisted. Cook himself did it."

"And?" Daniel asked, intently.

"It was there," Horace chuckled, seemingly in response to Daniel's captivation. "Soon the repairs were complete, the wind came back, and they sailed away."

"Were the sounds confirmed by anyone else?" Sylvia asked.

"Two years later, the Royal Navy sent a ship to the area and the noise was gone," Horace said. "They'd checked again a few years later. Again, nothing."

Horace rubbed his hand over his head and took a breath. He continued, "You both have done enough research to know how unrelated events could turn out to be connected. And this observation by the fabled Captain Cook is connected to the present."

"How so?" Daniel asked.

"Well," Horace said as he leaned back in his chair. He put his hands behind his head and grinned. "The noise has returned."

CHAPTER III

~ 1 ~

Saturday, 9 May (7:03 a.m. CST – Chicago)

Will's gut was as heavy as lead as he got into the SUV and started the long drive south. He had no appetite, and coffee only made his stomach burn. Being the weekend, at least he wouldn't have to fight traffic on his way through the city.

The sun shone brightly on the left side of his face as Interstate 57 South took him out of Chicago towards Memphis. He put on his sunglasses and turned off the scratchy AM radio, leaving him with only his thoughts and the sounds of tires and wind.

He and Denise had grown much closer than he'd realized, and leaving her behind was more difficult than he'd imagined. After his fiancé had deserted him, he thought he'd never trust anyone again. Denise was different.

The night before, she'd made dinner for him in her apartment. Afterwards, they split a bottle of wine and talked until well after midnight. She'd expressed her feelings without holding back, and he told her how he felt. There were many tears.

He'd explained why he had to leave – that she and Jonathan would be in danger if he stayed. Although they'd still talk regularly, she agreed that it was no way to begin a relationship. She'd taken it well – better than he did.

He turned the radio on and forced himself to think about something else. What would things be like in Baton Rouge after more than a decade?

Although he was okay with staying in a safe house for a while, the objective was not well defined. His case handler had told him that he'd partake in the surveillance of former Red Box inmates who'd been gathering in the area, but provided no details. The FBI didn't know what

54

the men were doing, or why they were in Baton Rouge. He knew another Compressed Punishment facility was being built in the city, but construction had been halted when the program was shut down.

The drive south on Interstate 57 was going to be long and featureless, but he was anxious to the get to southern Illinois and pass by Cordova, the little college town where he'd tried to cultivate a life and career. It was the place where, over a year earlier, he'd been falsely accused and eventually convicted of a horrible crime. Before he reached Cordova, however, he'd pass by Marion Prison, where he'd been incarcerated before going to the Red Box.

He shuddered. For an instant his thoughts conflicted: his instinct was to avoid the place where his life had plummeted into despair. But his curiosity trumped the darker emotions. He wanted to see it, this time from the outside.

~ 2 ~

Saturday, 9 May (8:42 a.m. EST – Antarctic Circle)

McHenry washed down the last bite of his breakfast with a swig of bug juice, a cool-aid-like drink that could double as a cleaning agent. They were closing in on their destination, and it would soon be time to violate every instinct of self-preservation that he had as a submarine captain. They'd reveal their presence to every ship in the area. He felt reassured, however, that a carrier group was on its way, and that other friendly subs were sleeping nearby.

There must be some genuine worry in Washington about whatever was making the noise. If he had to guess, it was a piece of lost scientific apparatus – scientists sent devices up in balloons all the time, many of which get blown out to sea, and then fall in the water and sink into the deep. It just seemed to him that exposing an attack sub was an overreaction. They should've sent a surface exploration team.

A young sailor entered the mess hall and approached McHenry.

"We're in position, cap'n," he said.

McHenry followed him through a maze of tight walkways and ladders to the sonar room. He stopped at a consul where his best sonar tech tapped away at a computer.

"What's the status, Finley?" McHenry asked.

"Located the source, same position as yesterday," Finley explained. "The sounders and detectors are in the lock and ready to be deployed."

"How long will we be vulnerable?"

"The array will be in passive mode until we get to depth," Finley explained. "As for active time, that depends on how many images you want."

"We'll see what they look like," McHenry said. "We aren't leaving until we have what we need – we don't want to do this twice. Let's get the show on the road."

Finley pushed a button. "Load-lock filling." Thirty seconds later he said, "Bay hatch open, winch unwinding, turning on bay camera." He clicked a button on the computer monitor opening a video frame. A mess of cords and pulleys appeared on the screen.

"Don't tangle anything," McHenry warned.

"Just have to do it in the right order. The source goes first," Finley explained and pointed to the screen as a white, beach-ball-sized, faceted sphere, lowered by cable out of sight and into the dark. He clicked another button. "And now the detector array."

The device resembled a large chandelier, with detectors in place of lights. "How much line do we have?" McHenry asked

"Five hundred meters," Finley answered. "Should be enough to get some good images. With our drift, we'll get a few perspectives."

If we're lucky, McHenry thought. He knew there was going to be some complex motion involved with the operation. The currents in the southern seas were notoriously strong and unpredictable. He worried that deeper crosscurrents might produce slack in the cables, resulting in a whiplash effect. The whole thing could end up on the ocean floor, and there was no retrieving it from that depth. But it didn't matter: his orders were to take whatever risks necessary to get the images. Loss of equipment and, by implication, lives, were acceptable risks in this mission. It was an internal conflict for him, the risk versus his curiosity. A similar anxiety was evident in the eyes around him.

"Everything is in position," Finley informed.

"Turn it on," McHenry ordered. "Let's see what this is all about."

Finley clicked a few buttons and typed parameters into the computer control program. "Detectors active. Standing by to energize the sounding source."

"Do it," McHenry said without hesitation. He was curious to see how the new active sonar imaging system performed. The *North Dakota* was filled with new, unproven equipment that was touted as "advanced." For him it was just another source of worry.

Finley clicked a button and said, "We're in active mode and collecting data."

A minute later an image formed in the data acquisition window.

"This is a direct overhead view," Finley explained. "Looks like there's an object at about 1,500 meters. The depth to the sea floor is 4,000."

McHenry stared at the gray-toned image. It looked like a sphere suspended in the water.

Finley clicked a button labeled Color Enhancement, and the image reformed with stunning clarity, a blue-green sphere over the darker background of the seafloor.

The sphere seemed to have a bulge on one side. "How big is this thing?" McHenry asked.

"About 25 meters in diameter," Finley answered.

Stunned, McHenry said, "That's enormous. How can that thing survive at that depth?" He knew no one had the answer. There were no known structures of that size that could survive the hydrostatic pressures at that depth – unless it wasn't hollow.

"We need a profile shot," McHenry said and grabbed a communicator device from his pocket that resembled a small cell phone. He pressed a button and spoke into it, "Get us to max depth, and 200 meters east of our current position. Go slowly – one knot."

"We have another 100 meters on the array. Shall we go to max depth on that as well?" Finley asked.

"Yes, drop it when we're stationary," McHenry replied. "Take images as we move."

Finley nodded and said with apparent hesitation, "They might be blurred."

"Do it. The more data we have the better. We'll get better images when we're stationary."

The first new image formed on the screen.

"That's not too bad," Finley commented.

The coloring made the object look very spherical, with no evidence of a bulge. A few minutes later, the next image appeared and the asymmetry was on the opposite side.

"That's odd," McHenry said, twisting his head to view the screen from a different angle.

The next image showed the bulge in the same place, but more pronounced. And the next even more pronounced, and slightly tapered.

A few minutes later, McHenry was informed that they had reached the desired location, and Finley turned to look at him.

"Lowering the array to maximum depth," Finley informed.

Finley repositioned the array and took an image. At first, what came up on the screen was baffling. But they quickly figured it out: the bulge was a misperception caused by their angle of view from above. It was actually a long stem that propped up the sphere from below.

"How far does that thing go down?" McHenry asked.

Finley responded by color-enhancing the image. The answer was obvious.

"The son-of-a-bitch goes all the way into the floor," McHenry gasped. "That's another 2,000 meters."

"Twenty-five hundred, sir," Finley corrected, and looked at him wide-eyed.

"How in the hell was that constructed?" McHenry asked, again knowing there wasn't an explanation. "We have the images?"

Finley nodded.

"Go silent and pull up the array," McHenry instructed. "Then get the data ready for transmission. We're getting the hell out of here."

They'd again have to risk detection by taking the *North Dakota* to transmission depth to send the image files. He wondered if his superiors in Washington were expecting what they were about to get.

~ 3 ~

Saturday, 9 May (12:03 p.m. CST — Southern Illinois)

Will shuddered as he passed the Marion maximum-security prison. The cold blue structures of the complex were unimpressive from the highway, but the razor wire glittering in the sunlight like strings of tiny mirrors reminded him of what was inside. At the time, it was the closest he'd ever come to hell. Marion Prison was as close to being a corrections facility as a slaughterhouse was to being veterinary clinic. He was convinced a well-behaved person might emerge criminally insane from such a place. He'd started along that track during his short stint there.

Twenty minutes later he passed the exit for Cordova, Illinois, where he'd spent six years of his life as a university physics professor. His thoughts turned to his ex-fiancé, Pam. They'd been engaged and living together for a year when he'd been arrested. The anger of her betrayal still burned in his chest. She'd turned on him the instant she learned of the allegations that he'd raped and tried to murder a teenage girl. It was the most cutting, irreversible insult that could be leveed upon a person. And her betrayal had affected the trial: it probably put the jury over the edge to convict him.

He took a sip of soda and chewed ice to get his thoughts to dissipate.

A few minutes south of the Cordova exit, the billboards and trees thinned out. To the west, a mile off the highway, the light poles of the football stadium he'd visited the night of the arrest loomed above a dense grove of pine trees. It was the crime scene. It was strange how different everything seemed in the sunlight. During the past two years his mind had made it out to be a much darker place. But there was darkness in everything, from the most beautiful tropical beach where a mother's child had drowned, to the magnificent house where a man comes home to find his family murdered. The sunlight couldn't hide such things. Each place was different for everyone.

He steered his thoughts to something more positive. Baton Rouge would be a welcomed change. The night before he'd dreamt of crawfish and gumbo – a stark difference from his usual nightmares. Escaping the unseasonably cool Chicago spring would also be a plus, and his new abode was touted as a vacation resort.

He shifted in his seat, gripped the steering wheel tightly, and tilted his head sharply to the left and right, stretching his neck muscles. His new arrangement was not sustainable: how long did the FBI plan to keep him there? He had no legal or operational knowledge of how to engage in an investigation. He'd only been trained to keep himself safe.

He suspected the FBI had given him the mobile phone more to track him than to contact him. He'd play along for the time being. After the Israeli's warning, it was best he went off the grid for a while. But the isolation would serve a purpose other than keeping him safe. A feeling of urgency was building in him to explore his new abilities and the hidden world to which they'd given him access. The current situation would give him the opportunity to do this.

A road sign indicated that Memphis was 245 miles south. He'd stop there for the night.

~ 4 ~

Saturday, 9 May (1:10 p.m. CST – Baton Rouge)

Zhichao Cho trembled as he stared at the package on his desk. He could hardly believe it had taken so little time to acquire. His stomach twisted with the idea that maybe they hadn't gotten everything.

He turned the heavy box so he could access the seams, cut the packing tape with a utility knife, and tore open the flaps. Each item he extracted had been carefully wrapped in plastic, and he arranged them on the table in three piles: bound documents, file folders, and two data storage drives. It was the latter that captured his interest.

Dates and numbers were written in red marker on a piece of paper taped to the top of each drive. The latter indicated the number of the treatment room in which the video had been recorded. He extracted the one with the earliest date from its case, and connected a cable between it and his laptop. A few seconds later he started the first video.

Cho squealed in delight when the first image appeared. It was the first time he'd seen a subject inside an operational Exoskeleton. Before he'd acquired Syncorp, the company had provided him with still images for demonstration purposes. They never had access to actual treatment footage. That information was highly classified and only available to authorized government personnel.

The video showed an overhead view of a man inside a horizontally oriented Exoskeleton positioned a few feet above the floor. The time rolled at the top right of the screen: the recording had started at 6:33 a.m. After about a minute a door opened and a middle-aged man and a young blonde woman, both dressed in white coats, rolled in carts filled with tools and gadgets. When they reached the Exoskeleton, a bundle of tubes and cables lowered from the ceiling. They connected them to receptacles on the carts, and the man grabbed a device that looked like an electric toothbrush and pressed a button on its handle. The device responded with a high-pitched whine that he immediately recognized. They were *dentists*.

The ensuing torture was nothing like he had ever seen. The dentists carried out procedures without anesthetics, and he found himself envying them. Cho had carried out some fairly gruesome things himself during his rising years in Chinese intelligence, but nothing under such extreme and controlled conditions. What he was witnessing was how it was supposed to be done.

For over two hours, the drilling and screaming was interrupted only to allow the subject to regain consciousness after passing out. Cho yawned, and then stood and stretched his legs as the video continued. What was he supposed to be looking for? The video had been deemed important for some reason. Did he miss it?

He walked away from the desk to a counter where an electric teapot steamed away. He selected a bag of green tea from a jar, put it in a cup, and filled it with hot water. When he returned to the computer, the blonde woman was on the floor and the dentist was standing over her, trying to help her to her feet. *What the hell happened? Did she pass out?*

He reset the video to the point when he'd gone for tea. The man backed away from the subject and let his assistant take over.

The woman selected an instrument and approached the subject, but before she even touched him, her head spontaneously jerked to the side and she fell to the floor, landing hard. It looked unnatural, as if she'd been struck on the side of the head.

Cho replayed the scene a dozen times. This was what he was supposed to see.

He went the computer keyboard and navigated to the file folder with the video files. The file names indicated they were all footage of the same subject: Number *523*.

~ 5 ~
Saturday, 9 May (3:41 p.m. EST – Washington)

Daniel closed the file he'd been reading for the past two hours and slapped it down on the coffee table. He sat on the couch, put his hands on his head, and massaged his temples with his fingers. What was he expected to do? Thackett had made it clear: nobody knew what was happening. In the meantime, he and Sylvia would work on the problem, guided by the grandmaster of all Omnis, Horace. But he and Sylvia would have to come up with their own, unbiased conclusions without knowing how Horace came to his. It wasn't clear that Horace had a logical path to his conclusions, whatever they were. Daniel suspected the man was working on a gut feeling.

He unwrapped a granola bar, took a bite, and chased it with a sip of water. Something bothered him: if Horace was who Thackett said he was – the country's greatest intelligence resource – then the old man's identity had been compromised. He wondered now if he and Sylvia would have to be eliminated once they'd served their purpose. Through his many years of classified research, he'd often crossed cases of preventive assassinations. So it was a possibility. Or did they trust him and Sylvia? After all, they'd eventually need someone to replace Horace.

Daniel sighed and shook his head. What was he going to do, quit?

The new project had elements that made it different from all the others, including a facet he'd not before experienced: time pressure. It was as if there was a race to solve some big puzzle.

He choked down the rest of his snack, picked up the file, and got back to Operation Tabarin.

He'd concluded that the Brits and Americans had initiated their respective operations as a response to something, and their response had to be related to the war effort. The Americans had initiated their mission after the war ended, so to whatever it was that they were responding had persisted after the war.

Up to this point, he hadn't turned up anything more than background information. However, he did find a clue in a Royal Navy logbook from a reconnaissance vessel that had been deployed in the southern sea before the war had begun. The British ship had followed a German vessel, called the *Schwabenland,* to Antarctica. No details were given about the reason for their suspicion of this vessel, nor anything they'd discovered about it.

Daniel submitted a requisition for top-secret documents and emailed it to the appropriate CIA address. He'd have all the available information about the *Schwabenland* in the morning.

He twitched. The urgency of the assignment had his mind tumbling with adrenaline. What he needed was a nap. Instead, he turned on the electric teapot on the windowsill. He hoped some tea would sooth his nerves and ready him for the long hours ahead.

~ 6 ~
Saturday, 9 May (7:58 p.m. CST — Chicago)

Lenny Butrolsky leaned his throbbing right shoulder on the wall of the balcony of his 19th floor hotel room. The even pressure spread the pain around so that it wasn't all in one place.

The sweet Chicago night air was poisoned intermittently by cigarette smoke that wafted up from a lower balcony. The enormous red moon dominated the cloudless sky above the Great Lake despite the lights of the city. The glittering ripples in the water made him think about better times, and the uncertain future.

He dialed the number on his secure mobile phone. A man answered after one ring.

"It's done," Lenny said, referring to his latest target, Kelly Hatley.

"We know," the man responded. "The funds will be deposited within 24 hours along with the first installment for your next job."

"Instructions coming by the same method?" Lenny asked.

"Yes," the man replied and hung up.

Lenny put the phone in his pocket and looked out over the water. Hatley had been taken out with a simple injection into her I-V. He felt hollow inside when he thought about her – she was in her late twenties, at most. Although, he thought, by virtue of her choice of employer she was no angel. He grinned and nodded as he took a deep breath. He could say the same for himself. But his actions damned him much more than anything the woman had done.

The Hatley job had been easy. He preferred it that way, as would anyone in his profession, but he'd become more aware of risks now that he was considering retirement. Maybe he'd just do a few more jobs. It seemed he could get all the work he wanted. He suspected his handler got orders directly from the former CIA Director, Terrance Gould, who'd been

64

desperately trying to dispose of Red Wraith personnel since his untimely removal four months ago.

Lenny was uniquely suited for such a cleanup operation. He'd been intimately involved in the project – he knew the major players, what they did, and what they looked like. It was fortunate for Gould that many of the most threatening people had already been eliminated – either by Lenny, or killed in the explosion at the Red Box. But there were others.

His phone buzzed. It was a text message indicating that a new email awaited him in a secure account. They never actually *sent* emails – it was too risky. Instead, they wrote drafts and saved them so that someone else could log in and read them. Afterwards, they were deleted. He navigated to the email account and read.

His next target was a Dr. Martha Epstein. Lenny immediately made the connection to her Red Box alias, *Dr. Smith*. She was a psychologist who had interacted with every patient as they entered the program. She knew what happened there, and could make connections to others, including Gould.

He read on and swore under his breath. He had to go Flint, Michigan. The woman didn't have the common sense to get out of the area, and now he'd have to return to the place where he'd already carried out multiple hits. Even though it would be difficult to link him to any of those jobs, it was downright risky.

So far, all of his targets had been Red Box personnel. *Was someone else eliminating people from the Long Island facility?* he wondered. He knew the man who had held the security post there, a position equivalent to his at the Red Box. That man had been well connected in upper government circles, whereas Lenny had been linked directly to the project head, Heinrich Bergmann. He bet that the other man was conducting cleanup operations of his own. Perhaps they'd cross paths.

The jobs would get increasingly more risky, and Lenny thought about upping his fee. But he'd wait on that until he had enough in the bank to quit the business. Besides, it was the former CIA Director who had arranged for his escape from the hospital. That was risky. Perhaps he owed the man some work.

~ 7 ~
Saturday, 9 May (10:45 p.m. CST – Memphis, Tennessee)

Will ate a late dinner of Memphis-style ribs in the hotel restaurant and then went up to his room. No matter how now nice they were, hotel rooms could be some of the loneliest places on earth. Like most things, it depended on one's state of mind.

He stepped through a sliding glass door onto the room's seventh floor balcony and looked out over the Mississippi River as a barge drifted under a bridge. He leaned against the railing and admired the stars shimmering in the night sky. They were brilliant despite the large red moon and lights of the city. Each star represented the possibility of a different world, but it was the blackness between them that gave him a sense of the infinite, the eternal, and, for some unknown reason, hope.

His phone vibrated in his jacket pocket. He pulled it out and looked at the screen: it was Denise.

"I miss you," she said before saying hello.

His chest tightened.

"I should have gone with you," she said.

Will wanted her with him, but it would have been selfish. "It's only temporary," he assured her. Even though that was true, he wasn't certain where he'd go next. Maybe he'd be in even deeper cover and be out of contact with her completely.

Her voice changed to a professional tone as she filled him in on the status of his civil case, and then on their hunt for Red Box personnel. What she told him next made his mind reel.

"Kelly Hatley passed away," she said.

He was speechless. The young dental assistant was sadistic and she deserved what she got, but it was also saddening. He felt cheated: he'd wanted her to survive so that she'd be confronted with her crimes and sent to prison.

66

"When?"

"Last night. She was overmedicated. She was murdered."

So it had started. He imagined a food chain with the government at the top hunting down all Red Wraith personnel. The upper-echelon Red Wraith figures were second in the chain, taking out the lower-ranked personnel before the FBI caught up with them and offered deals for their testimonies.

Where did he fit into the food chain? he wondered. *And what about Denise and Jonathan?*

"You and Jonathan better watch your backs," he warned. "You're prominent in the investigation. You're dealing with ruthless people."

She assured him that they'd be okay, and they ended the call a minute later, leaving him in a numbing silence.

To take his mind off of it, he reached for the television remote, but then reconsidered. It was time to practice.

He leaned back on the bed and put his arms at his sides. He closed his eyes and brought memories of agony to the front of his mind, concentrating on the pain of the dental treatments in the Red Box ... Kelly Hatley driving a sharp instrument under his left upper molar and into his jawbone ... the dentist cracking a wisdom tooth with a curved pliers ... the white hot pain surging through his entire jaw and leaching into his head and neck ... and then he was out ...

He looked down on his body from above. His face seemed relaxed. Only slivers of white were visible in his mostly-closed eyes. He moved about the room and *touched* things. He grabbed the remote, turned on the TV, and then turned it off again. He went into the bathroom, picked up a glass, and filled it at the faucet. As he brought it back into the room, he stopped at a mirror and looked in wonder. In the mirror were the reflections of both his body, flat on the bed, and the glass of water suspended in space. He stared at image for a few seconds, trying to decide whether it was real, and then moved along to the bed and put the glass on the nightstand.

After a few more minutes of moving around the room, and out and over the balcony, he returned to his body and opened his eyes. He sat up, grabbed the glass with his hand, and took a drink. He put it back on the nightstand and watched as the disturbance on the water's surface dampened to smoothness. He lived in two worlds: one constrained to the physics of matter and time, and the other bounded by neither. The latter caused him great angst. There was a purpose for it, for *him*. He had no idea what it was but, as the Israeli said, it was something that transcended the geopolitical. It was deeper.

His eyes were tired, and he'd need sleep if he were going to get an early start on the six-hour drive to Baton Rouge. He was returning to his past, but his purpose resided somewhere in the unknown future.

CHAPTER IV

~ 1 ~

Sunday, 10 May (4:01 a.m. EST – Antarctic Circle)

Captain McHenry walked around the sonar consul to another control station. He was on minimum sleep and maximum caffeine. His eyes burned as he squinted into a video monitor that lit up the face of the man testing the equipment. "Ready, Stuart?" McHenry asked.

"Going through some preliminary checks, sir," Stuart replied, focused on the controls. He pushed a button and the computer screen flashed white. The display then faded to a view of a load-lock bay containing a small submarine.

"The *Little Dakota* easy to operate?" McHenry asked.

"The right joystick steers, and the left directs the camera," Stuart replied. "The depth, speed, and lighting are controlled by the keyboard. Not too complicated."

"We'll be in position soon," McHenry said and then walked to the navigation station where a team of four monitored computer stations. A large screen displayed a map with a blue line that represented the *North Dakota's* past and projected course. Seeing their current location on a map had often amazed him. He'd been in so many strange places over the years: beneath the North Pole, the bottom of foreign harbors, and, now, inside the Antarctic Circle. But it had never felt like actually being there. It was like reading a book: his physical environment was unchanging, but his imagination filled in the gaps and gave him a sense of what was outside.

They were about 150 nautical miles southwest of Dronning Maud Land, in the Weddell Sea, near the Brunt Ice Shelf. Why anyone would expend so much effort to build a structure in such a place he couldn't fathom.

"We're in position," a navigator said.

McHenry made his way to sonar. "Finley, you getting the signal?"

69

"Had it locked in an hour ago," Finley replied.

"Stuart, ready the launch," McHenry said.

"*Little Dakota's* ready," Stuart replied.

"Go," McHenry ordered.

Stuart actuated the load-lock fill valve.

Other sailors jostled for position behind McHenry to get a line of sight to the video feed.

The load-lock bay flooded with seawater and quickly rose above the submersible. A few seconds later, the bay doors opened, and the clamps holding the *Little Dakota* in place disengaged. The mini-sub was free to roam.

"How much line do we have?" McHenry asked Stuart, referring to the umbilical cord providing remote control communications to the sub.

"About 2,500 meters of fiber-optic cable. But we have to be careful to avoid slack," Stuart explained. "The crosscurrents will snap the line."

The *Little Dakota* had two built-in emergency protocols. One made it blow its ballast tanks and go to the surface if its tether was severed. The other *filled* the ballasts and made it sink to its destruction. The latter option was selected for this operation.

It was a quiet vehicle, even more so than its parent, which made him feel better than he had during the noisy operation of the previous day. Returning to the same area after just 24 hours, however, made his stomach burn.

After a few minutes, Stuart reported, "*LD* is at 1400 feet, but still no visible on the sphere."

"We're coming at it from above," McHenry said. "Make sure we don't land on top of it."

He tried to suppress a thought that loomed in the back of his mind: was it possible that the thing was rigged – booby-trapped for an inquisitive cat like an American fast-attack sub? He'd brought up the idea hours earlier with Diggs, but they'd both dismissed the notion. First, it would be an exceedingly elaborate trap just to kill one sub. Second, it would mean war for whomever had set it. Still, the thought lingered.

"Stopping at depth, 1,480 meters," Stuart said. "It should be close by. Going to circle around and look."

Stuart tipped the camera downward with left joystick and circled the sub slowly with the right. About halfway around the circle, gasps and expletives spewed from the crew. "Recording," Stuart said.

The smooth, white sphere had no markings of any kind – no seams, rivets, paint, scratches – nothing.

"Get closer," McHenry said. "Don't hit it." He was more concerned with the noise it would make than with damaging it.

Stuart guided the *Little Dakota* closer until the screen filled with the white color of the object. "Fifteen meters away, sir," Stuart said. "Probably shouldn't risk getting closer. The current compensators might not be able to keeps us stable."

McHenry nodded, not averting his eyes from the screen. The surface was featureless. "Go all the way around."

Stuart piloted the sub along the equator of the sphere. The surface was bright white, at least in the lights of the mini-sub, but not shiny. It seemed like it had a texture similar to that of unglazed ceramic – like that on the backside of a bathroom tile.

"Let's look underneath, at the stem," McHenry said.

The sub backed off a few meters and then descended until the joint between the stem and bottom of the sphere came into view. The camera panned back and forth. The cylindrical stem connected to the sphere via a smooth joint – as if the whole thing, sphere and stem, were cut from one enormous piece of material.

"Move down the stem," McHenry instructed. It was smooth like the sphere, but he hoped there was a marking of some kind – a serial number or a company name – giving away its maker.

Stuart lowered the sub along the stem, panning the camera back and forth along the way. It revealed nothing but a smooth, white surface, but its radius increased gradually with depth. The *Little Dakota* stopped.

"We're at maximum depth," Stuart informed.

"Damn," McHenry cursed. "Where are we?"

71

"Twenty-three hundred meters on the tether," Stuart replied. "We started at 240 meters, so the absolute depth of *Little Dakota* is currently 2,540 meters."

"Christ, that thing goes on for another 1,500 meters," McHenry said. They needed a longer tether. "Bring it up, and let's get the hell outta Dodge." It was time to communicate the information back to Naval Command.

McHenry was acutely aware of the risks they'd been taking, and how easy it was to get used to such behavior. His father, a machinist, had often claimed the he'd been able to keep all of his fingers by sustaining a healthy fear of the powerful machines that he used every day. It was prudent to have a similar outlook as a sub captain.

But that self-preserving awareness was slipping away. The mystery at the bottom of the sea was taking over.

~ 2 ~

Sunday, 10 May (5:58 a.m. EST – Washington)

The sun warmed the right side of Daniel's face as he sipped coffee from his glass mug. His unusually early 6:00 a.m. arrival warranted something stronger than his usual cup of green tea. He'd been awake since 4 a.m.

Horace hadn't given him much to go on. However, the old man's words had kept him riled through the past two nights. *Existential implications.*

Something was sounding in the icy deep of the Weddell Sea, a little over 150 miles off the coast of western Antarctica. It had been two centuries since Captain Cook heard the same signal in approximately the same location. The noise must have been dormant for all that time; otherwise it would have been discovered by military ships, or by the multitude of scientists who studied that part of the world. *So why had it come back to life?*

72

Daniel concluded the previous evening that Operation Tabarin had been instigated by the voyage of the German ship, *Schwabenland*. And it seemed that that vessel had spurred events that extended many years into the future, maybe even to present day.

As if cued by his thoughts, there was a knock at the door. He opened it, and Sandy stood in the doorway with a large envelope. He signed the receipt, thanked her, and closed the door.

The size of the package disappointed him.

He sat on the couch and tore it open, removed the contents – about two hundred pages of individually bound documents – and set them on the coffee table in front of the couch. He sorted them by country of origin, and located the one that he sought: a report by Britain's Secret Intelligence Service, or SIS, now known as MI-6. It was the logical place to start, Tabarin being a British mission.

He finished reading the document in just under two hours and looked over his notes. The *Schwabenland* was an exploratory vessel. It had set out on its Antarctic expedition at the end of 1938, just before the outbreak of World War II. Herman Goering himself had authorized the mission, the official objective of which had to do with Germany's concerns about the whaling industry. It made sense since whaling was important for the supply of lubricants and food products. However, the Germans were more likely concerned at the time with another whale byproduct – glycerin for *nitroglycerine* to be used in explosives.

It was also suggested that, anticipating the invasion of Russia, Goering needed to test aircraft performance in extremely cold weather. The *Schwabenland* had been rigged with a catapult to launch small seaplanes from its deck, which could then be retrieved with an onboard crane.

The SIS report claimed that the primary objective of the *Schwabenland* was to scout for viable areas for U-boat landings, both in the Antarctic region of Dronning Maud Land and in the isolated Brazilian Islands of Ilha Trinidade, 1,000 kilometers east of Vitoria, Brazil. A British reconnaissance vessel had documented an awkward, open-sea meeting between a German U-boat and the *Schwabenland* in the Weddell

Sea, about 200 kilometers off the coast of Antarctica. The U-Boat was not identified.

Daniel got a chill and rubbed the back of his neck. A German U-boat in the Weddell Sea brought up many questions. *Had the noise been there in 1938? Had the U-boat detected it?* The meeting place could have just been a coincidence, but he doubted it.

He stood and looked through the window over the tops of the trees to the eastern horizon. That a device of any sort could have been positioned in one of the least accessible locations on the planet during the late 1700's was intriguing. But a machine of any kind operating for over two hundred years – and in *saltwater* – was downright fascinating. A hoax of this magnitude – even in current times – seemed impossible. Daniel was a skeptic by nature, but he knew this couldn't be a trick.

His desk phone rang. It was Director Thackett. They had more information, and were to meet at 4:00 p.m. in Room 713. He looked at the clock on his computer: 12:48 p.m. He'd forgotten to eat lunch.

~ 3 ~

Sunday, 10 May (1:52 p.m. CST – Baton Rouge)

Will took a right on the Jefferson Highway off-ramp and found himself in dense, stop-and-go traffic. He recalled that this part of town had been a horse ranch just a decade earlier. Now it was packed with stores, restaurants, and fancy houses.

He turned onto Corporate Boulevard and weaved his way through a labyrinth of high-end apartment complexes until his GPS guided him to the address he'd programmed that morning. He parked in a sparsely populated lot, and climbed several flights of outdoor stairs to a third floor apartment. He unlocked and opened the door, and the odors of new construction and carpet tingled in his nostrils.

He walked in and flipped a light switch. Bright lights, recessed in the high ceiling, illuminated a fully furnished living room, dining room, and kitchen. It was an open floor plan; the only thing separating the kitchen from the living room was an island with a large, double sink. Four barstools were lined beneath its black granite countertop.

He padded across the wood laminate floor and around the island. He pressed a switch that energized the lights hanging over the counter, and then opened the large stainless steel refrigerator: empty, clean, and new.

Exploring the rest of the flat, he found two bedrooms: one with a carpeted floor and a queen-sized bed. The other had wood floors and was set up as a study, furnished with a large desk, couch, upholstered chairs, and a coffee table.

He shook his head and sighed. The apartment was excellent.

He looked out a window into the bright afternoon and decided it was a good time to explore Baton Rouge and to pick up a few things to stock the fridge. He'd make a nice dinner and then find the swimming pool. He needed to decompress after the long drive.

~ 4 ~
Sunday, 10 May (3:58 p.m. EST – Washington)

Daniel was on time, but still the last to arrive in Room 713. He sat on the leather couch next to Sylvia, with everyone in the same seating arrangement as the first time they'd met. He wondered if all Omnis lives were ruled by routine.

Thackett glanced to Horace on his right, and then opened a laptop, clicked on the keyboard, and turned it toward Daniel and Sylvia. It was an underwater video, already playing.

"This is from the USS *North Dakota*," Thackett explained. "Footage of the object."

Daniel couldn't take his eyes off the computer. It was mesmerizing. The video seemed to be in black and white, but it was hard to tell in the dark water background and the white object. It resembled a spherical water tower.

75

"It doesn't move – just seems to make noise," Daniel said. "Is it a beacon of some sort?"

Horace shrugged.

Thackett snapped the computer closed and put it in a briefcase on the floor next to his chair. "Other than knowing what it looks like," he explained, "this video doesn't add important information. We've requested a sample of the material, the analysis of which should provide us with some useful information – the manufacturing company, country of origin, *something* – that should aid in your research."

Thackett nodded to Horace.

"Sylvia, Daniel," Horace said and then seemed to carefully formulate his next words in his head.

Daniel's intuition told him bad news was coming.

"My gut tells me your respective projects are closely related to the object, and to each other," Horace continued. "We know it's against every safeguard we have, but we've decided that you two should work together."

"I thought we already were," Sylvia said, vocalizing Daniel's thoughts.

Horace nodded and said, "Now we need you to interact." He opened his arms and looked about the room. "This will be your new office. There's enough space for you both to have your offices moved here, but maintain some privacy."

Daniel didn't like it. He was happy working alone. He could tell by Sylvia's expression that she felt the same.

"You both have reservations," Horace said, grinning. His eyes conveyed understanding. "But this project is too important for us to miss anything."

It seemed that Horace was implying danger, but Daniel wasn't convinced there was an immediate threat – the object had been there for centuries. He remembered the old man uttering the words *existential implications,* but it seemed farfetched. Maybe it was time for Horace to retire.

"You two can figure out the office arrangement," Thackett said. "There's enough room so you can each take a corner and have your offices arranged exactly as they are now."

Sylvia looked to Daniel and shrugged.

Daniel nodded.

"Good," Horace said. "You should get each other up to speed on your respective projects and update each other regularly. Brainstorm."

"Your offices will be moved after you leave tonight," Thackett said. "You'll report here first thing tomorrow."

Daniel cringed at the idea of sharing space, but nearly panicked at the thought of changing his routine. How would this affect his research? His concentration was fickle. When focused, he could make connections that most people would never find. If distracted, he might miss something. Thackett was new, but Daniel knew the CIA director understood this about him and the other Omnis. Horace had to know it as well.

They seemed to be panicking.

~ 5 ~

Sunday 10 May (8:17 p.m. EST – Antarctic Circle)

The USS *North Dakota* maneuvered to a position directly above the object. The *Little Dakota* had been fitted with sample collecting tools to extract a material sample for analysis. *LD* was ready and waiting in the load lock.

"Flood the chamber and let's get this show on the road," McHenry ordered.

Stuart filled the chamber and launched the min-sub.

In 20 minutes they had the same view of the object that they'd had over 12 hours earlier. Stuart inched the *LD* closer.

"Activating the arm," Stuart said and pushed a button.

A metallic, multi-fingered appendage came into view and approached the sphere. One of its fingers resembled a drill bit, and three others had thick rubber pads on their tips.

"What are those?" McHenry asked, pointing to the padded

fingertips that were now in contact with the surface.

"Suction mounts," Stuart said as he pushed a button. "An onboard pump will create a vacuum at the tips. The connection should stabilize the sub and allow us to mill into the surface."

"And the drill bit?"

"A diamond-impregnated end mill."

An end mill was much like a drill bit, but its tip was nearly flat. It could be used to plunge into metal to create a hole, but could also cut laterally to machine flat surfaces. A diamond mill could cut just about anything.

"Cut in no more than a millimeter," McHenry said.

Stuart started the motor and the tip spun up to a blur.

"How's the material collected?" McHenry asked.

Stuart clicked a button, and one of the free fingers on the appendage moved to a position close to the contact point between the tool and the surface. "That's a suction filter system," Stuart explained. "It sucks the debris and water in through a sieve which collects the pieces. Material might also be stuck on the cutting tool afterwards."

The spinning bit made contact, and McHenry strained his eyes to see if material was being removed. The cutting edge of the mill was undoubtedly in contact with the white surface, but didn't look to be cutting into it.

Stuart seemed to notice the same thing, and backed the tool away from the surface. "Didn't even make a mark," he said. "Let's increase the speed and put a little more pressure on it this time."

The cutter pressed onto the surface, but again didn't do any damage.

"Go to the highest speed and largest force you can apply without damaging the tool," McHenry said. He didn't like the *North Dakota* sitting in one place for too long.

Stuart changed some parameters and engaged the cutter.

Finley, who manned the sonar system at an adjacent station, pulled off his headphones. "Sir, we're making noise."

McHenry nodded. He looked back to Stuart. "Anything?"

Stuart backed the drill from the surface. "Nothing – no change in appearance whatsoever."

"Are there other options?" McHenry asked.

"There's a diamond grinding wheel," Stuart replied. "It should cut through anything. We'll make a lot of noise."

McHenry gave him the go-ahead, and then watched as the drill retracted and a dark wheel, about four inches in diameter, took its place. About a quarter-inch of the outer edge glittered with tiny chips of diamond. They faded into a blur as the wheel spun up to full speed.

"Here we go," Stuart said, and guided the grinder to the white surface.

The wheel made contact, and Finley turned to McHenry and put his hands on his headphones, indicating they were making a lot of noise.

"We're getting debris in the filter," Stuart said in an optimistic tone.

"We don't need much material," McHenry said, "but let's make sure we penetrate into the surface about a millimeter."

Stuart nodded and pressed the wheel in slowly. Finley warned again about the noise, this time motioning with his hands that his head was exploding.

"The filter indicates we have a lot of material, and we've moved in about a millimeter," Stuart said. "Back off?"

McHenry nodded. "Let's see what we've done."

Stuart retracted the grinding wheel and spun it down to a halt.

Confused, McHenry looked more closely at the monitor. "I thought you said we were catching debris."

Stuart squinted at the screen. "We did, sir. I don't understand ... there's not even a scratch."

"I see the problem," McHenry said and pointed to the screen. "Look at the wheel."

The diamond-impregnated outer edge of the cutting wheel seemed to be thinner, now only about an eighth inch of the outer edge glittered – it had worn down.

At that moment, Finley turned with a look concern. "Sir, there's another vessel in the area – a sub."

McHenry's vision faded and he felt dizzy for a second. "Get the *Little Dakota* back home now," he ordered. "Notify me immediately when the bay is closed. Be prepared to cut the line."

McHenry's neck muscles tightened as he made his way to the conn. This was exactly what he'd feared.

~ 6 ~
Sunday, 10 May (8:00 p.m. CST – Baton Rouge)

Will spent the afternoon exploring Baton Rouge and the campus of his former graduate school. He'd avoided the Department of Physics since he'd likely be recognized, especially if he crossed paths with his former research advisor who was near retirement age, but still there. The day had been a pleasant trip to the past, like walking through an old yearbook. But he could never go back to being the person he was at that time: positive, happy, and naïve.

He returned to his apartment at dusk and unloaded the groceries he'd picked up on the way back. He poured a glass of a cabernet recommended to him by a young woman who'd browsed the same display of wines at one of the stores. He couldn't relax in public, always keeping an eye out for possible pursuers. The woman had caught him off guard, and his interaction was nothing short of awkward.

He sat down on the couch and set the wine glass on an end table to his right. It was time to check out his neighbors. He took a deep breath, relaxed, and concentrated on one of his painful experiences in the Red Box. An instant later he viewed his body from the ceiling. His shoulders slouched, but his body remained upright. His face was blank, resembling that of death more than sleep. It had always given him an eerie feeling seeing his body that way. Sadness would set in quickly, and he couldn't remain in the separated state for very long. It was a feeling he could only describe as that of watching someone drown.

80

Passing through walls and other obstructions, he made his way through each room of his apartment and returned. His range improved daily. He lifted the glass of wine and moved it from the end table to the coffee table in front his body. He then *softened* his state, and passed an imaginary hand through the glass. An almost imperceptible ripple appeared on the fluid's surface, and a cool sensation washed around his fingers. He knew his fingers weren't really there, but his senses and perceptions seemed to follow those of his body. He wondered if it would remain that way when he'd have to leave his body for good.

His turned his attention to the wall opposite the couch. He passed through a flat-screen television and the wall to which it was mounted, and entered his study. He continued through the next wall and into the vacant bedroom of the adjacent apartment. Sounds of young children came from the next room over, which would be the living room if the apartment had the same layout as his. He pressed forward, through the next wall, where two young girls played on the floor while their mother and father worked in the kitchen. The aromas of baked fish and freshly cut lemon filled the air. He hadn't considered the idea of smelling things while separated, but now he knew it was possible. These neighbors would not be a threat.

A physical tugging and emotional falling indicated that he'd reached his limit – in distance, time, or both. He quickly retraced his path, returned to his body, and opened his eyes. He picked up the glass and took a sip. He was getting better.

Since his release from the Red Box, he'd had to continually convince himself that his ability to separate soul and body wasn't a hallucination. *Soul* was the only word he could use to describe what he was when away from his body. He'd used other words before – consciousness, perspective, self-awareness – but they were awkward. Soul was best because it described his essence. When separated, he still sensed stimuli to his body, but the sensations were tempered, and were only in the background. In the Red Box, separation had saved him from pain. It was pain that had driven him to separate. That had been their plan all along.

A total of about 1,200 people had been admitted to the Compressed Punishment facilities at Detroit and Long Island. Of those, over 300 died during the treatment, 500 were placed in mental health facilities upon completion of the program, 100 committed suicide within weeks of release, and 200 fell off the grid entirely. Not one went back to prison.

One thing he found strange, and frustrating, was that no one since his release had asked him to demonstrate his abilities. It wasn't that he wanted to reveal it to the rest of the world, but there were a handful of people who supposedly knew of his transformation, as it had been called in the reports, but they'd never seen it with their own eyes. Even Denise had never asked him about it. He figured that they either didn't believe him or they didn't understand what transformation meant.

After resting for a few minutes, he separated again and checked in with the other neighbors, all around, and above and below. No apparent threats – mostly families and young professionals. He did, however, suspect that the FBI had someone in the complex to keep an eye on him.

He changed into the swim trunks he'd purchased that afternoon and grabbed a towel. He'd been looking forward to a nighttime swim in his apartment complex's large pool, and perhaps a soak in the outdoor hot tub.

As he reached for the door, his phone chimed. He picked it up and read the message: *523.* The FBI was going to call. The phone rang a half-minute later, and the phone number had a Baton Rouge area code. "Hello?" he answered.

"No names," a man said. "Let's meet at the *College Palms Café* in *Corporate Lakes Plaza*, tomorrow at 10 a.m. Got it?

"Yes," Will replied and hung up.

He sighed. Maybe they actually had a plan for him – something for him to do.

He picked up the towel, slipped on his flip-flops, and headed for the pool.

$\sim 7 \sim$

Monday, 11 May (12:28 a.m. EST – Flint, Michigan)

The damp nighttime air made Lenny's shoulder ache. Even though the first half of his life had been spent in the coldest parts of the planet, he now hated cold climates. He often dreamt of a warm place to retire, maybe the Cayman Islands or somewhere in Central America.

It was unseasonably cold for spring in Flint, Michigan, and he had to circle the car around the block a few times to warm himself. He stuck his fingers inside the heater vents, and then did the same to his black leather gloves to soften them. He'd been waiting for over an hour for the woman's husband, an emergency room doctor, to leave for work. According to the file, he was supposed to have left by midnight. Also, her young children were supposed to be long asleep by then.

The info he'd been given on Dr. Martha Epstein, a.k.a. Dr. Smith, had been accurate. However, one could not account for unplanned delays or unseasonable ice storms, the latter of which was on the way. He'd been given an SUV for the job, but he was supposed to ditch it afterwards. If the storm hit, he might be stuck in it for a while. The four-wheel-drive might come in handy.

Lenny parked a block short of Martha Epstein's driveway and waited. At 12:40 a.m., her garage door opened and plumes of white car exhaust wafted over the cement driveway. He held an electronic device about the size of a car key remote up to the window and pushed a button, and a red light flashed near its tip. The white BMW SUV backed out of the garage and down the steeply sloped driveway into the street, where it hesitated until the garage door began rolling down. The red flashing light on Lenny's device turned to constant green, and he watched in the rear-view mirror as the SUV sped away and turned right at the first street.

He put the device in his coat pocket and grabbed a long, white zip-tie from the passenger seat. He fed its plastic tip through the slot on the other end to form a loop about a foot in diameter, and then pulled the tip until heard it ratchet a few times. He tucked the loop inside his coat and held it in his right armpit. His gun, silencer installed, was fastened to a Velcro holster under his left arm. Finally, he donned a black ski mask. These days there were cameras everywhere, so every job had to be done either in mask or disguise.

He got out of the car and crossed the street. The damp cement had started to freeze, making him slip and nearly fall on the sidewalk.

He passed the driveways of the adjacent houses in the dense residential neighborhood, and pressed a button on the device in his pocket as he approached the Epstein place. The garage door squeaked loudly as it lifted, and light shone through the crack that formed at the bottom. He turned left, up the driveway and, misjudging the slope, nearly slipped again.

The door fully opened as he reached the top of the drive and entered the garage. He pushed the button again and the door lowered behind him. It was a typical suburbanite garage, with bikes hanging on the walls, toys scattered about, and pool supplies and tools piled on shelves. Shoes of all sizes littered the stoop in front of the door that led into the house. He assumed the silver Volvo sedan belonged to Martha. Cat prints decorated the hood, and stick-figure stickers representing the members of her family, ordered largest to smallest from the left, were stuck on the back window. Evidently she had three kids and two cats. No sticker for a dog – that was good, since there wasn't mention of a dog in the file.

He slowly turned the knob of the door to the house. It was unlocked. He turned it as far as it would go, and pushed the door with his shoulder. It barely opened a crack, but made a loud squeak that he knew could be heard throughout the house. It didn't matter. He was at a point of no return.

He opened the door fully, and stepped into a foyer filled with more shoes, and coats on hooks. He closed the door carefully enough to avoid the squeak, but it didn't matter. A woman's voice chimed from deeper in the house.

"What did you forget?" she asked.

Lenny responded with a soft muffled grumble, after which scuffing footsteps came from the same direction as the voice. A second later a thin woman in her late-forties with short, gray-speckled hair entered the room. Her eyes widened behind wire-rimmed glasses. It was Martha Epstein.

Lenny struck her square in the nose with his fist, smashing her glasses and knocking her to the tile floor. He opened the door and dragged her by the collar into the garage, where he kicked her once in the stomach. He went back into the house, picked up her mangled glasses, and went back into the garage, closing the door behind him. He threw the glasses into a trashcan, and then turned back to Martha Epstein.

The woman gasped for air, but at the same time he thought he heard her try to ask, *"Why?"*

"You should know why, *Dr. Smith*," he said calmly.

The woman's eyes widened, first in recognition of her alias, then in horror.

"Yeah, that's right," he said as he pulled the large zip-tie out of his coat. "Did you really think you could just live life as if nothing happened? No one escapes, Doc."

The woman put up her hand and shook her head. Lenny lowered the noose down but the woman struck out, flailing violently. He grabbed her face with a gloved hand, squeezed as hard as he could, and pushed her head to the cold floor. He put a knee on her chest and slipped the zip-tie around her neck. He then stood, stepped on the side of her head with a heavy boot, and pulled the end of the zip-tie with all of his might. The woman's gurgling drowned out the ratcheting.

He backed off and left her writhing on the floor, rolling and clawing at the plastic band around her throat. It was hard to watch her bulging eyes, but it had to be done this way. He couldn't allow his jobs of the past months be connected by method. He had to mix it up. Besides, dead was dead. And, as far as dying was concerned, this wasn't the most painful way to go. He figured a drug overdose was the best way, but a headshot was probably the quickest.

What was different about his jobs during the past months was that he had intimate knowledge of the reasons for each of the hits. Every target had been involved in the Compressed Punishment program – which was much more sinister than the story the public was being fed about it. They all had blood on their hands in some way. They deserved what they got.

When the kicking stopped, Lenny walked over and looked into the lifeless eyes of Dr. Martha Epstein, touched one eyeball with his gloved finger – no reflexive response – and then walked around to the driver's side of the Volvo. He popped the trunk and shifted things around inside it to make room. He then picked up the body, put it in, and pressed the lid down slowly until it clicked closed. He thought it might take them a while to find it. The longer the better. And the cold might keep the stench at bay for a while.

He took one last look around. He spotted a paint scraper on a shelf, grabbed it, and walked to the back of the car. He scraped off the second stick-figure sticker from the left – the one representing Martha – rolled it into a ball, and tossed it into the garbage.

Convinced that he'd left nothing behind, he pressed the remote in his pocket and the door rolled upwards. When it was half open, he ducked under and stepped out. As he walked down the driveway, he pressed the button once to stop the door's ascent, and a second time to get it going back down. He got into the SUV, started it, and drove away.

Killing civilians had many advantages over killing professionals. Civilians weren't trained to fight or to take the precautions that professionals never overlooked. It was easy money. And there was more to be had.

A few more jobs like this, he thought, and he'd be done with it for good. He wondered how many others in his line of work had said those very words, and how many of those actually made it out.

He turned his attention to getting to the next destination, switching cars, and getting out of the area before the storm hit.

~ 8 ~

Monday, 11 May (12:42 a.m. CST – Baton Rouge)

Cho sipped on his second brandy and enjoyed the view from the balcony of his top floor condominium. The waves of the campus lake lapped against the shore just 100 yards to the north, and orange lights illuminated the bike and running trails that encircled it. The mild night had attracted runners, mostly students, who were amenable to such hours.

With his acquisition of Syncorp, Cho had arranged for a complete turnover of sensitive human resources. The giant conglomerate had been the former CIA chief's baby and, for a price, Gould had provided Cho with a list of sensitive contacts and operatives who had been developed to service the company. It was amazing what Gould had been able to accomplish, especially regarding the assets he'd turned within the FBI. In Gould's case, he needed to know what the FBI was doing because they had been investigating Red Wraith. Cho didn't care about any of that – the FBI had no influence in China. What he wanted was information about Red Box inmate 523: who he was, and his whereabouts. Cho was pleased to learn that his FBI informants had already provided him with man's identity.

The man's name was William Thompson, and he'd gone into protective custody after his release from the Red Box. Since then, he'd entered relocation program under the auspices of the FBI. Cho knew he'd obtain the man's location in short time, but how could he know if Thompson was the right man, and whether he was truly transformed? What was definitive proof of such a thing? It didn't matter for now. It was his only lead.

His phone vibrated in his breast pocket and he extracted it. It was a message: *XXX*. It was an indicator that the job scheduled for the evening had been successfully completed. Dr. Martha Epstein, A.K.A. *Dr. Smith*, was no longer a member of the living.

He smiled. The network that Gould had built was working well. It was fascinating that it worked independently of who gave the orders. He'd been given the reigns of a lethal machine capable of collecting information and removing threats. It was a dangerous notion: could this happen to a Chinese intelligence network? He shook his head. The Chinese intelligence structure was not as susceptible as that of the Americans – Chinese intelligence was truly centralized, leaving no room for independent action.

Cho sent a message to his second in command authorizing a hit on the next person on the list. Next, he'd press his FBI assets to acquire the whereabouts of William Thompson. Once he had that, he'd decide the man's fate.

CHAPTER V

~ 1 ~

Monday, 11 May (7:40 a.m. EST – Washington)

Daniel rubbed his eyes as the elevator took him to the seventh floor. Sleep had eluded him again.

He bristled at the added intrusion on his routine. He was out of his office of 20 years and, worse, sharing space.

The elevator stopped and opened. He checked in with the man at the front desk, and continued down the hall to Room 713. He hesitated. Should he knock or just walk in? He decided on the latter, but found the door was locked. There was a number pad next to the handle and he punched in the code for his former office. The pad beeped and the lock clicked open.

He entered, closed the door, and observed the new arrangement. In opposite corners of the large room were collections of furniture. One of them was his office – laid out exactly as it had been in its previous location, except for the window, which now made up the entire southern wall of the room. It was magnificent. They'd even reassembled the piles of books and sticky-notes as they'd been the night before.

Sylvia's office was in the opposite corner. She must have been neater than he was. The leather furniture and coffee table arrangement had not been altered. It was as if his and Sylvia's offices merged with original layout of 713. Maybe it was going to be okay.

A beeping sound came from the door. A few seconds later Sylvia walked in, head down.

"Good morning," he said.

She yelped and dropped her leather knapsack. "Oh my God," she said as she patted her chest with her hand. A half-smile of relief formed on her face.

"Sorry," he said and turned again to look at the room. "The office

89

arrangement looks like it will be okay."

She assessed the layout and nodded.

"Meet after lunch to get each other up to speed?" he asked.

She agreed and headed for her side of the room.

Daniel went into his office area, turned on his electric teapot, and pulled out the *Schwabenland* files. The Germans had sent the vessel out just before the onset World War II, a war they had been planning, to scout Antarctica for resources and potential U-boat bases. It made perfect sense. Under those conditions, the meeting between the *Schwabenland* and the U-boat would not be unusual.

Still, the suspicious part was the location of that meeting – that particular part of the Weddell Sea. The encounter lasted less than hour and the U-boat disappeared. But the *Schwabenland* had remained in the area, fighting rough seas, for a full day. *Why?* He concluded that they must have detected the noise.

He thought that if the *Schwabenland's* mission was the stimulus for Operation Tabarin, then Tabarin must have been connected to the beacon. But there was no mention of it in any of the Tabarin files.

It was all conjecture. Daniel knew he couldn't write any of his ideas in a monograph, unless he posed them as questions. He needed more facts, which meant more research. He looked at the files piled around his office. He had a long way to go.

~ 2 ~

Monday, 11 May (9:01 a.m. CST – Baton Rouge)

Will woke up early, exercised in the clubhouse gym, and took a swim in the pool. The spring in Baton Rouge was quite different from that in Chicago. The warm, sunny morning and the setting created by the palm trees that surrounded the pool should have been calming. But the peaceful environment contrasted starkly with his internal disquiet. The rendezvous with the FBI contact was in an hour.

He went back to the apartment, changed into jeans and a T-shirt, and drove out of the complex. He got onto Jefferson Highway, drove a mile south, and took a right on Corporate Boulevard. A quarter mile down he turned right, into a large collection of stores and restaurants called *Corporate Lakes Plaza,* and spotted the *Palms Café* on a corner.

He parked the SUV and walked through the parking lot, paying close attention to his surroundings for anyone tailing him. He pulled open the glass door of the café and went inside.

The place teamed with well-dressed patrons who talked loudly over the blasting espresso machines. He took his place at the end of the long line and casually searched for his contact. He identified two potential FBI agents: one was a man at a corner table reading a newspaper, and another in line a few places ahead of him had a cell phone of the same make and model as his own.

The line moved quickly, and a college-aged woman took his order. He asked for a medium-roast coffee, paid, and picked it up at the other end of the bar. He looked for a good place to sit as he crossed the room to another counter to get cream for his coffee. All of the seats were taken except for one that had an obstructed view. He spotted a few vacant tables outside through the large windows that made up the outer walls of the café. He walked out and took one that put his back to a wall, giving him a simultaneous view of the interior of the café and the parking lot. It was two minutes to 10: he was right on time.

At 10:10 a.m., a tall man dressed in khakis and a white, collared shirt walked out of the café. When he saw Will, he walked over to his table, set down his coffee, and held out his hand.

"Glad you made it, Will," the man said with a New Orleans accent that Will hadn't noticed during their short conversation the night before. "I'm Rick Jennings."

Will shook his hand. The man was a couple inches taller than him, probably 6'1", and fit. His short blond hair probably made him look younger than he really was – mid-thirties, he estimated. "Good to meet you, Jennings. FBI?"

Jennings put a finger to his lip and nodded. "The Chicago office told me that you might be able to help with a situation that's brewing here," he explained. "It has to do with the Compressed Punishment program. I understand you were involved."

Will nodded. He'd been more than *involved*.

"Some former CP inmates have been gathering in the area," Jennings said. "Don't know why – other than our governor lobbied to get one of the CP facilities built here. They actually broke ground just before the whole program was terminated. It was going to be a massive building, with a few levels below ground. Now there's a bank or a mall being constructed there. You should check out the mess on the corner of Acadian and Perkins."

Will knew about the plans for the third facility – Detroit's Red Box and the one on Long Island being the other two. He wasn't convinced the scrapped third facility was a good enough reason for the CP inmates to organize in Baton Rouge. "Is there a specific threat?" he asked.

"No. Just a lot of chatter," Jennings said. "That itself isn't unusual, but the communication between domestic and foreign terrorists groups is unique."

"Domestic terrorist group?"

"Well, the word *group* is misleading," Jennings said. "Less than a dozen inmates, we figure. Baton Rouge is a strange choice – there had been only one CP inmate from this area, and he's dead."

"What about the foreign terror groups?" Will thought it was strange.

"An obscure extremist group from Yemen," Jennings answered. "One was caught at the Mexican border with crates of plastic explosives. He was delivering them to the CP inmates. However, we're convinced that's the extent of the foreign involvement – to smuggle in explosives."

"Why not just round them all up?" Will asked. He figured it couldn't be too difficult a task.

"We can never catch them all in the same place," Jennings said. "Several come to Baton Rouge for a few days, and then scatter again, just to be replaced by others. Some go to Mexico. We suspect they're also bringing things back with them. We're too lean on personnel to follow them all."

"Again, why Baton Rouge?" Will asked. "Doesn't seem like the kind of population density terrorists target."

"Neither was Oklahoma City."

It was a fair point, Will thought.

Jennings continued, "Other than the third CP facility, a government contractor also set up shop here after the facility was approved. They'd developed much of the equipment used in the facilities."

Will had a sudden flash of memory. "Syncorp," he said. He felt sick.

Jennings looked back at him, wide-eyed. "You've heard of it?"

"The name was stamped on everything in the Red Box," Will replied. Cold adrenaline surged through body. He clenched his jaw and released it. "I had to see that damned tag every day I was in there. It was on the Exoskeleton, riveted to the top of my left forearm."

Jennings nodded and took a sip from his cup. "You think they want revenge on this company?"

"Yes," Will said as he looked around at the patrons of the café, imagining any one of them could be working for the evil company. He followed Jennings' eyes to his straining clenched fist, and let it relax.

"Syncorp makes a lot more than CP equipment," Jennings explained. "It's a huge defense contractor."

Will shook his head. "I don't know for certain why the CP inmates chose Baton Rouge, but I'd put money on them going after Syncorp."

Jennings pulled out his car keys and edged forward in his chair. "I'm starting to understand why they sent you here."

"Me, too," Will replied.

Jennings stood. "I need to do a little research. I'll contact you again in a few days."

Will watched as Jennings walked back into the café and merged with the crowd. A minute later he spotted him in a black BMW sedan, driving through the parking lot and then disappearing around the corner.

He took a sip of coffee and realized his hands were still trembling. If the CP group planned to go after Syncorp personnel, he'd have a hard time not sympathizing with them, especially if they went after the people at the top. On the other hand, he knew the production people probably weren't privy to purposes of the things they produced. In his book, they were still innocent – or innocent enough.

The CP men wouldn't need help from the outside to go after personnel. If they were collecting explosives, then they were going for something large-scale, which probably meant indiscriminate killing. This would be the only reason he'd try to stop them.

~ 3 ~
Monday, 11 May (11:49 a.m. EST   – Washington)

Daniel twitched at a thumping sound from the other side of the room. Sylvia must have closed the door to her mini-fridge. He glanced at his watch – 10 minutes to noon.

He rubbed his eyes to help them readjust from hours of reading. He'd made progress but hadn't answered any questions. It was clear that Operation Tabarin was a direct British response to Germany's *Schwabenland* mission. The next link in the chain was the American Operation, Highjump.

Highjump was a mock invasion of Antarctica by the U. S. Navy in 1946. It was a massive and expensive undertaking. Officially, its purpose was as a training mission to prepare for a possible Arctic battle with the Soviets. Skeptics had argued that they could have instead prepared in Alaska – an environment much more realistic than Antarctica.

The reports described conspiracy theories that had emerged about Tabarin and Highjump. Although both governments had tried, it was impossible to keep them secret – there were just too many people involved. The actions were out in the open, and difficult to conceal. The real objectives, however, were more difficult to unearth. In his gut, Daniel knew they were all tied together – the *Schwabenland*, Tabarin, Highjump, and the beacon.

94

As he finished eating his peanut butter sandwich, Sylvia approached. She stood at the perimeter of his office as if imaginary walls surrounded it – a gesture he appreciated.

"Chat?" she asked, and nodded towards the leather furniture between their two office areas.

He agreed, filled his cup with hot water, and scooped loose tea from a bag with a silver tea steeper on the way out of his office. He sat in Horace's chair. She sat on the couch directly across from him. He put his cup on the coffee table, and submerged the steeper.

"This is my third project as an Omni," Sylvia explained. "I've been working on it for six months, and found some things that might be relevant to your investigation."

"What topic?"

"Ex-Nazi networks in South America," she replied. "I think there are connections to Operation Tabarin."

Daniel knew there could be numerous connections – seemingly unrelated secret projects were often linked. The interrelationships between them were often obscured because they were connected by covert motives beneath the surface, like the intertwined roots of neighboring trees.

"Maybe I should get you up to speed on my project first, since I've been working on it for a shorter time," Daniel suggested.

Sylvia agreed, and Daniel spent the next fifteen minutes explaining his meager progress on Tabarin.

Sylvia sat back on couch and pulled her feet beneath her. "Since Tabarin is connected to the beacon, then all of this is connected to Horace's Captain Cook story?" she asked.

He noticed a hint of a smirk on her face. He laughed. "Sounds strange, but the fact is that Cook was there first. The question is whether it was the logs of his voyage – the report of the mysterious sound – that had piqued the interest of the Germans."

She nodded. "The missions you've encountered started before World War II and extended beyond it. I have some info that continues on from Highjump, further into the future."

"Let's hear it," he said.

"Did you know that the United States detonated nuclear weapons near Antarctica in 1958?" she asked.

"You mean *Operation Argus*," he replied.

"How do you know that?" she asked, shaking her head and smirking.

"I happened across it a few years ago. Spend two decades as an Omni and you'll have a lot packed away in your head," Daniel replied. "Refresh me of the details."

"They detonated three nuclear devices in the upper atmosphere."

"For what purpose?"

"To investigating how charged particles and radioactive isotopes affect communications, satellite electronics, and intercontinental ballistic missiles."

"I remember now," Daniel said. "They were also trying to see how quickly other countries might detect such an event."

Sylvia shifted in her seat and leaned in, as if she was going to whisper. "Have you heard of an operation code-named Blackfish?"

Daniel searched his mind for a few seconds and shook his head.

"In 1958, the American operations Argus and Blackfish were carried out simultaneously," she explained. Her eyes grew wider as she spoke. "Argus was the detonation of three warheads in the atmosphere. In Blackfish, two devices were detonated under water. It seemed that the atmospheric explosions were a diversion to direct attention to the sky, hundreds of miles away."

"Suppose that's true," he said. "What was the purpose? It seems that bombs detonated in the atmosphere carry larger risks – both in detection and radioactive fallout."

She shrugged and nodded. "But guess *where* those underwater weapons were detonated."

The skin on Daniel's forearm puckered like gooseflesh.

She nodded, knowing that he'd figured it out. "That's right – they were detonated in the precise location of our mystery beacon, in the Weddell Sea."

~ 4 ~

Monday, 11 May (5:18 p.m. EST – Antarctic Circle)

McHenry leaned over the shoulder of the pilot of *Little Dakota* and squinted at the computer screen. His eyes had been burning ever since they'd rendezvoused with a frigate to get the extended control cable for the mini-sub. Lack of sleep was taking a toll on everyone.

His nerves were a mess. He was certain they'd been detected by a foreign sub during their last visit to the area. "What's the depth?" he asked.

"Three thousand meters," Stuart replied, "and descending."

The stem of beacon widened with depth, but maintained the same shade of white and uniformly smooth texture as the *Little Dakota* descended. There were no visible seams or markings of any sort.

"Sir, we'll be at the test depth of *LD* soon," Stuart said. "Might end up short of the floor."

McHenry nodded. He knew that the crush depth exceeded the test depth by about 10 percent – in this case about an extra 400 or 500 feet. They had to keep going – they needed a picture of the object's insertion into the seabed. The *Little Dakota* was expendable.

Twenty minutes passed in silence as the men watched the stem gradually thicken as the camera went deeper.

Stuart broke the silence. "We're at test depth," he said. "Shall we use the *Little Dakota's* ranging sonar to measure the remaining distance to bottom?"

McHenry wanted to avoid using active sonar as long as they could. "No, continue to dive slowly," he said. "Keep an eye out for the floor."

The *Little Dakota* descended, and the stem continued to thicken. McHenry estimated that it was currently 40 or 50 meters in diameter at the current depth. It was enormous.

A beeping sound chirped from the computer.

97

"What's that?" McHenry asked.

"Hull sensors," Stuart replied. "*LD* is suffering severe stress. We're at the limit, but I think I see bottom."

Stuart panned *Dakota's* cameras and adjusted the bottom-view lights. It was clear: they were about 20 meters from the bottom, near the limit of their visibility.

"Snap some high resolution images, and let's get some wide-range stuff, too," McHenry instructed. "We have to see how this thing is mounted to the floor."

"I don't see anything that could be a mounting base," Stuart said after a few minutes of probing. "The thing seems to grow right out of the bottom."

"It's probably buried," McHenry suggested.

As Stuart panned around and took pictures, McHenry noticed a slight incline of the sea floor – it seemed to rise, going outward from the stem. "Turn and look outward from the stem."

Stuart turned the *Little Dakota*, and then adjusted the lights and camera. The sea floor rose steeply as it went outward. Being focused on the stem on the way down, combined with the limited visibility, they hadn't realized that the *Little Dakota* had descended into a crater. It gave the impression that the beacon had emerged from the earth, like a sprouting plant.

McHenry suddenly got a nauseating dose of adrenaline as a red light began flashing on the ceiling to his right. His communicator buzzed and he grabbed it. "McHenry."

The voice on the other end came back in an artificially calm tone. "Fish in the water, sir. Orders please."

Torpedo. Shit. McHenry turned to Stuart. "We have all the data on board?"

"Everything on board is low resolution; high-res data is stored on the mini-sub."

"Cut the line and close all ports," McHenry told Stuart. He then spoke into his communicator. "Evasive action. Battle stations – sound the warning. Ready countermeasures. I'm on my way."

Monday, 11 May (4:45 p.m. CST – Baton Rouge)

Will started at the clubhouse and walked around an asphalt running track that followed the perimeter of the apartment complex. About a fourth of the way around he noticed his shoe was untied and went to one of many wooden benches mounted on concrete pads just inside the track, spaced about every 200 feet. He sat down and tied his shoe, and then leaned back on the bench and took in the scene.

A few yards in front of him, just across the track, was a wrought-iron gate to an old cemetery. The late afternoon sun beamed through the branches of Live Oak trees that seemed to both weep for and celebrate those who had passed, and who now resided in graves arranged haphazardly over a couple of acres of land. Will thought that the graves were positioned to avoid the trees, although he had no idea of the age of the oaks.

He had normally waited until evenings to hone his skills, as it tired him, but he needed to develop the ability to separate in public, and with distractions. He straightened his posture and put on sunglasses. He concentrated on the memory of the pain of the bone-bending treatments he'd suffered while in the CP program and separated. He looked down upon is body – it seemed stable.

He turned his attention outward and elevated, going higher and higher until he was 10 to 15 feet above the treetops, more than 50 feet above his body. He faced west and looked directly into the afternoon sun. He felt no discomfort, and his vision didn't saturate. There were no physiological limitations. Although he'd been told there were other senses, he'd only experienced the standard five while separated.

He descended through the tree branches, looked south, across the track, and viewed his body from the front. It was slouching now, leaning heavily towards the edge of the bench. He spotted a runner making the corner about 200 feet from the bench, and approaching. He went back to his body, recovered his posture, flipped up his sunglasses, and took out his cell phone. Twenty minutes had passed since he'd separated.

The woman transitioned from jog to walk and passed by slowly, and then picked back up to a jog.

He looked back through the iron fence into the cemetery. He'd contemplated death often since his release. Perhaps it was because he'd technically been dead for a short time while in the Red Box – drowned – but they'd brought him back. Or maybe it was because he'd actually seen the soul of a dead man once while separated. The man undergoing a treatment a couple rooms away had died, and his hideous, ghostlike soul tried to attack him. It was both frightening and sad.

Will recalled conversations he'd had while confined to the Exoskeleton. He still wasn't sure with whom he'd been speaking – possibly himself – but the discussions had often led to dark places, and brought up questions that, although unanswerable, led to profound conclusions. If dead meant being "not alive," then he'd been dead already – for an eternity. Where he'd been before being born was as surreal a concept as where he'd go after he died. Why did people fear death? The unknown future was more threatening than the unknown past. He understood why that was, but it didn't mean that they were different. Maybe when he died he'd just return to the place he was before he was born. The real question was *why was he alive now?*

His thoughts turned to his conversation with Jennings in the café. It was unwise of the FBI to involve him in a case where he had such a strong emotional connected. He hated Syncorp, and knew it would be difficult to control that hatred if an opportunity arose.

~ 6 ~
Monday, 11 May (6:14 p.m. EST – Antarctic Circle)

McHenry rushed to the conn and stood next to Diggs. His first officer's bulging eyes darted around like those of a trapped animal.

"Status," McHenry yelled.

"It's a homer, probably Russian," Diggs said. "Possibly Chinese."

McHenry swallowed hard. It was a type of torpedo that was launched and then allowed to roam on its own. It used a combination of passive and active sonar, and only pinged when it got into the neighborhood of a target.

"Up 50 meters, and full speed ahead, bear 60° west," McHenry instructed.

Navigation personnel repeated the orders.

"Ready countermeasures," McHenry ordered. It had been decades since the Russians made advances in their torpedo technologies – there was even a good chance that this one would malfunction. He didn't know what to expect if it was Chinese. The U. S. Navy had made significant advances in countermeasures, but this did little to ease his nerves. The countermeasures were still crude devices – just drums of compressed air that released bubbles that sounded like propellers to passive sonar detectors and, en masse, looked like large objects to active sonar systems. The recent advances consisted mainly of sonar-jamming components, and new electronics and sensors that allowed them to delay activation and make a more effective decoy noise. The *North Dakota* also carried a new countermeasure, but it was untested in combat.

"Fish at 900 meters and closing," it was Finley's voice over the intercom.

"Launch two sound-makers," McHenry ordered. "Set to activate when the fish is within 200 meters."

"Fish at 800 meters and closing," Finely informed.

McHenry suppressed any outward nervousness by reassuring himself that they were following the correct evasive protocol. He waited as patiently as he could. Where were those countermeasures?

"Seven hundred meters."

A voice rang out from the intercom speaker. "Two countermeasures launched, bearing set to intercept at torpedo's depth of 220 meters in 1-2-0 seconds. Set to activate at a separation of 200 meters."

They wouldn't have much time if the torpedo somehow defeated the countermeasures. They'd only have one more shot. "Ready the proximity countermeasures," McHenry said, "all four aft tubes." It would be the first battle deployment of the US Navy's new, "hard-kill" torpedo countermeasure system, meaning that the devices were designed to destroy torpedoes rather than confuse them. He hoped they'd be alive to report the results.

A voice chimed from the communicator in the control room: "Countermeasures to activate in 10 ... 9 ... 8 ..."

"Stand by to launch proximity countermeasures, all four," McHenry said.

The response came immediately. "Standing by."

" ... 3 ... 2 ... 1 ... activated."

Now they would wait on edge for about 20 seconds. McHenry had experienced this kind of situation numerous times, but his men hadn't. Even his first officer wasn't old enough to have seen any real combat. The next 20 seconds would be the longest of their young lives.

Finley's voice came through the speaker. "Torpedo has activated its active sonar, stand by for new trajectory information."

McHenry crossed his arms. This was standard. They'd know in a few seconds.

It was Finley's voice, "Countermeasures failed. Fish's active sonar locked in on us. Repeat countermeasure –"

" – Launch proximity countermeasures, tubes 1 and 2," McHenry ordered.

" ... tubes 1 and 2 launched," Weapons replied.

"A hundred and fifty meters and closing ..." Finley said.

McHenry waited for 10 seconds and then gave the order, "Launch proximity countermeasures, tubes 3 and 4."

" ... tubes 3 and 4 launched," Weapons replied.

The next 10 seconds were quiet. He felt a certain level of peace: it would all be over in seconds, one way or the other.

He grabbed a rail and barely avoided being rocked to the floor by the multiple blasts: he was able to discern the first two, which happened nearly simultaneously, and then two more 10 seconds later. He went to the communicator. "Finley?"

"Searching," Finley replied. A full five seconds later Finely spoke again. "Fish destroyed. Repeat, fish destroyed."

The men in the control room cheered, but McHenry suppressed his outward emotions. This result was to be expected. He couldn't fool himself, but maybe he could give his men some confidence from the experience. "Nice job, men," he said to the crew. He went to the intercom. "Weapons officer, arm and load homing torpedoes in forward tubes 1 through 4." He turned to navigation. "Circle back, radius 2,000 meters, depth 200. Let's find out who attacked us."

McHenry nodded to his first officer to follow him. They'd go to the ready-room to discuss what had just happened, and what to do next. If it wasn't before, it was absolutely clear now: others were interested in the mysterious structure – *others who were willing to kill for it.*

~ 7 ~
Monday, 11 May (9:22 p.m. CST – Baton Rouge)

When Cho spilled his brandy on his lap, the final wisp of his patience evaporated. He threw the stack of files off the desk and strode to the window and breathed deeply. He'd been in his office reading the entire day and evening and found nothing in the files about Thompson's current location. In the afternoon, an FBI mole reported that they were having trouble getting access to the information. Maybe the Americans understood the value of what they had. They'd relocated him and were keeping his information safe.

There were resources that Cho could exploit other than the FBI. Thompson had friends and family. They'd be much easier to find, and it wouldn't be difficult to get information out of them if he employed the right techniques. That is, if they actually knew anything.

He sat at his desk and opened his laptop. It was time to get other assets involved. He had five new emails in his inbox, but the second one from the top made his throat tighten. It was from the Ministry of State Security. The MSS was the main Chinese intelligence agency, and for the past year, he'd interacted exclusively with its director. Their communications had been sparse, and for good reason: as the new CEO of Syncorp, there was to be no connection between him and the Chinese government. That the director was writing meant something was afoot.

He opened the email and read it. His vision blurred as his blood pressure spiked. The Director put a priority order on collecting William Thompson. How did he even know about him? Cho thought he alone was at the cutting edge of this information, and he'd only just learned Thompson's identity. The order set the first priority for Thompson's rendition, and the second, his termination.

The orders paralleled Cho's plans, but there was an added key phrase that made the hair on his arms stand like cactus spines. It was the Chinese phrase for "at all costs." The meaning was literal and absolute. He had never been given such a directive, but he knew it meant that his Red Dragon project could be sacrificed to accomplish the objective.

Cho stood from the desk, walked to the window, and looked out over the teaming city below. What was happening?

CHAPTER VI

~ 1 ~

Friday, 15 May (7:21 a.m. EST – Washington)

Daniel stared through his office window and shivered. The treetops swayed in a swirling wind infused with a freezing mist.

He was the first to arrive, just beating the brunt of the incoming weather. Sylvia's schedule was about a half hour behind his, which suited him. It gave him time to start his day without distraction. He recalled with nostalgia when his entire day use to be like that.

It had been a week since their first meeting in Room 713, and he was sure that Thackett was disappointed in their progress. He *had* to be – a carrier group had already entered Antarctic waters and a large-scale, geopolitical event was on the verge of exploding. The Omnis had, to this point, contributed nothing.

His left eye twitched as he sat on the edge of the couch and rested his elbows on his knees. He massaged his temples. By the look of her chewed fingernails, which he'd noticed the previous night, he could tell the pressure had been getting to Sylvia as well.

Despite the anxiety, seeing things unfold in real time was exciting. He was privy to the real motivations for the large-scale naval actions, whereas the general public was fed plausible misinformation. Snippets had been released through various news media: the Navy was conducting exercises, and the carrier group was heading to the southern seas to test new equipment. Of the billions of people on the planet, only a handful knew the truth, and Daniel was one of them – or at least he thought he was. He was cognizant of the possibility that even he wasn't told the complete truth, but he had to place his trust somewhere.

As usual in his research, he was overwhelmed with the names of operations, people, and, in this case, naval vessels, all with filamentary connections between them. He reminded himself that they were only in the

105

discovery stage, and things would become clear with time.

The carrier group securing the icy waters surrounding the beacon had provided some new information about the object, but they were mostly physical details that had, so far, not helped to determine why it was there, or how it got there. *When* it got there, however, was fascinating. If he hadn't read the Captain's log himself, he would've scoffed at the idea that Captain Cook had been involved. But it put a timestamp on it: the beacon had been there in the 1700's at the very latest.

The timeline of events was so complex that, two days earlier, he'd requested a whiteboard and a large corkboard to pin photographs, just to keep things straight. As usual, everything was ready to go the next morning. They'd even included an assortment of pins for the corkboard and colored markers for the whiteboard.

The whiteboard was already covered with notes, Daniel's in blue marker and Sylvia's in red. At the top, in blue, was a timeline starting with *Cook and crew discover beacon (November 1773)*. Next came the *Schwabenland Expedition (January 1939), U-Boat – Schwabenland Rendezvous (February 1939)*. And then *Operation Tabarin (November 1943)* followed by *Operation Highjump (Southern summer, 1946)*. Finally, *Operations Argus and Blackfish (November, 1958)*. The names of the major players, mostly military personnel, were written close by, and he and Sylvia had been trying to identify links between them.

He stared at the spaghetti of red and blue lines and scribbled words, some of which were circled or underlined for emphasis. He then turned to the corkboard and examined the photos pinned to it. Black and white pictures of people were placed in two columns, one for those associated with Daniel's investigation and another for Sylvia's. They hadn't yet made any connections between the columns.

Photos and schematics of the various Antarctic bases were organized according to their respective operations – but most were from Operation Tabarin. Some of the bases had been shockingly small – in some cases, just a single building and fewer than ten people. He thought those who'd occupied them must've been miserable dealing with the extreme conditions.

He inspected the images of the ships and equipment involved in the operations. Pictures of German and American submarines, British vessels, and various aircraft were grouped according to the dates the photos had been taken. Three photos of the *Schwabenland* were pinned in a vertical column, each showing the vessel from different perspectives. The British report described it as an 8000-ton floating airbase. It had two tall masts, which were actually antennae, and a catapult to launch its two seaplanes, *Boreas* and *Passat*. A claw-like crane was mounted on the rear deck to pluck the planes out of the water after returning from a flight. The *Schwabenland* had belonged to the German airline, Lufthansa, whose crews flew and maintained the planes.

He kept staring at the *Schwabenland* pictures. He walked closer to the board and examined each more closely. There was something …

The door beeped, far to his right.

Sylvia stepped in and inserted her wet umbrella into a clay pot next to the door. She nodded to Daniel, walked into her office area, and put her lunch in a small refrigerator. A few second later, she walked to his side of 713. An empty coffee cup dangled from her hand.

"May I?" she asked, and nodded in the direction of his coffee pot.

She looked disheveled, as if she'd been up all night. Her damp hair was the color of dark copper. "Certainly," he said as he walked to the back of his office, retrieved the pot, and filled her cup. "You look tired."

"Just what a girl wants to hear," she said and shook her head. "Couldn't sleep. My brain was in overdrive all night. When I finally managed to fade out, I dreamt of this stuff. I feel like we're behind."

"We are," he said and walked out of his office and towards the furniture arrangement in the center of the huge room. Sylvia followed.

He sat in Horace's chair, and she on the couch directly across from him.

"I think we have many pieces of the puzzle," he explained, "but something big is still missing."

"If this is so important, why aren't all of the other Omnis working on it? Why aren't they pooling together all of our resources?"

"Who's says they aren't?" Daniel replied.

"Why are you and I working together?" she asked.

Daniel shrugged. "Our projects have commonalities: Nazis, South America – the route to Antarctica was not direct from Germany or England," he said. "It was a long trek through South America and some island hopping."

She nodded. "The Nazi network I'd been researching spanned Argentina and included Deception Island."

"As a part of Operation Tabarin, the Brits put an outpost on Deception Island to spy on the Germans," he explained. "But why would the post-War network set up anything there? What interest could former Nazis have in getting to Antarctica? They'd be better off hiding in South America. Warmer, too."

"There were rumors about ex-Nazis and Antarctica," she explained. "One of my tasks was to find their origins and debunk them."

"What kind of rumors?"

"That the Nazis were regrouping. Hitler was still alive and building the Fourth Reich in a secret base in Antarctica," she said. "The best one was that they had come across extraterrestrial technology and were about to mount a new attack. There were even stories of strange aircraft sightings in newspapers."

Daniel fell into deep thought for a few seconds. "How else can we account for the beacon being there for centuries, and being beyond their technology – maybe beyond our *current* technology?"

Sylvia raised an eyebrow. "Are you suggesting it had an extraterrestrial origin?"

He huffed and shook his head. "I'm saying we can't take anything off the table. For now we have to keep all possibilities open, no matter how absurd they may be."

She nodded.

He continued, "We can't even identify the material the damned thing's composed of – can't even scratch it. And we certainly don't know its purpose." His legs muscles twitched like taught rubber bands and he had to stand. "I need to get back to work."

Sylvia went back to her office and Daniel went to the corkboard to reexamine the photos. His attention was again drawn to a large snapshot of the *Schwabenland*. One of the water planes, the *Passat*, was perched on the catapult. Its two propellers – push and pull – were blurred, so it must have been getting ready to launch. He stared at it for a few minutes and then moved on.

His focus turned to the German U-boats that the Brits had tracked as part of Operation Tabarin. One was of U-530, taken in July of 1945 at the Argentine naval base at Mar del Plata. He wondered how the men on those vessels coped with the cramped conditions; they'd been but a malfunction or depth charge away from a horrible death.

The adjacent picture was of U-530's young, smiling captain, Otto Wermuth. There were some strange facts regarding U-530. First, it had arrived with no torpedoes. Second, it had a skeleton crew – somewhere around twenty men – where its full contingent was 54. Third, the vessel's documents were destroyed before landing in Argentina. Finally, there were large barrels of cigarettes on board; a strange detail that had drawn speculation that they'd been intended for delivery at a base of some sort.

As he'd done at least 100 times in the past week, he examined the pictures of Otto Wermuth. Some had been taken after his arrival at Mar del Plata, and others snapped before his final mission. It was easy to tell the difference: he didn't smile in the later pictures.

He unpinned and took down two pictures of Wermuth to have a closer look. Both had been taken in the captain's quarters of U-530. He focused on a leather file binder in one of the photos. It lay open on a desk and contained file folders stamped with standard Nazi emblems. He could see swastikas on everything, and SS symbols were stamped on a few, but there was one he couldn't quite make out.

He went into his office and returned with a magnifying glass. The image was a little fuzzy, but clear enough. The hair on his neck bristled and the magnifying glass shook in his hand. The symbol was of a large bird of prey carrying an emblem that resembled a hash symbol with tails coming off from every other edge. It was like a swastika drawn with a tic-tac-toe board at its center rather than a cross.

He knew *exactly* what it was.

Friday, 15 May (8:54 p.m. EST   – South Beach, Florida)

This is more like it, Lenny thought, as he parked the rental car in a gravel parking lot in front of the restaurant. South Beach, or *SoBe*, as the locals called it, was exactly the type of place he wanted to live out the rest of his life. The heat made his aging and damaged body feel comfortable. He'd experienced too many cold winters in Chicago and Detroit, not to mention the long spans of time he'd spent in Eastern Europe.

Ivan Poliakov, M.D., Ph.D., was smarter than most of the others who had been involved in the Compressed Punishment program. The others hadn't run far enough away, or run at all. Poliakov at least made it to a place better than Detroit, but he didn't change his name. It was okay. It made Lenny's job easy.

He got out of the car and took a deep breath of evening ocean air marinated with the scents of seafood and spices. He donned a Florida Marlins baseball cap he'd purchased at his hotel the day before, and adjusted his loose-fitting khakis. He slipped on a light leather jacket over his open-collared white shirt. He'd fit in perfectly with the rest of the upper-class clientele.

The doctor was celebrating his fifth wedding anniversary, which was earlier that week. Poliakov had been low on the target priority list, but he'd been moved to the top when Jonathan McDougal started looking for him. Lenny had known of McDougal long before the catastrophic breakdown of the Red Wraith project. The do-gooder lawyer was the one who had shot him. Lenny longed for the day when he'd find McDougal on his target list. Now the law professor's DNA Foundation was tracking down everyone involved in program. He was certain McDougal intended to not only to round up the run-of-the-mill employees, like Poliakov, but to use them to get the people at the top.

Lenny knew he wasn't safe either, having blood on his hands, even though it was unlikely they'd get any solid evidence. Even the man who had ordered the hits, Heinrich Bergman, was dead. He wondered why McDougal wasn't a priority target: they could end the problem with one hit.

Poliakov was one of a team of three doctors who knew enough to put many people away. The other two had been killed in the explosion that had exposed the Red Box. Eliminating Poliakov would allow many high-level Red Wraith personnel to sleep more easily – and that included the former CIA Director.

Lenny walked into the Blue Dolphin Bistro, a restaurant-bar that was crowded on Friday nights because of their seafood and margarita specials. He asked a young woman at the host station how long the wait was for a table for two. There wasn't a second person, of course, but to dine alone in such a place would draw attention. Besides, he had no intention of being seated; he just needed an excuse to move about the place.

As he weaved his way through the crowd, he spotted Poliakov's wife, Jillian. She was a stunning woman, tall with dark hair and green eyes. She wore a green sundress and a thin, white sweater. According to the file, she was in her early thirties, eight years younger than her husband.

A bearded man, about four inches taller than Jillian, walked onto the scene holding two glasses of red wine. He handed one to her.

Lenny took a seat at the bar, his back to Poliakov, and ordered a beer. He watched the doctor and his wife in a mirror mounted behind the racks of alcohol and below a TV showing a baseball game. He glanced back and forth from the TV to the mirror as he sipped.

Poliakov's red beard was nearly as full as his own, and much thicker than it was the first time they'd met. Although Lenny had been beardless during their first encounter, he wondered whether the doctor would recognize him. He doubted it: when they'd met, Poliakov had just accidentally injected himself with some horrific chemical and was writhing in pain. How a person could accidentally inject his own thigh with a syringe of fluid, he'd never understand.

Even though Poliakov wouldn't recognize him, Lenny had to be careful. Most places had cameras. After being shot and captured, his identity had been well-cataloged – pictures, fingerprints, and DNA. He couldn't leave any evidence behind – and that included the beer bottle in his hand.

It was fitting that Poliakov would die by injection. The man had spent a good part of his so-called professional life administering various drugs and chemicals into the bloodstreams of hapless patients. *How many people had the man treated?* he wondered. *How many of those had died?*

Lenny was no hypocrite. He, too, was a killer. But the man had it coming, as did the others. The woman he'd terminated in Detroit was no better. Nor was the young woman in the hospital in Chicago. She was a psychopath whose goal was to become the dentist of the damned – a torture artist of the worst sort. None of these people belonged in the world, and Lenny was doing a service to society.

That was the thing about operating in the civilian world: he was almost always given justifications for his hits. In the professional world, there were only orders. In that case, he thought of himself as an instrument, and all guilt could be transferred from him to the entity that had deployed him. He was innocent.

Dr. Poliakov stood from the table and excused himself.

Lenny watched in the mirror as the man passed behind him towards the restrooms. He pulled his hat low on his forehead, gulped the last of his beer, and slid the bottle into his jacket pocket. It was time.

~ 3 ~
Friday, 15 May (9:20 p.m. CST – Baton Rouge)

Will pulled the SUV out of the apartment complex onto Corporate Boulevard. Why did Agent Jennings want to meet at such a late hour?

He turned left on College Drive and worked his way through a half dozen traffic lights. He made a right onto Perkins and, after a half mile, turned right again into a large complex of stores and restaurants. He

112

spotted a bar called the Bullfrog and parked about as far away as possible, in front of a Thai restaurant. He got out of the car and was confronted by the sweet tang of Thai spices.

Voices and music grew louder as he approached the bar's entrance, and the volume increased sharply as the door opened. Two young women, laughing as they walked out, saw him and held the door. He nodded and smiled, and went inside into a dark foyer.

The bar was loud, but milder than he'd anticipated. It wasn't smoky – Baton Rouge had a no-smoking policy for such places – and clean. A few wall-mounted screens were showing baseball games.

He spotted Jennings in a booth in the far corner to his right. There was a woman with him, but he couldn't see her face.

Jennings noticed him as he approached, and waved him over. "This is Natalie Tate," he said. "She's on our project."

Natalie looked up and nodded to him. Will returned the gesture. She looked like an FBI agent: conservative dress, dark-rimmed glasses, physically fit – possibly underweight – and a serious expression.

"You're wondering why we called you out," Jennings said and slid over to give Will room to sit.

Will nodded and sat.

"Our friends are back in town, and four of them are here," Natalie explained. "Can you identify them?"

Will scanned the room and immediately spotted the men at the bar. The bumps on their foreheads gave them away. It was clear that at least one of them had had cosmetic surgery, but it wasn't a good fix. One of the others tried to hide them with his hair, and the remaining two made no effort to conceal them. They were all Compressed Punishment victims.

"How'd you find them?" Will asked.

"Border control warned us," Natalie replied. "These guys showed up in El Paso a week ago, and we put a GPS tracker on one of their vehicles."

"That tracker," Jennings broke in, "is no longer active, but we've located their residence."

"Why not just round them up now?" Will asked.

"Nothing to go on," Natalie said. "What do we charge them with – being ugly?"

Will admitted they weren't exactly physically appealing human beings, and then wondered if he fit into that same category. "A little risky – bringing me here."

"Why?" Natalie asked.

"Can't you see them on my forehead?" Will replied. He'd had an excellent cosmetic surgeon, but remnants of the bumps were still visible in the right light.

He watched Natalie's dark eyes scan his head and focus first right, then left.

"You were an inmate?" she whispered, eyes wide.

Will looked to Jennings.

Jennings shrugged and looked to Natalie. "Now you know."

"If those guys see me, my cover will be blown," Will said.

"Do they look familiar?" Jennings asked.

"No," Will responded. "I've only met one other inmate – just before I was inserted into the program. He's not one of them."

Will caught the eye of Natalie. Her eyes shifted back and forth from his eyes to his forehead.

"What did they do to you in there?" she asked, seemingly both intrigued and horrified.

"Bad stuff," Jennings cut in. "I'll fill you in later. For now, we need to concentrate on what these guys are planning."

"Not sure how I can help with that," Will said. "Why did you call me here?"

"Just hoped you'd ID one of those guys," Jennings explained.

"And then what?" Will asked.

Jennings shook his head.

"You want to know what they're up to," Will said. "It's more than a coincidence that Syncorp is in Baton Rouge."

"The scope of our investigation has broadened," Jennings said and then nodded to Natalie.

"If we could get you into Syncorp," she said, "could you identify equipment used in the Compressed Punishment program?"

"To what end?" Will asked.

"Syncorp has been sold," Jennings replied. "The company has had numerous government projects – many of them were so-called black projects. We need to know which ones are still active after the takeover – especially anything connected to Red Wraith."

"Red Wraith?" Natalie asked, confused.

"Forgive me," Jennings said to Will. "I haven't brought her up to speed." He turned to Natalie. "It's the black project that's responsible for the CP program."

"You think they're still producing CP equipment?" Will asked.

"Not sure. They're not delivering anything inside the US," Jennings explained. "But a shipment of medical equipment arrived in China just three weeks ago."

Will's heart thumped so hard he felt it in his eyes. "And you think they sent CP equipment to China – *Exoskeletons*?"

Jennings shrugged.

If all it took was for Will to identify equipment in the facility, he was ready to go immediately. "Will there be arrests?"

"Likely," Jennings replied.

"When do we start?" Will asked, hardly containing his eagerness.

"There are some complications," Natalie said, and motioned with her eyes towards the CP inmates at the bar. "We think those guys are going to pull something. They'll ruin our investigation."

Will didn't mind if the CP guys acted first. He wanted to see the place burn.

"Contact me when you have a plan." Will said and stood. He left the bar.

He checked his phone as he weaved through parked cars towards his SUV. It was time to give Denise and Jonathan an update.

~ 4 ~

Saturday, 16 May (2:02 a.m. EST – Washington)

Daniel eyes were still wide open. All he could do was stare at the ceiling of his bedroom, dimly illuminated by the green lights of his digital clock. His wife snored lightly next to him.

The captain of the German U-boat possessed files with letterhead containing the symbol of the Nazis' Red Falcon project. Red Falcon and Tabarin were now connected. And the connection between Red Falcon and Red Wraith was already well established. A chill ran through his shoulders and neck inducing a single, spontaneous twitch. He didn't yet understand the implications or connections, but his subconscious poked at parts of his mind. Something was there.

The other thing that stole his sleep was the fact that the technology needed to construct the beacon did not exist. He did some research, and was aware of the amazing capabilities the oil companies had developed to access deep waters and drill into the seabed. There were also special research submarines capable of going to great depths. But this thing was different – it was enormous for something at that depth, and its base penetrated into the seabed. Adding to the mystery was that it was composed of an unknown, super-hard material. All of it was inexplicable.

Was the idea of extraterrestrial technology such a leap? He didn't think so; he'd come across evidence of such things in previous assignments – though nothing conclusive. But there were more drastic ideas swimming around in his head. What if it were even more bizarre than alien technology?

He didn't know why his mind asked him that question, but he'd done enough thinking for the night. His eyelids lowered, and his breathing deepened. It was time for dreams. Or nightmares.

~ 5 ~

Saturday, 16 May (9:50 a.m. EST – Antarctic Circle)

The Antarctic coast was no place for an attack submarine. Captain McHenry was aware of the dangers, but had his orders.

With a carrier strike force securing the area, they could study the beacon without threat. Three other U.S. subs patrolled the waters like hungry sharks. This freed up the *North Dakota* to explore the ice shelves along the coast closest to the beacon. Treacherous circumpolar currents characterized the dark waters, and the surface was rife with ice flows. The southern winter was fast approaching.

The waters were an acoustic wonderland. American teams had been mapping the ocean floor for days, and ships and submarines deployed active sonar on a regular basis. There was no attempt to keep their presence a secret – quite the opposite. It was made known to the world that the United States Navy was conducting war games in the Southern Ocean. For the sake of appearances, they periodically carried out mock maneuvers.

Twice since dodging the torpedo attack, the *North Dakota* had chased away the same Chinese submarine. Another American sub discovered a Russian sub sleeping under a protrusion in an ice shelf 170 kilometers from the beacon. They'd pinged it with a sonar blast, sending it scurrying away. He wondered which one of the two foreign subs had launched a torpedo at them. He wouldn't mind an opportunity to return the gesture.

The *North Dakota* was currently exploring the Brunt Ice Shelf. A floating body of ice extending from the western coast into the Weddell Sea, the shelf covered over 100,000 square kilometers, and spanned the coast of Coats Land to Dronning Maud Land. It was a vast inverted vista, riddled with nooks and crannies that made good hiding places for submarines. But the *North Dakota* was not there to ferret out sleepers.

He had to throw the self-preservation habits he'd developed as a sub commander to the wayside. The *North Dakota* was now playing the role of a science vessel – mapping the floor and currents beneath the shelf. Their pinging constantly broadcasted their position.

The floor sloped upward as they approached the coast, slowly pinching them between the rocky bottom and a ceiling of thick ice. If they grounded, or had a malfunction that immobilized them, they'd be in trouble. They wouldn't be able to break through the ice – it was over 100 meters thick.

After the first 12 hours of exploration, McHenry went to the mess room to get some scrambled eggs and coffee. Diggs joined him, and they chatted about their mutual discomfort with the situation: *noise was death*.

"We have other subs running silent," McHenry confided quietly. "We're in good hands."

Diggs nodded. "Mapping the floor like a science junket isn't very interesting. What do they expect – we'll find another beacon?"

McHenry shrugged. "Don't know." A vibration tickled his right hip, and he pulled a communicator from his belt and put it up to his ear. "Go," he said.

"Captain, you're needed at sonar," the voice said. "Something you should look at."

"There in five," he replied and set the communicator on the table.

He took a bite of eggs. They could wait a few minutes while he finished eating. It was the fifth time he'd been called. He knew they were approaching the coast, so he suspected they were getting shallow again. They'd need his permission to turn and start mapping outward.

They'd been scanning to and fro, toward the coast and out to sea, creating a full map of the sub-shelf floor. Rough maps already existed for the area, but it was clear that more detail was needed. And, as Diggs said, they were searching for abnormalities.

He finished his breakfast, bussed his tray, and topped off his mug with coffee. A few minutes later he entered the sonar room and was surprised to see a half-dozen men crowded around a computer monitor. "What's up?" he asked.

The men parted, revealing Finley at a chair in front of the sonar computer.

"Have a look at this," Finley said with excitement.

McHenry stepped closer, put on a pair of half-rimmed reading glasses, and studied the image. It took him a few seconds, but then he saw it clearly: it was a trench that led towards the coast. At the bottom of the trench, which gouged 50 meters into the seafloor, was a submarine. It was upside down, partially buried, and blended in well with the landscape, but he could still tell by its size and shape what it was: a World War II German U-boat.

~ 6 ~

Saturday, 16 May (12:22 p.m. EST – Washington)

Daniel sat with the others in Room 713. Sylvia sat to his left on the couch, and Horace and Thackett sat in the chairs across the table to complete the square.

Thackett filled them in on the current status of the beacon, a few close calls between American and both Chinese and Russian submarines, and the securing of the area by a U.S. carrier group. From the ensuing silence it was clear that the update provided them with nothing new.

After an awkward lull, Thackett's face flushed and he cleared his throat. "We're at a standstill," he admitted. "I'm under some pressure to get answers."

Daniel knew where Thackett wanted to go with the conversation, but didn't help the man.

Thackett continued, "I don't want to put too much pressure on you two, but –"

"– but we have no choice," Horace cut in. "Have you discovered anything?"

Sylvia answered first. "Incremental advances. Nothing significant."

"Like what, exactly?" Thackett asked, eagerly, not rudely.

"The so-called sightings of strange aircraft in Argentina have been definitively discredited," she explained. "I've found the sources of rumors – one was an author who had propagated false information to get notoriety for a book he was writing. I've found no connections to the beacon."

"That's fine, Sylvia," Horace said and looked to Daniel. "And you?"

Daniel shifted in his seat and set his cup on the table. "I've

119

recently found something," he replied. He walked to his office and returned with some photos and a magnifying glass. He handed the magnifying glass and a photo and to Horace. "I don't know how I managed to notice this – it's small and blurred."

"What am I looking for?" Horace asked as he examined the picture.

"The emblems on the files," Daniel replied and pointed out the general area on the photo. It was the picture of Otto Wermuth in his quarters on U-530.

It took Horace about ten seconds, and then his face took on a sickly expression.

"Now this one," Daniel said and handed him another photo.

He seemed to go back and forth between two points on the photograph, the same two, Daniel presumed, that he'd toggled between hours earlier.

"Extraordinary," Horace gasped.

"What is it?" Thackett asked.

"Have a look for yourself," Horace replied and handed the pictures and magnifying glass to Thackett. Horace sat up straighter and addressed Daniel. "I'm not sure what this means." Daniel detected a subtle trembling in Horace's voice, and then in his hands.

Horace continued, "The second picture was taken *before* the war – it's of the *Schwabenland* during its exploratory mission to Antarctica?"

"Yes," Daniel replied. "I thought it might have been doctored, but I found an independent photo in which the aircraft is missing. The crate and the emblem are still there."

"Someone please explain to me what I'm looking for," Thackett said. He was studying the *Schwabenland* photo.

"The emblems," Horace said. "They're a little hard to see, but definitely there – one the plane's fuselage and another on a crate on the deck."

It was Sylvia's turn to express frustration. "Could someone please fill me in?"

"It's from my previous assignment," Daniel replied. "The Red

120

Wraith project."

"I think I see it now," Thackett interrupted, still leaning over the table with the magnifying glass. "It looks like a complicated swastika."

"That's it," Horace confirmed.

"It's the same as the one on the plane, except the one on the crate is being carried by an eagle," Thackett said.

"It's a falcon," Horace corrected.

"A *leftward facing* falcon," Daniel added. "The direction means something."

"Yes, a leftward-facing bird of prey is a Nazi symbol of aggression," Horace explained. "We don't know the full meaning of the emblem, but it represents the Red Falcon project."

Thackett leaned forward and handed the pictures to Sylvia.

Horace continued. "Until now, it had been assumed that Red Falcon had begun after World War II had started."

"But these photos of the *Schwabenland* suggest it started before the war," Daniel explained, "and that the *Schwabenland's* mission might have been connected to Red Falcon."

"Well," Horace spoke in conclusive tone, "I think you'd better revive your research on Red Wraith and Red Falcon."

"We're missing a lot of information about Red Wraith," Daniel said to Thackett.

"How can that be?" Thackett asked.

"Red Wraith was a black project – perhaps the blackest of the all," Horace explained. "The government entities that ran it were considered rogue. The information might be hard to come by."

"It's hard to imagine that Red Wraith had been kept secret all this time," Daniel added. "It was a huge money sink, and active since the end of the war up to a few months ago."

"Where can we find this missing information?" Thackett asked.

"It was a lawyer in Chicago who'd exposed the Compressed Punishment program," Daniel explained. "But it was the FBI that finally brought it down – stormed the two CP facilities, and confiscated evidence. They'd also raided DARPA facilities." It was the information from the

Defense Advanced Research Projects Agency that Daniel coveted. He'd requested information from them just before his Red Wraith research was put on hold, but it had never been delivered.

Thackett rubbed his forehead with a flat palm, and then ran his fingers through his greasy hair. "So the FBI has it," he said and sighed. "I'll see what I can do."

Horace and Thackett left. Daniel and Sylvia remained seated.

"That was quite a discovery," she said.

"I just noticed the crate and plane this morning," he replied, detecting disappointment in her voice. He didn't mean to leave her out of the loop. "I hadn't appreciated the ramifications until now."

"You couldn't get the Red Wraith documents? I thought we had access to everything."

"Just when my investigation started to pick up, information got increasingly difficult to acquire," Daniel explained. "Sometimes I got messages saying that the files had been destroyed. Other times there was no response at all. The FBI obstructed almost every request."

"Strange," she said.

"There's mistrust between the agencies," he said. "Red Wraith was the CIA's baby, and they were highly protective of it. The CIA had even ordered hits on FBI agents investigating the project – they'd killed at least 20 over the years."

Her mouth opened and her eyes turned blank. "What could be that important?"

"I never had the chance to find out," he answered and shrugged. "It haunts me."

"So what if we can't get the information we need? What if Thackett fails?" she asked. She laced her fingers together and squeezed until marbled red-white patterns formed on her knuckles.

Daniel had come up with a possible solution to the problem. "As Omnis, we gather written documents and read them. Based on what we learn, we gather more documents and read them. This iterative process repeats until we have exhausted the topic we are researching, and we write the final monograph based entirely on written sources."

Sylvia shrugged. "So?"

"Have you ever used a *human* source?"

"You mean bring someone in and interview them?" she said shaking her head strongly. "It would be a security risk."

"The urgency of our situation warrants it," he argued. "Besides, we wouldn't bring anyone here."

Her head tilted to the side. "You mean go and talk to someone – on the outside?"

He saw genuine fear in her face.

"Daniel, we're not operatives."

"You're just like me," he said, although 20 years ago he'd been on the outside and dealt with human resources first as a CIA case officer, and then as a reports officer.

"Just like you?"

"We've become so reclusive that we fear anyone even seeing our faces."

"It's the nature of our work," she said in a defensive tone.

"It has become the nature of *ourselves*," he argued.

After a few seconds of reflective silence, she said, "You'll have to get permission from Thackett."

Daniel nodded.

"Who do you want to interview?" she asked.

"The man who brought down the Compressed Punishment program," Daniel answered. "The lawyer from Chicago – one *Jonathan McDougal*."

~ 7 ~
Saturday, 16 May (1:31 p.m. EST – Antarctic Circle)

"Is it clear enough for video?" McHenry asked. He wanted enough data to at least document the find.

"We'll need the lights," Finley answered.

123

McHenry was intrigued enough to send out the *Little Dakota*, but she was somewhere at the bottom of the Weddell Sea, and they wouldn't get a replacement anytime soon. They'd have to settle for the snake, which was just camera on the end of a long, flexible appendage. The snake was about 15 meters long and designed to inspect the outer hull for damage.

Being close to the coast, they were in relatively shallow water – 150 meters. The pilot lowered the *North Dakota* to within 40 meters of the U-boat and illuminated it with bright floodlights. It was a color camera, but the video still looked as if it were taken in black and white.

McHenry instructed Finley to maneuver the snake until he found what he sought: a gaping hole in the side of the sub.

Finley gasped. "Looks like they took a hit."

"Find the markings," McHenry ordered. "They'll want to ID this thing."

After a half-hour of probing they'd only found faint, eroded markings. There might have been more on the bottom and the buried parts, but he figured they had enough high-resolution video for the naval forensic experts. They'd do a sophisticated image analysis, and might be able to ID the vessel even without markings.

His attention turned to the trench. The sunken U-boat was not far from its starting point, less than two kilometers from shore. He wanted to see how far it went, and what else they might find in it. He ordered the pilot to position the *North Dakota* just above the trench, and to proceed slowly towards the continent.

The gouge became deeper as the sea floor rose towards the coast. It seemed as if it maintained a constant depth, but the walls to either side grew as it proceeded towards the continent, where the ocean floor would eventually merge with land. After more than an hour of careful navigation, it started to get tight.

"How would you like to proceed, Cap'n," the pilot asked.

McHenry knew the question was whether or not to descend into the trench. "Do we have room to turn around in there, Finley?"

"No," Finley replied as he pointed to the sonar image on a computer monitor. "For now we can still rise above it to make the turn –

that is, until we get to the coast. Otherwise, we'll have to back out. What if it goes inland?"

"That's what we we're going to find out," McHenry said. "Let's stay just above it for as long as we can, and keep an eye on the ceiling as we go. Notify me when we get close to the coast."

McHenry headed to the conn. He needed to discuss the situation with his first officer. *What would he do if the trench penetrated inland?*

~ 8 ~

Saturday, 16 May (10:11 p.m. CST – Baton Rouge)

Will was ready to go within minutes of getting Jennings' call. An hour later, he was in the back seat of a car and heading to Syncorp. They were getting him inside.

Natalie Tate sat to Will's left, and Jennings was in the passenger seat. Jake Adler was behind the wheel. He was a former Syncorp engineer who had moved up the ranks to Vice President – one of about 100.

Adler was on the hook; Jennings had convinced him that Syncorp was in big trouble, and the only way he'd avoid being rolled up in the collapse was to help them.

Adler turned left onto Perkins from College Drive and headed south. After a mile they approached a driveway on the left. A dimly lit Syncorp sign appeared as they made the turn.

The sign induced strong emotions – mostly anger – and Will's chest tightened to the point of physical discomfort.

They followed the well-groomed, two-lane road for a half of a mile through dense woods until they stopped behind a semi-truck.

"There have been shipments every night for the past month," Adler commented. "It won't take too long to get in."

Five minutes later they came to a gate connected to a concrete guardhouse. An armed, uniformed man approached the driver's side, and Adler rolled down the window and handed him some documents.

The guard went back to the booth, handed the papers to his partner, and picked up a red phone.

"Who are they calling?" Jennings asked.

"It's normal procedure," Adler replied. "We have clients in late all the time."

Natalie asked, "You sure you can get us into the right areas? You passed us off as pharmaceutical clients."

"Relax," Adler replied. "I've done this before. We show off what we have to convince potential clients to do business. They've all been through background checks. I managed to get you on the list of previously vetted guests."

The security guard returned with three plastic visitor badges, and instructed them to wear them at all times. The gate lifted, and Adler drove through it and onto a wider, well-lit road with a median. Along the way were orange signs warning drivers to keep their speeds between 20 and 30 miles per hour until they got to the parking facility.

"What's with the minimum speed?" Natalie asked, pointing to one of the signs.

"They don't want anyone being dropped off before they get to the complex," Adler explained. "The security is extreme – but most things are monitored electronically. As you can see, however, there are loopholes."

A few minutes later they entered a parking structure and, after navigating turns and card-actuated gates, Adler parked the car and turned off the engine. He took off his seatbelt and turned his body sideways, towards Jennings. He glanced back and forth between Will and Natalie. "You have the story in case we're questioned?"

Will and Natalie nodded. They worked for a Canadian pharmaceutical company, and were in the market for ultrasound components. Adler had assured them that no security guard would have the technical knowledge to expose them. *But what if they ran into an engineer?* Will thought. Things could get pretty hairy, even with his technical background.

They got out of the car, and Will followed the others to an elevator. After descending three levels to what he thought was ground

126

level, the elevator door opened to a wide hallway. They got out, turned right, and walked down a corridor lined with big windows that revealed large, brightly lit rooms. The people on the other side were dressed in white lab coats and milled around massive stainless steel tables. The tabletops were littered with intricate mechanical pieces that he couldn't identify.

"This is the robotic surgery section," Adler explained in a voice that seemed commercial. Will knew they were now on stage – cameras everywhere.

They continued down the hall and took a left into another corridor, identical to the first.

"This is the radiation oncology division," Adler said. "We've made significant advances in radiation therapy devices. Next is the magnetic resonance imaging – or MRI – division."

Will was impressed. Before his jaunt in academia, he'd conducted research at government labs. It was clear that Syncorp's laboratory facilities, and probably the research, eclipsed anything he'd previously seen. Then he remembered that Syncorp was a defense contractor: funding was not an issue.

After a half hour of touring and chatting nonsense, they reached an elevator door that required card access. Jennings turned to Will and made a face suggesting *this is it*.

Adler slid his card. They piled into the elevator, and went down a floor.

The layout was identical to that of the previous floor except that the windows were darkened so that they couldn't see inside the rooms.

They proceeded at about the same pace as the previous floor, and Adler kept talking as if he was trying to sell them something. Jennings asked questions appropriate for their cover. After five minutes, Adler stopped in front of one of the doors.

"Let me show you an example of some of our most advanced technical capabilities," Adler said and ran his card through a slot next to the door. It clicked, and he pushed it open.

The room was as large as a basketball gymnasium, but absent of people. Overhead cranes hung on rails suspended from the 40 foot ceiling, and milling machines, lathes, welding stations, and other fabrication tools occupied stations on the wall to the left. Electronics benches and fume hoods lined the opposite side. On the far end were stacks of casket-sized crates arranged on heavy, wooden pallets. There were 7 groups of 10 and 1 group of 4.

Their shoes clacked and echoed in the large room as Adler led them to the crates.

"Things are quiet here this week," Adler explained, addressing the absence of Syncorp personnel. "They'd just finished a large order and the night shift had been put on hold for a while. Let me show you one of our products."

Adler walked to a workbench and returned with an electric drill motor with a screwdriver attachment. He walked between two pallets to the stack of four crates and engaged the drill. After removing the 20-plus screws from the lid of one of the crates and putting them in his pocket, he set the drill on the floor, and walked to one side. He grabbed the edge of the lid and nodded to Jennings to grab the other. They lifted together and set it on the floor.

Adler struggled to remove yellow foam packing material that was sprayed in for a tight form-fit. After dislodging a large piece and tossing it to the floor, he waved them over.

Will looked into the crate and was nearly overcome with dizziness. In his mind, he'd been transported back to the Red Box, back inside his Exoskeleton. He fought the strong urge to separate from his body. He stood still for a few seconds until the urgency subsided.

Two pieces were visible: an Exoskeleton forearm and the corresponding upper arm. They were separately wrapped in clear plastic and pressed into cellophane-covered foam. He picked up the forearm and examined it, despite the nervous look he got from Adler. It was lighter than he'd expected, and had the exact metallic-blue tint he remembered. The arm sections were missing some components that he knew had to be assembled later. It had mounting provisions for pneumatic actuators, conduits for tubes and sensors, and extra joints in places where they should

128

not be – one in the middle of the forearm and another around the bicep position of the upper arm. The extra joints had been used to bend his bones, the pain from which still lingered in his mind. The most damning identifier was the metal tag mounted on the top of the forearm, near the wrist: Syncorp, Inc.

Will extracted another set of arm pieces, set them on the floor, and pulled out another level of foam to reveal a set of legs and feet. "Are there other pieces?" Will asked. He knew there should also be head cages, motors, actuators, biosensors, and other systems.

Adler's eyes bulged so that the whites were exposed all around. Will was approaching the limit of their cover.

"This department only develops the parts that you see here," Adler explained. "And also the support appendage that connects the device to a control track."

Will remembered the sinister-looking appendage to which Adler referred: it resembled a giant scorpion tail, and suspended the Exoskeleton, and its hapless victim, from the ceiling. It also provided all power, sensing, and feedback control.

A light film of sweat cooled Will's forehead. He looked at Jennings with an expression of confirmation. He then turned to Adler. "Where are these going?"

Adler looked confused.

This was off script, but was a question any inquisitive person might ask. If Adler kept his cool, their cover should be okay.

"Um ... I'm not sure," Adler stammered. "Overseas somewhere, I think."

"Shall we pack up and go?" Jennings broke in. He'd already grabbed the packing foam and gestured to Will to put the pieces he held in his hands back into the crate. As Will leaned over the crate, he snapped some blind pictures with his phone, mostly concealed in his jacket. He hoped for at least one good shot.

After everything was packed, Adler and Natalie replaced the lid. Adler drove in the all of the screws in just a few minutes.

They left the room, made their way back to the car, and were off

Syncorp property and heading north on Perkins by 12:30 a.m.

"Again, where are the Exoskeletons going?" Will asked Adler.

"China," Adler replied. "Just one week after our … uh … domestic demand evaporated, we got new management with connections to the Chinese government – unofficial, of course. We now ship more of these than ever before."

"Do you know what they're used for?" Will asked, agitated.

"I assume they have some medical applications," Adler answered.

"They're used to *torture* people," Will nearly screamed.

Natalie put her hand on Will's.

"Sorry," Will said, more to Natalie than Adler.

He felt better when they reached familiar territory. Jennings turned right, from Perkins Road to College Drive, and then finally into the parking lot of the International House of Pancakes where Will had parked his car.

"We'll be in touch," Jennings said just before he closed the door.

Will got into his SUV and started driving home. He was alarmed that the technology was being passed to China, but it was no surprise. The United States couldn't keep a secret. The subtleties of the Manhattan Project had been leaked out before the first bomb exploded. Klaus Fuchs – one of the Los Alamos scientists – had been the traitor. That one man might have been the sole reason for the Cold War. The National Security Agency lost all of its secrets: again, one-man, Edward Snowden. Now, the Red Wraith research had leaked and it was spreading like cancer. China, not exactly the pinnacle of human rights, would apply the program indiscriminately. And what if they succeeded? What if they created more people like himself?

Syncorp had to be stopped quickly. *And by any means.*

~ 9 ~

Sunday, 17 May (1:05 a.m. EST – Washington)

130

Daniel sat on a chair in the central area of 713 while Sylvia worked quietly in her office. He'd devoted the evening to investigating Jonathan McDougal. The man impressed him. He knew, however, that he'd also have to impress Thackett and Horace if they were to grant him permission to meet with the old law professor.

Besides teaching law, McDougal directed a legal entity called the DNA Foundation. The Foundation funded researchers and lawyers to investigate old cases in which DNA evidence could give definitive answers, and they'd exonerated over 50 people in the first two years of its existence.

McDougal had made his name as the driving force for the moratorium on the death penalty in the state of Illinois. This was enough to establish him as a good risk – he seemed like a good man – but it was impossible to determine what information the professor had about Red Wraith, and whether he'd share it.

Red Wraith was the most secretive project that Daniel had encountered, but also the most deadly. Countless people had been assassinated in addition to the FBI agents who had investigated the project. But that was about all he'd uncovered – just a bunch of cloak-and-dagger events that seemed to have no underlying purpose. He'd never discovered its true objective, and this loose end, he suspected, was a source of obsession for his subconscious mind. He hadn't slept well since being taken off the project, yet it was the first thought in his mind the instant he woke up every morning, despite being reassigned. He felt more focused now that Red Wraith was part of his current assignment.

He moved to the couch, leaned back, and rested his eyes. After what seemed like no more than an instant, he twitched and sat up. His watch read 7:50 a.m. He'd been asleep for over six hours.

A few seconds later, the door beeped and opened, thirty feet to his right. Thackett and Horace entered. Horace looked more vibrant than Thackett, despite being nearly a half-century older than the CIA director. Each man inserted a wet umbrella into the clay flowerpot next to the door, and took off glistening trench coats and hung them on a coatrack.

Sylvia walked in behind them, dropped her things off in her office, and sat on the couch next to Daniel.

"How long did you stay last night?" she asked. "You were napping when I left."

"All night," he replied and shook his head. "I just woke up."

Sylvia smiled. "I should've woke you before I left."

Everyone took their usual seats.

"Any developments?" Thackett asked.

Thackett looked hopeful. Horace did not. Perhaps the seasoned man better understood the pace at which Omni research was conducted.

"Not much new," Daniel replied. "However, I have an idea that might get us going."

Horace sat back in his chair, crossed his legs, and rubbed the gray stubble on his chin between his thumb and forefinger. "Let's hear it."

Daniel explained his interest in McDougal, and how he likely had important information that they needed.

"He's an activist lawyer who happened by chance to catch the CP program at the right time," Thackett argued. "What makes you think he's actually in possession of anything of value?"

"National Security Agency surveillance archives of phone recordings between McDougal, his wife, and his assistant indicate they might have had files," Daniel replied.

Thackett shook his head. "Civilians don't understand the utility of burner phones."

"Actually, they did. But they screwed up," Daniel explained. "The NSA was able to ID the burners since they'd forgotten to pull the batteries out of their personal phones. They correlated the phones by GPS location. Once that's accomplished, using the burner is the same as using the personal cell."

Horace sat forward. "You want to talk to him in person?" he asked with an expression of doubt.

Daniel nodded.

"And what if he doesn't have anything?" Horace asked.

"I think he also *knows* things," Daniel replied.

"Like what?" Thackett asked.

"Details about the Compressed Punishment program," Daniel explained. "And he was involved with the FBI, and possibly with a CIA operative who was killed in the explosion at the Detroit facility just before it was shut down. He was also in contact with a former CP inmate – the man whose case the DNA Foundation had been investigating at the time."

Horace sat back again and pulled on his lower lip. "Maybe we should bring him in," he suggested. "Question McDougal here."

Thackett nodded in approval.

"No chance," Daniel said. "He doesn't trust us. He knows that the CIA was deeply involved in Red Wraith."

"We cannot trust any rank-and-file personnel with this – too sensitive," Horace said. "So, again, you want to go meet with McDougal in person?"

Daniel nodded. "He should be in Chicago now. He teaches a law class this semester."

"You'll be jeopardizing your identity," Horace said. "Are you sure you want to do this? Your career and safety are at risk."

Daniel had already thought it through, and turned the question on Horace. "Is it worth the risk?"

Horace's eyes gave away that he'd come to a quick conclusion, or maybe a realization.

He sighed. "Yes."

Sylvia, who had been silent through the conversation, said, "I want to go with him."

Daniel turned his head in surprise. It wasn't a good idea – two Omnis sticking out their necks.

Daniel started to protest but was cut off by Horace.

"I want you both on a plane to Chicago this evening," Horace said.

It seemed that Thackett was now just a bystander in the planning. But then, ever since Daniel had met Horace, he surmised that Thackett had always been just the figurehead for the Omniscients. It took something urgent to flush Horace out of the dark but, now that he was exposed, he took the initiative.

Daniel had to go home and pack.

CHAPTER VII

~ 1 ~

Sunday, 17 May (11:58 p.m. CST – Baton Rouge)

Zhichao Cho was sitting on his balcony puffing a cigar when the call came in: it was the head of his local contingent of MSS operatives. Chinese intelligence had been under more scrutiny in the United States since the Cold War had ended, but their perceived threat had diminished again after the attack on the World Trade Center in 2001. American intelligence mostly focused on people from the Middle East.

Cho's man-in-charge went by the name Ximin, and he was the most senior operative in his commission. His calls were rare.

Cho listened for two minutes, and hung up. Things were getting complicated. The FBI was investigating Syncorp, and agents had already been inside the complex. One thing he knew about the transfer of information was that immediate action could often snuff it out before it could be used. This became more and more difficult to accomplish in the digital age, but he'd have to move fast.

They knew the agent's identity, thanks to an FBI mole and a loyal Syncorp employee, so it should be easy to coax him into a trap. But Cho didn't want to just levy a hit. Besides, his principal asset for that kind of work was currently occupied. Instead, he wanted to extract information. And what would be a better place for that than Syncorp?

He made a call and gave the order.

Cho smiled. Maybe he'd try his hand at dental work.

~ 2 ~

Monday, 18 May (9:59 a.m. CST – Chicago)

134

According to the professor's web page, he held office hours Monday and Wednesday mornings from ten to noon. Daniel and Sylvia had arrived promptly at 10 a.m., but the hallway was already filled with students. From the chatter, it was apparent that a graded exam had been handed back to them before the weekend, and it hadn't gone well for many of them.

Daniel thought Sylvia, at 36 years old, could still pass for a law student, although many of the students looked at both of them with suspicious eyes. They most likely recognized everyone in their class, and identified Sylvia and him as outsiders.

At 11:10 a.m. it was finally their turn. Daniel followed Sylvia into the large office and closed the door. Sunlight from large, southeast-facing windows lit up the room, and bookshelves lined the other walls from the floor to the high ceiling. A spherical light fixture hung over a large, wooden table near the center of the room, and another cluster of furniture was arranged at the far end. The faint scent of pipe tobacco deepened the ambience. The office seemed comfortable – important for a place where one came to think.

Daniel directed his attention to a man sitting behind a desk, typing away on a laptop computer. He was mid-sixties, with thick gray hair and bushy eyebrows.

"Name?" the man said without looking up.

Sylvia and Daniel glanced at each other but remained silent.

The man looked up and shook his head. "I told you, one at a time." It was then that McDougal must have realized that Daniel wasn't a law student, and then his suspicion seemed to transfer to Sylvia.

"Who are you?" McDougal asked, and then stood and walked around the desk. He was dressed like a professor, business casual and a jacket, and was taller that Daniel by a few inches.

"I'm Sylvia, and this is Daniel. We're investigating Red Wraith," she said softly. "We need your help, Mr. McDougal. Can we meet with you today?"

McDougal's eyes widened, but he kept his composure. "Who do you work for?" he asked.

"We can discuss that when we meet again," Daniel said. He nodded towards the door. "You seem to be busy at the moment."

McDougal seemed to disarm slightly. "Yes," he said and nodded.

"Can we meet tonight?" Sylvia asked.

McDougal stepped back behind his desk and looked them over. From Daniel's perspective Sylvia looked to be of no threat, and he thought he didn't appear to be, either. They were both skinny, casually dressed, intellectual types. But he knew that looks could be deceiving – either of them could be carrying a gun. Hopefully McDougal got the idea that the time, location, and conditions of their first meeting were chosen to be as nonthreatening as possible.

"Fine," McDougal said at last. "Seven o'clock. I'll have a colleague with me."

"Thank you," Daniel said, and then followed Sylvia out of the office. They pressed through the students scattered throughout the narrow hall. It would be an interesting evening.

~ 3 ~

Monday, 18 May (6:36 p.m. CST – Chicago)

After eating pizza at the *Capstone Bistro*, Daniel and Sylvia walked the half-mile to the law school. At 7 p.m. sharp they knocked on Jonathan McDougal's door.

Jonathan brought them in and led them to a cluster of furniture at the far end of the room. It was a set of two chairs and a couch surrounding a coffee table, not unlike the arrangement in Room 713 of the Space Systems building. Already seated in one of the chairs was a woman Daniel recognized from his research. He and Sylvia took the couch.

Jonathan set a carafe of coffee and four cups on the table while he introduced the fourth participant, Denise Walker. He then poured coffee for everyone and took his seat next to Denise and across from Daniel.

"Now, how can I help you, Mr. ..." Jonathan asked, obviously fishing for a name.

"Call me Daniel," he said in an apologetic tone. "Our anonymity is crucial."

"Who do you work for?" Denise asked, directing the question to both of them.

Sylvia nodded to Daniel to take the question.

"Sorry, Ms. Walker. Again, I cannot say."

Jonathan rubbed his face and exhaled impatiently. "So you come in here and tell us nothing and expect us to give you information?"

It was a question that Daniel anticipated. "I can tell you that we are part of a government entity that is investigating the Red Wraith project."

"FBI?" Denise asked.

Daniel shook his head.

"CIA?" she asked again.

"Not exactly," he replied.

"We're lawyers, Mr. … Daniel," Jonathan said, "and 'not exactly' is not a valid answer. Yet it reveals something."

"We'll have to stop with this line of questioning," Daniel said. "Depending on what you have for us, we could provide you with useful information in return. We don't expect something for nothing."

With that, Daniel saw a change in Jonathan's eyes to something more amenable. Although, he thought, the exchange might be asymmetric. Daniel had mostly historical information that, although it laid the foundations of the project, might not be useful to Jonathan's current objectives.

"I hate to disappoint you, Daniel," Jonathan said, "but we handed over all of our information to the FBI over six months ago."

"I requested files from the FBI three months ago," Daniel said. "I was told they hadn't received new information on Red Wraith in a decade."

For an instant, Daniel saw an expression of alarm on Jonathan's face as he glanced over at Ms. Walker, whose expression was even more pronounced.

"You must not have clearance," Jonathan said.

Sylvia laughed, and covered her mouth as if she started to cough.

Daniel smiled and nodded. "No one has a higher clearance than we do."

"That would imply that you are an Omniscient," Jonathan said, raising his eyebrows.

Daniel spilled his coffee on his pants. He stood quickly and put his dripping cup on the table, almost dropping it in the process. Jonathan handed him some napkins and Daniel patted the coffee spots, but they had already soaked in. Denise cleaned up the coffee pooling on the table.

"How do you know about Omniscients?" Daniel asked. He was horrified by the idea that they were known to anyone outside the CIA. The mortified look on Sylvia's face perfectly expressed the same degree of alarm.

"We can get information, too," Jonathan responded, smiling, convinced he'd hit his intended target. "Our investigations lead us to many strange places. I take it then that you're CIA."

Daniel nodded. He felt violated in some way. He wasn't good at this.

"Not to worry. Your secret is safe with us," Jonathan reassured. "Now, let's talk about Red Wraith."

~ 4 ~

Monday, 18 May (8:25 p.m. EST – Antarctic Circle)

They'd followed the trench all the way to the coast. At that point it became a tunnel, and the ceiling turned from ice to rock. They followed it a kilometer inland, and then backtracked and communicated their findings. McHenry awaited instructions.

He could hardly contain his concern that another sub would get in there before he did. He alleviated his anxiety by meeting with a supply ship and restocking. After a few more nervous hours at communication depth, Naval Command gave him the order to explore the cavern.

"There's our dead U-boat," Finley said and pointed to its image on the screen.

McHenry hoped the *North Dakota* wouldn't suffer a similar fate.

"Take it slowly," McHenry said. "When we start going inland, map everything – floor to ceiling. We'll want to make it back out."

"I'll do my best," Finley replied in a voice that didn't conceal his tension.

Thirty minutes later they'd penetrated as far inland as they had the first time, about a kilometer. At this point, the trench was about 100 meters deep, and just as wide. Since the *North Dakota* was over 100 meters long, this was unidirectional territory – they'd have to go backwards to reverse course.

Three more kilometers and the trench deepened to a 150 meters. In all his time as a submariner, this was the first time McHenry had ever felt claustrophobic. He left Finley to his mapping, and went to the conn.

The control room was quieter than normal even though the usual contingent was present. The sailors concentrated intently on their jobs. Displayed on banks of wall-mounted video monitors were live feeds from various on-board sonar and imaging systems. McHenry was most interested in the images from the forward sonar sphere, which was functioning in active mode and providing the details required for tight navigation.

"How are the currents?" he asked, not directed toward anyone specific.

A young officer replied, "We're bucking a weak flow, sir. Nothing complicated."

"Keep it less three knots relative to the floor," McHenry ordered. "Have you tried for a visual?"

"Yes, sir. Clear as a bell out there," the officer responded. "Wanna look?"

McHenry nodded, and a second later another screen lit up with an aerial view of the floor. It was as clear as he'd ever seen. So clear, in fact, that it seemed as if they were flying.

"One more thing," the officer continued. "Our detectors indicate we're in low-salinity water."

That was an interesting detail, McHenry thought. With the current pressing against them, it seemed that the trench funneled low-salinity water out to sea. There must be a freshwater source somewhere.

His attention turned back to the visual of the floor. The white light illuminated large, jagged terraces covered with brown sand.

"Have you looked at the walls and ceiling?" McHenry asked.

"Not yet," the man replied. "Having a look now."

Two monitors switched to live images of the portside wall and the ceiling of the cavern, both of which looked as if they had been chiseled out of solid rock. Just as he took a step to get a closer look at one of the monitors, a voice rang out from the navigation station.

"Sir, there's something ahead," a man said, his voice either panicked or excited.

"What do you see, ensign?" McHenry asked.

"Look at display number four," he replied

He found number four, took a close look, and shook his head. This was something he feared: it was a fork in the tunnel.

"All stop," McHenry ordered. "Hold position."

There was no obvious choice – both openings seemed to be about the same size.

He spoke loudly so that everyone could hear his instructions, "Study our options. We'll have to make a decision –"

"Something else you should see, sir," a voice broke in from behind him.

He turned around. It was Finley, away from his station.

"Have a look at monitor seven," Finley said.

McHenry walked closer. He saw it, but didn't believe what his brain was telling him. There it was, in the left fork: another dead sub. It had settled on its side, revealing its mortal wound – a gaping hole. The identification numbers on its conning tower were faded, but clear enough to read: *193*. It was an American, Sargo-class submarine – World War II-era.

140

McHenry stared at the screen, his mind reeling. *What did this mean?* It meant that the cave they were exploring with such urgency had been discovered long ago, and by the United States. Someone, somewhere, had more information about this place.

"Hold position," McHenry ordered. "I'll be back shortly."

McHenry went back to his quarters. He had to think it over.

He sat down on his bunk and put his hands over his face. He hadn't been given all of the information. He'd detected no deception during his conversations with the commander of the carrier group or with Naval Command. So it was likely that they, too, had no idea what was going on. But, long ago, someone had.

~ 5 ~

Monday, 18 May (7:31 p.m. CST – Chicago)

Daniel filled in Jonathan and Denise on what he knew about Red Wraith. "But one thing I never understood: what was the *purpose* of the program."

"What?" McDougal scoffed. "You mean you don't believe it was designed to improve our penal system?"

"That façade emerged only recently," Sylvia said, "when the facilities went active and they needed an official cover."

Jonathan pulled out a pipe and filled it with tobacco. "Mind if I puff a bit?" he asked.

Nobody objected, and Jonathan lit the pipe with a silver lighter. Soon a rich scent filled the air, like cherry incense.

"We might be able to help you," Jonathan said between puffs. "What do you have in exchange?"

Daniel had been prepared for the question, but didn't quite know how to play it out. "What would be useful to you?" Daniel asked.

Jonathan squinted his eyes and puffed slowly, either trying to read Daniel's angle, or thinking about the question. Daniel assumed he was doing both.

"What do you have?" Jonathan finally asked.

Daniel laughed, and then tried to squelch it. "Please, Mr. McDougal, be specific. We have access to many things that may be of use to you."

"Can you get us the identities of former Red Wraith victims?" Denise asked. "And their locations?"

Daniel sat back and rubbed his chin. He played it as cool as he could, but he knew it wouldn't be a problem. "Possibly," he said. "I'll have to run it by my boss. For what will we be trading?"

Jonathan leaned forward. "We still have copies of the most important documents that we sent to the FBI. You'll find the answer to your question in them."

"What kinds of documents are we talking about here?" Sylvia asked. "Recent or old?"

"Both," Jonathan answered. "Some as recent as last year, some from before World War II."

Perhaps it was because of McDougal's accomplishments, or that he was almost a public figure, but Daniel trusted him. "Let me make some calls and see if we can make an exchange," he said. "We'd like to get back home tomorrow – we're under some time pressure."

"Really?" Jonathan said, surprised.

It was a mistake, Daniel thought. Again, it was apparent that his field agent skills were rusty. But time was crucial, and giving up some information seemed inconsequential. He'd already made a huge leap that compromised his identity.

Jonathan pressed on. "Are you saying Red Wraith is still active?"

"No," Daniel replied. "But it might be connected to something else that's currently happing. I can't disclose anything more."

Jonathan stared at him for a few seconds and then nodded. "Okay," he said. "You get us the contact information of Red Wraith victims, and we'll give you what we have.

"How much are we talking?" Sylvia asked.

"More than a thousand pages," Jonathan answered. "It will take you a while."

Indeed, Daniel thought. It was time to get back to the hotel, call Thackett, and set up the deal.

~ 6 ~
Tuesday, 19 May (6:33 a.m. EST – Columbus, Ohio)

Lenny yawned and then glanced back and forth between his watch and his boarding pass. He hated being awakened at three in the morning, but a call of that sort usually meant a new job. The problem was that the new job preempted the one that was in progress. But it was okay – he'd gotten half of the payment for the lost assignment up front, and it was nonrefundable.

The new job was going to be *heavy* – on risk, and reward. There would be multiple hits and at least one of the targets was former military.

He sipped hot coffee through a plastic lid while he waited to board. They had him on a 7:30 a.m. flight from Columbus, Ohio, to New Orleans. From there he'd rent a car, drive to Baton Rouge, check into a fleabag hotel, and await instructions.

There was something about the conversation he'd had with his handler that made his stomach tighten. It was clear that this new job was a reaction, rather than a well-planned operation. This was also evident in the cancellation and reassignment.

He sensed of a change in leadership, and it just didn't sit well. Of course his former boss, Heinrich Bergman, had been killed six months earlier, and someone had to replace him. But that wasn't it. There seemed to be a change in *global* leadership. Things were starting to operate as they had when he'd worked for Russian intelligence, the origin of his professional life. The methods in which orders were given, mission tactics, and operational details such as weapon pickup locations and communication procedures were reminiscent of Cold War KGB protocols.

A woman's voice crackled over a low-quality intercom, and

people started to board the plane. When his group number was called, he stood, dumped his cup into a trashcan, and walked to the gate with his carry-on suitcase. Even though there was an element of trepidation in every mission, he felt some excitement. Either he'd have a huge payday, or he'd end up dead.

~ 7 ~

Tuesday, 19 May (6:35 a.m. CST – Baton Rouge)

Agent Jennings was dead.

Natalie Tate had called Will around 3 a.m. to deliver the news. Jennings' body was found in a small bayou on the outskirts of the city. All of his teeth had been drilled out – to the roots. Someone was sending a message.

The morning traffic was light as Will drove down Perkins Road. He felt safer in his car, and the driving eased his mind. He turned left onto Bluebonnet Boulevard and into a large commercial area that included numerous restaurants and stores.

He was confident that his identity hadn't been compromised since he'd arrived in Baton Rouge. He never used his real name for anything, and even electronic communications had been conducted through an alias account. But Jennings might have given away everything he knew, about Will and otherwise, as they tortured him.

Regarding the hit on Jennings, he figured there were three possibilities. The least likely scenario was that the CP inmates got wind of the investigation and caught Jennings following them.

Next, Syncorp may have identified Jennings during the visit to the facility, which made him wonder about the whereabouts of their inside guy, Jake Adler. The problem was that, if Syncorp was able to identify Jennings, then why not Natalie Tate and himself? It was more likely, however, that Syncorp had gotten to Adler, and he'd double-crossed Jennings.

144

The third possibility was the most disconcerting; someone in the FBI had betrayed Jennings. In that case, it was uncertain who was responsible for carrying out the actual deed of terminating the man. Was it Syncorp, or did some government thug make the hit? Either way, he or Natalie could be the next targets – the FBI knew them both and how to find them.

As he rolled to a stop at a traffic light, his phone beeped with the message *523*. He turned right into a crowded parking lot in front of a large bookstore. Natalie Tate called thirty seconds later.

"Adler's still alive," she said.

"Is Syncorp after him?" Will asked.

"Doesn't seem so," she replied. "He claims he knew nothing about the hit on Jennings, and there's nothing that points to Syncorp having anything to do with it. Besides, Adler went into work yesterday."

"Could it have been the CP inmates?"

"If so, we're going to come down on them hard," she said. "But before we get to them, we're going to get more out of Adler. He's still our ticket into Syncorp, and I think we should make a move."

Will's heart raced. "When?"

After an awkward silence, she replied, "When I get back from Chicago. I have to brief my superiors on what happened to Jennings."

"You're wasting time," Will said, not hiding his displeasure.

"My flight leaves in an hour," she said. "You'll be on your own for a while."

The phone went dead.

If the CP men had killed Jennings, then Will figured he wasn't in danger. But it also meant they might be ready to move on Syncorp. If they did, they'd jeopardize the investigation. If Syncorp murdered Jennings, then his identity might be compromised. But it didn't matter. Anyone coming to him with bad intentions would be making a grave error.

With the FBI wasting time, he'd have to take things into his own hands. He'd start with the former inmates.

~ 8 ~

Tuesday, 19 May (7:34 a.m. CST – Chicago)

Daniel took a bite of a toasted onion bagel slathered with cream cheese, and took a sip of coffee. He glanced up at Sylvia who was eating strawberry yogurt and reading a newspaper on the opposite side of the table. The little restaurant was busy with Chicagoans getting a quick bite before work.

The night before, he'd convinced Director Thackett that the information exchange with McDougal would be fruitful. It hadn't been a difficult sell – Thackett would part with just about anything as long as it advanced their investigation of the beacon. Besides, McDougal wasn't requesting government secrets that threatened lives or national security. To the contrary, the man was doing the country a service.

What Daniel already knew about Red Wraith disturbed him greatly. The project needed to be terminated and the people involved brought to justice. He was certain that the new information he'd be getting from McDougal would only strengthen that notion, as would the information going the other way. Synergy in intelligence was rare, but might be exemplified by their impending deal.

They took their time finishing breakfast and were at McDougal's office by 8:15 a.m. The large wooden door was propped open. Daniel knocked and they waited in the hall.

"Come in," McDougal said from somewhere deep inside.

Jonathan and Denise were sitting across from each other at a large wooden table. Denise gathered a bunch of papers spread out on the table and put them into a manila folder.

"Please, have a seat," Jonathan said. "We were just working on another case."

Daniel sat next to Denise, and Sylvia sat across the table from him, next to Jonathan.

146

"What's the verdict?" Jonathan asked.

"We have 43 names for you with location information," Daniel explained. "As of a week ago, each inmate on the list was alive and in a mental health facility of some sort. They're scattered about, but concentrated mostly in the Midwest and Northeast."

Daniel thought he saw Denise smile as she glanced over to Jonathan.

"I think we can do business," Jonathan said, grinning. "After months of searching, we'd only located five."

"And two of those were dead before we could get to them," Denise added.

"How soon can you get us the names?" Jonathan asked.

"I'll have them in an hour," Daniel replied. "When can you get the files?"

"They've been stored in electronic format," Jonathan explained. "I just have to make a phone call. We'll have them by noon."

The timing was perfect. Daniel and Sylvia had a flight out of O'Hare International at 2:20 p.m.

Daniel smiled. "We'll come back at noon and do the exchange."

Jonathan nodded in agreement and leaned back in his chair. "I have to say, Daniel, I'm interested in what's happening, and why you so desperately need this information."

Daniel shook his head slowly, and said, "All I can say is that it has *existential implications*."

CHAPTER VIII

~ 1 ~

Tuesday, 19 May (9:00 a.m. EST – Antarctic Circle)

Captain McHenry observed the sonar screen as Finley adjusted some settings.

"We're approaching the fork," Finley said and then pointed. "There's the sub."

Against the advice of his first officer, McHenry had decided to exit the tunnel and communicate their discovery to the carrier group. They'd responded within minutes with the identification of the sub. He'd also informed them of their choice of direction at the fork. That way they'd know where to start looking for them, if it came to that.

He examined the sunken SS-193 USS *Swordfish* on the monitor and wondered what secrets had died with it. They were now in the same position they were in ten hours before, but the new information they'd transmitted could be used by Naval Intelligence to help figure out what the hell was going on.

He pushed a button on his communicator. "Slow to two knots and proceed along the right fork." They'd determined that the left fork narrowed to unsafe dimensions a half-kilometer up the hole.

His order was acknowledged as he walked to the conn.

When he entered the control room the crew was eerily quiet. Most of the men concentrated intently on their computer screens, and their illuminated expressions conveyed both excitement and fear. What they were doing was serious business. One mistake and they could be stranded, or worse.

McHenry took a seat with a good view of the monitors displaying sonar and video feeds. The *North Dakota* was equipped with a wide assortment of lights and cameras, all of which were active and displayed. The forward camera presented the widest and best-lit view.

148

What he saw ahead of them gave him the same feeling he saw on his crew's faces. It also made him question, yet again, what the hell they were doing. He reminded himself that the *North Dakota* was the most advanced sub in the fleet, configured with capabilities that the others didn't have. Beyond the tight maneuvering and navigation advances, it could defend itself – something a science sub couldn't do. The *North Dakota* also had unlimited range, and could stay submerged or *stuck*, God forbid, and keep the crew alive for months.

After 20 minutes of slow maneuvering, the tunnel became uniform in shape and size. It was nearly circular and widened to over 100 yards in diameter. The light gray walls were marbled with veins of red and brown. Jagged boulders littered the floor on occasion, crumbled from the ceiling or walls.

After two hours, the dimensions hadn't changed drastically, but it was difficult to tell whether it was angled downward or upward with respect to the surface.

"What's our relative depth?" McHenry asked.

A young operator looked up from a computer consul. "A hundred meters. We're 20 meters deeper than we were at the entrance," the man replied.

"Keep an eye on the depth and let me know if there are any drastic changes," McHenry said. "We should have a three-dimensional map, including detailed depth data, for the return trip. How far are we from the entrance?"

"Twenty-one kilometers, sir," the man replied.

"Notify me when we get to 30, or if you come across anything unusual," McHenry said, and walked out of the control room. After 18 hours awake, he needed sleep. But first he'd discuss possible plans with his first officer.

~ 2 ~

Wednesday, 20 May (6:15 a.m. EST – Washington)

Daniel stared into the overcast morning from the window of 713. Flying had always exhausted him, and he wondered how he'd handled the frequent travelling when he was a CIA operative. He already knew the answer to that question but never wanted to admit it: he was *younger* then.

He was happy to be back to his normal routine. The trip had been good for him and also, he thought, for Sylvia. She was brilliant and hardworking, and he enjoyed her company. He hoped she had a similar impression of him.

He twisted a small, silver memory device in his fingers. It had a capacity of 256 gigabytes of data. It was amazing how much information that was – thousands of books – much more than everything he'd read or write in his entire lifetime. He just hoped there was something on it that advanced their investigation.

The coffee maker beeped, indicating that its product was ready. He filled his glass mug, sat at the computer, and inserted the memory device. He entered the password from memory and a long list of files appeared, the names of which weren't revealing. He started at the top and sent each document to a printer to produce two copies.

He'd been impressed with Jonathan McDougal and Denise Walker. They'd been cooperative, and even gave him advice on how to go about reading the files. They pointed to one specific file, dated recently. It was a report summarizing the progress of Red Wraith up to that point in time. He just hoped it would reveal the impetus of the whole thing – the underlying objective of the project. The truth.

When the printer stopped chugging out pages, he began sorting and stapling. The very first page caught his eye. It was on the unusual Nazi letterhead with the strange swastika-like symbol, identical to those in the photos of the *Schwabenland* and U-530. He fanned through the pages, and was sure he hadn't seen the document before.

A beep sounded from the direction of the entrance, and he turned just as Sylvia entered and pulled her knapsack off her back.

"Printing already?" she asked, smiling.

Daniel nodded. "Could hardly sleep."

"Me either."

"There's more here than I thought," he explained. "Some are long – reports and scientific works. Many in German."

Daniel handed two thick documents to Sylvia.

"You can start with these," he said.

He went back to his office and stood in front of the window. Strong spring winds generated swirling waves in the treetops that mesmerized him for a few seconds. His mind was overloaded and he had to force himself to concentrate on one thing.

He grabbed the thick report McDougal suggested he read first, sat on the couch, and flipped it open.

~ 3 ~

Thursday, 21 May (7:10 a.m. EST)

Daniel felt as if his eyes had been doused in lemon juice. At his age, pulling all-nighters wasn't good for anything – especially his brain.

The document McDougal had recommended revealed that Red Wraith had influenced almost every black activity since the end of World War II. The alarming thing about that fact was that he'd never crossed it in any of his earlier investigations. A secret of that magnitude kept for over a half-century was miraculous.

The content of the report was more disturbing than anything he'd read up to that point. That the world was filled with evil people who did vile things was not a revelation, and it no longer affected him as it had in his younger years. What troubled him was that the world was *fundamentally different* than he'd believed it to be.

The physical world was a distraction. During their finite lives, people concentrated on eating, gathering resources, and raising children. Not much different than animals. But he'd always suspected that there was something else in the world, something hidden, and it took something extraordinary to reveal it. In this case, it took extraordinary wickedness: Red Wraith, its Nazi predecessor, Red Falcon, and the people who had created them. Through their horrible actions, however, they'd revealed a facet of a hidden reality.

After reading hundreds of pages, Daniel found the information he'd sought: the true objective of Red Wraith. He had no doubt now that the meeting with McDougal had been worth it, and he'd pass that sentiment on to Thackett and Horace.

If what he'd learned during the past day was true, an entire plane of existence had been concealed from the human race. This knowledge would change everything, and probably not for the better. It was the most frightening idea he'd ever encountered.

"Are you coming?" a voice asked, startling him from deep thought.

He turned from his window to face Sylvia, who was standing at his office boundary. He looked at his watch: over an hour had passed – it was time for the meeting. He topped off his coffee, walked out of his office, and sat with the others in the central discussion area.

"Find any new connections between Red Wraith and the beacon?" Horace asked.

"No," Daniel replied, rubbing his eyes.

Next was Director Thackett. "So what has our risky trade of information brought us?"

"The purpose of Red Wraith," Daniel replied.

Horace shifted in his seat. "Explain."

Daniel took a sip from his mug and set it on the coffee table. "As you know, the Red Wraith project invoked the systematic torture of human subjects, many of whom died in the process," he explained. "But they hadn't been killed purposely. To the contrary, every measure had been taken to make sure they stayed alive and healthy. The objective was to cause severe, prolonged pain with minimal damage to the body. In the Compressed Punishment system, this was carried out using a device called an Exoskeleton, an automated skeleton-like apparatus into which the victim was inserted."

A prickly sweat broke out on Daniel's neck and he tried to rub it away.

"Please, its purpose," Thackett said, becoming impatient.

Daniel folded his hands on his lap and took a deep breath. "They were trying to separate the subjects' souls from their bodies."

Thackett's eyes turned glassy. Horace seemed unfazed.

"I don't understand," Thackett blurted out.

"They believed there is a state of duality in which a person's soul could separate from the body but remain connected to the physical world," Daniel said. "The purpose seemed to be for military applications: solders and spies penetrating walls undetected, or unleashing great physical power."

"Preposterous. Where did they get such an idea?" Thackett asked, his expression even more bewildered now.

Daniel continued, "It was based on the premise that, with the body subjected to great pain, and the mind convinced there was no hope of relief, the soul would leave a healthy body."

"Wouldn't they just die?" Thackett asked.

"Not if the body was still healthy," Sylvia replied. "Red Falcon had begun with the torturing of Jews and prisoners of war in the concentration camps. While executing long torture sessions that involved burnings and amputations, Nazi doctors had observed telekinetic-like events – toppling of furniture and the like."

"The most convincing event was a bizarre massacre – Nazi doctors and soldiers were killed," Daniel added. "Some tried to explain it away – saying that a guard who'd been observing the torture had snapped and killed those people. But the story didn't fit. Some of the bodies had been ripped apart – inexplicable wounds."

"So the Nazis got someone to separate?" Thackett asked.

"Maybe," Sylvia replied. "But there's no evidence it was sustained."

"And what about us?" Horace asked.

"The Red Wraith project was also unsuccessful, with one possible exception," Daniel replied. "Events resembling those observed by the Nazis are described in the treatment log of one of the Red Box inmates. But the file is incomplete, and the subject's treatments ended the day the explosion destroyed the Red Box."

It seemed that Thackett wasn't buying it. However, Horace nodded and his eyes revealed something that looked closer to epiphany.

"Let's get to the point," Thackett said. "How is this connected to the beacon?"

"No idea," Daniel replied. "The only connection we have is the photo of the *Schwabenland* – the symbols. And the same on the files in the picture of the U-boat captain."

"What does the symbol mean?" Thackett asked.

"It symbolizes separation," Daniel explained. "If you collapse the tic-tac-toe board, making the two sets of parallel lines merge to look like a cross, then the symbol turns into a swastika. The symbol for the Red Falcon project is a separated swastika."

"Nazis," Horace said. "What a blemish on humanity." He sat back and crossed his legs.

They sat in silence for a minute. It seemed that Horace and Thackett were both digesting the information, but Daniel knew it would take time. He'd known for over a day and still wasn't sure his mind would ever accept the premise.

Horace broke the silence. "What's next?"

"We'll continue with the Red Wraith files, and analyze whatever new information comes in about the beacon," Daniel said. "But we need to speak with one of the former Compressed Punishment inmates."

"The one who'd separated?" Thackett asked.

Daniel nodded.

"Do you know who it is?" Horace asked.

"Only his ID number," Daniel replied. "5-2-3."

"Perhaps Jonathan McDougal can help," Horace suggested.

"That's what we thought," Daniel said.

Thackett sighed. "We have little choice. Do it as soon as possible," he said and took a deep breath. "Now we have some news for you." He nodded to Horace.

"One of our subs was sent to explore the western Antarctic coast, about a 150 kilometers from the beacon," Horace explained. "They

154

discovered a trench beneath the Brunt Ice Shelf. They followed it to the coast, where it turned into a cavern that extended inland – an underwater cave leading into the Antarctic continent."

"Seems like treacherous business," Daniel commented.

"And proven so," Horace said.

"What do you mean?" Daniel asked.

"They discovered two sunken World War II-era subs," Thackett said. "One near the mouth of the trench, a German U-boat, and one inland – American."

Daniel wasn't surprised. Dead subs from the Second World War were found in all sorts of peculiar places.

"The importance of the find is not that the subs are there – even though the location is unusual," Horace explained, reading Daniel's thoughts. "The mystery lies in which specific subs these are."

Thackett reached into his briefcase, extracted two photographs, and handed them to Daniel.

The images were fuzzy. He could make out the shapes, but couldn't read the markings on their hulls. "I can't read this."

"No need," Thackett said. "We already have."

"And?" Sylvia said, tension in her voice.

"The American vessel is the SS-193, or the USS *Swordfish*," Thackett explained. "It's quite an historical submarine. It was the first sub to sink a Japanese ship in the war."

"Okay," Daniel said. "What's the mystery?"

"The *Swordfish* was sunk by a Japanese depth charge January 12th, 1945," Horace broke in. "In the Pacific."

"Oh," Sylvia gasped.

"Well that is a mystery," Daniel said. "And the other vessel?"

Horace raised an eyebrow. "U-530."

"That's impossible!" Daniel almost yelled, and jerked forward involuntarily. His face flushed with embarrassment. "U-530 surrendered itself at Mar del Plata, Argentina, after the war. That's the one in the pictures. The Red Falcon emblem was on Wermuth's papers –"

"Yes, yes, Daniel," Horace said, holding up his hand and trying to calm him.

"It was brought to the United States and sunk as a practice target in 1947," Daniel added, more softly now.

Thackett reached into his briefcase, pulled out another photo, and handed it to Daniel. "This is an enhanced image."

Daniel grabbed the photo and looked closely, even though it wasn't necessary. The number was clear: *530*. "I don't understand," Daniel said, shaking his head in disbelief.

"Neither do we," Horace added, grinning.

Daniel shook his head. He was now more lost than ever.

~ 4 ~

Thursday, 21 May (9:43 a.m. EST)

Daniel took a bite of an apple as he studied the scribbled words and timelines on his whiteboard. Almost every dark project he'd crossed in his career as an Omni was represented. Each had some connection to the beacon – some loose, some substantial.

He retraced the complicated timeline, starting with the journey of Germany's *Schwabenland* and ending with the American nuclear operations of 1958, Argus and Blackfish. The details of Blackfish were particularly suspicious, as two nuclear devices had been detonated in the ocean near the beacon. Were they trying to destroy it?

Now there were more details to add to the mess. A tunnel penetrated into the Antarctic mainland, and inside were two dead submarines, one German and one American. Both were misplaced, historically speaking.

Daniel sighed. He could explain nothing, and Horace's words constantly pressured him: *existential implications.*

He had an idea, and called Sylvia over to the meeting area.

"Find something?" she asked and sat on the couch.

Daniel took Horace's chair. "No," he replied, "but perhaps we can take a different approach – speculate a bit."

It contradicted their training. An unreferenced speculation proven incorrect in an Omni's monograph was a gaffe that could result in termination. Daniel didn't know what termination meant, exactly, but he was sure it would be something like being reassigned to some mundane analyst job. The possibility of being assigned to research the farming economics of a place such as Nicaragua, or Burundi, was a strong deterrent.

"What choice do we have?" she asked. "We're under time pressure. It would take years to go over everything we have. We're not writing a monograph here." She nodded for him to continue.

"My thoughts exactly," he said, relieved. "We start with the beacon and assume that, when all of this started, someone knew much more than we do."

"Seems reasonable – it's clear we're still missing information."

"And we have to assume we're not getting more."

"What's your theory?"

"We assume that everything we know about the history of that location, the Weddell Sea and the surrounding area, has to do with the beacon," he proposed. "The beacon is the center of everything."

"So the mission of the *Schwabenland*, and the U-boat with which it rendezvoused, was to do what?"

"The Germans knew of the beacon before the *Schwabenland* sailed," Daniel explained. "Its mission had nothing to do with whales, or even submarine bases. They were there because of the beacon – to study it with the hope that it could be useful."

"Pre-war or wartime, it was quite a commitment just to study it."

"They must've known something we don't," he suggested.

"Could they have constructed it?"

"No way," he answered. "It's unlikely that any country could it – even in the present day."

"Did they think it was a weapon?"

"Perhaps," he replied. "Or an advanced technology of some kind – like we do – maybe extraterrestrial. For the sake of argument, let's just assume that they knew it was important, and potentially powerful."

He winced and shook his head. It unnerved him to make assumptions he couldn't corroborate. "And I'm assuming their efforts weren't based entirely on Captain Cook's log – there must have been more."

She shrugged. "How was Red Falcon involved – as implied by its emblem on the crates and files?"

He shook his head. He stood and went to the whiteboard on his side of the room. Sylvia followed.

He mapped out what they had just discussed. The differences between the verified facts on the left side and the list of conjectures on the right were revealing.

"Supposing the beacon is the reason for all of this," he continued, "then why not jump into the deep end and say it was the underlying purpose of Red Falcon, and maybe even of the war itself?"

"The reason for World War II?" she asked with an expression of skepticism. "It's Unlikely. There would've been battles in the Antarctic region."

"Not if the Germans kept it secret."

She shrugged. "I don't think this is leading anywhere."

Daniel may have felt the same if his mind hadn't gone into overdrive. His subconscious was milling away at something his conscious mind was too distracted to notice. He looked at the board; something was hiding in that tangled mountain of facts and conjectures.

~ 5 ~
Thursday, 21 May (10:40 a.m. EST – Antarctica)

McHenry breathed heavily as he shook the sleep from his head and picked up his buzzing communicator.

"You're needed on the conn," the voice said.

He got up from his bed, pulled on his hat, and exited his quarters for the control room. As he passed through sonar he noticed the men were all staring intently at their computer screens. He arrived at the conn and joined a half-dozen others staring at the bank of monitors.

His first officer was leaning over a consul next to a navigator.

"What do we have, Diggs?" McHenry asked.

Diggs popped up his head. "Have a look for yourself," he said and pointed to the monitor of the forward camera.

McHenry studied the image as he walked closer. His stomach tightened immediately. It appeared that the tunnel narrowed drastically, like a pinched copper pipe. "Tight fit," he said. "The question is whether it stays that narrow, or widens afterwards."

"We've imaged the best we can using mounted sonar. There's a good chance that it's only a temporary constriction," Diggs explained. "But we can't tell for sure."

McHenry wished they still had *Little Dakota*. There was no way he was blindly taking the *North Dakota* into a tunnel with such little clearance.

"Send out the dive team, sir?" Diggs suggested.

"What's our depth?"

"Ninety meters," Diggs replied. "We've elevated slightly in the last few kilometers."

"Get as close to the ceiling as you can and send them out," McHenry ordered and turned to Diggs. "Let's talk."

McHenry followed Diggs to the ready room.

"I take it that we'll be continuing on if the tunnel widens again," Diggs said as they went inside.

"Yes," McHenry replied, as he closed the door behind them. "We'll take it as far as it goes."

"Where do you think it ends up – what's at the end?" Diggs asked as they sat across from each other at the table.

It was a question McHenry asked himself about every ten minutes. One answer was that it led to nothing, the tunnel would just terminate at a wall and that would be it. Then they'd have to find a way to turn the *North Dakota* around.

"There's something of significance in here – *or there was*," Diggs said.

"Possibly," McHenry agreed. "Or it could just be a case of two subs chasing each other and ending up in here – making it look like it has some importance."

"Pretty big coincidence," Diggs said, "being in such close proximity to the beacon."

"It's not that close." On a global scale 100 miles seemed close. But searching for something within 100 mile radius meant covering over 30,000 square miles.

"It's the closest landing point to the beacon," Diggs argued.

"It's just an ice shelf. What would be the utility?" If the beacon were active during that time, those subs were well aware of it. Diggs was right; it was about the beacon.

After an hour of consulting with Diggs and downing a finger of whisky, McHenry's communicator chimed. He picked it up. "Status?"

"Divers are back," the man said.

"What's the verdict?"

"Tunnel widens again after the constriction, but it will be a tight fit," the voice said. "Also, the divers want to talk to you, sir."

"Why?"

"They found some manmade structure on the other side."

McHenry twitched as his heart picked up pace. "On my way," he said and then turned to Diggs. "Looks like you might be right. Let's go."

~ 6 ~
Thursday, 21 May (10:01 p.m. CST – Baton Rouge)

The Bullfrog wasn't as busy as it had been the first time he'd been there, when he'd rendezvoused with Jennings and Natalie Tate. Now Jennings was dead, and Natalie was back in her FBI home office in Chicago. Will hadn't heard anything from his FBI handlers in days. His patience had run out.

He walked up to the bar and ordered a beer. Mounted high on the back wall above rows of liquor bottles were five large television screens, four of which showed sporting events. The fifth showed a CNN News report on naval exercises near Antarctica.

Five men sat around a tall rectangular table on the far side of the bar and drank beer. He recognized three of them from his first visit to the Bullfrog. The two newcomers also had bumps on their foreheads, like the others. They talked amongst themselves and didn't seem to pay much attention to what was going on in the rest of the bar.

Will searched for a place to sit where he could lean against something to keep him upright. He spotted a booth far from the men and with a view of the games. He walked over to it and slid in, close to the wall. He pulled his baseball cap down low over his eyes, and put his phone on the table so he had an excuse to lower his gaze. He took a swig of beer and concentrated. He separated, and looked upon his body from above. It looked stable.

He moved about 50 feet to his left to a position directly above the men and listened. At first the sound of music and patrons drowned out the men's voices. He moved closer and concentrated, filtering out the intruding noise.

One man talked about getting food and another about a movie that was playing at a local theater. It was small talk. They seemed to be waiting for something.

After some unknown time he began to feel tired. Just as he was about to go back to his body, one of the men looked up and said, "Here he is."

A scrawny, unshaven man walked towards them from the entrance. His gait was odd – as if his stride was too long for his body, making his head bob up and down. His black hair was thick and fell over his eyes, but it didn't conceal the blemishes on his forehead.

"We have everything we need," the man said as he sat down, directing his words to a massive man wearing a black bandanna and sitting directly across from him.

The other men nodded in approval.

"I want them all," the skinny man said, hardly above a whisper. "Management, engineers, accountants – *everyone*."

"Won't there be some in there that have no idea what the company has been doing?" the man in the black bandana asked.

"I know who the guilty ones are," the skinny man argued. "Only needed the names."

"You have them?"

The skinny man nodded.

Will suddenly found himself back in his body, staring blankly at a young blonde woman with a purple and gold bow in her hair.

"Sir?" she asked. "You okay?"

Will forced a laugh. "Must've dozed off waiting for my wife to call," he said, and glanced at his phone.

She smiled. "Did you need anything?"

He glanced at his half-full beer glass. "No, I better wait until she gets here."

The woman nodded and went to another table.

His thoughts went back to the conversation he'd just heard. The men had some plans and, better, they had names. At first he was tempted to let them go ahead with it, but then he reconsidered. As hard as it was for him to swallow, he acknowledged that there were innocents who worked for the company. That meant engineers and accountants – Syncorp also developed legitimate medical technologies. All he knew was that he wasn't going to turn these thugs in to the FBI. He only trusted Denise and Jonathan, and he wasn't going to drag them into anything yet. He needed more information.

He'd wait for the men to leave, and then follow them home.

~ 7 ~
Thursday, 21 May (11:55 p.m. EST – Washington)

162

The traffic was thicker than normal for a Thursday night in DC. As Daniel pulled in his driveway, he glanced at the clock on the dashboard and estimated that the trip took him 20 minutes longer than most nights. The house was dark. He got out and opened the back door of his Toyota Corolla, leaned in, and pulled his jacket and briefcase from the back seat. When he closed the door, he yelped before he knew what caused his reaction.

A man stood an arm's length away, staring at him.

Daniel tried to speak, but his mouth only expelled air, like what happened to him sometimes in nightmares – a common occurrence as of late.

The man spoke instead. "Daniel Parsons," he said. His voice was deep, and had a subtle accent. The streetlight glared just above and behind the man's right shoulder, concealing his face in shadow.

"Who are you?" Daniel asked. He was frightened by the panic in his own voice.

"Please," the man said. "I mean you no harm."

"What do you want?"

"To talk. There's a restaurant around the corner," the man said and tilted his head over his left shoulder. "Let's go sit in there for a few minutes."

Daniel stood still, considering.

"I have something that will help you with your investigation," the man added, "and might keep you alive."

"I have no idea what you're talking about," Daniel said, now worried that his Omni identity was blown.

The man grabbed Daniel's right arm with a large hand. "I know about the beacon."

Daniel had no words.

The man released his grip. "Please," he said, and again gestured in the direction of the restaurant. "Our interests coincide."

His brain seemed to freeze for a second before he finally agreed and reached for the door of his car to deposit his briefcase.

The man grabbed his arm for the second time. "I'm armed," he said in a low voice.

Daniel shuddered. "No, I … I'm not …"

The man let go, and seemed to watch nervously as Daniel leaned into the back seat. Daniel made sure his hands were clearly visible as he backed out again.

They walked down the driveway and turned right, toward a diner on the corner of his street and a larger boulevard.

They walked in silence for five minutes and then entered the restaurant. A young woman showed them to a booth. The smell of coffee and breakfast food soothed Daniel's nerves. The man removed his jacket and hat and sat across from him, finally revealing his face in the light. He had a dark complexion, black-grey hair and eyebrows, and intelligent, brown eyes that turned down at the corners.

"You can call me Avi," the man said.

"You're Israeli," Daniel said, recognizing the accent. The name clinched it.

The man shrugged, but did not affirm Daniel's assertion.

The woman who had seated them returned with a carafe of coffee and two mugs. Both men turned down food menus. The woman filled the mugs and left them alone.

"What's this about?" Daniel asked.

The man stirred cream in his coffee as he cleared his throat and replied, "I understand the sensitivity of your position. I don't want anything from you."

"I don't know what you mean by my *position*," Daniel responded, trying to maintain a look of ignorance.

"I can elaborate on the specifics of your work, if you like," Avi said. "Shall I begin with your title, or shall I describe some of your recent projects? Perhaps I could just mention a name: Jonathan McDougal, you know him?"

Daniel's skin puckered in goose bumps, and he fought a shiver.

"That's a yes," Avi said as he took a sip of coffee. "I also know you two made a trade."

Daniel remained silent.

164

"It's odd how we interact – our two governments," Avi continued. "We're allies – strong allies – yet we keep secrets from one another. Well, sort of. We're both familiar with the knowledge possessed by the other, if that makes sense, but the details we keep to ourselves. This practice would normally be okay – it keeps our relationship interesting. But the circumstances have become too serious to continue this way."

Daniel knew from his time as a CIA operative that what the man said was true.

"The puzzle is quite complex – the one on which you currently work," Avi said. "But it is impossible to solve if key pieces are missing."

"How do you know what pieces we have?" Daniel asked.

"Why must it always come to proof," Avi said, and took a sip of coffee. "Okay, I suppose it's good that you require some convincing. You already know about the Red Wraith project and now, I suppose, you've discovered its objective."

It was a question Daniel perceived as rhetorical. He nodded.

"So what's the goal?" Avi asked.

Daniel didn't want to answer the question. As it stood, he'd have to tell his boss everything that was happening, and he'd likely have to go through a polygraph screening to make sure he wasn't a further risk.

Avi waited for a full thirty seconds and then sighed. "It was to controllably separate the soul from the body. Correct?"

Daniel nodded. He flushed with embarrassment. He'd only made that connection recently. Either the Israelis knew of this fact long ago, or they'd acquired the information from someone inside the CIA. Either was a cause for concern.

Avi continued, seemingly conceding that Daniel would confirm nothing. "You're probably thinking the objective is to create beings with special powers so that they can spy, kill, wage war, and the like. And that's certainly possible. But you should know that there might be another purpose."

Daniel had no idea what was the man was talking about, but he'd suspected that there had to be more to it than making super-spies. "How do you know these things?" Daniel asked. "How could you know more than we do?"

"Why do you think Israel has been hunting Nazi war criminals for the past half-century?"

"Justice."

"Justice is secondary," Avi replied. "There's more."

"Yes?"

"Information," Avi said. "Why do you think so many Nazis were found in South America, Argentina specifically? It was undoubtedly a good hiding place for a while after the war. But many of them were there well *before* the end of the war – even before Germany started losing." Avi took a sip of coffee. "Why?"

Daniel didn't know the answer.

"It was convenient," Avi said.

"For what?"

"To get to Antarctica," Avi answered. "And what's there, Daniel?"

"The beacon," he blurted. "You said it already – by the car." He wanted to make it clear that he hadn't divulged any information – something to keep his mind straight for the polygraph test that was to come.

"Just the beacon?"

Daniel was confused, but silent.

"A base, perhaps?" Avi seemed to speculate. "More than that." He reached into his coat pocket and brought out a small data storage device. He set it next to Daniel's cup.

"What is it?"

"Every Nazi war criminal captured by Israel since the end of the war had been interrogated by Israeli intelligence – Mossad," Avi explained. "The uncensored transcripts of those interviews are on this device."

"Why are you giving this to me?" Daniel asked, suspicious. Even as he spoke he was tempted to grab the device and run for the door.

"I know who you are, what you do, and with whom you work," Avi said in a matter-of-fact manner. "I have been authorized to give this to you. After all, our two countries are friends."

166

"Why me?" Daniel argued. "Why not give this to the director of the CIA, or the President?"

"What happens at our level – the highest level of intelligence – is not known to our temporary leaders," Avi explained. "Presidents come and go, as do the usual intelligence operatives and appointed leadership. You and I ... *we* are in for life. We are the true protectors of our countries. We are the thinkers, and the protectors of our secrets."

He understood now: Avi was the Israeli equivalent of an Omniscient.

"This is a race," Avi said. "And Russia and China are in it – everyone is in it."

"What do they know?"

"Too much," Avi answered. "Why do you think Chinese and Russian subs are in the area? Why do you think someone launched a torpedo at your submarine?"

"We've been making a lot of noise there," he replied. "They're worried that we've laid claim to something that will make us more powerful – the beacon."

"It's more than that," Avi replied. "They know what you know, and are one step ahead of you. They're already looking for William Thompson. And you are not."

"William Thompson?" Daniel didn't recognize the name.

Avi stared back at him blankly for a few seconds. "You don't recognize the name?"

Daniel shook his head.

"He's the Red Box inmate who'd converted."

"Inmate 523?"

Avi nodded.

Daniel's heart seemed to drop into his stomach. The Israelis had already identified the man, and it was therefore likely others had as well. "We know he's important, but didn't have his name," Daniel confessed. But now he did, although he'd still have to confirm it – he'd probably ask McDougal to confirm it.

"He's the key to something," Avi said. "He was in Chicago a few months ago, but we lost him. Find him."

"I don't understand his importance," Daniel said.

"He can separate his soul from his body," Avi said. "He's the most advanced human being on the earth. And he's absolutely unique – there will probably never be another like him. It took over a half-century of torture to obtain him."

"Why does his ability to separate make him so important, and how is he connected to the beacon?"

"That we do not yet understand, but we believe he has a purpose," Avi replied. "You must figure it out." As he concluded his statement, he stood and put on his hat. "Wait for five or ten minutes before you leave."

Daniel nodded. He wasn't going anywhere. As Avi walked out Daniel slipped the memory drive into his pocket. He stirred his coffee and wondered   how   he   was   going   to   sleep.

~ 8 ~

Friday, 22 May (1:19 a.m. EST – Antarctica)

McHenry reclined in his bunk and pondered the new discovery. The structure the divers had reported turned out to be iron beams and rebar, and about 50 rusted pipes, 10 inches in diameter and of lengths that ranged from 10 to 20 meters.

The tubes added to the mystery. How had they gotten there? They couldn't fit into a German U-boat.

The *North Dakota* was moving forward cautiously, and was safe for the moment. But for the first time in his life, McHenry sensed the world collapsing in on him. He'd been under the polar ice caps and slept on the bottom of harbors. Now they were more than 75 kilometers into the Antarctic continent. If they bumped the walls, they might trigger a collapse, or rip a hole in the hull. There would be no escape.

The only thing he could conclude from the discovery of the tubes was that there had been construction of some sort, possibly further up the tunnel. Perhaps the Germans built a submarine base. But that would be strange: it would be more than inconvenient for a sub base, and much more dangerous for WWII-era subs than for the *North Dakota*.

McHenry's eyelids closed and his brain coasted to a halt. Sleep.

~ 9 ~

Friday, 22 May (12:59 a.m. CST – Baton Rouge)

Cho downed the last of his Cognac and breathed in heavily. The vapors penetrated his sinuses and made his nose tingle. He smiled and puffed on a soggy Cuban cigar as the smoke swirled around the balcony before heading out into the night. Things were progressing.

The late Agent Jennings had provided him with information and entertainment. Regarding the former, Cho was now aware of two things. First, a group of Red Box survivors were planning an attack on Syncorp. He was already on top of that problem. Second, another Red Box inmate was in Baton Rouge independent of the others: it was William Thompson – Inmate 523. Cho's Chinese Intelligence overlords would be pleased, and he wouldn't have to shut down Red Dragon. In fact, Thompson would be its newest acquisition.

Cho held back on that thought. The Ministry of State Security wanted the man, and it seemed urgent. Maybe he wouldn't get the chance to work with him.

Regarding the entertainment, Cho got to practice dentistry for the first time. He recalled how Jennings had screamed for mercy as he removed the teeth from the lower right quarter of his jaw with a large beak-like pincer. He chuckled. It wasn't easy pulling teeth: maybe he should have researched the technique beforehand. Most of them had cracked off at the base, but their roots were left intact – and he enjoying drilling them out. It reminded him of a root canal he'd had once, back in China.

Jennings was dead, Adler was loyal to Syncorp, and the other FBI agent, Natalie Tate, was turned. In her case it only took money. Now she and Adler would reel in Thompson, and Cho could make his delivery.

He savored another puff of the Cuban. Why did the MSS need Thompson, and why didn't they explain it to him? He was confident that he was the only expert China had on Red Wraith. Why else would they charge him with the construction of the Red Dragon program? Maybe the MSS was going let him in on the plan once Thompson was in custody. He shook his head. That had to be it. It would mean abandoning operations at Syncorp – at least temporarily.

He shivered and walked from the balcony into the apartment. Whatever was going on, it had to be big.

CHAPTER IX

~ 1 ~

Friday, 22 May (11:40 a.m. EST – Washington)

After explaining his encounter with the Israeli to Thackett, Daniel passed a polygraph test, was debriefed, and cleared.

The storage device Avi had given him was passed along to CIA specialists to search for viruses and spyware: the Israelis were our allies, but it was impossible to determine whether the man Daniel had encountered was legit. More alarming was the fact that the man had found him and had knowledge of his work. Thackett speculated that Daniel's identity had been compromised during the trip to Chicago. If that were true, Sylvia might also be at risk.

His meeting with the Israeli raised the danger level for everyone. If someone were able to follow them home, then they were at risk of being kidnapped or killed. Now the only place Daniel felt safe was where he was now – in the Space Systems building.

Daniel was pleased, as were Thackett and Horace, that they now had a lead on the identity of Red Box inmate 523. It still had to be confirmed, but he hoped McDougal might help with that, and also help to located the man.

The digital documents Avi had provided him numbered near 10,000 pages. They were mostly transcripts of Israeli interrogations of Nazi war criminals, although there were a few supporting documents. Daniel and Sylvia divided them: he started with the earliest, and she in the middle. They'd meet every few hours to compare notes.

He pushed his way through the questioning of concentration camp guards, engineers, and other minor players. Most of the men and women had been carrying out orders – *heinous* orders – but had no knowledge of the big picture. It was after reading more than 100 interrogation transcripts of seemingly irrelevant Nazi fugitives when he'd found one that seemed significant.

Untersturmführer – Lieutenant – Hans Demler, had been a low-level SS officer acting as a courier, and was in charge of selecting and transporting Auschwitz prisoners for treatment at a psychiatric facility called Kraken fifty kilometers west. The man denied that prisoners had been subjected to anything more than psychiatric evaluations. That was until the interrogator had informed him that mass graves had been discovered in a densely wooded area a half-kilometer behind the facility:

INTERROGATOR: Most had severed limbs. Why?

DEMLER: I do not know – I am not a doctor. I only transported people to Kraken –

INTERROGATOR: No – you also selected them. And, as you said, you are not a doctor. So how were you selecting them? What were the criteria?

DEMLER: I was instructed to choose those who were well-educated, but also in good physical health.

INTERROGATOR: How often did you do this? How many people did you transport?

DEMLER: Between 10 and 15 every week. We picked them on Sunday evenings.

INTERROGATOR: Every week? For how long?

DEMLER: Over a year.

INTERROGATOR: So, as an estimate, you selected between 500 and 750 people during that time.

~ silence ~

INTERROGATOR: You must speak. Nodding cannot be recorded.

DEMLER: Yes, approximately.

INTERROGATOR: Had anyone else been involved in selecting and transporting?

DEMLER: Only low-ranking guards to assist during transport. Different men every week. No one else was to know about the routine.

INTERROGATOR: Only you? No one else?

DEMLER: There was also the doctor.

INTERROGATOR: Who?

DEMLER: Dr. Mengele.

INTERROGATOR: Josef Mengele?

DEMLER: Yes. He was the leader of the project.

INTERROGATOR: What project?

(Demler does not answer).

INTERROGATOR: It is clear that you are complicit in nearly 700 murders – that is the number of bodies found behind Kraken. And they had been tortured. Your only hope to avoid being hanged is to tell us everything and hope that you give us something useful.

DEMLER: Okay. I was not supposed to know anything about this. Mengele would tell me things during our trips between Auschwitz and Kraken. He'd ride with me in the front of the truck on Sunday evenings to the asylum with the load of prisoners. And then I'd chauffer him back to the Auschwitz camp sometime in the middle of the week.

INTERROGATOR: What did he tell you about the project?

DEMLER: He said he was doing experiments with prisoners at Auschwitz to test procedures for his research at Kraken.

INTERROGATOR: What kinds of experiments – at Auschwitz I mean?

DEMLER: Medical experiments. Testing theories he had about pain, and tolerance to cold, pressure, drugs.

(Note to analyst: Demler's testimony regarding Mengele's medical experiments at Auschwitz has been verified. See reports AU518 and AU519).

INTERROGATOR: And what did he say about Kraken?

DEMLER: He did not give me details. However, he said they were making great advances in understanding pain. I never asked questions – I didn't want to know too much to be a liability. But I did ask him once about the purpose of such research. They did not sound like medical experiments to me.

INTERROGATOR: What was his answer?

DEMLER: I will never forget the smile that came to the doctor's face when I asked that question. I regretted it immediately. He told me, "We are embarking on a new facet of humanity, or perhaps we will transcend it." I did not want to learn more.

INTERROGATOR: Did you?

DEMLER: Yes. He said Germany had discovered something that would put the Aryan race in its rightful place in the world. But first there were puzzles they would have to solve.

INTERROGATOR: Puzzles? Like what?

DEMLER: They had deciphered some ancient document that revealed a special place on Earth – a place that, if accessed, would allow them to change the world.

INTERROGATOR: What document?

DEMLER: He called it *weißen Stein*.

INTERROGATOR: White stone?

DEMLER: Yes, white stone. There was an inscription of some sort. He didn't tell me what it   meant.

INTERROGATOR: Where is it?

DEMLER: I don't know.

INTERROGATOR: You mentioned that you were a courier. Did you carry documents?

DEMLER: Yes.

INTERROGATOR: Did you see any classified documents?

DEMLER: Yes, on occasion.

INTERROGATOR: Explain.

DEMLER: Mengele was generally careless with files – he'd read them in the truck, and often set them on the seat between us. I only caught a few words here and there.

INTERROGATOR: What did you see?

DEMLER: The most unusual were those that had the words "Top-Secret" and "Red Falcon" printed on their covers. An emblem of a falcon carrying a strange symbol was usually positioned in the center. It was strange because official documents usually had an eagle with a swastika on them.

INTERROGATOR: You said Mengele mentioned a "special place

on Earth?" Where is it?

DEMLER: He didn't give specifics, but he said it was in an uninhabitable place. It was cold there.

(Note: Subsequent interrogations of *Untersturmführer* Hans Demler provided no new information, but were consistent.)

A handwritten annotation indicated that Demler had died in prison in 1962.

Daniel bristled at the mention of the "special place on earth," and that it was cold there. It would have made no sense if he hadn't already known about the beacon.

The next file was the official transcript of Demler's interrogation – the one that would be found in the normal classified records. Every mention of Red Falcon, and Demler's testimony regarding a special place on earth, had been redacted. To have the complete and redacted versions of the files side-by-side was revealing. If Demler had been deemed crazy, or just fabricating information to save his own skin, there would have been no need to hide any of his testimony.

Subsequent transcripts indicated that, indeed, Israeli interrogators had initially concluded that Demler made up the story in order to give the appearance that he was cooperating. After all, he'd been fighting for his life. Demler was fortunate, however, that there had been other Nazis who had corroborated details of his story. The Israelis had really needed to find Dr. Josef Mengele, but, as was well known, it was not to be. However, it seemed that they'd gotten a break when the Israeli Mossad captured the Nazi fugitive, *Obersturmbannführer* Adolf Eichmann, in 1960.

Daniel leaned back on his couch and read.

~ 2 ~
Friday, 22 May (1:10 p.m. EST – Antarctica)

McHenry leaned over Finley's shoulder and studied the computer monitor. "How wide does it get?" he asked.

"Over 200 meters," Finley replied. "It looks like we're entering the mouth of a large chamber."

After days of weaving the *North Dakota* through the narrow tunnel, McHenry felt a sigh of relief. It was as if he'd fallen down a dark well and finally climbed out and lay flat on the surface with the sun beating down on his face. His moment of release was quickly squelched by the reality of their situation. They had no means of communicating with the outside, and would still have to navigate their way back through the treacherous tunnel.

"Orders?" Finely asked.

"Forward, keep center," McHenry said. "Map all surfaces as we go."

"We looking for something in particular?"

McHenry thought they should be looking for something related to the beacon. On the other hand, there were dead subs at the mouth of the tunnel, and other manmade debris further in, so they should be ready for anything.

"Anything resembling the beacon – or any unnatural structure," McHenry finally replied. Something else occurred to him. "Also look for side-chambers, or tunnels. And there could be mines."

Finley nodded, and then gave instructions to navigation and sonar personnel on the consuls around him.

McHenry went to his quarters. He put his head on a pillow, took a deep breath, and exhaled. It was a sigh of relief and exhaustion. After what seemed like just a minute, he sat up stiffly. His communicator buzzed. It was Finley.

"Sir, I think you need to come back," Finley said. "I recommend an *all stop.*"

McHenry rubbed his eyes. He hadn't been off the conn for 20 minutes. "I'll be right there," he said, and then communicated the all-stop order. *What the hell had they found?*

~ 3 ~
Friday, 22 May (1:35 p.m. EST – Washington)

Daniel refilled his mug with hot water and walked over to the window. The silver tea ball released brilliant green currents in his cup that matched the colors of the sunbathed treetops below. He set the cup on the coffee table and sat on the couch.

The interrogation of *Obersturmbannführer* Adolf Eichmann made Daniel's spine tingle as if his most primitive instincts were commanding him to run. His brain overrode the primordial urge, but he twisted and turned in his seat as he read.

Eichmann had been evil incarnate. He'd had the power and opportunity to carry out acts that defied the inviolability of life itself. Although known as the "desk murderer" for carrying out his heinous acts by action of the pen, Eichmann had done so without emotion or remorse and, in some cases, with denial. His numerous interrogation transcripts, especially those parts that had been redacted in other documents, had revealed something that scared Daniel more than anything else: *hope.*

Eichmann himself had used the word in defense of his actions. He'd had hope for something transformative to happen, something he'd been told by Hitler himself. He described something about a new facet of human existence – a metamorphosis – that would elevate humanity to the next stage. It sounded familiar.

The problem was that Eichmann had never mentioned specifics in the interrogations – not because he hadn't wanted to, but that he apparently hadn't known any. He'd explained that the purpose of the concentration camps was to exterminate Jews, and others the Nazis wanted out of the way, but the reasons were different from what had been assumed by the rest of the world. The Nazis wanted to clean the earth not for the Aryan race in its form at the time, but for the *transformed* race. He'd explained that there would soon be a refined race that transcended humans in their current form.

The second major purpose of the concentration camps, other than extermination, was for a source of healthy subjects to be used in experiments of the sort carried out by Dr. Josef Mengele at the Kraken asylum, and other such places. It was the transcripts of interrogations of Mengele that Daniel really wanted to read. It was most unfortunate that the evil doctor hadn't been captured. He'd lived in Argentina until the Israeli Mossad got too close, and then fled to Paraguay. Finally, Dr. Mengele had drowned off the coast of Brazil in 1979. They'd called him the Angel of Death for his participation in the selection of Jews for the gas chambers at Auschwitz – an operation that Daniel now suspected was just a discarding of the subjects he couldn't use in his torture and medical experiments.

Human twins were of particular interest to Mengele. His curiosity had stemmed from another Nazi researcher named Nestler who had conjectured that twins' souls were *entangled*. The entanglement in this sense was not of the sort suffered by two fishing lines that had twisted into an irreversible birds' nest. Instead, it was related to the entanglement described by quantum physics, the common example being the entanglement of two electrons. When two electrons were entangled in the quantum sense, they could feel each other's state from long distances – a phenomenon referred to as "spooky," even by physicists. So was the case with twins, according to Nestler and Mengele. The twins would be separated, Mengele would kill one of them in one room, and the reaction of the other twin, unaware of the fate of the other, would be observed in another. The results had been inconclusive.

Eichmann had referred to Red Falcon several times during the interrogation – the first instance initiated by him. The interrogator had obviously led him in that direction, but had never mentioned the name of the project. In the end, Eichmann hadn't known the details of Red Falcon. However, near the end of the interview, he'd made some chilling references. Eichmann described a New Order rising from cold waters. He called it the Last Reich. It was this Last Reich that would be the transformed version of humanity, and it was Eichmann's hope that it would rise before he was executed. He had also claimed that Hitler wasn't dead, nor were many of the others at the top of the Nazi hierarchy. They had escaped Germany through the secret Nazi SS operation called ODESSA, and would rise again from the south. Eichmann was executed in 1962.

~ 4 ~

Friday, 22 May (1:48 p.m. EST – Antarctica)

McHenry entered the control center. Whatever they'd discovered, it was big. Everyone was standing – some at their respective stations, others near the bank of overhead monitors.

"What do you have?" McHenry asked, his question directed at Finley.

Finley approached McHenry, grabbed his arm, and directed him to a monitor.

McHenry's heart pounded. He'd never been grabbed by a crewmember – and Finley's eyes were wide with either fear or excitement.

McHenry studied the monitor. It was an image from one of the *North Dakota's* forward cameras. The water was perfectly clear.

The tunnel terminated in an enormous cavern.

"What are the dimensions of this place?" McHenry asked, hardly believing what he was seeing.

"Irregularly shaped, about 800 meters in length, the same width, and the depth is over 1,000," Finley replied. "But that's not all." He nodded towards the screen. "The image you see there is with our external lights turned off."

It took McHenry a second to process what Finley had said, but then it was clear. "Ambient light from somewhere," he said. "An opening to the surface."

"Yes," Finley said. He instructed another crewmember to adjust the view. "The ambient light is coming from here," he said and pointed to a location on the opposite end of the cavern. "But while we searched for the light source, we found this." He pointed to two areas high on one of the walls, near the ceiling and at the edge of the opening to the surface.

McHenry gasped. There were human-made structures. "What the hell is it?"

"Don't know," Finley said. "We'll have to get closer."

McHenry nodded. His fatigue had all but dissolved away, the adrenaline taking over. "Go slowly." It occurred to him that there might be traps. He warned the crew.

As they inched closer to the light, the structure became more visible. Mounted to the cavern ceiling and wall, on the *North Dakota's* port side, were rectangular structures resembling the skyboxes seen in some football stadiums, but larger. Some were solid black – probably metallic or concrete – while others had windows. In all, there were over 50 of them. Behind the boxes, where the ceiling curved gradually downward into the wall, were six slots that resembled slips for submarines. Three were occupied.

As they approached the structure, the source of the overhead light became apparent. There was a colossal hole in the ceiling of the cavern. On the surface, McHenry realized, it must have looked like a lake. If needed, they could surface to confirm their position with satellite navigation, and communicate with the carrier group.

"Get closer to the structure," McHenry ordered. "We need to get pictures."

The pilot brought the *North Dakota* into the light, temporarily obscuring their view of what was ahead. Sonar kept them apprised of the cavern walls and structures. A few minutes later, they passed back into the shade of the cavern ceiling, and were now close enough to see the structures in detail.

McHenry swallowed hard, not believing what was before his eyes. It was a base. The protruding structures were indeed slips. The crew stared in silence at the decrepit Nazi U-boats sleeping in their slots like corpses in a crypt.

~ 5 ~
Friday, 22 May (3:40 p.m. CST – Baton Rouge)

Lenny Butrolsky soaked in the sun and sipped iced coffee at an outdoor café. Baton Rouge was well inland from the Gulf, but the scent of the sea imbued the warm breeze that filtered through his short hair.

His predicament had become complex. First, he was uncertain of the identity of his employer. Second, he was there for an operation that involved multiple hits: a bloodbath. He was supposed to make it look like one member of a large group had snapped and massacred the others. He was still awaiting the details of how it was supposed to go down, and when. It sounded like a cleanup operation. Cleanup was dangerous: everyone involved seemed to be nervous, and the authorities could swoop in at any time.

He shook his head and smiled to himself: his bank account was ballooning to retirement size. He hoped he'd have the opportunity to spend it.

Since he'd been freed from the hospital, his jobs had been assigned through the network in which he'd worked for over a decade. But, after the hit on Poliakov and the cancelation of his latest job, his handler admitted a "turnover in management." His suspicions were now confirmed: a Chinese firm that had purchased the companies connected to the project. His former boss, the late Heinrich Bergman, had worked for the American government, and therefore so had Lenny. Now it seemed he worked for China.

Lenny didn't care either way. He wanted out of the business and was getting close to having the funds to do it. The only problem he had for playing two sides – fully aware that there might even be more sides – was that it was dangerous. And his upcoming mission was going to be particularly hazardous.

At age 55 Lenny had experience on his side. He'd dealt with the

Chinese in the past. They had a reputation of tying up loose ends, and he knew he'd eventually be one of those loose ends. He planned on getting half the money he was due – the part that was paid up front – and forget the rest if they didn't transfer it. He'd complete his jobs, and then get out of Dodge. He wanted to be absent for the final wrap-up.

He took a deep breath and rubbed his shoulder. The warm weather was good for his body – soothing the dull aches from the many injuries he'd suffered over the years, as well as the natural deterioration of his aging body. He sipped his iced coffee and casually scanned the café. He spotted his contact: a tall, blonde female, forties, with a charm bracelet. The bracelet was supposed to have a small dodecahedron – a twelve-sided die, like the ones used in role-playing games.

The woman got in line, bought a coffee, and went to a small counter and mixed sugar and cream into her cup.

Lenny approached from her right and spotted the bracelet and charm on her left wrist as she grabbed a stir stick.

"Nice bracelet," he said. "Anniversary gift?" It was the phrase he'd been instructed to use.

"Yes," the woman replied and smiled. "I live a charmed life." She had a soft southern accent.

It was the correct response.

"Shall we sit outside?" he asked.

She nodded and followed him to a table far away from foot traffic.

Her face turned serious, and she handed Lenny a small memory device. "You'll find what you need on this," she said. "Your honorarium decreases after seven days. You'll get a bonus if you finish the job within the next five."

Rushing things for a multi-target job was risky. He needed time to study them, and plan the operation. "What kind of bonus?" he asked.

"Three fifty," she replied.

Lenny flinched. *Three hundred and fifty thousand dollars.* It would free him from his occupation. "Why is this so important?"

The woman ignored his questions. "Up to four more people will arrive in five days. Right now, it's likely that only the original five are present."

"Likely?" Lenny asked. He didn't like uncertainties.

"There's a constant flux," she said. "It's all in the file."

Lenny nodded.

The woman stood with her drink, smiled broadly, and walked away, leaving Lenny with the memory device and his thoughts.

~ 6 ~

Friday, 22 May (8:06 p.m. CST – Baton Rouge)

Darkness settled in as Will sat in the back seat of his SUV and waited. A gentle breeze carried the aroma of chicken from a small gathering of students cooking with a grill a few doors down. The night before, he'd tailed the former CP inmates from the Bullfrog to their house off of River Road, near the university campus. Dense traffic had provided adequate cover, and he'd followed them all the way to their door and parked his car on the street a few driveways down. He'd separated and observed them that evening, obtaining helpful information for this evening's activities – the alarm code and the combination to a safe hidden in a back room. The back of his neck stiffened at the thought of breaking in and carrying out his plan.

A door squeaked open somewhere on the right side of the house, and then banged shut a few seconds later. Five men emerged and piled into a red Honda Civic, one of three cars parked in the driveway. The car backed into the street and exited the subdivision, out of sight.

Will separated. He entered the house, unlocked the door, turned off the alarm, and punched the numbers into the keypad of the electronic safe. He wanted to set up everything to minimize his time in the house.

He returned to his body, got out of the SUV, and closed the door quietly. He looked for potential observers, saw none, and then walked up the driveway and followed a walkway along the right side of the house.

He stopped on a concrete stoop and examined the entrance. A

rusted screen sagged on the warped wood-framed door, and he was sure the tears in the corners let in mosquitoes. As he pulled the door, it creaked with a metallic ringing that he followed to a large spring that functioned to snap the door closed. He pulled it open as slowly and smoothly as possible until he was able to squeeze his body in and turned the knob of the inner door. He pushed the door open, and stale air from the cool interior breezed gently over his sweating hand. He entered, making sure to let the screen door close gently. The smell of stale beer and dried ketchup filled his nostrils. He was in a filthy kitchen.

He had to fight to stay calm even though the men would probably be out for hours. He made his way into one of the three bedrooms, opened the closet, and removed the blankets and clothes that covered the unlocked safe. He turned the handle, opened it, and pulled out three manila folders, each with 10 to 20 pages of documents. He removed the contents of one of the folders and laid the pages in a row on the carpeted floor. He turned one of three light switches on the wall by the door, energizing a light fixture. He adjusted the dimmer switch until the illumination was sufficient.

He pulled a small digital camera from his pocket and snapped pictures of the documents. He did this several times, checking periodically to make sure the images were clear. When he was finished, he packed the documents back into the safe and closed the door and locked it. As he piled the blankets and clothes back into their original positions, he discovered an Army-green metal box about the size of a carry-on suitcase.

He unbuckled two latches and opened the lid. It was tightly packed with small bricks of an off-white material that he was certain was the plastic explosive C-4. He snapped some pictures, closed the box, and put it back in its original position. He searched the rest of the closet and found detonation cord, detonators, and a box of cell phones – bomb materials.

He returned all of the items to their original positions and covered them. He closed the closet door and a headed for the kitchen. Just as he was about step onto the greasy linoleum floor, a noise made him freeze in place. It was the metallic screech of the screen door. *Someone was entering the house.*

He found a coat closet, slid in, and pulled the door closed.

184

The metallic jingle of sloshing keys persisted until one was inserted into the lock. A moment later, the screen door slammed closed, and the floor creaked in the hall just outside the closet. He held his breath as the floor creaked just out side the closet and footfalls continued on into a back room.

He felt no fear, but he had to be calm and still. Maybe the man just forgot something and would leave. Will had locked the door when he'd entered the house, but hadn't reset the alarm. It seemed that the man hadn't noticed. Will's attention turned to his voice. It was a one-sided conversation that he couldn't quite make out. He was on a phone. Even though it was muffled, the one sided conversation seemed to turn into an argument.

Will now worried that the others might return. He had to do something before the situation got more complicated. He sat down beneath hanging coats and shirts, and settled his rear on a pile of shoes. Once he was sure his body would remain propped in the corner, he separated and found the man in a back room. He recognized him from the Bullfrog. He'd been one of the less vocal ones, although that wasn't apparent from the animated cussing he currently delivered into his phone. It was clear that he was looking for something in someone else's room but couldn't find it. After a few minutes of arguing, it was clear that the person on the other end of the conversation was coming back to the house. Will would have to make a move before the others returned.

It was a tricky situation; he couldn't just run. The man would hear him, and then they would know they'd been compromised. Harming the man would have the same effect. He had to *incapacitate* him – without him knowing what happened.

He decided to choke him until he passed out – a blood choke, or sleeper hold. And he'd have to administer it without the man feeling like he'd been attacked.

In the separated state, Will could either stiffen his interaction with matter in order to manipulate it, or soften it to pass through things. He'd never tried to pass though someone's body.

The man ended the phone call, walked into the one of the three bedrooms, sat on the bed, and began untying his shoes. Will descended upon him slowly and focused on the side of his neck. Focusing on small things had the effect of reducing his size, like miniaturizing himself, so that he could also manipulate things at that scale.

He reached through the surface of the man's neck. It was a warm sensation, but much different than passing through a wall. Something inside seemed to resist his movement – it was something he'd never experienced when passing though inanimate objects.

He pressed into the throat area, and muscles, tendons, vertebra, and blood vessels came into view. He found the two large vessels he sought – the carotids – and pinched them closed.

He backed out to see what was happening to the man while he maintained the pressure on the arteries. The man flinched and grabbed his throat, and Will hoped he'd grabbed the right blood vessels – a mistake could be lethal.

The man lurched backwards onto the bed, struggled for a few seconds, and passed out. Will kept the pressure on the arteries for a few seconds longer, then returned to his body.

He stood from his position in the closet, opened the door, and made his way to through kitchen, out the back door, and down the walkway to the street.

Just as he got into the SUV and closed the door, a vehicle turned down the street and proceeded in his direction. A brown van cruised in and turned into the driveway. Now there were four vehicles; the men must've met up with others and brought them back with them.

Five men piled out of the van and filed into the house.

Will was lucky how it worked out; the other men would find their colleague asleep on the bed. No signs of a struggle or break-in.

The utility of Will's unique abilities was becoming clear to him. If he wanted to kill someone discretely, all he'd have to do is sever an artery, or damage an organ such as a spleen, spinal cord, or brain. He could do it undetected, and from far away. The Nazis and the US government had had the foresight to see this potential from the beginning.

He drove the SUV out of the subdivision and turned right onto

River Road. A mile north, with the Mississippi River on his left, he turned right onto a larger street where the traffic thickened. His path across town to his apartment was impeded by numerous stoplights, and he stopped behind a long line of cars. It didn't bother him, however. He needed time to think, and to calm down. He was in a strange state of mind: adrenaline was flowing in his system, and he had no fear. It was a dangerous combination.

He forced himself to think about something other than what had just happened. He recalled something an old physics professor had told him back in college: "If something were possible, humans would eventually do it," the professor had said. "Even if it meant destroying themselves." The atomic bomb was an example. Others included the high-energy particle colliders and genetic experimentation. Now their endeavors had expanded to a new dimension. They'd happened upon a new world or, perhaps, to the next one: they were manipulating the soul.

Will nearly jumped through the roof of his SUV in response to a horn blast that came from the vehicle behind him. The light had turned green.

He stepped on the gas and crossed through the intersection where the road turned from one lane to two. He pulled into the right lane to let the vehicle pass, but it changed lanes as well, now tailgating him. The vehicle was large and its high beams glared through his back window. He turned his rearview mirror away from his eyes and tapped the brakes. His follower responded by laying heavily on the horn.

His first thought was that the men had figured out what happened back at the house and somehow caught up with him. He dismissed it immediately, even though the vehicle seemed to be tall, like the brown van.

As they approached the next stoplight, it turned yellow and Will slowed to a stop. This seemed to anger the driver behind him who again laid on the horn, and then pulled beside him. It was a large, black pickup truck with a giant tires and its frame jacked up to an unsafe height. It growled loudly through two chrome exhaust pipes that extended above the backside of the cab. The tinted passenger window rolled down and a man stuck his head out and glared at Will. He was in his mid-twenties, wore a purple baseball cap with the bill facing backwards, and had a lump of chewing tobacco in his lower lip. Will rolled down the window.

"You got a problem, asshole?" the man said, and wiped tobacco drool from his lips with a hairy forearm.

"Stay off my ass," Will said. The adrenaline concentration in his blood started to increase again.

A click from the driver releasing his seatbelt drew Will's attention past the passenger and deeper into the cab. Another man, same age, similar look but with a beard, leaned over from the driver's seat.

"How'd you like to get your ass kicked, asshole?" the driver said.

Will pointed to a restaurant one street up. "Why don't we meet over there?"

The passenger responded by gyrating in excitement. "We're gonna kick the shit out of you," he yelled and then spit a disgusting brown slurry of tobacco juice at Will, missing low and hitting the door a few inches below the door handle. Will rolled up the window and the driver blasted the truck's engine, making the exhaust flaps flutter.

This wasn't going to be a good night for them. Will had no intention of driving into a parking lot and drawing attention to himself.

He shifted the SUV into park. He closed his eyes, concentrated, and separated from his body. He passed out of his vehicle and into the cab of the pickup. The men were talking, but he had no interest in what they were saying. The light was still red, but the intersection had cleared. Will simultaneously pulled up on the brake pedal and pressed the accelerator all the way to the floor.

The vehicle accelerated away from him, and his grip on the accelerator and brake slipped as the truck lurched forward. It gave him a moment to hear the reactions of the two men, their truck now in the middle of the intersection.

"What the hell are you doing?" the passenger yelled.

"I didn't do it!" the driver replied.

Will recovered his position and grip on the control pedals. He yanked the brake and jammed the accelerator to the floor. The engine screamed and the truck blasted through the intersection. This time he concentrated on moving with the truck as it accelerated. The men yelled in what sounded like fear and confusion as Will grabbed the steering wheel and turned the truck sharply to the left, forcing it over a curb and crashing into the large windows of a storefront, where everything slammed to a halt. An instant later, he took in the view from his own vehicle, still at the light, which was now green.

He drove through the intersection and examined the aftermath of what he'd just done on the sidewalk to his left. Half of the truck's bed stuck out of the storefront. The tailgate had opened during the collision, and the bed was covered with tiny pieces of broken safety glass. The driver was slouched over the steering wheel and the horn was blaring. He wasn't moving. Will figured the man hadn't put his seatbelt on after their exchange at the light. The passenger moved slowly, trying to open the door. It was jammed.

Will drove off. Although he hoped the men would be okay, he felt no remorse for what he'd done. His mind was numb.

After a mile, two police cars passed in the opposite direction with their sirens howling. Will smiled spontaneously. It frightened him.

Fifteen minutes later he pulled into his parking space at the apartment complex. His thigh muscles trembled as he climbed the stairs to his flat, a symptom of the adrenaline in his blood and the need for food.

He decided to relax for a while before eating and continuing his work. He poured a glass of red wine and sat on the couch. He'd learned a lot in one day – about the plans of the CP men and about his own capabilities. He could have killed the men in the truck. He could have killed the man in the house. He came to the realization that killing was something he might have to do. Again. *It was too easy.*

~ 7 ~
Saturday 23 May (2:08 p.m. EST – Antarctica)

It could only make sense if it wasn't exclusively a submarine base, McHenry thought. Antarctica was a horrible place on the surface; it would be extremely difficult to transport anything substantial so far inland. There were no roads, the land was riddled with crevasses, and the environment was horrifically cold and windy. The only things missing were polar bears.

Traveling under water, however, would be the same year round. But he was sure that subs of that era, with their diesel engines and some battery power rather than a nuclear reactor, couldn't get through the tunnel without surfacing for air. Yet, here they were.

The *North Dakota's* crew had spent the previous 24 hours mapping and photographing everything, the primary purpose of which was to find booby-traps. After they deemed the area clear, McHenry gave the okay to approach the structure.

As they ascended towards it, more details came into view. Each slip was fitted with a large vertical tube, about a meter in diameter, that hung from above. In the three occupied slots, the tubes were fitted over the hatches of the subs. In the center of the bank of slips was a gap so that there were three slips on each side. In the ceiling above the gap was a set of enormous steel doors. The opening they covered looked to be large enough for a sub to enter.

"Orders?" Finley asked.

"Let's get a look at the lake," McHenry replied. "How thick is the ice?"

"Thin, if anything," Finley said. "The water is brackish, and 7° Celsius near the surface."

The cavern was probably fed by some deep volcanic source, McHenry thought, but he didn't know much about the geology of the continent. "Go to periscope depth," he ordered. "Let's have a look around."

The crew watched the periscope view on one of the monitors. As it broke through the surface, the camera adjusted for the low-lying sun and its reflection from the quiet lake. To the portside, which was toward the geographic South Pole, the lake extended about a half-kilometer, ending at the steep rise of a rocky cliff. The precipice was well over 200 feet high, and sloped downward along the perimeter of the lake, terminating gradually to the water level at points directly forward and aft of the *North Dakota*. It was as if the oval-shaped lake was carved into the slope of a rock mountain. To the starboard side, the lake gently blended into a snow and rock shoreline that sloped gently upward into the horizon. The crew stood in silent awe of the landscape.

"Any manmade structure?" McHenry asked, breaking the silence.

After a few seconds, Finley responded, "We took high-res images. We'll have to study them carefully."

"Get GPS coordinates and dive," McHenry ordered. "Do we have any shots of the floor?"

"It's over 1,000 meters, sir," Finley replied. "We'll need to do an active scan to image it."

"Go to 200 meters and do it – full spectrum sonar," McHenry said. "Meanwhile, where does GPS estimate our location?"

"We're 262 kilometers from the coast. We'd estimated 264 kilometers," a man replied.

McHenry was flabbergasted. He'd not been paying much attention to the total distance traveled.

Finley indicated that they were at depth for floor scans.

"Commence," McHenry said.

"Starting multi-frequency imaging," Finley confirmed and pushed a button on the touchscreen display. "Imaging."

Twenty seconds passed and then Finley's face distorted. He tilted his head at the screen and then put on a set of headphones.

McHenry didn't like his look. "What is it?" he asked, hoping his sonar tech wasn't going to respond with *fish in the water*.

"There's another source," Finley responded. "Mechanical – multiple frequencies."

A sailor pointed at one of the monitors that displayed the visual overhead view. "I see it," he said.

McHenry walked closer. He couldn't believe his eyes. It was the large steel doors in the gap between the slips. *They were opening.*

191

~ 8 ~
Saturday, 23 May (2:50 p.m. EST – Washington)

Daniel sat with the others in the central gathering area with a mug of coffee to get him through the mid-afternoon drag.

Thackett started the meeting. "As we've learned from Daniel's encounter with the Israeli, Russia and China, and certainly other countries are involved in this. They know about Antarctica and the Red Wraith project." Thackett rubbed the stubble on his face. It was clear that he was sleep-deprived. "The Chinese have sent operatives here to find the ex-inmate from the Red Box."

"William Thompson," Daniel blurted out. "Red Box inmate 523."

"They'll all be looking for this man," Horace said. "And they're all ahead of us. We have the resources to pursue multiple leads, and we better get them activated."

"Where do we start?" Thackett asked.

Daniel shook his head. "McDougal might know where he is."

Thackett crossed his legs and leaned back in his chair. He looked to Sylvia and Daniel. "You two will get on a plane to Chicago tomorrow morning, talk to McDougal, and get everything he knows about Thompson. If he wants something in return, call me. We need to move on this."

"This will slow down our research," Sylvia argued. "We have thousands of pages to read."

"We can't send anyone else," Thackett responded. "Your research will wait."

"How about calling?" Daniel suggested.

"If McDougal is being watched, and you can bet he is, every communication device he owns is compromised," Thackett explained. "Get him out of his office – meet in a public place."

"Isn't this getting risky?" Sylvia asked. "I mean, for us."

192

"CIA personnel will be watching over you," Thackett assured them. "You'll be in good hands."

Daniel believed him, but this trip would be much more nerve-racking than the first.

"McDougal might appreciate the warning," Horace added. "He seems to be a careful fellow, but he's in over his head."

So were he and Sylvia, Daniel thought.

~ 9 ~

Saturday, 23 May (3:48 p.m. EST – Antarctica)

McHenry had to decide: surface and communicate their status to the carrier group, or move in to explore further? The former came with the risk of revealing their position and, therefore, the position of the base. If foreign parties intercepted their communications, something he suspected had been occurring for a long time now, they'd lose whatever advantage they had, and put the *North Dakota* in danger. On the other hand, if something happened as they explored, the information that they'd collected, including the knowledge that the base existed, would be lost. So the choice was to risk letting *everyone* know about it, or risk having *no one* know about it. He decided on the latter.

"Get to a position 30 meters directly below the bay doors," he ordered. "Ready the dive team."

"Do you think someone's in there?" Finley asked. "Or did we actuate some automated system?"

The thought hadn't even occurred to him that there might be someone inside. "My guess is that our sonar activated some sort of remote control." His thoughts went back to Finley's question. He got on his communicator. "Tell the dive team to go in armed." Surely there was no way there were Nazis inside. But what if one of their geopolitical competitors had already secured it?

He gave the dive team orders to examine the bay area, determine if

193

there were any threats, and measure the slip and bay dimensions. If the base was as large as he suspected, they'd dock and explore it.

The dive team was back within an hour. McHenry and his first officer, Lieutenant Diggs, met with them in the planning room.

The dive team leader, a sinewy man named Critch, explained what they'd found. "The bay doors open to a vertical tunnel, 25 meters in height, leading to an internal dock. It was designed for subs. It'll be tight, but it's large enough for the *North Dakota*."

"What's the state of the internal structure?" Diggs asked.

"There was no light," Critch answered. "From what we could see with flashlights, the place seemed to be in good shape. We didn't go beyond the dock, as instructed."

McHenry nodded. "Good work, gentlemen, you are excused."

The men left, leaving McHenry and Diggs alone in the planning room.

"What do you think?" McHenry asked.

"Sounds like we should get moving," Diggs said. "Dock and send teams out to explore."

"Agreed," McHenry said.

"Do you think this base, or whatever it is, is connected somehow to the beacon?"

"Yes," McHenry replied. "Too much of a coincidence. And we need to gather as much information as we can."

"If we find something important, will we communicate with the carrier group?"

"Depends on what we find," McHenry explained. "But I don't think we should transmit at all."

Diggs agreed.

McHenry stood up and opened the door. "Let's get this show on the road."

CHAPTER X
~ 1 ~
Sunday, 24 May (7:50 a.m. CST – Chicago)

Jonathan McDougal was regretting taking on a summer class, even though it was only a six-week course. He sat at his desk and took a break from grading the last few of over 40 papers he'd promised to return to his students by ten the next morning.

He stood, walked over to the windows, and gazed into the small courtyard below. Leaves had started to fill in the skeletons of the trees that had been dormant for longer than usual this year. It had been a cold winter and a busy spring semester teaching, mentoring two law students, and running the DNA Foundation.

His thoughts were interrupted by a knock on the door. It was Denise.

He waved her in and said, "I don't have too much time."

She nodded and set her backpack on a chair at the large wooden table, pulled out a laptop, and turned it on. As she pulled her hair into a ponytail, she said, "You have to see this. It's from Will."

"Oh?" he said and walked over to the table.

"He sent some pictures to our joint email account," she explained as she downloaded the files. "He said action is imminent." She pulled up the photos.

Jonathan looked on as she paged through them. Some were photos of documents – lists of names, maps, building layouts, and instructions on how to build bombs. Others were pictures of cars and license plates, houses, and men with bumps on their foreheads – five of them. One was a photo of a case of plastic explosives.

"The men are former CP inmates," Jonathan said. "Looks like they're planning to carry out some assassinations – with bombs."

"There's more," Denise said, opening another set of photos.

Jonathan looked them over and was flabbergasted. "Are those what I think they are?"

"Exoskeleton parts," she said, nodding. "These are from the Syncorp facility in Baton Rouge. They're shipping them to China."

He sat down and rubbed his chin. "Those Syncorp bastards are like cockroaches."

"Will thinks the CP men are planning to attack the Syncorp facility – and assassinate the upper-level personnel," she said.

"I have a half a mind to let them carry it out," he said.

"What should we do?"

"There are only a few people we can trust in the FBI," Jonathan said. "Let's turn the info over to Agent Carver – "

Jonathan turned his head in response to a knock at his office door.

A young woman stood in the doorway, mid-thirties, glasses, reddish hair pulled back in a bun. He recognized her, and his heart picked up pace.

"Professor McDougal?" Sylvia said.

"Back already?" he answered, "please, come in."

Sylvia walked in, handed him a folded piece of paper, and walked out.

Jonathan and Denise sat in silence for a few seconds, looking at each other. He unfolded the note as she walked around the table to his side:

Please meet us at Bridges Café in Logan Square today 2:00 p.m.
Do not speak or write of this.
Do not take your cell phones. You are being watched.
You may be in danger.

Denise spoke first. "Here we go again."

Jonathan nodded as a chill crept up on him. Why were the Omnis back in Chicago?

~ 2 ~
Sunday, 24 May (9:12 a.m. EST – Antarctica)

McHenry watched the video monitors as the pilot feathered the *North Dakota* into the gap between the slips, and then upward, through the open bay doors. It was fortunate that the port was large enough to accommodate the *North Dakota*, as it was much larger than the German U-boats. After about 10 minutes of fine position adjustments, they ascended through the vertical tunnel and surfaced inside the structure.

Four teams of four men each had been assembled. The first team would exit and establish a perimeter. McHenry desperately wanted to go himself, but that was ill advised: protocol dictated that the captain stay on board until everything was secure. He decided he'd go after the fourth team dispatched. His first officer would stay onboard.

The crew operated in shifts, but not one man on the *North Dakota* was asleep. The first team exited the hatch, and everyone who could get close to the video monitor watched it, even though they couldn't see anything more than scanning flashlight beams on a black background. There was much excitement, and too many people in the control room: McHenry ordered non-essential personnel to leave.

Twenty minutes later, after the perimeter had been established, the remaining three teams exited through the hatch to the platform. One team set up floodlights on the deck, and the others searched the extended area for booby-traps. A half an hour later, McHenry climbed out of the *North Dakota* and onto the steel dock.

The place seemed to be carved out of solid rock, and was much larger than it looked on the monitors. The ceiling rose to more than 100 feet, giving the space a cathedral-like feeling. The air smelled like wet cement, and it was warmer than he'd expected.

Every noise echoed, making it difficult to hear people speak. McHenry walked over to a team leader who was rigging additional

197

spotlights. "Find anything unusual?" McHenry asked.

"It's *all* unusual, sir," the man replied. "Did you notice the banner on the far wall?" The man pointed towards the far side of the cavern, opposite the slip where the *North Dakota* was docked.

The floodlights caught only a part of it, so McHenry pointed his flashlight to illuminate the rest.

The wall was about 250 feet away. Hung on it was an enormous, blood-red banner with a black swastika inscribed in a white circle. Looking more closely, he realized the symbol was not a swastika – it was more complicated, like a modified tic-tac-toe board.

"What the hell is that?" he said under his breath. He turned to the man who had pointed it out. "Get an electrician and find the power source for this place," he ordered, pointing to the lights hanging from the ceiling. "See if we can rig something from the *Dakota*." That was something that made modern subs different: the power plant. They had nuclear reactors, and therefore virtually limitless power. The question was whether it was possible to interface the *Dakota* with the facility's power grid.

Beneath the banner was a row of six steel doors, each at least 10 feet tall and 5 feet wide. It looked as if they were embedded in the gray-brown rock. Suspended from the ceiling were two overhead cranes, and tracks to position them anywhere in the bay. He figured they were used for loading and unloading, although they looked strong enough to repair damaged subs. About 20 feet up the far wall, near the banner, was a long, corrugated-metal walkway, behind which were a dozen large windows and a few doors.

There was almost too much to explore. He decided that half the crew should always be on the *Dakota*, along with either himself, or his first officer, Diggs. That meant there would be around 70 men in the facility at any time.

Establishing a perimeter, and dealing with other logistics, like power, were straightforward tasks. But he wasn't sure what to do after all of that was accomplished. He called over Chief Petty Officer Gonzales who was running cables for lights. "Take your team and start searching for filing cabinets, locked rooms, or anything that might tell us more about this place."

Gonzales nodded, handed his cables to another man, and started walking away.

"And, Gonzales," McHenry added, making the man turn to face him again, "don't get lost."

Gonzales smiled and nodded, and then continued on his way.

McHenry walked around the main bay area, which was almost as large as a football field. The floor was solid stone that looked as if it had been ground smooth. He thought it was too perfect and level to be a purely natural feature. It might have been a natural cavern that the Germans had altered. Even so, the construction of the place had been an awesome undertaking. It was a mystery that he thought might rival that of the beacon.

A young crewman, an electrician, approached McHenry and informed him that they had located the power grid. They'd have to rig up a converter to interface with it, but it should be straightforward.

"What about cables?" McHenry asked.

"Everything's here," the man replied. "We found an electrical supplies storage room near the main power bank. We have everything we need – that is, if the insulation in the cables is still good after all this time."

"Okay – check it out," McHenry said. "Better be careful not to start an electrical fire with the aged wiring."

"We'll go circuit by circuit, sir," the man replied and then left to carry out his task.

McHenry examined the walls and ceiling. Behind the beams and other steel support structures was bare rock. Like the floor, it looked as if there had been a lot of excavation to form the cavern. At first, he wondered where they would have put such a large volume of material, but it was obvious: they pushed it out the bottom. There was a kilometer-deep cavern beneath them.

He walked to the side of the bay that was to the right of the wall with the banner. Near its center was a set of sliding bay doors, about 20 feet tall and 30 feet wide. He tried to peak through the crack between them, but couldn't see anything. He then forced his fingers between them and pulled, but they wouldn't budge. He backed away. They'd have to get inside when they had power.

To the right of the sliding doors was a large freight elevator. He aimed his flashlight through its small window, revealing the elevator's control panel, its six buttons labeled with numbers and German words. *Six floors.*

He turned in response to footsteps pounding behind him. It was Critch, the man who'd led the first exploration team.

The man breathed heavily as he tried to deliver his message. "Sir, you have to see this."

"What is it?" McHenry asked. Critch seemed spooked.

"Not sure," he replied. "There are bones. *Human.*"

The place immediately took on a different complexion. It seemed even darker and more menacing than it had just seconds before. He glanced up at the strange emblem on the banner as he followed Critch towards one of the doors directly beneath it. *What in God's name had the Nazis done here?*

~ 3 ~
Sunday, 24 May (1:58 p.m. CST – Chicago)

Jonathan followed Denise into the Bridges Café in Logan Square. He spotted their contacts at a small table near a window.

As they approached, Daniel stood and stuck out his hand. "Thanks for coming," he said, and shook each of their hands. Sylvia did the same.

"Seemed urgent," Jonathan said, wanting to get to the point. "We met just last week."

"Things are escalating, Mr. McDougal," Daniel said. "You're being watched. Red Wraith is connected to something much larger."

"Larger than Red Wraith?" Denise asked with an astonished look.

Daniel and Sylvia remained silent.

"You expect us to trust you," Denise continued. "But you don't trust *us*."

"My supervisor seems to trust you," Daniel said. "And so do I. But the protocol required for sensitive information, something I've been subjected to for most of my life, is difficult to bypass."

"Who is your supervisor?" Jonathan asked.

"The director of the CIA," Daniel replied.

"Your direct supervisor?" Jonathan asked, surprised.

"Yes," Sylvia affirmed. "We interact with him exclusively – we're not supposed to know the identities of the other members of our group."

"We know you're wary of the CIA," Daniel said. "It's a complicated entity. The right hand never knows what the left is doing. And sometimes a cancer can form that isn't discovered until it's too late."

"And what part of the CIA are you?" Denise asked. "Malignant or benign?"

"We're a combination of its memory and subconscious," Daniel said. "Ever solve a problem, or experience an epiphany, subconsciously – while dreaming maybe? We serve that function for the CIA. We're that tiny part of its brain, if you will, that mulls over details of the past without boundaries. We digest information from every classified source and analyze geopolitical events and dissect operations. While the rest of the CIA is dealing with current events, we're remembering and dreaming. Thinking."

"So why are you are out in the light?" Jonathan asked. "Why did they send you?"

"Because it's important," Sylvia said.

"What do you want from us?" Jonathan asked.

"We need to find William Thompson," Daniel replied.

Jonathan tried to respond with a blank stare as if he didn't recognize the name, but he was sure his expression was coming off as awkward. He looked at Denise: her face had already reddened.

Jonathan spoke quickly to head off Denise's response. "He's a former CP inmate. Why do you need to find him?"

"We don't know exactly," Sylvia replied.

"You don't know?" Denise repeated. "Then why – "

"Because he's in danger," Daniel explained. "People are looking for him."

"Why?" Denise asked.

"He may have acquired to ability to separate," Daniel responded.

"He's safe," Denise said.

Jonathan glanced at Denise, hoping she'd take the hint and stop talking. "The fact of the matter is that we don't know where he is exactly," he said. It wasn't technically a lie. They only knew the city. "We can get a message to him. But I doubt that he'll cooperate with the CIA – that is, unless we give him more information." Jonathan worked to contain his curiosity. "You'll need to tell us more."

Daniel looked to Sylvia, and then back to Jonathan. "We should leave this place. Can we meet someplace private that you're certain isn't bugged?"

"I know a place," Jonathan said.

Denise smiled. "The old library."

Jonathan gave Daniel and Sylvia directions, and they split up with plans to meet in an hour. Jonathan and Denise left the café first and got into his car. Denise seemed upset.

"You okay?" he asked.

"Worried," she said. "Will's somewhere in Baton Rouge, but I'm not sure I'd trust anyone with that information."

He agreed. "We should warn him," he suggested. "Perhaps we should hear what our visitors have to say first."

She agreed.

Her hands trembled as she checked the messages on her phone. "Nothing new from Will," she said.

Five minutes later he parked the car in front of the law building and headed for his office to get a notebook. As they exited the stairway and stepped onto to his floor, he spied two people standing next to a door near the end of the hall. It was the door to his office.

As he got closer, it was clear that they were males, probably mid-thirties – definitely not students – and Asian. Their attire and body language communicated that they were professionals of some kind.

Jonathan and Denise stopped 10 feet in front of the men.

"Jonathan McDougal?" the taller of the two asked.

Their accents were thick, and Jonathan could tell they were Chinese. "How can I help you?" he replied.

"I am Zhang," the taller man said and nodded towards his shorter partner, "this is Wei. We were wondering if we could speak with you for a few minutes."

"About what?" Jonathan asked.

"Please," Zhang said. "Can we step into your office?"

Jonathan reluctantly agreed, and they went in and sat at the table with him and Denise on one side, and the strangers on the other.

"We have some questions regarding your investigation of the Compressed Punishment program," Zhang said.

"Who are you?" Denise asked.

Wei answered, "We work out of the Chinese embassy. We are diplomats."

"I can't talk about an ongoing investigation," McDougal said.

Zhang seemed to ignore his statement and continued. "We need to know the location of a man who was at the Detroit facility – the Red Box."

It was clear who they meant. McDougal was surprised that his CIA visitors' warnings were already materializing. "It seems strange that a Chinese *diplomat* would a need to talk to former American prisoner."

"He is wanted for crimes against the people of China," Wei said.

"That's preposterous," Jonathan replied. "You should make a request to the Department of Justice."

The men squirmed in their chairs.

"We are prepared to pay handsomely for any information helping us locate him," Zhang said, speaking more quickly now.

"I don't recognize the man's name," Jonathan lied. "Perhaps you should check some of the mental health facilities in the Detroit or Long Island areas."

Zhang's face reddened, and his breathing became heavier, which was quite noticeable since he breathed through his nostrils. "You are lying!" he exploded.

Jonathan stood up. "Leave," he said loudly and pointed to the door. "Now!" He was surprised at their outburst as well as his own. The men were either not professionals, or poorly trained.

"You haven't even heard our offer," Zhang said, trying to calm himself.

"Not interested," Jonathan replied. "Even if I had such information, it wouldn't be for sale."

The two men stood slowly. Zhang spoke slowly. "We will come back later, after you have thought about it."

"That would be fruitless," Jonathan replied, showed them out, and walked back to the table.

Denise's normally dark complexion had turned pale.

"Let's go," he said, and picked up a leather briefcase containing his laptop and notebooks.

They walked up two flights of stairs, and then down a wide hallway strewn with pallets and boxes. "Still doing renovations," Jonathan said.

"They were supposed to be done by the spring semester," Denise added.

They came to a pair of tall wooden doors. Jonathan pulled one of the oversized handles and the heavy door creaked – but opened easily – and they walked inside. The enormous room was dimly lit, even though the wall on the far side was composed entirely of windows. A plastic sheet the size of a tennis court hung from the ceiling, separating the library into two parts. Jonathan led the way through a slit in the partition, and they emerged in a clean, furnished room, close to the north-facing windows.

He set his bag on a circular wooden table, proceeded to the windows, and looked at his phone. "They should be here soon." He then powered it down and took out the battery.

He looked out the window, one he thought provided the most beautiful view of the campus, and waved Denise closer. "I'm concerned," he started.

Denise's looked at him with worried eyes.

"We've entered a realm in which we have no experience," he

204

explained. "Those men were not diplomats, they were operatives. The fact that they would be so brazen as to expose themselves, and to attempt a bribe, means they are desperate. And desperation means danger."

She nodded. "The way that man exploded – "

"At first I thought that maybe he was not well trained," Jonathan said. "But now I think he was under immense pressure."

"By their government?"

"Perhaps," he said. "Something big is happening, and our CIA visitors know what it is."

"We need to find out," she said. "Everyone is after Will, and he doesn't even know it."

"I wouldn't worry too much about Will," he said, trying to calm her. "He's been trained, and knows people are looking for him. He's a smart guy."

She gave him a look indicating that she knew what he was trying to do.

"We'll warn him after we meet with these people," he added. "Okay?"

She nodded.

The library door creaked open, then closed. Two smeared figures moved behind the plastic sheet. Now, he hoped, they would learn more.

~ 4 ~
Sunday, 24 May (3:43 p.m. EST – Antarctica)

McHenry followed the young sailor through the doors and up a corrugated metal stairway. It seemed that the darkness swallowed up the light from their flashlights as they continued along a corridor deeper into the rock. After a few turns, and up another run of stairs, they turned into hallway with lights flickering in the distance. Flashlight beams tracked them as they approached.

A few men stepped aside to give McHenry access to a door on the right. He followed Critch into the room and panned around with his flashlight.

The room was long, like a hallway, with steel doors lining the walls, 20 on each side. McHenry thought it resembled prison, or a mental ward. The ceiling was at least 15 feet high, although it was hard to tell exactly with the flashlight beams. There was a door on the far end, opposite the entrance – closed, like all the others.

"Have a look in one of the cells," Critch said, pointing to the closest one on the right.

McHenry hesitated when he saw the man's expression – the scattered light from the multiple flashlights amplified the stress in his face.

The handle screeched and clicked as McHenry turned it, and he pulled outward. The door opened with some resistance, and the grinding coming from the rusted hinges made it seem as if they might break. He walked into the cell.

The smell hit him like a punch in the face. It reminded him of the stench wafting from the slaughterhouse he'd passed every day on his way to and from school as a kid. It was the smell of old death.

The half-dozen flashlights that beamed around in the darkness confused his eyes at first, and it took his mind a few seconds to piece together the strobe-like visual information. The cell was larger than he expected, and packed with strange equipment. On his right were a metal table and a tall bank of shelves. Hand tools were laid out on the table in an orderly fashion, some of which he recognized, such as pliers and cutters, and others he'd never seen before. On the far end were a large sink and a manifold of valves with pipes sticking out in all directions. His eyes caught something hanging from the ceiling; it was a motorized winch with a cable dangling to a point about 10 feet above the floor. Something was connected to it.

He directed the flashlight beam downward along the cable and focused on what hung from it. He first recognized a skull; a part near the left eye socket was chipped out. It was a nearly complete human skeleton contained in some sort of mechanical device. It looked like an intricate cage, tightly fitted around the bones, with parts formed to fit like an open, iron suit.

The top of the cage was connected to the cable, and the bottom was anchored to a winch fastened to the floor. Every appendage teemed with gears and electrical contacts, and there were many joints and other moving parts. On the bottom of the device was a large electric motor.

On the wall near the entrance was a control panel with buttons and levers, and three circular screens resembling those found on old oscilloscopes.

"What is that thing?" Critch asked, nodding to iron suit.

McHenry shook his head slowly, keeping his eyes on the cage. "Not sure. Same scene in the other rooms?" he asked.

"Similar."

McHenry walked closer to the cage. The upper left arm of the human skeleton looked to be amputated, and about half of the right foot was missing – cut at an odd angle, lengthwise. His eyes were then drawn to a fixture mounted on the right forearm of the victim. That arm of the cage had been replaced by a steel track, extending outward a few feet from the shoulder region of the frame.

The victim's right arm was fed through a steel sleeve mounted to a carriage on the track. The sleeve was composed of two, 5-inch-long half-cylinders, separated by adjustable bolts. *One size fits all*, McHenry thought. A circular blade, about 8 inches in diameter, was mounted to an arm on the carriage. The arm was designed to lower the blade flush with the end of the cylinder, where a hand had once protruded. His stomach twisted in reaction to something his mind had already figured out but wasn't yet telling him.

A power cable led from the sleeve device to an outlet mounted on the neck section of the body cage. He followed the wires from the outlet, through loops on the outer part of the cage, to metal conduits hanging from the ceiling to a point 3 feet above the head. At that point, the wires joined a bundle of others leading from other parts of the cage, and continued upward, through the conduit, towards the ceiling. A few feet below the ceiling, the conduit took a turn at an iron support bracket, and then another turn when it reached the wall about 15 feet away. It finally terminated at the control panel on the wall near the entrance.

McHenry directed his flashlight back to the saw device on the victim's forearm. Dried, leathery, material was still lodged in its rusted teeth. A brownish discoloration on the floor directly beneath it looked like a linear spray pattern from the blade. He then noticed numerous stains on the stone floor, crisscrossing at various angles as if they'd been created with a can of reddish-brown spray paint.

The device rode on the carriage that was mounted to the track, allowing it to be positioned anywhere along the length of the limb. Directing the flashlight to the floor, he noticed a pile of 1-inch pieces of bone directly beneath the saw. On the other side, beneath the amputated left arm, was a larger pile. He looked closer and realized that a gear drove the carriage on the track – it was *motorized*. It seemed that the sleeve-saw could be set to automatically ride along the track, amputating the limb inch by inch, like an automated meat slicer.

He felt ill as he turned his gaze to the face of the broken skull in the head cage. He imagined its open mouth was the remnant of its last scream.

"What is that thing?" Critch asked again.

"The worst torture device you could ever imagine," McHenry answered softly.

"Who were they torturing?"

McHenry saw fear in the face of a young man who had probably seen much worse in movies. "No idea," he answered. "You say these things are in every room?"

The man nodded.

McHenry knew that no one could survive such a torture for a sustained period of time, so he wondered what the Nazis had done with the bodies. At first he thought that there might be an incinerator, but he dismissed it immediately. They wouldn't want smoke to give away their location. Their power source would give them enough trouble. His best guess was that they weighted down the bodies and threw them into the deep.

Before he left, he ordered the men to keep exploring the rooms, map the area, and take pictures of everything.

On his way back to the *North Dakota* he contemplated what he'd just seen. Why had the Nazis been so obsessed with such grotesque medical experiments, torture chambers, and the like? What was the purpose? He could understand the occurrence of a few psychopathic individuals – such people existed in the present day. But why had the Nazis done it on such a large scale, and with such organization?

And, he wondered as he emerged into the bay beneath the Nazi banner, *what the hell was the purpose of this place?*

~ 5 ~
Sunday, 24 May (3:30 p.m. CST – Chicago)

At the last second Jonathan realized something and panicked as the two smeared figures approached from behind the plastic sheet. He sighed in relief when Daniel and Sylvia emerged through the slit rather than the two Chinese operatives.

"Interesting place," Sylvia commented, apparently admiring the thick wooden beams that crossed high above their heads. She walked over to the large window. "Nice view."

"Shall we get started?" Jonathan said and motioned to the table. "Please."

Daniel and Sylvia sat facing the window, and Denise and Jonathan sat across from them, facing the entrance. Jonathan meant to keep an eye on the door, even though they'd hear it creak if anyone entered.

"We were just visited by two Chinese diplomats," Jonathan said.

Daniel's face turned white, and Jonathan saw fear in his face.

"Diplomats?" Daniel repeated.

"They were looking for Thompson," Jonathan said. "I told them nothing, but they'll come back. I assume you have protection."

"We have people close by," Daniel said.

Jonathan nodded. "Now, why are you looking for Thompson?"

Daniel looked down and took a breath. "Again, we're not sure."

"Well *something* had to instigate your search," Jonathan argued.

"The short answer is that we're looking because everyone else is looking," Daniel said. "And by everyone, I mean intelligence services of foreign countries."

"Like China," Denise said.

"I think you need to give us some background," Jonathan said.

Daniel looked to Sylvia, who nodded.

"We're prepared to disclose some general information, which is all we have," Daniel explained. "Red Wraith and the Compressed Punishment system, both foci of your own investigation, are a part of something much more massive. I'll explain, but you must swear to nondisclosure – this is top secret information."

"Understood, and agreed," Jonathan said, nodding.

"My connection to this project started when I was assigned to research the Compressed Punishment program over a year ago," Daniel explained. "It was different that my usual historical work, considering that the whole thing blew up in real time, figuratively and literally. My research led to the Red Wraith project, but, just as I was making significant advances, I was reassigned."

"It's unheard of in our work," Sylvia added. "I was reassigned as well, and the fact that Daniel and I are now working together is also unprecedented – Omnis aren't supposed to know each other."

Over the next two hours, Jonathan listened as Daniel and Sylvia described a series of historical events, starting with Captain Cook's logs, the voyage of the *Schwabenland*, and the discovery of a beacon in the Southern Seas.

"Fascinating," Jonathan said. "So these so-called naval exercises are just a cover?"

"There's more." Daniel said. "Do you recall the Nazi symbol for their Red Falcon project?"

"It's a falcon carrying an emblem in its talons," Denise said.

"Precisely," Daniel said. "We found a photo of the *Schwabenland* during its pre-war Antarctic expedition. A large crate on its deck had the

Red Falcon emblem on it. The photo was taken in 1938."

Jonathan was hooked. "Red Falcon started before the war."

Daniel continued. "The Brits and Americans carried out multiple operations in Antarctica after the war. In the 1950's, the Americans detonated nukes in both the upper atmosphere, and also deep in the southern sea."

"Near the beacon," Denise said.

Daniel nodded. "And now one of our subs discovered a tunnel leading deep into the Antarctic mainland. It set out to explore it, but we haven't heard anything from it for days."

"Were they expected to report back by now?" Jonathan asked.

"Not necessarily," Daniel answered. "Only that they were to communicate when they were finished exploring. So, either they have discovered something, or they're lost."

"Or sunk," Jonathan added.

"The Russians and the Chinese are involved, and probably others," Daniel continued. "And they're all looking for Thompson. Other than him showing signs of separating during his treatments in the Red Box, we don't know why they want him. Finding him is our top priority."

Jonathan looked to Denise, who gave him a nod to go ahead.

"We don't know where he is exactly," Jonathan said. "But we can contact him. It will be up to him whether or not he'll cooperate with you."

"That's all we can ask," Daniel said, and then cleared his voice. "Well, there is one more thing."

"Yes?" Jonathan asked.

"We want you to work with us – in a more formal capacity," Daniel said.

"I'm not sure what that means," Jonathan said.

"We may ask you to join us in DC for a time, depending on how things play out," Daniel explained. "Would you be amenable to that?"

Jonathan glanced at Denise and sighed after a few seconds of silence. "We'll get back to you on that," he finally said. He thought about his teaching duties – there was over a month left in the semester – and his work at the Foundation.

"Think about it. In the meantime, it might be a good idea for the two of you to get out of Chicago for a while," Daniel said. He gave Jonathan a card with a hand-written phone number. "Give us a call when you've decided."

Jonathan and Denise watched their visitors navigate their way out. The library door creaked as they exited.

"What do you think?" Jonathan asked, already knowing how she'd answer.

"We should do it," Denise replied immediately. "But we have to warn Will that he's in danger."

"You take care of that," Jonathan said, "and I'll look at the information he sent on Syncorp and the CP men. We need to decide whether or not to forward it to the FBI."

"We have to trust someone," she said.

"At this point I trust our new CIA contacts more than the FBI."

"Are we going to work with them?"

He nodded.

~ 6 ~
Monday, 25 May (12:11 a.m. EST – Antarctica)

A knock sounded.

McHenry glanced at his watch; it was after midnight. He wasn't getting any sleep. "What?" he asked loud enough for whoever it was to hear him through the door of his quarters.

"They're ready to power up, sir," Diggs replied.

McHenry looked again at his watch and smirked to himself. Those guys were good – from the nuke engineers to the electronics techs to the sonar specialists. If ever there was a collection of people who could get a half-century-old Nazi base up and running, it was a tech-savvy submarine crew. He had handpicked his men, an honor bestowed upon the captain of a new sub. "I'll be right there."

He dropped from his bunk and put on a fresh pair of pants. He took a long swig of water from a bottle on his desk and headed out. Diggs and the man who had managed the power-up were waiting for him on deck.

The head electrician spoke. "It was a good thing the Germans were so organized," he started, "we've identified the emergency power circuits and have them ready to energize on your go-ahead."

"Fire it up," McHenry said.

The man barked into his radio for an "all clear." In a few seconds he got return messages from four teams. They were ready.

"Pull the switch," the main electrician ordered.

A few seconds later, a loud metallic clank boomed through the bay area, followed by a ramping hum. One of the overhead lights exploded, raining sparks and glass onto the stone floor, and making McHenry nearly jump out of his shoes. A few of the other lights began to glow, and soon warmed to bright yellow incandescence.

"We had to convert to 240 volts AC," the electrician explained, and then went through diagnostics with the other teams over the radio. "A lot of burnt bulbs," he said a few minutes later, "but the emergency systems seem operational."

"Could we power up the entire facility?" McHenry asked.

"If the main circuits are intact, yes," he replied. "We still have to find the other power panels – this place is huge."

McHenry walked off the *North Dakota* onto the steel platform, and then onto the stone floor of the bay. The space looked much larger than it had in the floodlights. It was as if he were in another world – another time. The giant Nazi banner reinforced the notion: it was like those he'd seen in old black-and-white documentary films. In this case, however, the illumination brought out the banner's deep red color, reminding him that he was really there.

The crew teamed around the facility for the next few hours, going in and out of the many doors in the bay, carrying equipment, and talking loudly. One man rode on a cable hanging from one of the overhead cranes and replaced lights. Light shone through the high windows on the far end of the bay, opposite the *North Dakota* and above the upper-deck walkway. Silhouettes of his sailors sporadically appeared and disappeared as their cameras flashed.

So far, the elaborate torture facility was the most disturbing find, but hardly a surprise considering it had belonged to the Nazis. But did any of it have to do with the beacon?

A young ensign ran up to McHenry. "Sir," he said, out of breath. "Lieutenant Jenkins sent me to get you."

"What is it?"

"A vault," the young man answered. "A big one."

"Let's go," McHenry said, and followed the man up corrugated stairs to the second-level walkway.

They went down a long corridor, up two more staircases, and then along another dimly lit hallway. The semitransparent covers of the emergency lights were a dingy yellow, giving the walls the ominous hue of decay. They passed more than a dozen doors before entering an open doorway on the right. Lieutenant Jenkins faced him as he entered, with three other crewmembers pilfering through desk drawers and filing cabinets.

"Where is it?" McHenry asked.

"This way," Jenkins said, and then turned and walked deeper into the room.

At the opposite end was another door. They passed through it and into a small foyer. In front of him was a stainless steel door that didn't give away its age. It was a walk-in vault.

"How on earth did they get that thing here?" he wondered aloud.

"What do you want us to do?" Jenkins asked.

It was a tough question. They certainly didn't want to damage its contents, which ruled out a cutting torch.

"The SEAL team has explosives on board, C-4 and some other stuff," Jenkins suggested, "I think we could blow the hinges, and then grind away whatever is left."

It would have to do. Time was a factor, and they couldn't take the vault with them.

"Do it," McHenry said and walked back to the first room.

Another man approached him. "Sir, we found a room filled with books and papers."

"Show me," McHenry said, and then followed him through a labyrinth of walkways. He entered the room and stopped in his tracks, stunned. There were rows of floor-to-ceiling shelves stacked with books, like a small library. On the front wall, to the left of the entrance, was a square map, ten feet on a side, illustrating terrain he'd recently seen – the Southern Sea and the tunnel that had led them to the base. His eye caught a detail: the beacon.

"Take pictures of that," he said, pointing to the map. "And make sure you get every inch in high resolution."

Three lights hanging from the high ceiling illuminated a sturdy wooden table, 6 by 12 feet, located at the front of the room near the map. Papers and notebooks were strewn about its surface, as well as more than a dozen bound books, a few of which lay open as they had for over a half-century.

He stood over the table and examined the materials, careful not to disturb them in their fragility. The papers and notebooks were covered mostly with handwritten German script, along with symbols that resembled hieroglyphics. The bound books were exactly that – on the topics of hieroglyphics and other ancient languages.

"Get pictures of all of this, but don't disturb anything," McHenry ordered. As he walked around the table to have a closer look at the map, he noticed a canvas on the wall. Black symbols resembling hieroglyphs were arranged in five concentric circles. It seemed like the Germans had been trying to decipher something.

"Get a few shots of this right now," McHenry said, pointing to the canvas.

He left the room and headed back to the *North Dakota*. They'd take another day or two exploring the base until they were sure they weren't missing anything, and then they'd get the hell out of there. The more he learned about the place, the more he wanted to leave.

~ 7 ~

Monday, 25 May (11:45 p.m. CST – Baton Rouge)

Will reread the troubling email Denise wrote and saved in their mutual account. First, she informed him that Jonathan had given the FBI the information he'd sent regarding the CP inmates' plans to hit Syncorp. Will wondered if that was wise. Next, she notified him of a meeting she and Jonathan had with CIA operatives who claimed that he was in danger. He trusted the CIA even less than the FBI. Lastly, and most disturbingly, she described their encounter with Chinese "diplomats" who inquired about his whereabouts. It incensed him that she and Jonathan were being dragged into his mess.

It didn't alarm him that people were looking for him; the FBI and the Israeli had warned him that would happen. What disturbed him was that people knew where to look, and whom to contact, in order to find him. Next, he feared, they'd track down his family members to get information.

He understood why he was being hunted; it was the reason that eluded him. What purpose did they have in mind for him?

It reminded him of something that had happened to him while being tortured in the Red Box: he'd heard voices. Considering the extreme pain and psychological stress he'd endured during that time, it wouldn't be surprising if his mind had malfunctioned to that degree. But it wasn't as if he'd heard unintelligible whispering or ramblings. To the contrary, it was perfectly articulate and was always the same voice. And it had a name: *Landau.* He'd never seen Landau, and so had never been convinced that the conversations were real. His mind had gone to strange places during that time.

Landau, the voice, had claimed that Will had a purpose, that there was a reason for what had been happening to him, and that his abilities would be a crucial part of it. His powers of separation had emerged during that time, and had expanded greatly since then, but he had no idea of their

216

limitations. Will even thought that new ones might emerge over time. But if there was a purpose for him and his talents, he had no idea what it was. Was he meant to do things like prevent the attack on Syncorp? No. He couldn't believe that the purpose of such extraordinary powers was for such ordinary results. The FBI could just go in and arrest those guys, and it would be over – nothing special needed.

Besides, he was neither vigilante nor superhero. He had too much anger. He wanted revenge on Syncorp as much as the CP men did. The guilt from giving them up made his stomach knot up, but he found solace in knowing that their efforts wouldn't be for naught. Denise and Jonathan had the Syncorp lists, and would act on them—as would the FBI.

But Will also had the information, and now he'd decide whether or not to use it.

~ 8 ~
Tuesday, 26 May (1:33 a.m. EST – Antarctica)

McHenry poured a splash of whisky into his coffee cup and handed the bottle to Diggs, who poured some into his own. "We should get every bit of information that we can, and get the hell out of here," McHenry said.

"We have a lot to map," Diggs said. "One of the teams has been out of contact for hours. The place has six floors – it's the size of a large office building."

McHenry nodded. "Communicators don't work well in here, either." Although he wasn't concerned that the men had gotten lost, he did worry about booby traps.

"Can you believe this place?" Diggs said, smiling and shaking his head. "They have a power plant, supply stores, barracks, a library, kitchen, a sub base, running water, and I bet we find more."

"You forgot *torture chambers*."

Diggs nodded and his face turned more serious. "How many

people you think were based here?"

There were various barracks-like sleeping quarters and many private rooms. There were slips for a half-dozen subs, so they'd need to accommodate the crews. The staff of the base itself could be much smaller. All of that was assuming it was exclusively a submarine base. The enormous torture facility, and the research rooms, suggested it was more than that. "I'd say around 300 to 500 personnel, but maybe up to 1,000," he said.

"My estimate as well," Diggs agreed. "Still, what was the purpose?"

McHenry knew he was referring to the torture facility. "I don't know, but we might get some insight into that when we get into the vault."

As if he'd willed it to happen, McHenry's communicator buzzed. They were ready to blow the vault door.

Leaving the second officer in command of the *North Dakota*, McHenry and Diggs made the walk deep into the facility, arriving at the vault ten minutes later. Mounds of plastic explosive and detcord were mounted along the hinge side of the door and symmetrically around the locking mechanism in the center.

"Is this the safest way to do this, assuming there's paper inside?" McHenry asked, wanting reassurance.

"Yes, sir," the explosives expert responded. "The door is hollow around the locking mechanism, so we calculated the charge so that it won't penetrate into the vault itself."

"What about the hinge side?" Diggs asked.

"We're more uncertain about that," the man answered, "but we have men with fire extinguishers on the ready."

"Do it," McHenry ordered. There was no point in waiting. They weren't leaving without the contents of the vault.

Everyone walked out of the vault room, into the adjacent corridor, and covered their ears. The explosion thumped McHenry's chest like a base drum and set his ears into a high-pitched ringing. Two men with fire extinguishers rushed in, and McHenry and the others followed closely behind.

There was some smoke, but almost no dust, and an ammonia-like odor filled the air. The vault door, now tilting at a sharp angle as if it hung from a thread, was deformed on the hinge side, and had a gaping hole where the locking mechanism used to be. The blast did not seem to penetrate into the vault.

Two men pulled on the door, and jumped out of the way as the massive piece of steel hit the floor and eventually settled.

"All clear, sir," a man carrying a fire extinguisher informed him. "No fire."

"Nice job," McHenry said as he walked into the vault doorway, found a light switch, and turned on an overhead light.

He was astounded by both the size and layout of the vault. Shelves were mounted on the wall on the left, and large cabinets lined the one on the right. The wall straight ahead of him, opposite the door, was composed entirely of file drawers.

The shelves contained books similar in topic to those in the library. He walked to the file drawers and opened one at random. It rolled out nearly six feet, and was packed with file folders.

He pulled out a file at random and examined it. Its yellowing tab was labeled with German words that he knew meant "top secret," and had the image of a bird of prey carrying the same swastika-like symbol that was on the banner in the submarine bay. He opened it and tried to read, but it was in German. His eyes tracked to the name typed in the upper-left corner. His mind reeled; it was Josef Mengele, the infamous Nazi doctor. It made sense. Mengele had carried out monstrous medical experiments in the concentration camps. The same kind of horror, probably worse, seemed to have been carried out in the base. What didn't make sense, however, was that the document in his hand was dated July 5th, 1948. The war had ended in 1945. *What the hell was this?*

He pulled another file. It was signed by someone other than Mengele, but dated 1947. The dates weren't a mistake. He returned the second file to the drawer and slid the Mengele folder under his arm.

He walked to one of the cabinets and opened it. On the bottom shelf was a circular object, 2 feet in diameter and about 4 inches thick, wrapped in cloth. With some struggling, he pulled it out, put it on the floor, and unwrapped it.

It was a disk, the surface of which was smooth and white, except for black symbols inset into its surface, arranged in five concentric circles. He recognized it immediately: the symbol pattern was identical to that on the canvas on the wall in the library. It seemed the Nazis had been studying the object.

"Wrap it up and bring it along," McHenry instructed.

He examined the other objects in the cabinets, but didn't deem them important enough to take with them. He didn't have time to figure it all out.

"Take pictures of all of this," he ordered. He figured the extensive photos should be enough to convince his superiors that a return trip was necessary. They'd take the file and the disc back with them.

It was time to get the hell out.

~ 9 ~

Tuesday 26 May (2:44 a.m. CST – Baton Rouge)

If the last light hadn't gone off when it had, Lenny was going to make his move anyway. The best time for a job like this was between two and three in the morning. Most people were in deep sleep by then, and the third shift workers were well into their workday. Not many people would be on the road – although that could have its disadvantages.

He was sure they had guns in the house, but he couldn't risk it. He'd have to bring two of his own. He threaded a silencer on the first one and put it on the passenger seat. He did the same to the second and put it in the side pocket of his long jacket. He pulled a flashlight out of a leather bag on the floor behind him and grabbed the first gun from the seat. He was ready.

He weaved around the four cars parked in the driveway, and crept along the left side of the house to the side entrance. He knelt on one knee and cursed under his breath as the screen door squeaked. He turned the knob of the inner door: it was unlocked. He wouldn't need the toolkit he brought.

Having scouted out the house and targets for the past few days, he thought he was as prepared as best he could for the operation. Even though he'd be in and out quickly, he hoped they'd forgotten to set the alarm. Otherwise he'd have just a minute to work before it went off. It would be enough.

He pushed on the door. After opening it less than half an inch, a continuous, high-pitched tone sounded from somewhere inside. There was no going back.

He stepped in, closed the door, and found himself in a dark kitchen. He moved next to the refrigerator and crouched. He had a good view of the lights on the alarm control panel near the front door and of the side door he'd just entered.

Rustling and swearing came from the back rooms, and the sound of feet on carpet indicated someone was coming. A few seconds later, someone stepped in front of the panel. He was about to click on the flashlight and take his first shot when he decided to wait and see if the man would punch in the code and deactivate the alarm.

To his delight, that was what happened.

In a zombie-like shuffle, the man checked the side door without even looking in Lenny's direction, and then went to the front door and tugged on it.

"What the hell's going on out there?" a man yelled in a groggy voice from somewhere in the back.

"Side door was unlocked," the man replied on his way back to his room.

It couldn't have worked out better.

He waited until he heard snoring, which took less than 15 minutes, and then moved quietly towards the back. He peered into the first room on the left. His eyes had adjusted to the dark, and the green light of a digital alarm clock illuminated the room well enough to see. Two men slept in small beds. The man in the bed closest to him was on his back, the other on his stomach. He walked in and closed the door.

He yanked the pillow out from under the head of the closest man, put it over his face, and jammed the barrel of his gun into the pillow. He fired twice, hardly making a sound. The man on the far side continued snoring.

He pulled the pillow off of the first man and examined his green-tinted face. One bullet hit him in the forehead, above the left eye, and the other went into the eye. He was dead.

Lenny took the bloody pillow and walked over to the next bed. He jumped on the man's back, put the pillow over his head, and shot twice. The man kicked sporadically, so Lenny fired a third time. All was still. He pulled the pillow up and a chunk of the man's skull fell down onto the sheets.

Two down.

He walked to the door and listened for movement outside. Nothing. He pulled out the second gun and slipped the first one into the holster. He opened the door, went into the hallway, and spied on the next room to the left, making sure no one in the third room, on the right, was awake.

He slipped into the room on the left and closed the door. These men slept in the same bed, both on their sides and facing away from each other. This one he'd have to do differently.

He shot the man closest to him in the temple and then immediately fired a bullet into the second man's head, across the bed. The first man was silent, but the second one wailed out and stood straight up on the bed, leaning his back against the wall. Lenny didn't know how this was possible as the bullet struck him above the right eye. He shot him again, this time in the forehead, and the man tumbled off the opposite side of the bed, crashing onto a lamp and nightstand.

The man closest to him twitched again, and Lenny snuffed the spasms with another shot.

A few seconds later, someone pounded on the door. "What the hell's going on in there?" a man's voice said from the hallway.

When the man pounded again, Lenny shot though the center of the door, chest-high.

The man cried from the other side.

Lenny took out his flashlight and pulled the door open. He flicked on the light and shone it in the face of a man sitting in the hallway with his back against the wall, bleeding. He was hit in the shoulder. Lenny shot him twice more in the head.

There was one left, and he heard him rustling around in the dark in the last room on the right. Lenny turned off his flashlight, crouched down, and entered the room. He felt around on the wall for the light switch, located it, and turned it on. A ceiling-mounted light fixture lit the room just as the man pulled a gun out of a dresser drawer and turned. They shot simultaneously. Lenny's bullet ripped through the middle knuckle of the man's shooting hand and into his shoulder. The man's bullet nicked Lenny's right ear.

The man dropped the gun and fell back against the dresser, holding his disfigured hand and screaming. Lenny walked around the bed, and shot him five times: twice in the head, and once to the chest, hip, and right leg.

Now he had to move quickly. The neighbors might have heard the blast from the other man's gun, sans silencer. He took gun number one out of his coat, put in a full magazine, and went to the dead man the hall. He put it into the man's hand and fired it multiple times with the shooting finger, putting holes in the floor, doors, walls and ceiling. He then shot him a few times in random places with gun number two.

He went to the second room, shot the men a few times with gun number one, and then dragged one of them into the doorway. He reloaded gun number two, fired it a half dozen times with the man's twitching hand, and left it there. He then put gun number one back into the hand of the man in the hallway.

Lenny stood and did one more walk around, just to make sure everything was set up as he'd planned. It looked like a shootout – as if one of the two men killed all of the others, but they fought back and killed him. A thorough investigation would reveal that something was amiss, but it would take time, and he'd be long gone.

The stench of emptied bowels and urine permeated house. He assessed the damage to his bleeding ear with his right hand as he glanced at his watch. It was 2:59 a.m. More important was the date: he'd made the deadline for the bonus.

As he exited the side door, the alarm panel emitted a continuous beep. He knew he had a minute to get in his car and get out of sight before the alarm activated. He was gone in 30 seconds.

CHAPTER XI

~ 1 ~

Tuesday, 26 May (8:17 a.m. CST – Baton Rouge)

The sun shining through the kitchen skylight warmed Will's shoulders as ate cold cereal. He was speculating about when the FBI might make their move on the CP men when the phone rang. It was Denise.

"Where are you?" she asked.

"What do you mean?" Something was wrong.

"You haven't heard? There was a shootout – the CP men in Baton Rouge."

Dazed, Will turned on the television and found the local news.

"They're all dead," she said. "It's being reported that they killed each other in a skirmish, but it's not true. It was a hit. It happened at about 2 a.m. this morning."

There was nothing on the news. Of course it was a hit, he thought. "Who did it?" After a few seconds the silence on the other end became awkward. "Denise?"

She cleared he throat. "Where were you last night?"

It took Will a few seconds to understand the context of the question. "Sleeping," he said, finally.

"The FBI is going to question you," she said. "Can you prove you were home?"

"No." His blood seemed to freeze in his veins as a feeling he'd experienced in the past set in. He wasn't a killer, but it was hard to prove a negative.

His phone beeped in his ear, indicating he had an incoming message: it read *523.*

"Gotta go," he said.

"Wait, there's more," she said loudly before. "You read my email? Chinese operatives came to us asking where you are."

225

"I know. It's good that you don't know where I am," he replied.

"And the two CIA operatives," she added, "they want you to work with them."

"I'm sure they do," he replied. "Goodbye, Denise."

He hung up just in time to catch the incoming call. He answered.

"Thompson?" a female voice asked.

"Natalie. You're back?"

"You hear what happened?"

"Yes."

"I contacted Adler and told him he's also in danger. We have to move on Syncorp now, or lose everything."

"Syncorp killed those guys," Will said.

"Probably," she replied. "We have to get into the complex and get all of the information we can. If they knew enough to put out a hit, they might be getting ready to pack up everything and move."

"When do we go in?"

"I'm meeting Adler tonight to make plans," she replied. "In the meantime, get a burner phone. There's a leak at the FBI and they're tracking you. Call me on your new phone tomorrow morning."

He confirmed her phone number and they ended the call.

It was time to go off the grid.

~ 2 ~

Thursday, 28 May (7:59 a.m. EST – Washington)

Daniel had read hundreds of Mossad interrogation transcripts since his return from Chicago. Between those and the files they'd gotten from McDougal, he'd made some loose connections to events in the southern hemisphere, but no breakthroughs. Thackett had scheduled a morning meeting, but Daniel had nothing significant to report.

Thackett changed the routine and brought them into another part of 713. Daniel sat next to Sylvia and across from Horace at a wooden conference table located at the far end of the large office space, near the entrance. Thackett walked to the front, started up a projector, and lowered a screen. Daniel could tell by the look in his face that something was coming.

As the projector warmed up, Thackett poured a glass of water and downed it in a few giant gulps. He refilled it, took another sip, and set it in the table. He wiped his lips with the back of his hand, and spoke.

"As you know, the *North Dakota* had been out of contact for nearly ten days," Thackett said. "It has returned."

"What you are about to see is one of the most frightening finds in recent history," Horace said and nodded to Thackett to start the show.

The first slide was a photo of what seemed to be large loading bay with a dock. A giant banner with the Red Falcon emblem hung from the wall on the far end.

"What the hell?" Daniel asked, flabbergasted.

"It's a Nazi submarine base located at the end of a tunnel that extends more than 150 kilometers into the Antarctic continent," Thackett explained, and then described the *North Dakota's* mapping of the trench and discovery of the base. "They explored the facility, but only spent two days there – one of which was needed to get the power grid up and running."

Horace cut in, "What they found was nothing less than fascinating. There's an elaborate torture chamber, a research library, and a vault," he explained. "Show them the photos, Thackett."

Thackett advanced the presentation through pictures of the torture facility.

Daniel was shocked by the crude similarity of the device to the modern Exoskeleton. Even more disturbing was the victims' skeleton still trapped inside it. He wondered whether the person had been killed or just left to die when the Nazis deserted.

"Why did they do it there? Seems inconvenient," Daniel commented. "They'd have to transport them."

"We don't know why they'd chosen the location, other than its proximity to the beacon," Horace explained, "but the information found in the vault and research library might reveal something." He nodded again to Thackett, who then navigated to the relevant photos.

There were pictures of a library, and of the books and papers on the library table. Although Daniel had some knowledge of semiotics and symbology, he didn't recognize most of the characters in the photos, although many were reminiscent of hieroglyphics.

Thackett clicked to the next photo, which was of a white disk. It was approximately 2 feet in diameter and 4 inches thick, and was being tipped on its end by two sailors. Covering its surface were black, hieroglyphic-like symbols arranged in five concentric circles.

"There was a sketch or print of the same in the research library," Thackett said. "The object itself was found in the vault."

"What is it?" Sylvia asked.

"It might be a decoder of some kind," Thackett said.

"More likely it's what they were trying to decipher," Horace said. "We think it's composed of the same material as the beacon. It's impossible to tell since we can't obtain any of the beacon's material. But, like the beacon, the disk can't be scratched."

"There's more," Thackett said and flipped to the next slide. "This is the cover page of a file extracted from the vault at the base."

It was on Red Falcon letterhead and written in German. Daniel read what he could – it was the cover page of a report. He saw the signature.

"Josef Mengele was at the base?" he exclaimed.

"Look at the date," Horace instructed and nodded towards the screen.

Daniel read: 5 *July 1948*. "That must be a mistake."

Horace shook his head. "There were other files dated after the war."

Daniel's mind spun like a wheel in the mud. He glanced at the others. There was a tension in the room that was amplified in Sylvia's expression. Horace's face also deviated from its normally calm appearance. Thackett tilted his head downward and stared blankly at the table as if he were gathering his thoughts.

Daniel couldn't take it anymore. "What's going on?"

Horace looked to Thackett and nodded, as if he knew what Thackett was supposed to say.

"As you can see," Thackett started, and gestured to the projector screen, "it's very likely that the answer to our mystery lies in that place."

"Yes," Daniel agreed. "We need all of the information they can get."

Thackett glanced to Horace, who smiled and looked down at the table.

"There's too much, Daniel," Thackett said, making eye contact with him. "It would be a massive undertaking, even if it were just down the road. A submarine crew can't handle it. It would take time – time we don't have."

"And there would be something lost – *context*," Horace added. "You want to see the whole picture in its undisturbed state, in its original environment. Tearing it apart destroys information."

Daniel stared at them.

Sylvia laughed. "You're a little thick sometimes, Daniel."

He remained silent.

"They want us to *go* there," she finally blurted, and reached over and smacked the top of his hand.

"What?" Daniel looked first at Horace, who was smiling, and then to Thackett, who stared back blankly. "You're serious?"

Horace nodded.

Daniel sat back and processed the information. It would complicate things. "We won't have access to our resources. Our information –"

"You'll take whatever you need in electronic format," Thackett said. "Your primary task is to determine the purpose of the base."

Horace looked first to Daniel and then Sylvia. "Get your affairs in order. We leave tonight."

229

~ 3 ~
Friday, 29 May (10:38 a.m. CST – Baton Rouge)

Will found the bagel shop and parked the SUV. The aromas of scrambled eggs and onion bagels hit him as he entered. He wasn't hungry.

He spotted Natalie Tate in a booth, walked over, and sat across from her.

"I'm supposed to question you regarding your whereabouts when the CP men were massacred," she said.

"It happened around 2:00 a.m. I was sleeping. I can't prove it," he replied. "I would've been more apt to let them carry out their operation than kill them. I have no motive." He still couldn't believe that, for the second time in his life, he was being considered as a suspect in a heinous crime.

"We know," she said. "You're cleared."

Will nodded. He felt relieved, but was still on edge. "Any leads?"

"No, but it's connected to the hit on Jennings."

"Now, what about Syncorp?"

Natalie nodded. "Adler is going to get us in."

"You trust him?"

She reached into black leather knapsack on the seat bedside her and pulled out a packet of papers. "He gave me these," she replied and pushed it across the table.

The first few pages contained a list of Syncorp employee names and addresses. Others listed more than a dozen companies connected to Syncorp. The last page was a detailed map of the Syncorp facility.

"Why don't you just use this information and start arresting people?" Will asked.

"That's not evidence. What we need is on their hard drives," she said. "As soon as we'd make a move to arrest any of the people on that list, the data would be moved or destroyed. We need to acquire the digital

230

information before we do anything else."

"Why doesn't Adler get it?"

Natalie raised an eyebrow and smirked. "This is too sophisticated for Adler. We need the storage drives themselves – copying them will take too much time. And we now have a window of opportunity: the computers are located in temporary storage. Syncorp is building a high security facility for digital media, and they will be moved there soon. Once in the new building, they'll be nearly impossible to obtain."

"How much time do we have?"

"A week," she replied.

"Are there more agents coming?"

"No, it's only us," Natalie explained. "You'll go in, and I'll be on the outside in contact with you in case something goes wrong."

"How am I getting in?"

"Adler will smuggle you into the parking garage. The temporary storage building is right next to it."

"Sounds risky."

Natalie nodded.

The danger didn't bother him – he could protect himself – but was more concerned with failure. It was a unique opportunity. "When do we move?"

"Depends on Adler," she replied. "It will take a few days to set up, but be ready to go at any time."

Will didn't want to sit around and wait, but he had no choice. In the down time he'd send Denise and Jonathan the new information Adler turned over.

~ 4 ~

Saturday, 30 May (8:25 p.m. EST – Antarctic Circle)

Daniel was staggered by how quickly he'd been transported halfway around the globe, from the late spring of Washington, DC, to the late fall of Argentina. It started with a commercial flight from Reagan International to Buenos Aires, followed by a cold helicopter flight to the aircraft carrier USS *Nimitz*. The next hitch unnerved him, even though the pilot had promised a gentle flight. He rode in an F/A-18F Superhornet fighter jet from the *Nimitz*, somewhere in international waters off the coast of Argentina, to the deck of the USS *Stennis*, floating in the darkness of the Weddell Sea in the Antarctic Circle.

Daniel, Sylvia, and Horace gathered in the mess hall on the *Stennis*, awaiting their rendezvous with the fast-attack sub, the *North Dakota*. Sylvia seemed to have faired the trip well, despite the sleep deprivation. Horace, however, looked as if he might expire at any time.

They'd barely finished their meals when a group of sailors whisked them away for the final, and most treacherous, leg of the trip.

They were bundled in waterproof slicks and floatation harnesses, and loaded onto a helicopter. The chopper elevated to a few hundred feet above the deck of the *Stennis* and then turned and moved into the darkness. In less than two minutes, the side door slid open, and a wind colder than anything Daniel had imagined seemed to whistle through his bones. The crew slipped a harness over his shoulders and strapped him in, while another man secured himself in another harness.

Connected to a cable, the man latched Daniel onto the front of his own harness and bear-hugged him. "Hang on," the man yelled over the noise, "and don't touch anything. I'll release you at the right time."

Daniel wasn't going to argue. A drop into the water would mean certain death.

Seconds later he was suspended in a wind so cold that he thought he might flash-freeze. He looked down upon the black shape of the deep-sea predator beneath him. Submarines had always given him an uneasy feeling – he didn't know if it was the way they stalked their prey and attacked without warning, or the idea of being inside such a beast. He'd never felt comfortable in close quarters, but being submerged in hundreds of feet of water, and in danger of drowning or being crushed to death, didn't sit well with him either.

As they got closer to the *Dakota's* deck, the air blasting from the helicopter blades sprayed a freezing mist of seawater into Daniel's face. The taste of the salt awakened him to the reality of what was happening: he was boarding a submarine that would take him into one of the most secluded and unique finds in modern times. He'd be traveling into a dark history. He'd of course experienced such things in his mind, or seen them on paper, as his job required. But this time he'd actually be there.

Just before his feet hit the deck, a pair of strong hands grasped his harness and reeled him in. The man who'd been riding tandem released the latch, transferring him to the *North Dakota's* deck. Daniel was than shuttled inside and down a ladder. At the bottom, another man grabbed him.

"Welcome aboard," the young man said, pulling him along. "Let's get you into some dry clothes. Ever wear a poopy-suit?"

Daniel had no idea what in hell's name the man was talking about, and must have conveyed that in his expression.

The man laughed. "You look like a medium," he said, and handed him a folded blue garment. "What's your shoe size?"

"Nine," Daniel responded.

The man reached in a locker and pulled out a pair of sneakers. "These are 9 ½ s, closest we have."

The sailor led him to a room smaller than a bathroom on a commercial jet and instructed him to change clothes. "I'll come back in five minutes and take you to the planning room where you'll meet with the rest your group," the man said. "You'll meet the captain there." He closed the door, leaving Daniel to change.

The so-called "poopy-suit" was a blue, one-piece garment that reminded him of the overalls the mechanics wore at his oil-change garage in DC. He sighed and smiled to himself. With all of the research and writing that he'd done for the past twenty years, something always seemed to be missing. Perhaps this was it: actually *doing* something, *going* somewhere.

The overalls fit comfortably, if not a little loose, and the shoes were just right. They'd given him an assortment of other clothes as well – a tee shirt, boxer shorts, and comfortable socks. It struck him funny that they'd be giving Sylvia the same attire. Even more so, it would be the same for Horace. He wondered how Horace would fare the exchange from the helicopter to the *North Dakota*. From what he knew of Sylvia, she'd find it exhilarating.

He wondered how long it would take to get to the Nazi base. He wanted to be there already. Something was beginning to stir deep inside him. Maybe this was the most important thing he'd do in his life. It was as if everything he'd ever done had merely been preparation for what he was about to do.

~ 5 ~

Saturday, 30 May (8:05 p.m. CST – Chicago)

The scent of cherry pipe tobacco filled Denise's senses as she walked into Jonathan's office. He was smoking and staring out a window into the night. She cleared her throat to let him know she was there.

As he turned, he toked on the pipe from the corner of his mouth. "Ah, Denise," he said. "Have a seat."

She remained standing. "Will sent us more information."

He nodded as he puffed. "What did he get this time?"

"Lists of Syncorp personnel, locations of Syncorp branch companies, and a map of the Baton Rouge facility – updated to include some new construction," she explained. "This goes far beyond what he got from the CP inmates. It came from a Syncorp employee."

"Great work," Jonathan said. "We'll need to hire more people just to keep up with him."

"He asked about how to go about large data transfer," she explained. "The person on the inside is going to get him access to data storage drives."

"Hmmm ..." Jonathan walked from the window and put his pipe in an ashtray on the coffee table. "A place like Syncorp would have cutting-edge security for such things. And the files will be encrypted. Why

234

doesn't he let us come down there and help?"

"He won't," she said.

He nodded with an expression that Denise had seen many times – an indication of stubbornness. Sometimes it was a good trait.

"And he wants to know how we can protect his source," she added.

"Tell him I'll to talk to a few people and see what we can do."

"Have you been watching the news?" she asked. "China and Russia have joined the training exercises around Antarctica."

He raised an eyebrow. "It's heating up down there."

"You think it could lead to war?"

"Of course," he replied. "When was the last time the U.S., China, and Russia all had such massive military forces in the same location? Why can't the media see that something is going on down there?"

Denise shrugged. She was used to the media missing things. When the Red Box went down, they'd fallen for the story that a gas leak had caused the explosion. The initial stories of torture had been squelched; they'd claimed earlier reports were rumors propagated by conspiracy theorists. "You think Daniel and Sylvia are involved in some way?"

Jonathan shrugged. "Maybe we'll find out at some point," he said. "In the meantime, you should verify the information that Will sent, starting with the satellite companies – see if they exist and what they do. Then dig up anything you can find on the employees."

She agreed and went to her office, pulled up the lists on her computer, and selected the first company on the list of over a dozen: *Pangor Bioengineering Solutions*, Waukesha, Wisconsin. It was a good place to start. And the sooner she verified the data, the sooner they'd get to the next step, which she hoped would involve some action.

~ 6 ~

Saturday, 30 May (9:51 p.m. EST – Antarctic Circle)

235

McHenry looked over the three people sitting in front of him: a man in his forties who looked too weak to climb a ladder; a young woman who, except for the red-highlighted hair, looked like a librarian; and a frail old man ancient enough to have designed the Nazi base himself.

For an instant he felt ashamed, then suppressed his superficial assessments and gave them the benefit of the doubt. He took a seat at the small table, making it a total of five, including himself and Lieutenant Diggs.

"My name is McHenry, the captain of this vessel," he said, "and this is my first officer, Lieutenant Diggs."

Diggs nodded.

"We'll arrive at the base in a little more than three days," McHenry continued. "I've been instructed to show you the important features along the way. That means dead subs and manmade structures. There are also subs in the slips below the facility."

"Do you by chance have the markings on those subs?" Daniel asked.

"We'll get them for you," Diggs replied.

"We have two German translators on board if you need them," McHenry said.

Horace nodded. "We all read a little, but we'll need them."

"Do you have any idea of the purpose of that place?" McHenry asked, trying to soften the formal tone of their interaction.

Horace coughed and took a sip from his mug. "We can only speculate," he said. "But we think it's connected to the beacon."

"The emblem on the Nazi banner in the bay area is significant," Daniel added.

"How so?" Diggs asked.

"It's from a secret Nazi project called Red Falcon," Daniel responded. "It's also consistent with a torture chamber being in the facility."

"Did the base have any other obvious functions?" Sylvia asked. "Other than repairing subs, that is."

"In my opinion, the functionality of the base was for torture.

Maybe they were trying to get information from people – they seemed to be trying to break some kind of code." McHenry explained. "It being exclusively a sub base was unlikely. The mechanical facilities aren't geared for that purpose, and the location is inconvenient."

Daniel nodded. "We have quite a puzzle to solve. Good thing the Nazis were so organized – I saw the pictures of the library and the vault."

"Did you have a look at the file we brought back with us?" McHenry asked.

Daniel nodded.

"I just pulled one out at random," McHenry said. "Signed by Josef Mengele himself."

Daniel nodded. "I'm not surprised he had a hand in this."

"And the date," McHenry said.

"After the war ended – 1948," Daniel said. "If that's correct, it must've been why the US launched Operation Highjump around that time. They knew the Nazis were there."

"Highjump was just an exercise," McHenry said, recalling the operation from his naval history class at the Naval Academy.

"You mean like the one that's being conducted right now?" Horace countered.

McHenry nodded and smiled. "I suppose so," he admitted. "We should learn a lot in the coming days. Now, it's time for you three to get some rest. We'll be at the mouth of the tunnel at 09:00."

The civilians were escorted to their bunks, leaving McHenry and Diggs at the table.

"What do you think?" McHenry asked.

Diggs shook his head. "I don't like it, Captain. Not one bit."

McHenry nodded. He'd gotten word just before they'd submerged that Russian and Chinese forces had been spotted on the Antarctic coast, and inland, just tens of miles from the base. Such maneuvers were both costly and dangerous in such horrible conditions, which implied they knew something. It also meant the *North Dakota*, and its contingent of civilians, might have less time to accomplish its mission.

American subs and destroyers were guarding the mouth of the

tunnel. A sonar detection vessel was also there, lighting the place up like the sun. No one else could get into the tunnel. He also assumed that there was no way that the Russians or Chinese could know the exact location of the base; it was the right call not to radio from the lake when they were there the first time. Now they'd have to keep radio silence until they solved the mystery.

There seemed to be a lot at stake, he just didn't know what exactly – and neither, it seemed, did anyone else.

~ 7 ~

Sunday, 31 May (8:36 a.m. EST – Antarctica)

"I've been shaking you for a full 30 seconds," the young man said. Daniel rubbed his eyes and stared up at him. "We're approaching the tunnel."

Daniel looked at his watch. He'd been asleep for eight hours, which was twice that of most nights. He rolled out of his bunk, dressed, and realized he had no idea where he was supposed to go. He walked out of his quarters and the sailor was waiting for him.

He followed the man through narrow walkways and up steep steps to a room filled with electronics and visual displays. Captain McHenry, Horace, and Sylvia were already there and staring at one of many monitors suspended from the ceiling.

McHenry spotted him and waved him over. "One of the dead subs," he said, nodding to a monitors. "A German U-boat."

He'd already known about the sub, but it was surreal to actually see it.

"It's intriguing," McHenry said. "The American sub further up the tunnel is the SS-193 *Swordfish*."

Daniel thought it was even more interesting that the U.S. had falsified the records of SS-193. It meant that, long ago, someone had known about the tunnel, and maybe the beacon. It could have been one of those secrets that was so well kept that it really did fade away. It was rare. People always talked – that is, if they didn't die first. "We've been briefed on both," Daniel said. "The German one is U-530. It was captured in Argentina, and eventually scuttled by the U.S. The *Swordfish* had supposedly been sunk by the Japanese in the Pacific."

"The way I see it, there are two possibilities," McHenry explained. "Either U-530 was not destroyed after its capture, which I seriously doubt, or the Germans made duplicates."

It was an interesting idea, Daniel thought. One sub assigned to conventional war activities, while the other ran secret missions.

"How were these subs destroyed?" Sylvia asked.

"I could be wrong but, by the looks of them, the U-530 was scuttled and the *Swordfish* was sunk by torpedo." McHenry said. He cleared his voice and changed tone. "I don't think we should lollygag here," he said. "The next checkpoint is about a day away – some structure in the tunnel for you to observe – and a few more places along the way. My orders are to get you to the base as soon as possible."

"Agreed," Horace said.

"You three should get to the mess hall and get some breakfast," McHenry said, his suggestion sounding more like an order.

The last thing on Daniel's mind was food. But he had to calm himself – the trip was going to take a few days. He decided he should pass the time by reading the mountain of information that had been scanned and loaded onto his computer.

He felt like he had as a kid just before Christmas – hardly able to concentrate on anything. His mind yearned for the information at the base. It was going to be the biggest challenge of his life and, as his subconscious somehow conveyed to him, the most important.

~ 8 ~

Tuesday, 2 June (2:55 p.m. EST)

It took three days, but Daniel had finally adjusted to the cramped quarters of the *North Dakota*. One thing he hadn't anticipated was the smell: it was like that of an old locker room, bringing back unpleasant memories of his youth. Lieutenant Diggs had told him that the *North Dakota*, being new, smelled much better than older subs.

He was getting used to everything – even the food – and it gave him confidence. He thought that, when the mission was over and he got back to his normal life, simple trips to the grocery store would no longer cause him anxiety. His heart sank a little, however, when he realized it was only the beginning. He didn't know what to expect once they got to the base, and wasn't sure if he'd ever get back to normal life.

He, Sylvia, and Horace, passed the time reading files and discussing what they'd learned. They'd failed to make any new connections, but were confident they'd make progress once they got to the base. That there were files there from the infamous Dr. Mengele himself, and dated after the war had ended, made them all expectant. Maybe they'd unravel the entire mystery.

It was 3:01 p.m. when a crewman notified him that they were approaching the base. He met Sylvia and Horace in the control room where McHenry and members of the crew watched a video monitor. McHenry waved them over.

The tunnel opened into a gigantic cavern. The ceiling had two peculiar features. One was a manmade structure composed of six slips – three occupied by subs – and a set of large bay doors. A bank of observation windows lined the steep wall above the slips. The other feature was a large, smooth-looking area on the ceiling of the cavern. It was an opening to the surface, and must have looked like a small lake from the outside. McHenry informed them that the water in the cavern was both warmer than that of the rest of the tunnel, and brackish. Finley, the sonar operator, suggested that warm freshwater came from vents in the floor, about 1,000 meters below. The same was also responsible for the current they'd bucked all the way in from the fork.

Finley pinged the bay doors, and they opened slowly, like a coffin.

McHenry explained that the doors moved more quickly than they had the first time, probably because the power source that was used for this purpose was now fully charged since they'd energized the emergency grid during their first visit.

"I'm surprised they even opened the first time," Sylvia said. "Any batteries would have been dead after seventy years, right?"

McHenry shook his head. "We don't know – it's something our engineers are going to look into. They suspect it's some sort of capacitive storage, rather than a conventional chemical battery." He chuckled. "We were a little confused when we were about to depart from the base the first time and the bay doors had closed beneath us. Turns out there's a spring mechanism that closes them automatically."

The *North Dakota* rose towards the now fully opened bay doors. Daniel examined the three Nazi subs sleeping in the slips as they passed. One was U-505. He pointed and said, "That one's on display at the World War II museum in Chicago. It operated in the Atlantic."

"Another duplicate," McHenry said, shaking his head.

After 10 minutes of fine maneuvering, the *North Dakota* surfaced and docked. McHenry sent a scouting team out to secure the area. Next, a group of engineers energized the emergency power grid using the *North Dakota's* power plant. Daniel was impressed that the sub could power the entire facility. This time they brought all of the equipment needed to construct a permanent electrical setup capable of powering everything – not just the emergency circuits. They'd stick with the submarine power; the old German generators, if they could even get them running, would be noisy and produce exhaust that would have to be filtered and expelled at the surface. The last thing they needed was a heat signature, or smoke, to reveal the location of the base.

An hour later, McHenry cleared them to go ashore.

From the instant he emerged from the *North Dakota*, Daniel's gut seemed to tie itself in knots. His eyes tracked to the large banner with the Red Falcon emblem on the far wall. It was time to find some answers.

The base could have been the eighth wonder of the word. It was hard to believe that it was the work of humans; it was as if it were carved out of solid stone. Its musty smell, reminiscent of wet cement, permeated his sinuses. His eyes adjusted to the now well-lit bay; Diggs informed him that the engineers had replaced most of the burnt bulbs in the light fixtures hanging from the 100-foot ceiling. The air swirled gently through the space.

Even though the entire crew wore sneakers, their work produced noises that echoed as if they were in a cathedral. The only other noises were that of the water slapping gently on the sides of the *North Dakota*, and the faint, 50 hertz hum of the electric lamps.

McHenry walked over. "I thought I'd give you the basic tour so that you can get a feel for the layout," he said. "After that, you'll be on your own."

As they walked through the bay, McHenry explained how his engineers had configured power grid. "We could run this whole place at full power for months on the *North Dakota's* reactor, and not create wisp of evidence on the outside that the place was in operation. We'll still have to be careful of our heat signature, so space heating will be used sparingly."

McHenry led the way, followed by Sylvia and Daniel. Horace lagged behind. They entered the wide, double doors directly below the Nazi banner, and proceeded down a wide corridor until they reached a steep staircase, which they climbed to a mezzanine level with many doors.

After five minutes of walking, they came to a door with German words stenciled on it: *Der Tod ist der Hirte der Menschheit.*

Daniel knew too little German to interpret it, so he turned to Sylvia, who stood frozen, staring at the phrase. "What does it say?" he asked.

Sylvia moved her lips, but there was no sound.

Horace walked up, looked at it, and spoke. "It says, *death is the shepherd of mankind*."

The words sent a twisting chill up Daniel's back. "What does *that* mean?" he asked.

"No idea," Horace replied.

"Let's go inside," Daniel said to McHenry. He knew what was there from the pictures.

McHenry's face turned solemn as he twisted the door's heavy handle. The door squealed as he pushed it open.

They entered what looked like a mental ward. Doors lined both sides of a long room, with about 20 on each side, and one door on the far end, opposite the entrance.

McHenry led them to one on the right, opened it, and ushered them inside.

Daniel entered with wide eyes. It seemed different from the pictures. It was as if Mengele was in the room with them – he could almost see the monster at work.

A human skeleton was confined to a medieval cage-like device. Heavy electrical cables branched off from the various appendages – the head and extremities mostly, although some led to other places on the body. Electric motors and hand-operated levers were riddled throughout the structure. He knew exactly what the thing was: it was a crude Exoskeleton. It was nowhere near the level of sophistication of the modern device, but it had been *born* in this place.

"See the little pieces of bone," McHenry said, pointing to the floor and then to the saw mounted on the arm of the Exoskeleton. "Looks like some kind of automated amputation mechanism."

Sylvia walked closer and examined the one-inch pieces of bone. "It's awful," she said, but stepped closer.

At that instant, a heavy clunk boomed from somewhere overhead, and the control panel near the entrance sparked with white-hot electricity. Simultaneously, the saw on the Exoskeleton screamed to life and lowered through the nub of arm bone sticking out of a steel cuff that might have fit tightly around the bicep had there still been flesh. Sylvia screamed, and Daniel thought he had as well, although it might have only happened in his mind.

McHenry went to the control box and flipped switches. The saw wailed for a full 30 seconds before Daniel spotted a red button on the wall across from the Exoskeleton and pushed it. The saw powered down and coasted to a halt.

"They must be powering up the main circuits," McHenry said, and seemed to smile in relief. "That'll wake you up."

Horace looked paler than usual, and Sylvia's eyes were still as wide as soccer balls.

"How many of these things are there?" Daniel asked.

"About 40 rooms just like this, with minor variations" McHenry replied. "Examine those on your own later. Now let's go to the library."

They weaved their way through the complex, which McHenry explained had six levels above the submarine bay, extending into the cliff overseeing the lake. Teams from the *North Dakota* were still exploring, looking for exits to the surface, among other things.

After about ten minutes of walking and climbing stairs, they entered the brightly lit library. It smelled like the musty stacks in the old CIA archive where Daniel had done his first Omni research. The room was clean and the books looked to be in good shape. There seemed to be no humidity, despite the lower level being a submarine bay, and bugs weren't a problem in Antarctica. So the books should have been well preserved, despite their age.

The large area rug that covered the rock floor was similar in design to the banner in the bay, although the colors had faded. Daniel had often wondered why the Nazis had gone to such great lengths to overplay symbolism: it must have taken a long time to weave a custom rug with the Red Falcon emblem in the center. They'd cut no corners. It was something that he found disturbing.

Over a dozen books were scattered about the table, many of which were open – some face down. He knew the bindings would be ruined after 70 years in such a state. It seemed like most were about ancient languages and semiology, written in a variety of modern languages. And he was sure that some would be considered rare, and quite valuable.

"Was this the way the table was when you found it?" Horace asked.

It was a good question. It would give them an idea of the last things the Nazis had been researching when they'd deserted the place – which seemed like it may have been in a hurry.

"We disturbed nothing," McHenry said.

On the wall at the end of the room, closest to the table, was a large map. Daniel stepped closer and saw it was a map of the local area, including the tunnel and the base, although the details of the latter were missing. Various points were labeled in German, a few of which were repeated, nearly equally spaced, along the tunnel.

"What are these?" Daniel asked, pointing to the repeated points.

Horace squinted and spoke. "*Atemzug*: it means *breath*," he said.

"My God, of course," McHenry said. "We found them on the way back through the tunnel during our first trip. They're ten-inch pipes with flanges on the ends."

"What are they for?" Sylvia asked.

"The U-boats needed air," McHenry explained. "They weren't as sophisticated as modern subs – no air scrubbers. And they had diesel engines which also needed oxygen."

"Interesting," Horace added, "It also gave them more protection. Any sub pursuing them into this place would have to turn around before they ran out of air. The German subs, knowing there were vents ahead, could keep going."

McHenry nodded. "We don't have such a protection – now everyone has subs that can stay submerged for months."

For a microsecond, Daniel thought he saw worry in McHenry's face. It made him feel like they needed to get moving.

He noticed something on the wall to the left and adjacent to the map. He recognized it from the pictures – it was the print of the disc. The writing was completely foreign to him. "Do we have access to the original?" he asked, pointing to the canvas.

"We put it back in the vault room, exactly where we'd found it," McHenry said. "Shall we go there?"

Daniel glanced to Horace and Sylvia. They both nodded, and they followed McHenry out of the library.

They walked for about five minutes. It was as if they were in the hall of a large office building, passing many doors on both sides. They turned a corner and McHenry stopped at one on the right.

"Here we go," McHenry said and led them in.

The first thing Daniel noticed was the blown vault door, and was concerned that the contents had been damaged.

McHenry seemed to read his expression. "We were careful to contain the blast," he explained. "If we'd had time, we might have done it another way. But, as you know, time is one thing we don't have."

McHenry opened a cabinet, revealing an object wrapped in cloth. He removed the cloth.

Daniel stepped closer. The stone was off-white with black, inset markings. It was unblemished in any way – no chips or scratches – and the script of the writing was flawless. "Same material as the beacon?"

McHenry shook his head. "Can't confirm. We tried to scrape a sample from the backside to send for analysis, but we couldn't get anything – even with a diamond scribe. In that sense, the two are similar."

McHenry replaced the cloth and closed the cabinet. "Now for the files," he said. "Follow me."

The group walked deeper into the vault. On the far wall was a bank of file drawers, floor to ceiling. McHenry grabbed a file from a small table next to the wall, and handed it to Daniel.

Daniel opened the folder and examined the papers. The first one was written on Red Falcon letterhead, and was in German. It was dated 1948 and signed – Josef Mengele. He wanted to read it immediately, but needed it to be translated. His attention was drawn back to the file drawers. "Which drawer did this one come from?" Daniel asked.

McHenry pointed to it and Daniel slid it open. The first thing that struck him was the depth of the drawer: it rolled out about six feet, and was packed solid with files. He extracted one at random and opened it. This one was also signed by Mengele, dated December 12th, 1949. "How can this be?" Daniel asked and handed it to Sylvia.

"There are a lot of other peculiar things in this place," McHenry explained, "but my feeling is that you were meant to spend most of your time in the rooms I've shown you."

"What other things?" Horace asked.

"This is a self-contained facility," McHenry said. "There are sleeping quarters, food preparation facilities, a power grid, running water, and a sewer system. And there's a lot we haven't gotten to yet."

"I'd be interested in anything you find in the living quarters," Daniel said. "If there are books, handwritten materials, or anything out of the ordinary."

McHenry nodded.

"I'd like to get started in the library," Daniel said.

"Okay," McHenry said. "Find your way?"

Daniel nodded. The best way to learn the layout was navigate it himself. Motivation stemming from the fear of getting lost would make him learn quickly.

~ 9 ~

Wednesday, 3 June (12:04 a.m. EST)

The information in the library was unlike anything Daniel seen before. Each book contained an insert that described its authenticity, including the date acquired and origin. Some had been collected before the war, but most were stolen from places the Nazis had conquered. Nazi SS teams had also obtained tomes from places like Israel, Egypt, the Middle East, and South America. It seemed that the Nazis' *Ahnenerbe* had collected much of the materials, and it suggested that Himmler's research institute might have been formed with the sole purpose of collecting information to assist with Red Falcon. It was yet another thread in the dark web of Red Falcon that had been concealed for nearly three quarters of a century.

The books filled 12 floor-to-ceiling bookcases, and fell into a few basic categories, the predominant one being ancient languages and symbols. The rest were a mishmash of occult, folklore, and ciphers and code breaking books. He estimated there were between 6,000 and 8,000 volumes in the library and realized his life was too short to read them all.

A much larger, multilingual team, with experts in ancient languages would have been needed for a thorough investigation. Horace and Sylvia had the same impression, and agreed that they should concentrate their efforts on the things on the table, which included 13 bound books, 21 notebooks, and over 30 file folders.

Although reluctant to disturb anything, they finally assembled around the large table and collected and organized the materials. Silvia started with the books, Horace the file folders, and Daniel the notebooks.

The heavy wooden chairs around the table had high backs, forcing them to sit erect. Very Nazi-like, Daniel thought.

He selected a notebook at random and was shocked by what he saw on the very first page. It was a hand sketch of the beacon, with squiggly lines around its bulbous head as if it were transmitting a signal. It must have just been a doodle, as the next pages were filled with symbols and translations, but it proved unequivocally that the people at the base had been aware of the beacon. This one had the name Handel Schluter written in the inside cover. Daniel didn't recognize the name. He put a sticky-note on the notebook, labeling it as "Number 1," and wrote a description of it in his own notebook. Later, he'd transfer his handwritten notes to his computer. Although each of them had some knowledge of German, Horace being the strongest in this regard, it was clear they'd need the translators.

The next notebook had belonged to Josef Mengele. His name was written in the inside cover and dated May 10th, 1946. If anything, the mystery of Mengele's disappearance after the war was partially solved. He'd been spotted in Argentina, and other South American countries, but South America had not been his only home.

Mengele's notes focused mostly on the torture facility. Prisoners restrained inside the cage-like devices had been told to do the impossible: push over an object out of their reach, or read something that was visually obstructed. Each time they failed, something awful would happen – they'd be burned, shocked, or a body part would be amputated. The cages – crude Exoskeletons – had built-in mechanisms that could be cranked with a wrench to break bones.

The worst thing Daniel ever imagined was described in Mengele's handwriting as his own invention. It was the device that had scared the hell out of them when the main power circuits had been energized. Mengele had called it the *Nascher,* the best English translation being "Nibbler." It was a cuff-like device that fit around a subject's appendage, with a circular blade that would pass flush against the opening of a steel cylinder, cutting off whatever protruded. After making a cut, a motor would slide the device up a preset amount and saw off another piece. The Nibbler would slowly eat its victim alive. The operator would simply set it up in the evening, starting at the tip of the fingers or toes and, when he'd come back in the morning, said appendage would be piled on the floor in neatly cut pieces. In order to stop the victim from bleeding to death, the device compressed the limb, acting like a tourniquet. They'd thought of everything. Daniel shuddered.

Subjects could turn off the Nibbler any time they wished. A large, red "stop button" was on the opposite wall, just 10 feet away. All they had to do was push it, as Daniel had done when the device powered up in the torture room. The problem was that the Nazis' subjects had to do it while confined to their Exoskeletons. The only way to stop the torture was to *separate*. Only the person's soul could turn off the horrific machine. According to Mengele, it had happened multiple times, but he'd never directly witnessed it. It had always occurred overnight, and was only repeated by one unnamed subject.

Mengele's frustration was apparent in his writing. He'd become so irate at one particular subject for not explaining how his device had been turned off that he'd gone into a rage and shot him multiple times, killing him.

The facility had been operated by a team of torture specialists. Mengele had mentioned the individuals by name in his notes, and they had their own notebooks – there were at least four others. He wondered if any of them were still alive.

Daniel looked away from his reading as one of the crew entered the library. "Captain wants you all to come in for the night," the man said.

Daniel looked at his watch and was surprised to see it was 1:15 a.m.

"He said you all should get some food and rest," the sailor added.

They'd taken a break for dinner around 6:00 p.m., but the time had flown by since then. Sylvia stretched her arms above her head and yawned. Horace looked exhausted and somewhat peaked.

"I'm ready for both," Sylvia said as she picked up a book with yellowing papers sticking out of it and stuck it under her arm.

Horace stood tucked a file folder under his own. He looked a bit better after he straightened himself to his full height.

They went to the *North Dakota's* mess hall. The odor of the sub's interior was more obvious after being outside for a while, but the smell of food masked it.

While they ate, they discussed what they'd learned from the day's work.

"The symbols written on the white stone are a set of instructions," Sylvia said. "The Nazis had decoded a part of it – but I've only located fragments and short phrases, all written in German. We need to bring a translator tomorrow."

"Were you able to read any of it?" Horace asked.

"The term 'drum' had been mentioned several times," Sylvia said. "But I don't understand the context."

"How were they able to decode it?" Daniel asked.

"Some of the symbols were a variation of Egyptian hieroglyphics," Sylvia explained. "But there were more hieroglyphs – entirely new or modified – than what were known at the time."

"Strange," Horace said. "If true, it means whoever translated it had more knowledge than they should have had at the time, or they'd simply made guesses."

"I doubt they guessed," Daniel said.

"What have you learned, Daniel?" Horace asked.

Daniel told them about what he'd found in the notebooks.

"It's consistent with what I've been reading," Horace said. "The files on the table were those of the most promising subjects – those who had demonstrated unusual behavior during their treatments. The Nazis had collected those files for some reason."

"A planned event?" Daniel speculated.

250

"Perhaps," Horace said. "But what?"

Daniel shook his head. "It seems they vacated on short notice."

They finished eating and then went to their respective quarters. Daniel wondered if he'd be able to sleep and, if he did, what nightmares would torment him through the night.

~ 10 ~
Wednesday, 3 June (1:42 a.m. CST – Baton Rouge)

Zhichao Cho set down the phone and walked out to the balcony of his apartment. His heart thumped a dull pain into his eyes and he took a drink of scotch. He pulled out a Cuban cigar, lit it, and then put it out. He had to be patient, but the hardest thing to do was wait – especially considering the prize that awaited him. At first, he hardly believed how easy it was. But then he realized that the man was seeking him as well. They were like two charges of opposite sign finding their way to each other. Thompson had already been on the Syncorp site.

Cho relit the cigar, took a drag, and blew it out through his teeth. He was going to collect the man he'd been ordered to obtain at "all costs," and, for the moment, also preserve Syncorp. Red Dragon would soon be operating at full-bore in the homeland.

Another shipment of Exoskeletons was on the water, so he'd only need to arrange two more. More importantly, they'd begun disassembling Syncorp's fabrication equipment. This included the specialized machining systems – computerized milling machines, lathes, and welders. Once it was all in China, his people could reverse engineer and then produce them, and Red Dragon would be completely independent. Better yet, the United States would have lost the technology, and would have to start over from scratch – if they could stomach it.

He shook his head and smiled as he thought about what was to transpire in the next 48 hours. Why were the Americans so easy to buy? The FBI agents on his payroll weren't rich, but they weren't poor either.

251

Why sell out for a couple of years of salary? They risked their freedom and, more shamefully, their honor. And for what? They weren't friends of China – they didn't even understand the country. In the end, if their own authorities didn't discover them first, their lives would end in shame and dishonor. And they'd deserve it.

The next couple of days would be pivotal. The trap was set.

CHAPTER XII

~ 1 ~

Wednesday, 3 June (6:40 a.m. EST – Antarctica)

Daniel followed Horace and Sylvia up to the library. Two sailors fluent in German were supposed to join them within the hour.

They continued with their individual tasks – Sylvia on the translation of the "White Stone," as it had been referred to in the documents, Horace on the files, and Daniel on the notebooks, although he'd passed two of them to Sylvia since they were notes on deciphering the stone.

Most of the notebook entries had been by Mengele. However, other handwriting appeared from time to time, mostly in German. An hour later, the translators arrived. They transcribed long passages very quickly, and he could tell that they were disturbed by what they read.

Mengele wrote numerous page-long diatribes about seemingly tangential topics. It was these streams of consciousness that Daniel thought had the highest potential of revealing the Nazis' objective. The idea that they'd been attempting to build an army of super soldiers, or spies, was now bunk. They'd had something else in mind from the beginning, but, up to this point, the truth had eluded him.

In one of Mengele's passages, he'd speculated about the possibility that a person's soul might not only leave the body, but also leave any physical structure that contained it – the Exoskeleton, the room, even the entire base. There was no reason to assume that it was physically confined. Mengele had suspected that, in the cases where the Nibbler device had been turned off, someone in an adjacent room could have done it.

The idea was not new: Daniel had read similar things in the Red Wraith files just weeks before. What did catch him off guard, however, was Mengele's final line: *If true, we are closer to our objective than we*

253

previously thought. But it was only a teaser. Mengele went on to describe how he had "interviewed" the prisoners in the adjacent cells, to see if they had carried out the deed of turning off the Nibbler. But Daniel thought it was unlikely; why would they save someone else before freeing themselves from the same?

At lunch, Daniel reported to the others what he'd learned, and Horace corroborated the information with what he'd gleaned from the victims' files.

Then it was Sylvia's turn. "As I said before, the message on the White Stone is a set of instructions. The Nazi researchers were able to make some guesses based on the work of François Champollion in the 1820's on interpreting hieroglyphics."

"So the code is broken?" Daniel asked.

"No," Sylvia replied. "Hieroglyphics are complex. The writing is figurative, symbolic, and phonetic all at once, and subject to interpretation. But the real problem is the unknown hieroglyphs – if that's what they are."

"How many are there?" Horace asked.

"Dozens," she replied. "One that I think is significant is the symbol the Nazis had interpreted as *drum* – since that word appears so often."

"By 'drum' they mean the beacon?" Daniel asked.

Sylvia nodded.

"Any indication as to why the Nazis were so obsessed with it?" Daniel asked. "Any hint of its purpose?"

Sylvia shrugged and shook her head.

"Anyone with the slightest inquisitive nature would be intrigued by the beacon," Horace said. "It's a mystery for many reasons. But the obsession goes beyond scientific curiosity. The Nazis *knew* something."

Daniel agreed. He had a once-in-a-lifetime mystery on his hands. Under normal circumstances, he'd savor the process. Not this time. Something was bearing down on him. The multinational military involvement that was forming in the waters near the beacon caused some anxiety, but it was more than that.

It was always in the back of his mind, what Horace had said when they'd first gathered in Room 713: *existential implications*. It occurred to him that Horace might know more than what he was sharing.

~ 2 ~

Wednesday, 3 June (5:44 p.m. CST – Chicago)

Denise tugged at her hair, strands of which tangled in the hinge of her glasses. Rain blew against her office window and it was as dark as midnight outside despite the early hour. Her search for the personnel and Syncorp satellite companies on the list Will had sent was fruitless after a couple of days of work. The home addresses given for the personnel either didn't exist, or led to commercial locations such as malls and movie theaters. The company profiles seemed to be legit, unless their covers were just well managed.

She walked into Jonathan's office. He was on the phone and motioned for her to have a seat.

She sat down and watched through the large windows as the rain tore through the trees in the courtyard below. Jonathan ended the conversation that, from what she'd overheard, had to do with data encryption and recovery.

"Any luck?" he asked as he walked over to her. By the look in his eye she could tell he already knew better.

She shook her head. "I can't verify anything, and I'm two-thirds through both lists."

"Nothing at all?"

She shook her head.

Jonathan's face became serious to the point where she thought he looked worried. "What's wrong?" she asked.

"Nothing," he said, and seemed to shake away his expression. "The companies – any of them close to us?"

"There's one here, in Chicago, and another in Waukesha, Wisconsin," Denise replied.

255

"What's the one in Chicago?"

"A biotech company – nutrition enhancements," she replied. "Not sure what that means."

"Sounds nondescript enough to fit the profile of a Syncorp affiliate," Jonathan said. "Make a visit and see what they're doing."

"Just walk in?" Denise asked.

"Be creative," Jonathan said, grinning. "You've done this before."

Denise recalled the time she'd conned her way into a forensic testing facility in southern Illinois while investigating Will's case. That adventure had ended with the facility in flames, a car chase and, most disturbingly, two dead people. Compared to that, she figured, this should be a piece of cake.

"I'll start planning," she said.

"Get it done tomorrow," Jonathan instructed. "We need to evaluate this information as soon as possible."

Denise again sensed something in Jonathan's voice. "Something wrong?"

"I hope not," he said.

She walked back to her office and pulled up the webpage for Nutrition Enhancements, Inc. Maybe they had some job openings.

~ 3 ~
Wednesday, 3 June (6:55 p.m. EST – Antarctica)

After dinner, Daniel and Sylvia went back to the library with the translators. Horace stayed on the *North Dakota* to rest.

Daniel continued his work on the notebooks. The more he read, the more he despised Mengele. He was supposed to be able to emotionally detach himself, but it was impossible. The man was a brutal sociopath who had been given the opportunity to exercise all of his heinous whims. It was a shame that the Israelis hadn't caught up with him.

He finished with Mengele's first notebook, which started in

December of 1943 and ended in November 1944. At the time, the Nazis had to know the war was lost, but there was no such indication in Mengele's notes, even in the streams of consciousness that were now beginning to read as the babblings of a madman. The second notebook logged events of the same nature as the first: gruesome, drawn-out torture treatments, strange observations construed as telekinetic events, and ideas for new horrific experiments.

After a few hours, the translators left for a break and, on Daniel's request, to check on Horace. He caught Sylvia's gaze.

"I want to go to the vault," she said. "I need to look at the disc."

"You find something?"

She shook her head. "There's a mark on the print that's too faint to read," she said. "I just want to verify it. That's all."

As they navigated through the hallways and staircases, the underlying darkness overshadowed the bright lights. Even the crew bustling about, working on things and taking pictures, didn't temper the feeling of being watched. It was nonsensical, but it was hard to separate the place from what had happened there. Were the tortured souls still running about? He brushed it off. He'd debunked quite a few ghost stories in his early years as an Omni.

He tried to imagine what it had been like for the prisoners that had been brought to the place. They'd been delivered by submarine to the bottom of the world to have the most horrible things happen to them. They were being brought to hell.

They went through a door, and Daniel led the way through the first room and into the vault. He opened a cabinet on the right, revealing the large object wrapped in a blanket.

Sylvia reached in and uncovered the stone. With her finger, careful not to touch the surface, she traced the circular pattern on the third ring in from the outside. She tilted her head and looked closely at a symbol. "The print missed a subtle feature," she said. "Good thing we came." She pulled out a small, digital camera from her pocket and took a few shots.

They rewrapped the disk and closed the cabinet doors.

Sylvia turned to go out, but Daniel's attention was drawn to the bank of file drawers that filled the entire wall opposite the vault door. There were 49 of them – an array of 7 by 7. He grabbed the handle of one near the center and rolled it out. It was about six feet long, and packed solid with files. He didn't even bother to pull out a file; they didn't have time to read anything more than what they had, and he didn't want to disturb the organization for those who would come later and research the place in detail. It would take years, and he only had days.

He closed the drawer and opened others, just to see if they all were packed just as densely. Opened, closed. Opened, closed. After about 20 repetitions, he opened one from the middle right of the array that he knew was mostly empty from the moment he pulled it. All it contained was a cubic metal box, about 10 inches on a side. He pulled it out – it wasn't very heavy – and walked it out of the vault and set it on a desk in the adjacent room.

"What is it?" she asked.

"It's locked," he replied. He examined it for a label but found nothing. "Damn," he said, looking at his watch. "I'll ask the captain to get one of his guys to open it. Let's get back to work."

She remained still, staring at the box.

"What?" he asked. He read fear in her expression.

"I don't know," she replied. Her eyes darted around, looking at the walls, and then the ceiling. She crossed her arms tightly into her midsection and bent over. She took her right palm and pressed it tightly against the center of her chest, near her sternum.

"You okay?" he asked, touching her shoulder with his right hand.

She flinched violently. She stood erect and backed out of the room and into the hall. Daniel followed.

"Sylvia, what's wrong?"

"Let's just go."

"Okay," he said, trying to keep up with her as she hurried down the corridor.

After a minute, she slowed but was breathing heavily. He didn't say anything, but just walked with her. By the time they got to the library she was back to normal

When they walked in, Horace was already back and working. "Exploring the area?" he asked.

"We went to the vault room," Daniel replied, and then told Horace about the locked box. He asked one of the translators to go ask McHenry to have it opened.

"What happened to you back there?" Daniel asked Sylvia, her face still pale.

"I don't know," she replied, shaking her head. "I was overcome with the need to run – to get the hell out of there. It was a dark feeling, Daniel, like fright and depression. My chest hurt, and I still feel like throwing up."

Daniel had felt something as well, but for him it wasn't as strong. Perhaps it was from knowing what had happened so many years ago – from the files it was clear that many hundreds people had been tortured to death.

When Sylvia seemed settled, they got back to work. Daniel continued reading Mengele's third notebook. Most of the pages were covered with dense writing mixed with hand-drawn sketches and graphs. He finished a page explaining a new torture method that would tap into the nerves of a subject's lower back. He flipped to the next page that, to his surprise, was mostly blank.

In the middle of the page dated June 2nd, 1945 was written a phrase that Daniel was able to translate himself: *Der Führer ist heute angekommen.* He got light-headed for few seconds, and rubbed his eyes. He took a deep breath and read it again, slowly. There was no other interpretation.

The Führer has arrived today.

~ 4 ~

Thursday, 4 June (1:38 p.m. CST – Chicago)

Denise walked into Jonathan's office with a cup of coffee and sat down at the large table.

Jonathan hung up his desk phone, and walked over. He gave her a strange look.

"What?" she asked, confused.

"What's that smell?"

"I smell?" she asked, sniffing her sleeve, and then her hair. "No wonder the people at Moose Beard Coffee were giving me odd looks."

"What is it?"

"Cheese," Denise replied. "The suspected evil Syncorp partner I visited makes concentrated cheese products. I now know more about cheese than I ever wanted to."

"A front for something else?"

"I don't think so," Denise replied. "I posed as a job candidate and the owner took me on a tour of the entire facility. No place to hide anything."

"I have people checking out a few other places. Now I want you to focus your efforts on finding the Syncorp personnel on the list," Jonathan said. "I have a fundraiser tonight. Let's meet after that, say ten?"

Such late meetings weren't unusual. Jonathan would often work past 2:00 a.m. But this time she saw something different in his eyes. He was worried about something.

"Ten o'clock it is," she said and went to her office. She went to work on Will's list of Syncorp employees and, after two hours, confirmed nothing – not a single name. *Something was wrong.*

~ 5 ~

Thursday, 4 June (8:41 p.m. EST – Antarctica)

Daniel ate dinner while Horace and Sylvia discussed the day's findings with Captain McHenry.

"Certainly you aren't suggesting that Hitler was alive at the time," McHenry said.

"After seeing this place, would that really be such a surprise?" Horace asked.

Daniel could tell by Horace's tone that he wasn't completely serious. McHenry seemed to catch on.

"I suppose not," McHenry replied, and chuckled. "Have you made headway on anything else?"

After they finished giving their updates, McHenry spoke. "Now I have an update for you. We've discovered a porthole to the surface. It was used by the Nazis to extend an antenna. If we hadn't discovered it, tomorrow we'd have to take the *North Dakota* out to the lake and extend an antenna of our own."

"I thought we weren't supposed to communicate," Daniel said.

"We're not supposed to transmit," McHenry corrected, "but we can receive." He paused a few seconds and continued. "We put an antenna up the hole and got a message from the carrier group. Chinese Special Forces have moved closer – they're within five miles."

"How do they know what they're looking for?" Daniel asked. "And where to look?"

"I don't think they know exactly where to look," McHenry said. "That's our advantage, and we'll keep radio silence as long as possible."

"How long do we have?" Sylvia asked.

"If they don't find us, then we have until we run out of food," McHenry answered. "In that case, we have about three months."

"What's realistic?" Daniel asked. "How long will it take them to find us?"

"Ten days, tops," McHenry replied. "That is, if the weather holds up. It's getting pretty ugly out there right now."

"And if they find us?" Sylvia asked.

"We'll need to use force to secure the base. The President will have to decide whether or not to risk war."

Daniel's feet tingled. Sleep was going to be impossible. The time pressure made the conditions unfavorable for undistracted thought. "Did you open the box?"

"I have someone working on it right now," McHenry replied. "It

261

will be straightforward – we'll just drill out the lock – once we've determined it's not booby trapped. Do you think it's important?"

"Important enough to put into the vault," Horace said.

McHenry nodded.

They finished eating and McHenry went to the bay to check the progress on the box. Daniel filled his coffee mug and stood at the end of the table. "I'm going back to the library," he said.

"I really need sleep," Sylvia said, "but I don't see any other way."

Horace agreed.

Daniel was impressed by the old man's resilience. "Horace, I've been meaning to ask you something."

"Go ahead."

"I had the impression when we'd first met that you had some insight regarding what is happening right now," Daniel said. "Do you?"

After a few seconds of still silence, seemingly mulling over in his mind how to respond, Horace nodded slowly. "I've had suspicions since the end of the war," he replied. "You see, I participated in Operation Tabarin."

Daniel was stunned. Horace was indeed ancient. "But that was a *British* mission."

"I have dual citizenship," Horace replied. "I was OSS and SAS and, later, MI-6 and CIA."

"How were you cleared to be an Omni?" Daniel asked, astonished.

"The ties between the US and UK run deeper than most people realize," Horace answered.

"What happened in Tabarin?" Sylvia asked. "What did you learn?"

"Nothing," Horace replied.

Daniel was confused. "You said all of this had *existential implications*. What did you mean?"

"I'd led a recon group to a location probably within 50 kilometers from here," Horace explained. "We were looking for a Nazi SS task force."

"Did you find them?" Sylvia asked.

"Yes," Horace said. "At first we thought they'd frozen to death –

262

but 12 soldiers don't just freeze to death all in the same place. We searched their site and found a note explaining that they had poisoned themselves – committed suicide."

"Why?" Daniel asked.

"They were frightened," Horace said. "The note explained that the Nazis had found a way to bring back Hitler, and that he'd possess powers beyond imagination. They were aware of what Hitler had done in the extermination camps. They felt that, if he did return, they'd be responsible. They thought that Hitler might be the devil himself."

"It's preposterous," Daniel said. "The SS wouldn't fall for such idiocy."

"I disagree," Horace said. "The SS was a strange organization, deeply rooted in the occult."

"What do you believe?" Sylvia asked Horace.

"When we returned from our mission with this information, we were quickly debriefed and ordered never to speak of it again," Horace explained. "Of course, we talked about it amongst ourselves. But it wasn't until 1960, when I met a former American submarine captain, drunk in a London pub, that I'd become suspicious to the point of paranoia. He was telling a story to some fellow drunks of how he'd been tasked with sinking a Nazi sub off the coast of Antarctica because it had been feared that Hitler was on the vessel. He'd said that that occurred in 1946, during Operation Highjump – the so-called American invasion of Antarctica."

"You believed him?" Sylvia asked, her face showing both surprise and skepticism.

"No," Horace said. "But I wish I had."

"Why?" she asked.

"Now I remember some details of that conversation," Horace replied. "He'd mentioned a secret tunnel, and an underwater object – a secret Nazi weapon. When I asked him questions, he clammed up. My impression at the time was that he was making up stories."

"Too many correct details," Daniel said. "Probably not a coincidence."

"What's happening now *does* have existential implications,"

Horace said. "I believe that."

"And now, with Mengele's notes about the Fürher arriving ... well, I suppose we have to consider every possibility," Daniel said in disbelief of his own words.

McHenry rushed in. "Come with me," he said, breathing heavily.

"What is it?" Daniel asked, his heart thumped hard in his chest. His first thoughts were that Chinese forces were knocking on their door.

McHenry waved for them to follow him. "We've opened the box."

~ 6 ~

Thursday, 4 June (9:12 p.m. EST)

Daniel followed McHenry down the roped-guided ramp from the *North Dakota* to the dock and onto the bay floor. Horace and Sylvia followed.

Four sailors stared at the box at their feet. A dusting of metal shavings glittered the floor beneath the lock, and the lid was open. Daniel stepped into the group and looked down.

Inside was a leather-jacketed ceramic canister with its lid held in place by four metal clips, like a candy jar. The sheath was fitted with rings through which leather straps were threaded to hold the canister in place. The inside of the box, including the lid, was padded and upholstered with a dark red fabric.

"What is it?" Daniel asked.

"No idea," McHenry replied. "We haven't touched it – only took pictures. It's not booby trapped." He pointed to a cardboard box of latex gloves.

Daniel grabbed the end of a glove and tugged until it came out of the box with a snap. Two gloves were stuck together so he peeled them apart, put them on, and squatted close to the box.

He struggled to release the brass clips that held the leather sheath in place. Even through the latex gloves he could tell that the burgundy padding was slippery like satin. It reminded him of the inside of a casket.

After releasing the four clips, the ceramic vessel was free. He slipped it out of its leather jacket, and examined it at arm's length. It was the size of a pickle jar, but heavier. He turned it slowly, but his attention was diverted to Sylvia, whose expression became distorted in what Daniel thought was fear – not unlike the expression he'd seen on her face while in the vault.

"Look!" she said in a hoarse voice. "Turn it around."

He turned the vessel and read the words etched on its bulbous midsection. It read: *Adolf Hitler, 20 April 1889 – 30 April 1945.* The vessel was an urn.

Daniel felt dirty – violated in some way. "This can't be true," he said, and looked to Sylvia and Horace for something to ease his agitation. They offered nothing.

"Why not?" McHenry asked, and glanced at Horace. "Look at this place. We're in a Nazi base in Antarctica. I'd think anything was possible. At least this confirms Hitler was dead when he arrived."

Daniel's mind bombarded him with a thousand thoughts at once. What was going on here? What was the point of bringing Hitler's burnt remains to the base?

Horace donned some latex gloves and took the urn. He rotated it slowly and then lifted it up to examine the bottom. His eyes widened. "My God," he said.

"What?" Daniel asked as he crouched to get a look underneath. He read it aloud, his words sounding like they came from someone else, "Vatican City, 8 May, 1945."

"Vatican City?" Sylvia said, her face more pale than before. "I thought the allies recovered his body in Berlin."

Daniel shook his head. "It was never confirmed," he said. "His body was burnt beyond recognition."

"But it makes sense," Horace said. "An ODESSA ratline ran through the Vatican, or so some speculate. This might be proof."

"I understand why the Nazis set up escape routes for living war criminals," Sylvia said. "But why would they go to such great lengths to smuggle a corpse out of the country?"

"The SS was an odd group, with a cult mentality," Horace said. "Who knows what strange rituals they had planned, or what mystical value they'd given to the remains of their leader."

Horace then gave Daniel and Sylvia a look indicating he was going to open it. "Shall we?" he asked as he set the urn on the floor and secured it between his feet. He disengaged the four wire clips that held the lid in place. A crust had formed between the urn and its lid, but he pried it open carefully.

The four of them, including McHenry peered down, between Horace's feet. The urn was about two-thirds filled with light gray ash and small pieces of bone. Horace replaced the lid, secured it with the clips, and set it back in the padded metal box.

No one spoke for a full minute.

"This is an interesting discovery," Daniel said, "but we better get back to the library and figure out what the hell was going on here, and why the rest of the world is trying to find this place."

McHenry snapped the leather holders in place, and closed the lid. "I'm taking this to the *North Dakota*, and I think we should start moving the other important artifacts there as well. We could get the order to evacuate at any time."

That McHenry was even mentioning evacuation made Daniel's heart race.

"Let's go," Daniel pleaded and got them heading to the library. "We no longer have time to go through this methodically. We should start from the end – the latest information – and work backwards."

"I've been doing that," Sylvia replied. "And I don't understand anything yet."

It seemed to Daniel that she was still shaken about something – ever since the incident in the vault. "It's okay. Keep going," Daniel said. "I'll start at the end of the last notebook. I probably should have been doing that from the start."

"That's not how you were trained," Horace interjected, out of breath and holding his chest as he walked. "Your skills weren't developed to deal with time pressure. They were meant for accuracy and revealing obscure connections. But you're right. We must deviate in this case."

They arrived at the library and went to work. They weren't letting up until the Chinese knocked on the door.

Daniel opened Mengele's final notebook, and went to the last page, dated August 22nd, 1958. It was the book that had been strangely truncated – incomplete. Something clicked in his head, and he turned to Sylvia. "When were operations Argus and Blackfish carried out?" he asked.

Sylvia looked up and pulled off her glasses. "The first detonations were at the end of August, 1958 – the 27th I believe. The last was September 6th."

Was it a coincidence that the Mengele's last entry and the nuclear explosions were so close – both in time and location?

He paged backwards, ignoring Mengele's calculations, and reading only his maniac diatribes. Mengele never ranted about the progress of the war, and hardly mentioned it even as Germany surrendered. It was as if the war didn't matter, other than to set the stage for the Antarctic base and its unknown objective.

Daniel stood and stretched. He walked back to the stacks in the rear of the library and paced as he gathered his thoughts. Mengele was excited that his Führer was arriving because he thought he was on the verge of a breakthrough. His Führer, however, was in a compromised state – being in the form ashes at the time. Why would Mengele be so excited about that? He returned to the table and, after another hour of reading, he finally found the answer in a long dialog.

They thought Hitler's soul would follow his ashes. It wasn't the primary objective of the base, but the Nazis thought that if they could get the soul of one of the torture subjects to leave his or her body, Hitler's soul could enter it and take over. Live again.

When the war had turned against Germany, the Nazis devised a plan. If Hitler were in danger of being captured, he was to commit suicide. His body was to be cremated and he – meaning his soul – was to follow his ashes wherever they went. They'd smuggle them to the base and put them in a room with a separated subject, giving Hitler's soul the opportunity to occupy the subject's body. Once he'd successfully taken over, he was supposed to utter a specific phrase to confirm that it was really him: *Der Tod ist der Hirte der Menschheit.*

Daniel shuddered. *Death is the shepherd of mankind.*

~ 7 ~

Thursday, 4 June (9:31 p.m. CST – Chicago)

Denise ate dinner in her apartment and returned to campus at ten minutes to ten. She'd been able to verify nothing on the lists of names or companies that Will had given her. The names were all of a common sort; every search had given results in multiple states, and none matched the associated addresses. This was in stark difference to the information he'd collected from the CP men – all of that was legit.

The companies on Adler's list were all real, but similar in size to the company she'd visited that morning. Jonathan had arranged to have a few of the companies inspected by his contacts in other cities, and she was eager to hear the results.

She logged into the email account she shared with Will to see if he'd made an update. There was a new one in the draft folder, and she opened it. The message was short: "Getting the hard drives. Give you an update tomorrow."

Denise read it again. What did it mean? Was he doing something tonight – at Syncorp? Was he crazy?

The clanging of keys from the hallway broke her from her thoughts. She jumped up and met Jonathan before he could unlock the door to his office. She waved him into hers.

She pointed to the screen as he walked in.

He pulled a set of half-rimmed glasses from his front pocket and leaned in close. After a few seconds, he leaned back, shaking his head. "This is bad," he said.

268

"What do you mean?"

"Were you able to corroborate anything on those lists?"

Denise shook her head.

"I had people in Milwaukee and Detroit visit some of the companies," he explained. "None are Syncorp-related."

"Will recovered bogus intelligence," she concluded.

"Someone must've known what he was doing," he said.

"So what's happening now?" she asked, nodding to the message on the computer screen. She knew what he was going to say.

"He's getting set up is what's happening."

She felt light-headed and sat in a wooden chair next to her desk.

"You okay?" he asked.

"What are we going to do?" she asked.

"Call him."

She grabbed her phone and placed the call. "It went directly to voicemail," she said.

"Could he have his phone turned off?"

"Never happened before."

"We can't call the police or the FBI – we might get him killed," Jonathan explained. "But the Foundation has friends in New Orleans. I can send them up to Baton Rouge."

"What will they be able to do?"

"Not much, I'm afraid," Jonathan replied. "There's no time. You need to send him another email – immediately – in the off chance he reads it before he sets out on his operation."

Denise switched chairs and wrote a quick message: *You're being set up! Call me!* She saved it in the drafts folder and then prayed that he got it before it was too late.

~ 8 ~

Thursday, 4 June (10:57 p.m. EST – Antarctica)

"That the Nazis tried to reincarnate Hitler is mindboggling," Daniel said, mostly to break the silence. He'd been pacing in the stacks again. He took his seat at the table. "And if that wasn't their main objective, what in the hell was?"

"I've found more pieces of the Nazi translations," Sylvia said. "It's clear they thought the beacon had some special function, and the White Stone gave instructions on how to access that functionality."

"The instructions included torture?" Daniel asked with skepticism.

"Not exactly," Sylvia explained. "Each concentric circle is encrypted differently, and each requires different knowledge or techniques in order to decipher it. The outermost ring was the easiest: it was coded in known languages of the time. It revealed the location of the beacon."

"They got the location from hieroglyphics?" Daniel asked.

"Not all of the symbols are hieroglyphics – it's more complicated than that." Sylvia explained. "The translation gives the angles for longitude and latitude in units of radians, rather than degrees. Zero latitude starts at the equator, as usual, but the prime meridian – zero longitude – goes through Giza, Egypt."

"What's special about Giza?" Horace asked.

"It's where the White Stone had been discovered in January of 1932," Sylvia explained. "The Germans stole it six months later."

"Hitler's rise to power came soon thereafter," Daniel added.

"What about the second ring?" Horace asked.

Sylvia paged through her notes and selected a page. "The most comprehensible translation I've found is 'The one who harnesses the power of the drum must suffer in body and mind.'"

"They interpreted that as an instruction to torture people?" Daniel asked in a tone of contempt.

Sylvia shrugged. "An alternate interpretation replaces the words *suffer in* with *transcend.*"

"Transcend body and mind," Daniel said. "Sounds too general to get any definitive meaning."

"Perhaps that's why they went with the first one," Horace said.

"Fragments of the third ring translations were in another

notebook," Sylvia said. "The handwriting is different for each – it seems that different people were assigned to each ring."

"And?" Horace said.

"It reads, 'Pass through the barrier and displace to transcend this world.' The word 'displace' can be replaced with 'turn.'"

"First transcend body and mind, and now the world. Makes no sense," Daniel said. "What about the fourth and fifth rings?"

"Nothing yet," Sylvia answered. "But there's something disturbing about the dates the first two rings had been interpreted."

"After the war," Horace said.

"No," Sylvia replied. "Both were deciphered *before* the war – between 1935 and 1937."

Daniel's brain went into overdrive and quickly formulated implications. It conjured up something he and Sylvia had conjectured while they were in DC. "This – the beacon, Red Falcon – was the *reason* for World War Two," he said, staring blankly at the map on the wall.

"It's possible," Sylvia said.

"So the location of the beacon was known sometime before 1937," Horace said, "and the Nazis sent the *Schwabenland* out to explore the area in 1938."

"Yes," Sylvia replied. "At about the time they'd deciphered the second and third rings."

"Hitler thought they were on the verge of discovering the beacon and started the war earlier than planned," Daniel suggested.

"Speculation," Horace said.

"What's the stone telling us to do?" Sylvia asked.

"The first ring provides the location of the beacon," Horace replied. "Perhaps the second tells us how to *access* it, and the third how to *activate* it."

Something tripped in Daniel's mind. "Yes," he said quietly. Then louder, "yes."

"What?" Sylvia asked.

"The beacon is made from an indestructible – impenetrable – material," he vocalized his brainstorm. "It maybe even survived a nuclear

271

blast during Operation Blackfish."

The others remained silent.

"Red Falcon and Red Wraith were designed to produce someone who could separate soul from body," Daniel continued. He stood up and walked to the map. "None of it had to do with creating super-soldiers or spies. It had to do with this!" he exclaimed and hit his fist on the map where the beacon was marked. "The only way inside the beacon is for a human to separate soul from body and pass through it. They wanted to get *inside* it."

Silence.

Sylvia pushed her chair back and stood. "Why?"

"They though it had some sort of power. They wanted transcend this world, or whatever the third ring told us," Daniel replied.

"Control this world," Horace said. "Hitler wanted to rule the world."

"But there's nothing specific in these translations," Sylvia said. "It was a gamble – one the Nazis lost."

"Because they couldn't get someone to separate," Daniel said. "But *we* were able to get someone to separate. They did it in Red Wraith."

Horace nodded. "And that's why the whole world is looking for William Thompson."

"We have to find him," Daniel said. "Before someone else does."

"Don't you think you're overreacting?" Sylvia asked. "The idea that he can separate is just rumor – there's hardly any more evidence that he has this ability than there was for the Nazi victims' alleged abilities."

"There's a lot of circumstantial evidence here," Horace argued, patting the pile of files in front of him. "Strange thing is that I don't think they were embellished. They'd isolated three hopefuls during the time between 1946 and 1958, two men and a woman. They'd wasted the first one – tortured him to death with Hitler's ashes, hoping to reincarnate him. But they had two more at the end."

"What happened to them?" Daniel asked.

"Unknown," Horace replied, "other than that they were to be taken away by submarine. That was near the end of it all – near the date of the final entry in Mengele's last notebook."

"They were taking them to the beacon," Daniel concluded. "The final date in Mengele's notebook was 21 August 1958, about the time Operation Blackfish was executed. They must have nuked the area – and maybe the beacon – to stop them."

"We need to get Thompson," Horace said.

After a full minute, Sylvia broke the silence. "We need to talk to Captain McHenry. We have to tell Thackett to collect Thompson," she said.

Daniel nodded. "I'm going now," he said, heading for the door. As he exited, his gait accelerated into a jog, and then to a run. He weaved his way down the corridors and around Navy personnel. He just hoped they weren't too late.

~ 9 ~

Thursday, 4 June (10:22 p.m. CST – Baton Rouge)

"It'll be a bit a little tight in there," Adler said as he pointed with a fat finger to the black bag Will carried in his left hand. "What's that?"

"Tools," Will replied. "To extract the storage devices." He turned to Natalie Tate. "You'll get a text if I sense trouble."

Will made sure the ringer on his phone was turned off and crawled into the trunk of Adler's BMW 5-series sedan. Adler closed it gently and everything went black. The car rocked as the heavy man got into the driver's seat and slammed the door.

Will wondered if Syncorp had increased its security in response to the hit on the CP inmates. He was sure the company was behind the massacre, so they must've known about the gang's plans. According to Adler, outside visitors were no longer allowed on the Syncorp campus, hence the ride in the trunk. He found it odd that they didn't check the trunks of cars as they went in and out.

The car's frame creaked as it went over the speed bumps in the road that ran through Adler's closed-gate subdivision. A half-minute later, he bounced as the tires rumbled over the guide track of the security gate. He sensed the right turn onto Kenilworth Parkway. Kenilworth led to Perkins Road, where they took another right.

It was a good thing the trunk was empty: he'd felt every bump along the way, part of which was through unfinished road construction. He followed the bends in the road, and knew they'd arrived at the Syncorp entrance when the car slowed to a gentle halt at the gate. There was a muffled exchange with guard and then the car moved forward onto the facility grounds.

After less than a minute, they slowed and took a sharp left. A metallic clanking sound along with a jolting bump on the front end, followed by the same on the rear, indicated that they had passed over a gate rail and into the parking facility. The echoes of their squeaking tires inside the building confirmed it.

After a few turns, they made a sharp left and stopped. The pitch of the engine elevated as Adler shifted it into park. A second later, all was silent, except for the ticking of the cooling engine and exhaust pipes.

Will breathed heavily and a bead of sweat trickled into his ear. He hadn't realized how the anxiety had sneaked up on him – he wanted to get the operation moving.

All was quiet for over two minutes. Was there was a problem? Maybe someone was nearby, and Adler was waiting for them to leave. Another half-minute passed before the driver's door opened, and the car shifted upward with the reduced weight. The door slammed closed.

The echoes from Adler's heels seem to come from all directions as he walked from the side of the car to its rear. Will sensed him standing next to the trunk. What was he waiting for?

A few seconds later, the clacks of shoes echoed from a distance, and got louder. There were at least two other people out there, maybe more. Will's heart thumped hard. He was tempted to separate and survey the situation, but decided against it. The footfalls came to a halt at the trunk. He pulled out his phone, the bright screen illuminating the entire trunk. He sent a short text to Natalie: *Trouble*.

An instant later, the trunk flew open and Will squinted into bright lights. He held his hand up to shield his eyes, but there were two or three sources, all at different angles so he couldn't get a look at anyone. A thick hand grabbed his upper arm and yanked him out of the trunk. In the next instant he was face to face with a man that seemed to be more gorilla than human. It was a face he recognized from the Red Box. The top of his right, pig-like ear had a flesh-colored Band-Aid on it.

The man stepped back and pointed a gun at his chest.

"How's that leg doing?" a man asked from behind Will and to the left.

He recognized the voice, and turned to verify it. It was the man he'd met during his FBI training.

"Roy," Will said. "Glad you're here to help us bring this place down."

Roy smiled and shrugged. "Sorry."

Will turned to the others. The first face he crossed was Adler's. He looked into his eyes to see what was there: no fear, but smugness. *Adler set him up.*

Next there was a greasy-haired Chinese man in a suit who he did not recognize and, finally, a woman who kept a light on his face. He put up his hand to shield his eyes and got a glimpse of her. It was Natalie Tate.

Natalie reached into her pocket and pulled out a vibrating phone. She smirked and showed Will the text he'd just messaged.

Will shook his head. "I guess I now know what happened to Jennings," he said.

Natalie glanced at Cho and looked down.

The Chinese man spoke with a subtle accent. "I am Cho, the new CEO of Syncorp. I am glad you came, Mr. Thompson. We are in need of your services." The man was a few inches shorter than Will, maybe 5' 7", with black hair that was slicked back with some kind of gel. His brown teeth dimmed his wide smile.

"That's Dr. Thompson to you," Will said, "and my services are not available."

Cho continued, "It's a good thing we vet our employees

275

thoroughly," he said, nodding towards Adler. "Came to us right away when Jennings contacted him."

Adler looked at Will and smirked. "Idiot."

Will took a step towards Adler, who immediately retreated.

Roy stepped in, obstructing any further advance. "Let's not get out of control here."

"Lenny," Cho said and nodded to the gorilla man.

Lenny nodded and walked to the tailgate of a box truck parked next to Adler's beamer. He shoved the rear door upward on its tracks, and then reached inside and pulled out a four-foot-long roll of plastic sheet and dropped it onto the painted concrete floor, near a drain. He put on a pair of latex gloves, rolled out the plastic sheet and cut it with a utility knife, and then motioned for Adler to help him unfold it. When they'd finished, the plastic spanned an 8 x 12 foot area with the center of one edge near the drain.

Will knew what was going on – he spotted the saw in the back of the truck. They were going to kill him and then dismember his body. He was going to have to separate while standing – his body was going to take a fall. He'd take out the gorilla first, and then Roy. He'd have to improvise with Cho and Natalie. He'd save Adler for last.

Lenny pulled a handgun out of his coat and threaded a silencer on its barrel. He then turned and shot Adler in the middle of the forehead. Adler remained wide-eyed and standing. Lenny pushed him on the shoulder, and Adler tipped like a tall tree and landed squarely in the center of the sheet. Lenny stood over Adler's twitching body and delivered two more bullets to his head. The shots were silenced, but still loud.

The thug put the gun back in his jacket, jumped into the back of the truck, and pulled out a wet-dry vacuum cleaner and set it next to the plastic sheet, which was already pooling with blood. He ran an extension cord from an outlet in the back of the truck to the murder scene, and then returned for an electric knife and a small handsaw. When he came back, he set down the tools and started undressing Adler's corpse.

"Now," Cho said, "while my specialist prepares Mr. Adler's corpse to be dissolved in acid, let's talk business."

"Not interested," Will replied. He was going to take them all out.

"I'm afraid you don't have much of a choice," Cho replied.

Will nodded toward mess. "If you think that can sway me, you're mistaken."

"We're not going to threaten you, Mr. Thompson – not yet," Cho explained with a haughty expression. "You're much too valuable to us alive. We expect you to cooperate for other reasons."

"I don't think so."

"Perhaps you'll cooperate to save your friends," Cho said, smirking now.

"What friends?"

"Denise Walker and Jonathan McDougal, of course," Cho replied. "Two of my operatives are tailing them right now."

Will looked over to Roy.

Roy confirmed Cho's statement with a nod.

Jonathan and Denise were careful and resourceful, but he didn't know how they'd fare against professionals set on assassinating them.

Maybe it was best to let it play out for a while. He had Cho in his sights: the CEO of Syncorp was a primary target. But maybe there were people above him – maybe he'd have a chance to get everyone at once.

~ 10 ~
Thursday, 4 June (11:28 p.m. EST – Antarctica)

As Daniel ran through the bay towards the *North Dakota*, he thought about his two lawyer friends in Chicago. If foreign governments already knew what Daniel and his cohorts had just figured out, then Jonathan and Denise were in great danger, as was William Thompson.

He slowed as he went over the ramp from the slip to the deck of the sub, and then increased pace again until he got to the hatch. He climbed down and weaved his way through the narrow corridors and around crewmembers who flattened themselves against the walls when they saw him coming. He spotted Lieutenant Diggs, and asked for Captain McHenry.

Diggs informed him that McHenry had gone to rest in his quarters.

Daniel insisted he bring him to the Captain.

A minute later, Diggs knocked on McHenry's door.

There was rustling behind the door – as if the Captain was getting dressed – and grumbling.

Diggs looked to Daniel. "I hope this is important."

Daniel nodded.

The door opened a crack, and McHenry poked out his head and squinted through reddened eyes. "What's going on, Parsons?" he asked, his expression changing from annoyed to concerned.

"Can we talk in the planning room – soon?" Daniel asked.

McHenry nodded. "Be there in 10 minutes," he said and closed the door.

Daniel headed to the mess to get coffee and something to eat. He was sitting at a table organizing his thoughts when Sylvia and Horace joined him.

"Five minutes in the ready room," Daniel said and took a bite of scrambled eggs. "You guys should eat something."

Horace nodded and left to get something, but Sylvia stayed.

"Do you think you might be moving too quickly on this?" she asked.

The thought had already gone through his mind a dozen times. "I could be wrong," he admitted. "But if I'm right, this is a race. And if we don't move now, we lose. And if we lose … well, I don't know." *Existential implications.* "What do we lose if I am wrong?"

Sylvia shrugged. "Credibility?"

Horace returned with juice and two nutrition bars. He gave one to Sylvia.

Daniel led the way to the ready room. Diggs was already there. A minute later, McHenry entered and closed the door, and they all sat around the small table.

"What's going on?" McHenry asked.

Horace and Sylvia looked to Daniel to start the conversation.

"We think we may know what's going on here," Daniel started.

"The purpose of the base?" McHenry asked.

"Yes, and the purpose of the research – the *real* purpose of Red Falcon," Daniel said, his words picking up speed as he spoke.

"Let's hear it," McHenry said.

"This base was built to torture people until they acquired the ability to separate their souls from their bodies," Daniel said, just spilling it. He knew McHenry was well aware that something heinous was going on, but from his expression, he knew it caught him off guard.

"It was also the purpose of the American Red Wraith project," Horace added. "You know, the Compressed Punishment program that had recently been exposed."

McHenry shook his head but remained silent.

"This was no great surprise to us," Daniel said. "We knew all of that before we got here."

"Why separate the soul from the body?" Diggs asked.

"Separation is a unique state of existence," Daniel explained. "In this state, the soul can interact with the physical world in peculiar ways."

"To what purpose?" McHenry asked.

"We originally thought they'd been trying to create super-soldiers or super-spies," Daniel explained. "You see, the physical interaction is expected to be quite powerful. Also, the soul can presumably pass through walls undetected. You can see the utility in this ability for a spy."

McHenry nodded. "Of course. But why expend such resources on the very slim chance that this was even possible?"

"Because it had nothing to do with spies," Daniel answered. "The Americans never figured that out."

"Then what?" McHenry asked.

"The White Stone gave instructions on how to find, enter, and activate the beacon," Sylvia said.

"Enter?" McHenry asked.

"Yes," Daniel replied. "But, the problem is that the beacon is made from an impenetrable material – there's no known way inside. No *conventional* way."

McHenry's eyes widened and he nodded. "But a separated soul could get in."

"Precisely," Horace said.

"We know that the Red Wraith project produced one subject who had supposedly acquired the ability to separate," Daniel explained. "The Chinese are currently pursuing him, and they're looking in the right places. Finding the base is one important objective for them; they probably want the White Stone and any other useful information. But they know enough already to be on the continent looking for the base, and are in the Antarctic seas positioning themselves near the beacon. They know what we know – probably more."

"What do you want me to do?" McHenry asked.

"We need to get a message back to the CIA – to our director," Horace said. "He must find this man before the Chinese collect him."

"Or before the Russians do," Daniel added. "We need him in protective custody. If the Chinese get him first, they'll bring him to the beacon."

McHenry shook his head in what seemed to be both skepticism and confusion. "What is the threat? So far, the thing has only made noise."

"It's alien to our current technology," Horace said. "Who knows what it was meant to do."

McHenry sighed, closed his eyes, and nodded reluctantly. "If you're telling me it's imperative that we get this message out, then I will arrange it. But it will mean that we have to pack up and leave. Sending a message from here will reveal the base."

"We can take everything we need," Daniel said. "We'll take the White Stone, all of the important books and files."

"I'll arrange it," McHenry said. "I want the three of you supervising – make sure we take everything that's even remotely important."

McHenry turned to Diggs. "Organize two groups, one for the library, and one for the vault. We need to pack and move everything we can fit onboard."

McHenry looked back to Daniel. "I hope you're right."
Daniel nodded. "Me too."

~ 11 ~
Thursday, 4 June (10:40 p.m. CST – Baton Rouge)

Will watched in disgust as Lenny grabbed the ankles of Adler's naked corpse and turned it so that it lined up with the creases in the plastic sheet. The blood that had pooled behind Adler's head smeared into a wide half-circle, and was already starting to coagulate.

Although the man deserved what he got, Will would've stopped the assassination if he could have. But there was no way – there had been no warning. He wondered whether the same could have happened to him. He recalled when he'd been shot at during his last conscious moments inside the Red Box. The moment the man pulled the trigger it was as if time had stopped. The bullet, although on target, hadn't gotten to him. And the shooter had been eliminated. But now, even with confidence in his own safety, his nerves tingled. He was aware of every movement.

With Lenny cutting away in the background, Cho explained his take on Will's situation. "As you can see, you have little choice," Cho said. "One of your investigator friends is in danger at this very moment. It only takes one phone call from me and she will be killed."

Will thought about killing the man on the spot – all of them at that very instant. There would be no phone call.

He found it was strange how the same people kept showing up – particularly Roy. He'd had a strange feeling about the man when they'd met in Chicago. And he recognized Lenny from the Red Box. How could that animal still be loose? McDougal had shot the thug in a skirmish months ago, and he was supposed to be in police custody. How had he escaped? Maybe it would be best to kill Lenny right now, he thought. Eliminate a killer from the world and cause a diversion at the same time.

"Don't get any ideas," Cho warned.

It was as if Cho had read his mind.

"My people are on kill orders," Cho explained. "If they don't get a call from me, they carry them out within 24 hours. I have to reset it every day. In fact, it's time right now."

Cho pulled out his phone and pushed a button, and the ringing on the other side was loud enough to hear from a distance. After two rings, someone picked up and grunted something he didn't understand. Cho said something in Chinese, they went back and forth a few times, and Cho ended the call.

"Your lady-friend is working late in her office," Cho said. "She'll be safe for 24 hours."

Cho was an idiot. Will could kill him in an instant, scramble his brains like eggs in a blender. Twenty-four hours was more than enough time to kill them all, get to Chicago, and warn Denise and Jonathan.

He was tempted, but then they'd be right back where they started, no closer to exterminating Syncorp and the Red Wraith project. They'd just scurry away like cockroaches and set up camp somewhere else. Then he'd have to find them again, and more people would die in the meantime.

He glanced over to Lenny, who had removed Adler's right arm and slapped it down on a clean part of the plastic sheet. It sounded like a butcher dropping a slab of meat onto a piece of wax paper. The man *was* a butcher, Will thought. Killing him again entered his thoughts, but he figured Syncorp had 100 more just like him operating around the world. They'd just replace Lenny with someone else.

The echoes of clacking heels turned Will's attention to two men descending the ramp that led to the next floor of the parking facility. They were Cho's men – Asians with slicked back hair and wearing dark suits.

"These men will escort you to your transportation," Cho said.

One of the men opened his coat, revealing a gun.

Will held back a smile. It was a reaction he thought to be strange, although he understood why he had it. He had no fear of these people.

"I regret that I must leave you now. I have other business to attend to. But you'll see me again soon," Cho said with a smug grin and then nodded to the men.

They grabbed Will's arms and led him up the ramp to the third floor of the parking garage, and then up a dim stairwell and onto the roof. His eyes adjusted to the darkness, and the silhouette of a helicopter came into view against the lights of the city.

In front of chopper was the shadow of man with the glowing tip of a burning cigarette near his face. The cigarette brightened for a second, and then arced into the air and landed on the roof in a hail of sparks. The man climbed into the pilot's seat and said something to the co-pilot as he slammed the door. The engine started a moment later.

The man on Will's right trained his gun on him while the other retrieved a pair of handcuffs from his coat pocket. The man with the gun prodded Will to turn around as the second pulled his arms behind his back and ratcheted the cuffs around his wrists. It wasn't going to be a comfortable flight. They led him into the passenger cabin, closed the doors, and strapped him in. One man sat directly across from him and the other on his right.

The memory of the last time he rode in a helicopter came to mind. He'd been in handcuffs that time as well, but it had been so cold that he'd thought he was going to die. It was the trip from Marion prison in Illinois to the Red Box in Detroit. It was late December. He still didn't know how he'd survived the ordeal, from that first freezing helicopter trip to the final explosion nearly forty days later that ended the Red Box.

The helicopter engines revved, and the craft lifted from the roof of the parking garage and headed northeast. They approached downtown Baton Rouge, and passed over the capitol building. Ten minutes later they landed next to a hangar at the Baton Rouge airport. The men led him out to the tarmac where they stood while one of them went inside the hangar.

A minute later, the hangar's large, sliding doors squealed opened and the man emerged. Three new Asian men followed him and met up with the group. There was a short conversation, and then two men grabbed Will by his cuffed arms and led him into the hangar, where others were loading supplies onto a small jet. They dragged him up a ramp and into a lush passenger cabin, furnished like an airport lounge with leather seating and low tables. They directed him to a seat and then occupied the seats around him. His escort detail had grown from 2 to 7.

Fifteen minutes later they were in the air and heading south.

CHAPTER XIII

~ 1~

Tuesday, 9 June (7:51 a.m. EST – Mar del Plata, Argentina)

Will's captors fed him on the second leg of the trip, from Houston to Guatemala, and he'd slept most of the way from Guatemala City to Buenos Aires. From there it was a four hour ride in the trunk of a car to the port city of Mar del Plata, where they'd kept him in a safe house for two days. During that time he'd seen at least 20 people pass through; it seemed that Chinese intelligence was extremely active in the area. The next leg of the trip was a long, chilly ride in a motorboat to a Chinese frigate.

His nerves were set on edge once the ship set out to sea and land was out of sight. He'd never liked the idea of being at the mercy of a boat. It was odd since he'd never feared flying, where a minor mechanical failure could be catastrophic. At least a boat would still float if the motor died. The constant rolling of the frigate caused him no seasickness – the Red Box had prepared him for such conditions. His land-legged escorts, however, were as green as avocados within hours.

Although the sun was low in the sky during the short daylight hours, he could tell they were heading generally south. It was clear he wasn't being taken to China.

His captors took off his handcuffs, and he was free to move about. It didn't matter – he wasn't going anywhere. Anyone who set foot onto the deck was immediately soaked with a freezing ocean spray. Ice had formed on every external surface, making it treacherous as well.

It had occurred to him that he might have made a critical mistake. He'd gambled that they'd bring him right to the heart of Red Wraith – to the *people*. If he got the opportunity to chop the head off the beast, he'd do so without hesitation. But he needed to keep his confidence in check. He wasn't invincible. He had to keep his body healthy. That's why being on the ship made him nervous. If something happened to the ship, or if he were thrown overboard, there would be nothing he could do. His body would die.

He didn't fear pain or death, but he was mortified by the idea of consciousness without influence. He'd seen the soul of a dead man once – a Red Box inmate who'd died a few rooms over. Will had separated and witnessed the hideous thing search about and flail in rage. That wraith had gone away – Will didn't know to where – but he was sure that souls hung around after their bodies died.

After many hours on the water, he stood and stretched his legs. He looked through a forward-facing window and saw their destination. The silhouette of an aircraft carrier loomed on the southeastern horizon. It was like a hazy, gray mountain that blended with the sea and overcast sky. He shuddered. Did they have a torture facility on the ship? He knew that the Chinese navy only had a few carriers, most of which were retired vessels from other countries. Devoting one of them to such a venture was a significant commitment.

As they got closer, a helicopter lifted from the deck of the carrier and headed their way. His captors then marched him through the cold wind on the frigate's deck and loaded him into a large metal container. Two of the guards joined him.

As the door slammed shut, the helicopter approached and a loud metallic clank indicated that something latched onto the roof. The men sat down on the floor and directed Will to do the same. The box creaked and swayed as it was hoisted from the surface of the frigate, and wind noise picked up quickly. A few minutes later they landed heavily and someone climbed on to the roof of the box and released the latch. The sound of the helicopter faded.

The door opened and Will was face-to-face with one of the Chinese crew. Six others stood behind him. They took him into the bowels of the ship and delivered him to a large room. Chinese military personnel, and a few others in plain clothes whose faces he couldn't see, surrounded a rectangular table.

Cho was at the head of the table. "Welcome, Mr. Thompson," he said. "I hope you had a comfortable journey. I'm sorry I couldn't join you.

I was busy getting a crash course from our intelligence service on recent events."

Will didn't respond.

"I suppose you are wondering why you are here," Cho said.

"He already knows," a man said. The man had his back to him.

"Where are we, Roy?" Will asked, recognizing the voice.

"The Southern Sea, just off the coast of western Antarctica," Roy replied, and swiveled his chair to face him.

"Please, sit down," Cho said and pointed to a chair.

Will sat directly opposite Cho. Roy and his FBI accomplice, Natalie Tate, were to Cho's left. The others, including two Asian women, filled the rest of the seats for a total of eight in addition to Will.

"Let's hear it," Will said. "You've taken some risks – especially you, Roy. They paying you well?"

Roy's face flushed.

"Mr. Thompson," Cho broke in, "this transcends espionage and geopolitical skirmishing."

"This should be good," Will huffed. He wondered what kind of bullshit the man was going to feed him.

Cho started by describing a mysterious object protruding from the seafloor.

~ 2 ~

Tuesday, 9 June (8:12 a.m. EST – Weddell Sea, Antarctic Circle)

Daniel sat alone at a table in the mess hall of the USS *Stennis*. The comforting aromas of bacon and maple syrup filled the air. He sipped orange juice as he thought about their abrupt departure from the base. He worried that they'd overlooked something – he didn't want to leave anything that might be of use to the Chinese.

Captain McHenry had explained there were no unnatural features on the surface that would reveal the base – only the lake might draw attention. There was also a chance that the Russian and Chinese forces would cross each other and interfere with their respective searches. However, if they were persistent enough, it was only a matter of time before they found the base.

It took the *North Dakota* less than four days to navigate the return through the tunnel, and they were back on the carrier 12 hours later, along with everything they'd taken from the base. He and Sylvia were given quarters close to the room where the artifacts from the base had been stored. Horace was placed closer to the medical facilities, as he'd come down with something that took hold on the return trip. The man looked as if death could take him at any time, although that wasn't very different from the way he looked when he was feeling well.

Daniel didn't know exactly what to do next, but he knew they had to get William Thompson onto the ship. If anything, it would keep him from falling into the wrong hands. It made him think of Jonathan and Denise. They were in danger, too. Since they were experts on the Red Wraith project, he'd request that they be collected along with Thompson.

Daniel was surprised that the Red Wraith project leaders had missed the true purpose of Red Falcon from the beginning. He was also astonished at how the Nazis had been able to keep so many secrets – the whereabouts of Dr. Mengele, the successful transport of Hitler's ashes, the base, and, most importantly, the beacon. The world would have been a better place had those secrets died with them. Instead, just enough information had been discovered in Germany after the war to entice the Americans to create Red Wraith. They'd plugged forward without knowing the true purpose of what they were doing, nor the consequences.

He shook his head and sighed. He and the others in his group were no better: they were pressing forward without knowing where they were going. There were still many unanswered questions, such as *what was the purpose of the beacon?* The Nazis thought it was a source of power to help them to conquer the world. There was no evidence for or against that. The two innermost rings of the White Stone had not yet been deciphered, and the information the Nazis *had* obtained revealed nothing regarding its purpose or function.

Someone tapped him on the shoulder. He turned around to see an older man who was in his early fifties, wearing a khaki Navy uniform and a blue baseball-style hat with "USS *Stennis*" written on the front in gold letters.

"Mr. Parsons," the man said. His face was friendly, but serious. "I'm Grimes, the captain of this ship."

Daniel stood and shook the man's hand.

"You wanted to talk," Grimes said.

"Yes, sir, thanks for meeting me," Daniel responded. "I'm not sure how much you know about what's going on with the base and the beacon."

"McHenry briefed me," Grimes said, "and I got more detailed information from Naval Command. The information came from your director."

"Then you understand why I've requested to have a man brought to your ship."

Grimes   nodded.

"There are two others who should be brought here as well: Jonathan McDougal and Denise Walker. They're experts on the Red Wraith project, and have dealt with William Thompson directly," Daniel explained. "They're also in danger."

"I'll send a request to Naval Command," Grimes said and started to walk.

"One more thing."

Grimes stopped and turned back to face Daniel.

"Tell them to find McDougal first," Daniel explained. "He'll know how to find Thompson."

Grimes nodded and went on his way, leaving Daniel to his thoughts. The next question was what were they going to do with Thompson once they got him on the ship. Should they take him to the beacon? He figured they'd have to. Someone would eventually get to it with a person who could penetrate its walls. Even though he didn't really trust any government with the responsibility of what might be discovered there, he preferred that responsibility *not* be placed in the hands of the Chinese or the Russians.

Daniel shivered as a chill crawled up his spine. Their competitors were well-informed. They'd been a step ahead the entire way – until the *North Dakota* stumbled upon the tunnel. It was sheer luck that they were in a controlling position – locating the base and securing the beacon. But there was one more crucial piece to be acquired.

Daniel hoped desperately that William Thompson was still safe.

~ 3 ~

Tuesday, 9 June (8:16 a.m. CST – Chicago)

Jonathan hung up the phone and looked across his desk to Denise who was sitting in a hardwood chair with her legs crossed.

"What's going on?" she asked, intrigued.

"That was James Thackett, CIA director," he said.

"Yes?"

"He wants us to contact Will and bring him in," Jonathan explained.

Denise shifted in her seat and a concerned expression formed on her face. "Will's in trouble. It's been days."

Jonathan nodded. He was more worried than he led on. "There's more. When we find him, they want us to go with him."

"Where?"

"Buenos Aires."

"Oh."

"Closer to where everything is happening."

Denise pulled her laptop out of her backpack and turned it on. A minute later she sighed. "Still nothing from Will. What should we do?"

"We get on the first flight to Baton Rouge and find him," he replied.

"Where do we start?" she asked.

"I don't know, but waiting here isn't productive," he said. "We have phones and computers – we'll track him down somehow. We may have to get into Syncorp, since that's where he was going."

"I'll book the tickets," she said and left for her office.

He considered not bringing her along on this one. He had a bad feeling about it; she'd only been on the job for a year and needed more experience. But he knew it would never fly. She'd appeal to his wife, and he knew how that would turn out – in Denise's favor.

He smiled and sighed. He turned his chair around and opened up a safe hidden behind a wooden panel in the wall behind his desk. He retrieved his and Denise's passports, a DNA Foundation credit card, and his gun.

~ 4 ~

Tuesday, 9 June (9:28 a.m. EST – Weddell Sea)

Will took a sip from a bottle of water and looked to Cho. "So let me get this straight. The Nazis deciphered some ancient script on a stone –"

" – the White Stone," Cho added.

"And it gave them instructions on how to find this mysterious object located in the ocean near Antarctica," Will rehashed. "The object makes noise. Surely submarines and science vessels would have detected it long ago."

"It doesn't beat continuously," Cho said. "We're not clear on what makes it come out."

"Come out?"

"It periodically goes dormant and retracts into the seabed."

"Why do you need me?"

"You must separate and go inside it."

"Not sure what you mean."

Cho stared at him in silence for a full 10 seconds. "So, is it going to be like this?"

"Like what?" Will said. "I'm not a diver."

291

Cho shook his head. "Mr. Thompson, I suggest you cooperate. You know exactly what I'm talking about."

"Please, explain it to me."

"We have seen the videos of your … *events*," Cho said. "You're the only successful conversion of the Americans' project."

Will stared at him blankly.

"It's interesting how history repeats itself," Cho continued, his expression turned smug. "The United States creates the atomic bomb, expending an astounding amount of resources, and China just takes it after you've figured it all out. Then there was the nuclear test ban treaty. Your country develops a computer code that allows you to design new devices without testing, and China just steals it – just one person properly placed."

"Los Alamos," Will said. He recalled the report of a Chinese man, a Los Alamos employee, who had set up the electronic transfer of the computer code to China. The U.S. never learned about security.

"And they let the guy go," Cho laughed. "A true Chinese patriot and hero."

Will's eyes burned and he pressed a finger on in his temple.

Cho continued, "And we've just introduced the world to our improved version of your latest stealth fighter."

Will hadn't heard that one yet – but it didn't surprise him. The world would be a much different place if the United States could hold onto its secrets.

"And now we've stolen Red Wraith," Cho said and smiled broadly. "It has all been absorbed into China's project, *Red Dragon*."

Will's was grateful for the project name. Now he had a new target.

"And now," Cho said, with an arrogance that made Will want to rip his face off of his skull, "we have you."

"I still don't understand," Will said, although he understood perfectly.

"Please," Cho said, smirking. "We know you're well informed about Red Wraith. Why else would you try to take down Syncorp? I saw you on the security tapes. So just end your feigned ignorance." Cho leaned on the table. "Your pathetic country spent more on Red Wraith than it had on the Manhattan Project, and they continued to expend great resources on it since its inception at the end of World War II. And, once again, *we have it all*."

"I wouldn't say that you have *it all*," Will replied.

"If you are referring to the technical aspects," Cho said, "we most certainly do. We have all of the mechanical plans, the people, and we've purchased the most important industrial partners. If, on the other hand, you're referring to yourself, I'd surmise that you are certainly in our custody."

"That assumes I'll cooperate," Will said, staring Cho directly in the eyes.

Cho leaned back in his chair. "We're prepared to exhaust every means we have to make sure that you do."

"Such as?"

"We could always start with ... well ... *physical* tactics."

"You can't really believe that that's going to work," Will said. "Do you have any idea what I've been through?"

"We'd start with less gentle means than what Red Wraith had imposed on you," Cho said. "You obviously haven't suffered amputations or permanent damage. But we could also impose such things upon your friends – or your family. We'd just need to bring them to visit our Baton Rouge facility."

Will thoughts turned to a place devoid of light. He could kill them all.

"But we'll start with something that appeals to your humanity – love of country," Cho said. "We have tactical nuclear weapons at our disposal. We'll take out your carrier group if you don't cooperate. They're in our way as it is."

Will's mind whirred. "What carrier group?"

Cho laughed loudly. "Your navy has cordoned off the seas near the beacon – a carrier group and a multitude of submarines. We're on the verge of war."

"You drop a nuke and there *will* be war," Will said. "You willing to risk that?"

"Absolutely," Cho replied without delay.

"What do you think is inside the beacon?" Will asked. "What could be so important that you'd sacrifice your country?"

"It's more than just my country, or yours," Cho replied. "The entire world will fall into war. Russia has its finger on the trigger as well."

"Again, why is the beacon so important?" Will repeated.

"We don't know."

"You've done all of this – killed people – over an unknown?" Will asked, almost yelling.

"The White Stone came from the pyramids, Mr. Thompson," Cho argued, "and it predicted the location of the beacon. These things are before their time – they're out of place – and must have come from somewhere else."

"What are you talking about – extraterrestrials? Gods?" Will scoffed. "Ever think that it might all be a hoax?"

"Impossible," Cho replied. "The beacon had been detected centuries ago. It is composed of a material beyond current technology."

It was intriguing, Will admitted, although he hadn't actually seen any of the evidence himself.

"Hitler thought the beacon was the source of great power," Cho continued.

"And you want to give that power to me – let me pass through its wall and claim what's there," Will said. "You think I'll follow your orders once I'm all-powerful?"

"Your body will be in our hands," Cho said, his face reddening. "If you don't follow our orders, we'll kill you. If you don't get into the beacon, we'll kill you. If there's nothing of value in the beacon, we'll kill you. And if you don't do what we tell you to do right now, we'll kill everyone in that carrier group – and your family and friends. Does that sum it up well enough for you?"

Will stared at the man and didn't break eye contact. After an awkward span of time he said, "Who is in charge of this project?" He was going to decapitate Red Dragon.

Before Cho could answer, a Chinese officer entered the room, whispered something in Cho's ear, and left.

"I want to talk the person in charge, or I'm not going to cooperate," Will said.

"It seems that your location has been leaked," Cho said blankly. "American destroyers are headed this way."

Will smirked. "Looks like the jig is up." He was relieved someone knew where he was.

"I don't think so," Cho said. "This is an all or nothing game. And they don't realize what we are willing to do."

Cho spoke in Chinese to Will's guard detail and then left the room. He was then escorted to another, smaller room located nearby, and locked inside, *alone*. They had no idea of the threat he was to them. They would have been better off keeping him out in the open, where someone could get a shot at him.

He didn't know what they were going to do, but he couldn't allow them to launch a nuclear strike on the American carrier group. He'd have to make the first move.

~ 5 ~
Tuesday, 9 June (9:43 a.m. CST – Chicago)

Jonathan and Denise slogged their way through security at Chicago's O'Hare International Airport. He passed his gun, which was packed in a locked case, to a woman he knew in security who would put it in his checked luggage after it was scanned. It always paid to make contacts.

With an hour to burn at the terminal while they waited to board their flight to Baton Rouge, he walked to a Starbuck's kiosk to get coffee. Denise stayed behind with their bags.

While in line, searching through email on his phone, someone tapped him on the shoulder. He turned and faced a dark-complexioned man whom he didn't recognize: mid-fifties, dark hair, dressed in khakis and a navy-blue polo shirt.

"Can I help you?" Jonathan asked.

The man put his right hand on Jonathan left arm and squeezed gently. "We have to talk, Mr. McDougal," the man said in a slight accent. "It's urgent."

"Who are you?" Jonathan said and pulled away gently.

"A friend," the man replied.

The man was Israeli, probably Mossad, Jonathan thought. He'd dealt with Mossad agents on two occasions – they'd saved his ass both times. But it was always a gamble trying to figure out who to trust. By their very nature, intelligence services were deceptive – especially those that dealt with human resources. Operatives were trained to earn the trust of people from whom they were to extract information, or to get them to do things.

They walked to an empty terminal and took a seat close to a wall of windows with a view of a runway. The Israeli sat in silence as a jet took off and then began. "I am Avi," he said. "Your friend, William Thompson, has been captured by Chinese agents and taken to Argentina. We lost track of him there."

Jonathan was flabbergasted. "How do you know this?"

"The same way I know that there are two Chinese agents following you right now," Avi replied. "They booked the same flight to Baton Rouge. Your communications have been compromised, and your office is bugged."

Jonathan immediately recalled the visit from the so-called Chinese diplomats. Perhaps their belligerent behavior was a distraction; their objective was to bug his office.

"You were to continue to Argentina once you had Thompson," Avi continued. "Go there now – skip Baton Rouge. You must get the message to the CIA Director that they're taking Thompson to a Chinese aircraft carrier in the Southern Sea. He's probably already onboard."

"What about our tails?"

"I managed to obtain their names – at least as they appear on their passports," Avi said and smiled. "My agency put them on the international no-fly list. They weren't able get through your security, even though they have diplomatic immunity."

"Clever," Jonathan said in approval. "They'll have a backup plan."

"They already have operatives set to pick up your trail in Baton Rouge," Avi said. "Take a direct flight to Buenos Aries. The CIA wants you on the USS *Stennis* as soon as possible."

Jonathan shook his head. "The aircraft carrier?"

Avi nodded. "They need you to help with Thompson"

Jonathan nodded. "What can we do?"

"He trusts you," Avi replied. "My government warned your leaders about this situation months ago, and how crucial it was to protect the man. They didn't heed the warning, and now it might be too late."

"Too late for what?" Jonathan asked, confused.

"I better be going," Avi said and stood. "Call the CIA director."

"How do you know I – "

"We've bugged you, too," Avi said and shrugged. "You need to get up to speed on security." He winked and then turned and walked out of the terminal, disappearing into the crowd.

Jonathan walked back to the gate for their flight to Baton Rouge.

Denise looked up from her phone. "Where's the coffee?"

"Change of plans," he said, grabbing his bag and indicating to Denise that she should do the same.

"What's going on?" she asked as she stood and pulled her knapsack over her shoulder.

"We're going directly to Buenos Aires."

~ 6 ~

Tuesday, 9 June (7:39 p.m. EST – Weddell Sea)

Cho's men left Will caged in the room for many hours, during which Will separated multiple times to spy on what going on. Now things were happening and he knew he had to move.

Will separated, passed through the ceiling into a storage room, and continued into a large bay where scores of men tended to aircraft. They were fueling, and attaching missiles to the undersides of their wings. It seemed they were going to follow through on their threat to attack the American ships that were confronting them.

He rose to the ceiling of the bay, and pressed through it and into open air. He sensed the change of temperature and the wind, and could see despite the darkness. He ascended to a point 150 feet above the deck. Now at the greatest distance he'd ever separated from his body, weakness invaded him, and he fought hard against the urge to recombine with his body.

A group of men rolled two fighter jets into position on the launch deck. He scanned the horizon in all directions: no sign of the US warships.

He returned to his body and analyzed the situation. If those jets launched to intercept the U.S. destroyers, it was unclear whether they would attack, or just threaten them. If they attacked, people would die. He couldn't allow the planes to launch. He had to get his body closer to the launch deck.

He separated and passed through the wall, into the corridor. Two plain-clothed men stood guard, one on each side of the door. He pinched an artery in the neck of the man on the right, just as he'd done to the ex-CP inmate. The guard collapsed, and Will repeated the action on the second man. He unlocked the door, returned to his body, and was out and running down the corridor. He had to get close enough to the planes so that he could maintain his separation. He was already fatigued.

A hundred feet down the hall he came to a steep stairway leading up to the next floor. He climbed two steps at a time, turned left into a corridor, and passed by two of the Chinese crew. They glanced in his directions but otherwise ignored him. He knew that carriers held crews of a few thousand, so most of the people he'd cross would have no idea who he was. Even though he stood out by appearance, there were other Caucasians in civilian clothes on the ship who were not prisoners. If he remained cool and acted like he belonged there, he'd be okay.

He climbed another flight of stairs and emerged in the large bay where men readied the fighter planes. He crossed to the wall on the far side of the bay, which was lined with doors. Men walked in and out of the rooms, and on a steel-grate walkway just above them. He checked the rooms until he found a small custodial closet. He ducked in, closed the door behind him, and snapped on a light switch. The door had no lock.

He rummaged around and found a plastic tarp riddled with splotches of dried gray paint, and then dragged it to a corner behind a shelf. He pulled a few empty cardboard boxes around him and covered himself with the tarp.

He separated and pressed upward, through deck and above the carrier's runway. Just a few yards from him, two jets pulsed their engines and seemed to be ready to launch. As he tried to determine how to damage the first plane in line, its engines blasted and the steam-powered catapult engaged. The fighter accelerated down the runway.

Will, panicked, reacted entirely upon instinct. In an instant, he was in the cockpit with the pilot, accelerating along with the jet – the distance from his body increasing quickly. The jet blasted off the edge of the deck and lifted. Will did the only thing he could do; he grabbed the stick and jammed it forward. The screams of the pilot seemed to ring in his ears as the plane plunged into the sea.

Next thing he knew, he was back in the closet, light-headed and weak. He pulled the tarp from over his head and found a bucket just in time to avoid vomiting on the floor. Having almost nothing to eat in the past day, not much came up except a burning concoction of mucus and stomach acid. He spent the next few minutes dry-heaving. When it had finally subsided, he went to a small sink and rinsed out his mouth with cold, brackish water. He'd separated from his body by more than 250 yards.

He sat down behind the boxes and tried to determine whether what he'd just experienced had really occurred. If so, the Chinese captain probably wouldn't launch another jet until they'd determined what had happened. They wouldn't figure it out.

A feeling of darkness and dread hit him hard. The pilot hadn't had time to eject – he was dead. He'd killed him. It was too easy.

Another bout of nausea overtook him, but he didn't use the bucket

– there was nothing in his stomach. He dry-heaved for full minute before it subsided. His hands trembled and his nausea turned to a sickly exhaustion. Although he was famished, he knew the weakness was caused by the extreme separation. It was like stretching a rubber band beyond its limit, causing an irreversible distortion. Although he was already recovering, he couldn't help thinking about what might've happened had he separated beyond his limit. Would he be dead?

He wondered now about Cho. If he'd been aware of his abilities, why did he leave him alone? The answer was that Cho didn't really understand. If so, he would've known they were in danger from the beginning.

His thoughts turned to what to do next. First, he'd disable the mechanism that launched jets down the runway. After that, he'd sabotage the lift that took planes from the bay to the deck. Finally, he'd destroy the propulsion system of the carrier. He wondered if the ship had a nuclear reactor. If so, he'd render the vessel a floating radioactive ruin.

~ 7 ~
Wednesday, 10 June (4:55 a.m. EST – Mar del Plata, Argentina)

Jonathan struggled to keep his eyes open by the time they'd reached the Argentine naval base at Mar del Plata. By her silence, he could tell Denise was also exhausted. And they were both freezing.

He rubbed his runny nose with the back of his cold hand as they sat on an iron bench inside an open Quonset hut, awaiting the next leg of the trip. Two CIA operatives paced at the wide opening that faced the sea. After an hour of half-frozen, intermittent sleep, the chopping sound of a helicopter rose above the sounds of the waves that lapped against the rocky shore. Jonathan strained his eyes to locate its red and white blinking lights in the sharp background of stars.

Just as the helicopter made its final approach, its engines whined and it flared back into the air. The two CIA officers screamed in

300

Jonathan's direction as they scrambled for cover. Jonathan looked into the rear of the Quonset hut and spotted an open door and two shadowy figures. There were two men, one crouching behind an old boat and the other behind a stack of wooden crates.

The first shot struck the thick metal arm of the bench. Denise yelped and bent over, falling onto the gravel floor. Jonathan fell on top of her as dark blood mushroomed rapidly around the frayed tear in her jeans.

After that, everything seemed to move in slow motion as the two CIA operatives charged in the direction of the shooters. Jonathan rolled Denise onto her back and placed her hand on the wound on her thigh.

"Press hard," he yelled.

Keeping crouched as low as he could, he dragged her by her feet behind an old tractor. He then fumbled under his coat only to realize he didn't have his gun – couldn't get it on the international flight. More shots rang out, some hitting the tractor frame, scattering lead and paint in random directions.

The CIA men maneuvered around old marine equipment and returned fire. One of them took a bullet to the shoulder, and settled on his rear behind a pile of bricks. The other rushed to him, but sprinted away a few seconds later as the wounded man covered his advance. Ten seconds later a flurry of shots ended the conflict: both attackers were dead.

The two CIA officers yelled back and forth a few times, and the wounded man radioed the chopper. Jonathan turned his attention to Denise, whose face was pale, and her pant leg soaked with blood. He pressed his hand over hers to put more pressure on the wound. She grunted in pain.

"You're going to be okay," Jonathan said.

"Those bastards shot me!" she yelled with a look of rage in her face he'd never witnessed before. She tried to stand.

"Stop," Jonathan said. "You need a medic."

She relaxed and started to go unconscious. He grabbed her face and shook gently. "Stay awake," he said. He didn't want her to go into shock.

He examined the wound but couldn't assess the damage.

Ten minutes later they were on board the chopper and heading out to sea.

The wounded man looked to be okay. The other operative looked more closely at Denise's thigh. "She'll be okay, but you're lucky we're just minutes away," he said.

"You guys did well back there, thank you," Jonathan said. "Who were they?"

"Chinese operatives," the man replied. "No identification on them, but we were warned about Chinese interference. They looked the part."

"They're dead?" Jonathan asked.

The man nodded. "Would've been better to bring one back alive, but that's not the way it worked out."

Jonathan nodded and looked forward, past the pilots and through the front windshield. They were approaching the USS *Stennis*.

~ 8 ~

(Unknown time)

Will awoke but remained still until he figured out where he was. Light filtered in through the dirty gray tarp that covered his face and body. The air smelled like paint, and the pungent taste of puke coated his mouth. He must have passed out, or fallen asleep. The extreme separation had drained him. The last thing he remembered was rinsing his mouth out with horrible-tasting water from the sink in the utility room, and then covering himself with the tarp.   He was still in the utility room. He was lucky they hadn't found him.

His stomach grumbled and he felt weak, like he had a hangover. He needed to find food.

~ 9 ~

Wednesday, 10 June (5:10 a.m. EST – Weddell Sea)

The helicopter landed gently on the *Stennis*. Jonathan tried to follow the medical crew who whisked Denise and the wounded CIA operative away, but a sailor stopped him – he'd only get in the way.

Four heavily dressed men guided him and the other CIA officer along a green line painted on the deck, leading them away from the landing pad and into the interior of the ship.

He was then handed off to two sailors wearing khaki jumpsuits and blue baseball caps who led him to a room where he met the ship's captain, and two others that he already knew. Daniel and Sylvia looked distraught.

Daniel shook his head. "Sorry, we had no idea –"

"– we were aware of the risks," Jonathan cut in.

"I was hoping to have Will Thompson here as well," Daniel said, and then sat down and gestured for Jonathan to do the same.

"Why the frantic scramble?" Jonathan asked.

Daniel pulled a laptop from a leather knapsack at his feet. "We're close to the beacon," he explained as he turned the screen towards Jonathan. "It looks like this."

It looked as he imagined it from Daniel's description during their meet in Chicago, except the bulbous top portion seemed small compared to its long, tapered stem. It was like a stretched chess piece – a pawn with and undersized head. "Fascinating," Jonathan said. "Have you determined its purpose?"

"Only guesses," Daniel said. "We'll learn more when we get inside it."

"Inside?" Jonathan asked. "Did you find a hatch?"

"No, and it's physically impenetrable," Daniel replied. "That's why we need Thompson."

Jonathan gasped. He knew immediately what Daniel was thinking.

"What?" Daniel asked.

"You believe that he can separate," Jonathan said.

Daniel stared at him intently. "Can he?"

Jonathan didn't know the answer to the question. He had a vague idea what separation meant, but hadn't considered that it was really possible.

"You ever ask him about it?" Sylvia asked.

"No, not directly," Jonathan replied. "I've read reports from the Red Box that described some strange things, but they could all be explained by, well … other means. We'd assumed he might have been having hallucinations at the time and – "

"Have you seen the videos from the Red Box?" Daniel asked.

"They disappeared before we could obtain them," Jonathan answered.

Daniel nodded. "Well, we have," he said. His face reddened and his voice gained volume. "In one, a woman – a dentist – got thrown to the floor by some invisible force. In another, Thompson read numbers out of his field of view. I saw him, while confined to the Exoskeleton, incinerate thousands of hornets in midflight – brilliant flashes of white light. The final events, and the explosion that ended it all, were nothing short of terrifying."

Jonathan sat back in his chair, looking at Daniel and thinking. Having been focused on the legal issues and the investigative aspects of the case, he'd pushed all of the crazy stuff into the background. And Will hadn't offered any information on his own.

"We need to get him back," Daniel said, "and make sure the Chinese don't to use him to get inside the beacon."

"How will they do that?" Jonathan asked.

"A submarine – to get him close," Daniel replied. "But that will be difficult with our ships in the area."

"But suppose they *do* get access," Jonathan said, "and Will separates and gets inside. Do you even have a guess as to what's there?"

"No," Daniel replied. "But we might find answers in the information we took from the base."

"Base?" Jonathan asked. What the hell was he talking about?

Daniel nodded. "Remember I told you that one of our subs found a cavern?"

"Yes."

Sylvia smiled. "There's a lot we need to tell you."

Jonathan's fascination was quelled by another invading thought. Denise was like a daughter to him. He stood. "Please take me to sick bay. I need to see her."

~ 10 ~
Wednesday, 10 June (7:35 a.m. EST)

Jonathan woke up slouched in a chair in the sickbay waiting room. He must've dozed off while they worked on Denise. He stood from his chair and looked through the small window in the surgery room door. They were gone.

He walked out of the waiting room and found a nurse who directed him to the recovery room. When he arrived, Denise was already dressed and sitting in a wheelchair next to a cot. She wore loose shorts over her bandaged right leg.

"What are you doing?" Jonathan asked. "Aren't you supposed to – "

"I'm not sitting in here all day," she said. "I'm fine. Just not supposed to walk on it for a day."

A doctor walked in and Jonathan turned to her. "Is that true?" he asked.

She nodded and smiled. "She was lucky. She was hit with two small fragments. Caused some tissue damage and a lot of bleeding, but it missed the large vessels. If she can handle the pain, she can walk on it tomorrow."

"See?" Denise said, smiling. "You worry too much."

"How's the other fellow?" Jonathan asked, referring to the CIA officer that was hit in the shoulder.

The doctor smiled. "He'll be back on the job in a few weeks," she said and nodded towards Denise. "I'll see her tomorrow morning. If all's okay, she'll be cleared to walk."

Jonathan shrugged. "Breakfast?"

Denise nodded.

He rolled her out of the sickbay towards the mess hall. "So what's it like being shot?" he asked.

"I'll tell you tomorrow when the pain sets in," she said. "Have you ever been?"

"Yes," Jonathan replied.

Just as he was about to elaborate, Daniel and Sylvia turned the corner and joined them on their way to the mess hall.

They ate as Daniel and Sylvia got them up to speed on the beacon and the Nazi base. An hour flew by in what seemed like minutes.

Afterwards, Jonathan pushed Denise behind the others as they made their way to meet with Captain Grimes. They met in a large ready room with a rectangular table at the center.

Grimes described the recent events on the Chinese carrier.

"Crashed into the ocean immediately after takeoff," Jonathan repeated the captain's words, astonished.

"That happened yesterday and they haven't attempted another launch," Grimes added. "Seems like they haven't ironed out all of the problems with their carriers."

Jonathan looked to Denise on his right, and then to Daniel and Sylvia across the table. He wondered if they were thinking the same as he was: there was more to the pilot's demise than an equipment malfunction. What was he thinking – Will had a hand in it? It was preposterous.

The captain told them that he'd keep them apprised of any new developments, and walked out. Jonathan and Denise were now up to speed regarding the beacon and the Nazi base.

"They were trying to reincarnate Hitler?" Jonathan asked, trying to keep his skepticism at bay.

"That's what Mengele wrote in his notes," Daniel said as he fidgeted with his hands on the table. "The idea was that, if Hitler's soul traveled with his ashes, and they could get a soul to leave a body that was still alive, then Hitler could occupy the body – like a possession. But that's just a side story. The beacon is the more urgent matter."

"We need to decipher the inner two rings," Sylvia added, and then shook her head and sighed. "Even if we had a team of experts, it could take months."

"We need to recover Will, and get him down there," Jonathan suggested. "He'll have to get inside before we've figured it all out."

"The Chinese would kill Thompson rather than allow us to acquire him," Daniel argued.

"Then we're stuck," Denise said.

Jonathan flinched as the first officer of the *Stennis* burst into the room.

"The captain wants you to come with me," he said.

"What's going on?" Daniel asked.

"The Chinese carrier is on fire," the officer replied.

"Did we attack?" Denise asked.

The young office shook his head. "I don't know."

Jonathan then wondered if the ship was being attacked from the inside.

~ 11 ~
Wednesday, 10 June (8:58 a.m. EST)

Setting the lower deck ablaze had been easier than Will had anticipated. He'd separated and ripped a hole in a fuel tank of one of the jets, spilling its contents to the floor. He'd done the same to a portable fueling vehicle, and then ignited it all with an arc-welder. Jet fuel wasn't as easy to ignite as gasoline, but once it got going, it spread like wildfire and was difficult to extinguish. He figured at least four planes had been destroyed. His estimate increased after secondary explosions rocked the ship.

Next, he located the piston that drove the aircraft launching mechanism and punctured it, releasing a burst of high-pressure steam that could cut through flesh. Jets could no longer be launched.

He then ripped out the hydraulic hoses that actuated the lift that raised planes from the lower bay to the deck. With hydraulic fluid spraying like blood from a severed aorta, he crushed the central hydraulic cylinder, rendering the entire system nonfunctional. Now the planes couldn't even get to the upper deck. The Chinese carrier was now just a useless platform.

He returned to his body and nearly vomited. His body sickened again from the extended separation, but he recovered more quickly this time. He was feeling better since he'd found food – canned goods – after moving from the utility closet to a storage room a few doors down. Although he'd been unable to read the cans, most had contained seafood of some kind. He'd also choked down a can of slime that he guessed was pureed sea cucumbers.

He was satisfied with the damage he'd caused to the carrier's launch capabilities, but he wasn't finished. His next objective was to render the carrier dead in the water – he'd destroy the propulsion system.

He was in the upper-middle part of the ship, just below the launch deck. The propulsion system would be aft and below him. It was too far for him to separate, so he'd have to move his body closer. He could tell by the noise that there was a lot of action outside – they'd be looking for a saboteur. If they were looking for a plain-clothed Caucasian, he'd be identified immediately. He had to find a way to blend in.

He separated and searched the adjacent rooms. Two doors down, he found a rack of overalls – the type mechanics wear. He unlocked the door of the room from the inside, and returned to his body. He exited the supply room, walked along the wall and into the room he'd just unlocked, and closed the door. The light was already on.

He sorted through the rack of dark blue overalls. He found one that was too large, but the remaining six or seven were too small. He slipped it on over his clothes and buttoned it. He rolled up the sleeves and cuffed the legs. It had Chinese characters embroidered on the left side of the chest. In a locker on the far wall was a box of baseball-style hats with flexible bands. He found the largest one and put it on, pulling the bill down low over his eyes. It was a good fit.

He walked out of the room into the bay where sailors rushed about with tools and fire extinguishers, responding to officers barking orders

308

through bullhorns. Although he understood nothing of what they said, there was panic in their faces and urgency in their actions. He tried to put himself in their place: one of their fighters had recently plunged into the sea, and their capacity to launch the others had been eliminated. Worse, fires had spontaneously broken out on the lower deck. He wondered how they'd feel when their ship was dead in the water.

He weaved his way through foot traffic across the bay to the same staircase he'd climbed earlier. He descended two levels, turned left, and followed a corridor towards the rear of the ship. As the pungent odor of diesel fuel filled his nostrils, it became clear to him that the carrier did not have a nuclear reactor. When the smell was strong, he entered a room at random, and was relieved to find it vacant.

A set of three-level bunks hung from the walls on both sides of the quarters. He climbed into the upper bunk of the one on the right, lay on his back, and pulled a wool blanket over his head. After one breath he yanked the blanket back – the body odor that saturated the bedding was overwhelming. Instead, he turned on his side and faced the wall in case someone came in the room.

He knew what he was going to do, but didn't have a plan for what to do afterwards. Eventually, he'd have to get off the ship – not an easy thing to do in the freezing seas at the bottom of the world. Once the carrier was rendered helpless, maybe Cho would hand him over to the U.S. fleet. If not, maybe he'd eliminate Cho. Maybe he'd eliminate Cho either way.

He separated, passed through the door and into the corridor, and proceeded towards the back of the ship. After passing through a few rooms, he found what he sought: giant diesel engines, two rows of three separated by a corrugated-steel walkway. A half-dozen men monitored a wall of gauges and displays, while a team of three worked on one of the six engines. Engine parts were laid out in an orderly fashion on a tarp next to the men.

Will passed through the housing of the first engine and examined its innards. It was running, its 16 pistons pounding at a blurring pace. The question was whether he should make subtle damages to the engines, or tear them to pieces. He decided on the latter.

He reached towards one of the pistons and noticed something peculiar. As he concentrated on the moving pistons, *they seemed to slow down*. As he got closer, the pistons slowed to a standstill. He grabbed one and ripped it through the cylinder. He backed out to observe the consequences of his modification.

The engine sputtered and a violent metallic grinding sound emanated from its innards. Two of the engineers rushed to the now squealing engine and then screamed at the men at the control panel, who frantically adjusted knobs and levers and finally turned off the engine.

Will turned to the other engines and performed the same operation, and did the same to the one that was undergoing repairs. After a horrid stretch of screeching and grinding that lasted about 30 seconds, all of the engines were dead. It was time for the next phase.

He located the fuel lines of the engines and tore them out, spewing diesel fuel over the floor of the engine room. He tracked the lines to a valve manifold, and then followed the main fuel line to a colossal fuel tank deep in the belly of the ship. He ripped out the main fuel supply flange from the tank. Diesel spewed out like water from a fire hydrant, quickly flooding the large room. He opened the door to the corridor, giving the rushing fuel a place to spread.

The same as with the jet fuel, he'd need something to ignite it. He looked around, but found nothing. Then it occurred to him that he'd done it before – burned something while in the separated state. The first time had been the flies in the Red Box. Just minutes later, he'd burned thousands of attacking hornets. The third time, a man had been aiming a gun at him. Will had melted the gun in the man's hands, and then incinerated him.

He focused on a steel beam on the ceiling above the center of pooling fuel. He concentrated and summoned the anger he'd had while burning the man in the Red Box. He thought of the thug that had killed Adler in the parking garage, and how he'd dismembered the body with an electric knife. These people had no regard for life. The pipe glowed red, then orange, and then almost white before orange-white droplets fell into the diesel fuel. The first few just fizzled out, but then a large molten clump fell in and ignited the pool. It quickly spread into the corridor.

He tore the room's half-dozen doors from their hinges – the fire would need oxygen. Black smoke billowed out of the room and into the corridor. He followed the corridor back towards his body, destroying every door that could be used to isolate the fire along the way.

He awakened in his body. The floor rumbled as men ran though the corridor outside, in the direction of the fire. He smiled as he thought about it. He'd single-handedly disabled an aircraft carrier. Every day he gained a better understanding of his powers. There could never be another like him. He wouldn't allow it to happen.

~ 12 ~

Wednesday, 10 June (10:12 a.m. EST)

"Are you sure it wasn't attacked?" Daniel asked, staring at the satellite images displayed on a large monitor. Sylvia, Jonathan, and Denise crowded behind him along with a few of the crew.

"Not by us," Captain Grimes replied. "It's dead in the water. Two of their smaller vessels are taking positions as tugboats."

"How does this work to our advantage?" Daniel asked.

"Not clear," Grimes answered. "It's a hostage situation, not a naval battle."

"Where are the destroyers?" Daniel asked.

"In position and standing by," Grimes replied. "If we're attacked, they'll counter on the carrier."

"Will is on that ship," Denise said in protest.

"We'd disable the carrier rather than sink it," Captain Grimes responded. "But it seems that has already happened." He shook his head. "I've never seen a ship self-destruct like that."

Daniel looked to Jonathan, who shrugged and raised an eyebrow. He knew they were thinking the same thing: it was Will. Maybe the Chinese took on more than they could handle.

"What are our options?" Daniel asked. "The importance of this man is becoming increasingly apparent. For Christ's sake, he's an American citizen being held captive on a Chinese ship."

Captain Grimes nodded and closed his eyes for a second before responding. "We have the area contained. No vessels or aircraft have tried to enter or leave the area since Thompson was delivered," he explained. "We have aircraft in the air right now, circling their crippled fleet like buzzards, and another carrier group is on the way."

"Have we made any demands?" Jonathan asked.

"Not yet," Grimes replied. "We're getting presidential approval to make the next move."

"We don't have time to wait," Daniel said.

"That Chinese carrier group has nukes," Grimes said. "Time is a problem, but we need to be careful."

The mention of nuclear weapons conjured up something in Daniel's mind: Operation Blackfish. Nuclear devices had been detonated in this precise area in the 1950's, and now the same was being threatened again. History might be repeating itself.

"Could a nuke take out the whole carrier group?" Daniel asked.

Grimes's expression flashed with annoyance, and then to deeper thought before he responded. "Yes," he replied. "But that would lead to all-out war."

"Suppose the Chinese thought that it was worth all-out war," Daniel said. "They could destroy all the ships in the area in one shot, load Thompson onto a sub, and go for the beacon."

"That would be the biggest gamble I've ever heard of," he said.

"Yes," Daniel said. "All or nothing."

"There's no way they'd get Will to cooperate with them," Denise interjected.

Jonathan nodded in agreement. "I'd be inclined to let them take him to the beacon. If there was some sort of power associated with it, he'd control it and wouldn't help the Chinese."

Daniel shook his head. "Too risky."

Captain Grimes concurred. "I've been given orders not to let any foreign vessels near the beacon."

A young officer entered to room and spoke. "Sir," the young man said, "the destroyers reported that the fire on the Chinese carrier is getting out of control. Two new fires have broken out."

"Spreading from the fuel reserves below the flight deck?" Grimes asked.

"No, sir, mid ship and lower decks," the officer replied. "Isolated from the first."

The officer left and Grimes turned to the others. "Unusual to have two isolated fires break out on a ship that's not being attacked."

Daniel had a different impression: the ship *was* being attacked.

~ 13 ~
Wednesday, 10 June (10:32 a.m. EST)

Will found a secure room and sat on a chair behind a worktable. He thought about what he'd just done as he recovered from the extended separation. He wondered if he'd wake up unexpectedly one day in an insane asylum and realize he was dreaming it all.

It was time to find Cho, but he didn't know where to start looking. He was sure Cho was looking for him as well. Will hadn't killed the guards outside his door when he'd escaped, so he was certain they had reported it as soon as they'd regained consciousness. Now the question was where did they expect *him* to go? Were there lifeboats on a carrier?

Flickering lights distracted him from his thoughts. He watched as they dimmed and then went out completely. They must have switched to emergency power, and he wondered if he'd now have to destroy generators or batteries.

The sound of helicopter blades chopped just above the threshold of background noise and, for one hopeful moment, he thought it might be American. He separated and ascended through two levels to the flight deck. The sky was in twilight, and the only artificial illumination was that of the dim lighting of the jet runway. A helicopter with Chinese markings was about to lift off from a helipad.

Will passed through its rotating blades and though the armored shell of the cockpit. Two pilots flipped switches, preparing for takeoff.

He passed into the passenger cabin. Two plain-clothed Chinese men sat on one side, and Natalie Tate and Roy sat on the other. *Where in the hell did they think they were going?* Will thought to himself. Anger welled up inside him. He couldn't let them go back to the states and continue their work. They had blood on their hands.

The helicopter ascended about 100 feet above the pad and drifted over the water. Will went into cockpit and grabbed the stick. The pilot shouted as he struggled with the controls. Will directed the chopper over the bridge of the carrier and then forced the stick forward. He rode it down until he awoke in his body and sensed the explosion from that vantage point. It was like thunder rumbling above him.

Killing was becoming easier.

~ 14 ~
Wednesday, 10 June (10:40 a.m. EST)

"What the hell was that?" Captain Grimes exclaimed. There was surprise and fear in his eyes.

"What?" Daniel asked.

Grimes pointed to a monitor displaying the live video feed from a camera on one of the destroyers. It was a green-tinted, night-vision video that was mostly saturated – overloaded with light.

Grimes instructed one of the crew to rewind the video and replay it. It was clear: a helicopter crashed into the bridge of the carrier, producing a brilliant explosion.

"I've never seen anything like it," Grimes said softly, shaking his head.

"Perhaps we can offer assistance," Jonathan suggested. "Time to get in close."

"They'd never allow it," Grimes said.

"Then how are we going to get Will off of that ship?" Denise asked.

"What if we sent a helicopter to the carrier?" Daniel asked.

"They'd shoot it down," Grimes said.

"Not an appropriate action for a distressed ship in need of assistance," Daniel replied.

"They have other ships," Grimes replied. "They don't need our assistance, and wouldn't accept it if they did."

Another explosion lit up the screen.

Grimes shook his head in disbelief. "We'll try to radio them." He walked out.

Daniel watched the screen as smaller, secondary explosions flared up from the carrier's bridge. Could one man really cause that much chaos?

CHAPTER XIV

~ 1 ~

Wednesday, 10 June (10:46 a.m. EST – Weddell Sea)

Will pulled his cap down tight over his face, and went into the corridor. The thick stench of burning fuel burned his nostrils, and he used the smoke as an excuse to cover his face as sailors ran past him in both directions. He fought through strong fumes as he plodded in the direction of the burning bridge, hoping to cross Cho along the way. What he really needed was a satellite phone – something to communicate his location to Denise and Jonathan. He hoped they could help him establish communications with the American ships.

It had been a mistake to allow Cho to take him. He was now in an impossible position. He had no end game. He could sink their carrier, but he'd be on it when it went down. Even if he were able to sneak away on a life raft, his body wouldn't survive the cold for long. Even with the ability to separate, it meant death.

He entered the lower bay area, avoiding people as they scurried about. He picked up his gait to look as if he was scurrying with them, and avoiding the fire that had spread to six or seven of the jets in the center of the bay. He wondered if the missiles under their wings could explode under the heat.

He crossed the bay, entered a wide hall, and climbed the first set of stairs he found. He searched until he found another flight and climbed them, and then another.

The bridge was ablaze. Burning electronics, plastic, and fuel produced a toxic concoction of smoke that billowed through the passageways, chasing sailors from the area. He trudged forward as far as he could and peered into one of the rooms, but soon wished he hadn't: the charred remains of bodies were strewn about. Some were fused with the chairs in which they sat when the helicopter had crashed in on them. *What*

316

had he done?

A sharp object poked into his lower back, near his kidney. He turned. A Chinese man in plain clothes stood an arm's length, covering his face with a cloth with one hand, and pointing a pistol at Will's abdomen with the other. Cho was 20 feet back, giving the man instructions in Chinese.

The man tipped the gun, instructing Will to follow Cho, who was now talking on his phone. Will didn't resist, and followed Cho a long distance away from the fires, ending up in the same ready-room to which he'd been taken when he arrived on the ship. Cho ordered him to sit.

"The others will be here shortly." Cho said as he walked to the head of the table and stood. "Who helped you escape – your FBI cohorts? If so, you should know they are both dead."

"I already know that," Will replied.

"How?"

"How did they die, or how do I know?"

Cho looked confused. "How do you know?"

"I killed them," Will replied.

"They were killed in a helicopter crash."

Will nodded.

Cho shook his head in disbelief, as if trying to assess Will's mental state. The door burst open and two military men entered, both officers.

"This is Captain Zhang and his political officer, Wu," Cho explained and then turned to the captain and nodded.

Zhang, who spoke in nearly-accent-free English, said, "As you can see, Mr. Thompson, we are in a vulnerable position. We have been sabotaged and are in standoff with the American Navy."

Will smiled.

"Perhaps you don't understand the gravity of the situation," Zhang said. "It pushes us towards the nuclear option."

"Your planes are grounded," Will said. "You plan to launch a missile?"

Zhang raised an eyebrow. "From a submarine," he said.

"And what will that get you?" Will asked. "All-out nuclear war?"

Cho grinned. "I doubt it would come to that. Perhaps they would counter, but your country would not attack mainland China."

"That's a big gamble," Will replied. "For what? To acquire some object at the bottom of the sea? You don't even know what it is."

"We'll clear the surface ships of your carrier group in one blast," Cho said with a smug expression. "Then we'll take out your subs with six of our own – or at least chase them out of the area. We'll then take you to the beacon."

Will smiled and shook his head slowly. "Your plan has some flaws," he said. "First, your submarines are no match for ours."

Cho looked to Captain Zhang, whose face had flushed.

"That's what you've been told," Cho said. "Along with many other falsehoods propagated by your government."

"And suppose everything works out and you get me on a sub near the beacon," Will said. "You really think I'll cooperate?"

"You'll be under immense pressure," Cho said.

"Really?" Will scoffed. "I don't think you understand what I've been through. There's nothing – "

"We will kill your friends," Cho said. "And your family."

For an instant, Cho's words put him in a state acute panic. He calmed himself. He understood that he couldn't protect everyone, but he could stop Cho from killing anyone. It had become a life or death situation.

"What would happen if you were all dead?" Will asked.

"Is that a threat?" Cho laughed and looked to Captain Zhang. "What do you think, Captain, are we in danger?"

The captain replied with a tentative shrug.

Will was convinced that Cho had no understanding of separation abilities. "You are gravely mistaken on this point," Will said and extended his arm. "Now give me your phone."

Cho stared back blankly before responding. "You're delusional."

Will sat down. "Your phone and your gun, on the table, now," he commanded.

Cho pulled out his gun and pointed it at Will's chest. "You are the one in danger, Mr. Thompson."

Will separated, grasped Cho's gun-wielding arm and snapped it at the mid-forearm with a sound like that of a cracking lobster shell. Cho screamed as the gun fell from his twitching hand, which now hung at an awkward angle. The gun clunked heavily onto the table.

Will returned to his body, snatched the gun, and pointed it at Captain Zhang who had started for his own pistol in the holster on his hip. Cho whimpered as he cradled his broken arm against his chest. Will ordered Captain Zhang to put his gun on the table.

Zhang capitulated, and Will snatched the weapon and threw it on the floor behind him.

The third man, Wu, snapped his pistol from the holster, trained it on Will, and started to squeeze the trigger.

The reaction was automatic. Instantaneously, Will was outside of his body and everything seemed to freeze in time. The next thing he knew he was back in his body, and the man's head exploded as if a hand grenade detonated inside, spraying blood, brain matter, and skull fragments all over the room.

Cho screamed.

Zhang looked confused and slowly wiped the wet debris from his face. His hand seemed to catch on something in the middle of his right cheek. He grasped it between his thumb and forefinger, and gingerly pulled it out and looked at it. An inch-long shard of skull had pierced his face.

Will was horrified by what had just happened – what he'd just done. He wiped blood and brain matter off of his own face and turned to Cho. "Your phone," he screamed, holding out his hand.

Cho seemed to be in shock.

Will pointed the gun at his head. "Now!"

Cho, his torso leaning heavily on the table, rolled to one side to access his inner jacket pocket with his good hand. He extracted the phone and threw it onto the table.

Will picked it up and opened it. The screen lit up and prompted him for the password.

"Password," Will said.

Cho hesitated.

"Password!" Will yelled, pointing the pistol at his face.

Cho listed a seven-character password. The question now was whether he could remember the phone numbers.

~ 2 ~

Wednesday, 10 June (11:09 a.m. EST)

Jonathan took a sip of coffee and looked at his watch: it was after 10 a.m., Chicago time. His bones ached from lack of sleep, and his eyes no longer maintained focus. These weren't new sensations for him, but he worried about his ability to think clearly. A vibration disrupted his thoughts, and he lifted the offending phone from his coat pocket and looked at the screen. It was from an unknown number, so he terminated the call and put it back in his pocket.

"Who was it?" Denise asked as she took a bite of her lunch.

"Unknown number," he said.

Daniel and Sylvia joined them and immediately dug into their food. It was clear that they were as hungry and tired as he was.

His phone buzzed again and he pulled it out. It was the same unknown number, and he cut it off and put it back in his pocket. "Persistent bastards. I'm on the no-call list," he muttered and set the phone on the table next to his plate.

He swallowed a few bites of his breakfast and was chewing on another when the phone buzzed a third time. He looked to Denise, rolled his eyes, and set down his fork. He picked up the phone, looked at the screen, and almost choked on his food. It was a text message.

"My God," he said, covering his mouth with a napkin. "It's Will."

Everyone seemed to stop chewing at the same time. Denise started to stand from her wheelchair, but winced and settled back into her seat.

"Where is he?" she said, flustered.

The phone vibrated again, this time it was an incoming call.

"We'll see," Jonathan said and tapped the screen and put it up to his ear. "William?"

"Yes. Jonathan?"

"Where are you?"

"You're not going to believe it but – "

"You're on a Chinese aircraft carrier off the coast of Antarctica," Jonathan interrupted. "And it's ablaze. What's your status?"

Will's silence conveyed confusion. After a few seconds, he replied, "I'm in control of the situation. I have the captain of the ship, Zhang, and a man named Cho here with me. Where are you?"

Jonathan looked to Daniel. "Get the captain – hurry!"

Daniel sprinted away.

"We're on the USS *Stennis* – a carrier group a few miles from you," Jonathan said.

"Good to hear you evaded Chinese intelligence," Will said.

"Barely," Jonathan said. "Denise took a bullet to the leg, but she's okay."

The silence on the other end made Jonathan regret relaying that information.

"Is she there?"

"I'll put you on speaker," Jonathan said, initiated speaker mode, and put the phone on the table. "There are others here, too."

"Will?" Denise said.

"You okay?" Will asked, sounding agitated.

"I'm fine," she said. "I'll be walking tomorrow."

"We need to get you off of that ship," Jonathan broke in.

"They're talking about hitting your carrier group with a nuke," Will said. "They're trying to get access to something the *Stennis* is protecting."

"The beacon," Jonathan said. "They want to take you to it in a submarine."

"Yes," Will replied. "Do you know why?"

"They want you to get inside the object – they think you have separation abilities," Jonathan said. He wanted to ask him if that was true, but decided to ask a more indirect question. "You have anything to do with the Chinese carrier's misfortunes?"

A pounding sound came through the phone, like someone knocking on a door.

"Gotta go," Will said. "I'll call back. Inform the *Stennis'* captain of the threat."

The call ended, and he looked at the screen for a second before Daniel's voice broke his trance.

"What did he say?" Daniel asked as he and Captain Grimes rushed to the table.

Jonathan informed them of the potential nuclear strike.

Grimes turned pale. "This is a game changer," he said. "I need to talk to Naval Command."

"What are you going to do?" Jonathan asked.

"We've been ordered to keep our position at all costs," Grimes explained. "Evidently there are people at the highest levels who think the beacon is worth it. We may have to engage the Chinese carrier group."

"It could escalate into war," Daniel said.

Grimes nodded.

"We need to get Thompson off of that ship," Jonathan said.

"I don't know if that's possible," Grimes said.

"It's *imperative* that we get him into our custody," Sylvia reiterated.

"I'm not sure that's true," Grimes said. "Our first priority is to get him out of Chinese hands. That might mean ... well, it's not pretty."

Jonathan didn't like it, but he knew Grimes was right. Killing Will would satisfy the minimum requirement of not allowing the Chinese to use him. "There's no way Thompson would cooperate with them."

Grimes nodded. "I'll get back to you after I talk with Naval Command," he said and walked away at a hurried pace.

Jonathan thought that Will should be informed of their plans; maybe it would give him a chance to get out of the way. But he knew that was unlikely. There was nowhere to flee.

~ 3 ~

Wednesday, 10 June (11:21 a.m. EST)

Will pointed the pistol at Zhang and put his back against the wall next to the door. "Tell them to go away," he whispered and then nodded at him to open it.

Zhang pulled the door open and said something to the man on the other side. The conversation went back and forth a few times and Will realized he'd made a stupid mistake. He couldn't understand what Zhang was saying and now he couldn't let the other man leave.

Will sprung into the doorway with his gun ready. The man was already aiming and pulling the trigger. Will felt himself leave his body as the world slowed down around him. An instant later, he recombined with his body. He was still standing.

It took him a few seconds to process the scene before him. The man's head was gone and his body leaned against Zhang. Blood spurted out from the man's frayed neck and into Zhang's face.

Will had just killed the man in an instant, and couldn't remember doing anything. His head pounded. "You stupid fuck!" he yelled and grabbed Zhang's ear and dragged him into the room. He grabbed the collar of at the headless sailor and dragged his twitching body into the room and closed the door. He looked back to Zhang and pointed to the two headless corpses on the floor. "That is your fault."

Will punched Zhang on the side of the head, and grabbed his collar.

"Where are the nukes?" Will asked. "Where will they be launched?"

Nothing.

He dragged Zhang to the side of the table, and forced his hand onto its surface.

"Tell me," Will said. His patience was gone.

Zhang said nothing.

Will's anger had boiled over. He slammed the handle of the pistol onto Zhang's fingers with great force. Bones broke, and the flesh around one of them split, yellow slivers of bone jutting through the skin.

Zhang responded with a delayed scream.

Will grabbed the man's ear and twisted hard. "Where are they?" he yelled.

He brought the pistol up high and slammed the hand again. The pinky finger was now mangled, bent at an awkward angle and bleeding. The nail of his ring finger was completely removed, stuck to the bottom of the gun handle.

For a split second the darkness that filled Will's thoughts faded to shame. The feeling disappeared quickly: what Zhang was experiencing was nothing compared to what he had endured in the Red Box. *And they shot Denise.*

Will brought the pistol up again, but before he brought it down, Zhang yelled out. "Wait. I'll tell you whatever you need to know," he said, half screaming, half crying. "There's nothing on this ship."

"What about the other surface ships?"

Zhang shook his head, blood dripping from where he'd bitten his lip. "Only submarines."

"How many subs are carrying nukes?"

"There are six subs; one of the six carries nuclear warheads," Zhang said.

He let go of Zhang's arm and the man slipped off the edge of the table, holding his damaged hand tightly with the other.

Will turned to Cho. "Your men shot one of my friends," Will said. "You killed the CP men. You killed Adler, and who knows how many others. Now you plan to murder thousands, all in the name of the Red Wraith project. You know people. I want names."

Cho didn't answer.

"You see what's happening to this ship?" Will said, looking Cho directly in the eyes. "The plane crashing into the sea, the fires, the helicopter – that was all me." He then nodded towards Captain Zhang, who was still on the floor, clutching his fingers. He looked back to Cho and pointed to the two dead men on the floor. "I swear I'll do the same to you."

Cho nodded. "I will write them down for you."

Will searched drawers and cabinets until he found a technical manual of some sort and tore off the cover. "You have a pen?" he asked.

Cho nodded and pulled one out of his shirt pocket.

"I want your superiors in China, anyone involved in Red Wraith – or your Red Dragon project. I want the moles in the U.S., and any foreign connections," Will said.

"There are three people above me in China," Cho said, "I only know of two high-ranking people in the United States. One is dead."

"Write," Will said and put the paper on the table in front of him. He then stepped behind him so he could see what he was writing and keep an eye on Zhang at the same time.

"I can't," Cho said. "My arm."

Will grabbed the pen and stood next to him. "Talk."

There was only one name on the list that he recognized: Heinrich Bergman. He was the first person Will had killed his last day in the Red Box.

He asked questions as Cho talked. The other American VIP on the list was CIA, but that was no surprise. "Now, the name of the thug who killed the man in the parking garage," Will said.

Cho said the name.

"What about the two FBI agents – where were they in the hierarchy?" Will asked.

"Low-level operatives to deal with personnel matters," Cho replied. "They were to be eliminated. They were about to be dropped into the sea, but then the helicopter crashed."

Will folded the paper, reached inside his blue overalls, and put it in his front pants pocket. He turned to Zhang. "Now I need to get off of this smoldering piece of crap," he said and pulled out Cho's phone.

~ 4 ~

Wednesday, 10 June (11:58 a.m. EST)

Jonathan answered on the first ring, and sat down at the small conference table. He put it in speaker mode and set it in front of him so that the others could hear.

"Go ahead, Will," Jonathan said. "Everyone's here, including Captain Grimes."

"I have the captain here – his name is Zhang," Will said. "He's agreed to release me."

"Are you on speaker phone?" Grimes asked.

"No."

"They're not going to release you, Thompson," Grimes said. "Israeli intelligence tells us that their orders are to either use you, or kill you – at all costs. They're not to give you up under any circumstances, even if it means losing their entire carrier group."

No response.

"William?" Jonathan said.

After a few seconds, he replied, "I'm still here." His voice was softer. "I understand."

"What are you going to do?" Denise asked. A tear rolled down her cheek to the corner of her mouth.

"I'll think of something," Will answered. "Before I go, there are some names you should be aware of – people involved in Red Wraith, and FBI and CIA leaks to investigate." He read the list to them. "The two FBI moles were with me from the beginning – starting in Chicago. The leak there is serious. Trust no one."

"Put your phone in speaker mode," Grimes said.

After a few seconds Will informed him that it was ready.

"Captain Zhang," Grimes said, "this is Captain Grimes of the USS *Stennis*. Your carrier is dead in the water and burning. You have

326

threatened a tactical nuclear attack on our vessels, and we have been given authority to launch a preemptive strike. Surrender William Thompson to us immediately and move your group out of the area. We can offer assistance to tug your disabled carrier."

"Regretfully," the Chinese captain replied. "I do not have that authority."

"A lot of people are going to die," Grimes said.

"That is not my choice," Zhang replied. "If you leave the area, no one will die."

"I've heard enough," Will broke in. "What can I do to assist you, Captain? I can sink this ship."

"That won't be necessary," Grimes replied. "It's disabled. The support ships in their group are conventional – no nukes. We're only concerned about their subs."

"Zhang says there are six in the area," Will explained, "and that only one is carrying nukes."

"We've already identified their subs," Grimes said. "Turn off the speaker."

Something clicked on the other end and Will followed with, "Go ahead."

"Our destroyers are going to move in at fourteen hundred hours," Grimes said. "That's in two hours."

Jonathan was taken off-guard by Grimes's disclosure.

"Go to the carrier's helipad area at that time," Grimes continued. "We'll have to improvise, so be prepared for anything."

"I'll be ready," Will said.

Jonathan picked up his phone and shut down the call.

Denise put her head on the table and remained silent.

"What's the plan?" Jonathan asked Grimes.

"First, we're going after their subs," Grimes replied. "Next, we'll sink every surface vessel that stays to fight, save the carrier. Then we'll raid the carrier. I hope Thompson can hold on for that long."

Denise lifted her head off the table. "I'm pretty sure he can handle anything, save the sinking of the carrier." There seemed to be hope in her voice.

Jonathan nodded. "I agree." He put his hand on Denise's shoulder. "He'll be fine." He looked to Grimes. "When does it start?"

Grimes stood and straightened his hat. "It already has."

~ 5 ~

Wednesday, 10 June (12:17 p.m. EST)

As Captain, McHenry had never been given a real search-and-destroy order. The *North Dakota* had the advantage of being stealthier and carrying better armaments, but the Chinese subs outnumbered those of the Americans 2 to 1. To complicate matters, Russian and British subs were also in the area, and it wasn't clear whether they would engage once the action started.

Taking out a sub was a serious matter. Unlike the sinking of a surface ship, where the crew at least had a chance to get into a life raft or be picked up by another vessel, everyone on a sinking sub was doomed. McHenry had not yet informed the crew, or even Diggs, of the orders. They were to commence the mission in 90 minutes, so he decided to hold off for another 20 minutes with the hope that the orders might be rescinded. He knew that was unlikely, but they'd remain at communication depth until it was time to move.

He was apprehensive not only about the taking of life, but for the lives of his crew— many were younger than 25 and had families. He trusted that there was a confirmed threat to prompt his superiors to give the order to attack.

He made his rounds, sipping strong coffee from an oversized stainless steel mug, and chatting with the crew as he went along.

When he got to Finley, he asked, "What do you hear out there?"

"A lot," Finley answered. "Eight signatures."

"Anything new?"

"Yes," Finley answered and pointed to a sheet of paper on the

328

consul.

McHenry picked it up. It was a list identifying various subs by country and type: 6 Chinese, 1 Russian, and 1 British. Of the Chinese subs, only one was nuclear-capable. The others were sub hunters – hunter-killers. The *North Dakota's* primary target was the nuke-capable sub, but they'd likely have to engage the others – or be engaged by them.

"Anything unusual?" McHenry asked.

"One of the Chinese subs seems to have left the area – toward the direction of their carrier group," Finley explained. "Two of the Chinese subs went quiet. The remaining three Chinese and the Russian are moving about – patrolling."

"I want you to seek out that nuke sub, and keep an eye out for another," McHenry said. "It's important – I'll tell you more later – but it's crucial you keep them marked. Understand?"

Finley raised an eyebrow, and then his face became serious. "Aye aye."

McHenry looked at his watch as he walked away. It was time to inform Diggs of their orders.

~ 6 ~
Wednesday, 10 June (1:18 p.m. EST)

Will tried to avoid looking at the two headless bodies on the floor, but it was as if his own guilt forced him to do it. Both men had threatened him, and his reactions had been spontaneous – out of his control. Crashing the jet had been a conscious effort, but justified in his mind. Crashing the helicopter was another story. That Roy and Natalie had deserved their fates eased his conscience, but it wasn't enough. He had every right to judge, but not to sentence and execute.

The blood that had pooled on the floor was now coagulated and dark, and the growing stench of death was unmistakable.

With only minutes to wait, he twitched with anxiety. He'd have to incapacitate Cho and Zhang. He considered killing them both, especially Cho, but assassination wasn't a path he wanted to take. He looked again at the headless corpses. He wasn't a killer.

He'd damage the carrier's weapons systems once he started towards the helipad, and he'd continue to do so until the Americans either raided it or sent it beneath the waves. He wondered if, once things got going, the Chinese would launch a nuke. He thought Cho was gravely mistaken in his assumption of a mild retaliation. The Chinese would be wagering their entire existence on whatever was behind "door number three," which, more often than not, was worthless. The beacon was a complete unknown.

It was time. Will stood and listened at the door.

"What are you going to do with us?" Zhang asked, still clenching his damaged fingers with his healthy hand.

"Take off all your clothes except for undergarments," Will replied dryly.

"Why?" Zhang asked.

"You too, Cho," Will added. "Now."

The men hesitated.

Will pointed the gun at each man and demanded that they comply. He then tied them up using their belts and shoelaces. Then, using their pants and shirts, he gagged them and then tied each man to one of many thick pipes that ran vertically along the wall opposite the door. They were now out of each other's reach, and should remain bound until they were discovered. By then he hoped to be off of the ship.

Will sat in a chair, separated, and passed into the hall. All was clear. Time to go.

He exited the room and walked at a hurried clip towards the helipad.

~ 7 ~

Wednesday, 10 June (1:29 p.m. EST)

"You certain, Finley?" McHenry asked.

"No doubt, sir." Finley replied. "It's their newest boomer."

"Any other boomers?"

"Unknown, but doubtful," Finley replied, "They've all been on the move in the past 48 hours, and we've tracked all six subs. The others are all fast-attacks."

McHenry's concern was that there was a seventh Chinese sub, another boomer sleeping in the dark. He couldn't afford to sink one and then have another launch on the carrier group.

He picked up his communicator. "Load forward torpedo tubes, 1 through 4. Load aft countermeasures, 1 and 2." They'd launch and run. It wasn't clear whether or not the Chinese fast-attack subs could hear them, but they might launch in the general direction of the *North Dakota* and let their torpedoes do the hunting.

He received affirmation that everything was ready.

"Status?" McHenry asked.

"Boomer went silent," Finley replied. "Assuming the same location."

McHenry spoke into his communicator. "Launch torpedoes 1 and 2."

~ 8 ~
Wednesday, 10 June (1:44 p.m. EST)

Will climbed a flight of stairs, opened the door at the top, and emerged on the carrier's upper deck. The wind pierced his clothing like frozen needles, and his body went into spasms of shivering. He pressed forward, breathing in the salty, freezing mist that was expelled into the air by the massive waves that crashed into the side of the ship. The deck was slippery, and he grabbed a hold of whatever he could as he moved along.

He headed toward the bright flames that still reached high into the sky above the bridge, fluttering in the wind like loose sails. About halfway to his destination, he noticed something on the deck that he recognized. It was dome-like object covered with a tarp, and he was sure it was a multi-barreled gun used to shoot down incoming missiles, modeled after the American Sea Wiz weapon. Yet another stolen technology, he thought.

He sat cross-legged on the deck and separated. As he approached the gun from the top, he realized it was much larger than he'd anticipated. He penetrated the plastic tarp and examined the gun. It had six barrels mounted on a spindle attached to a gear mechanism. The entire weapon was on a rotatable platform, and an internal gearbox aimed the weapon. All he had to do was pinch the barrels closed. A few seconds later, the task was completed and he was back in his body and heading for the helipad.

He knew that most aircraft carriers could launch missiles, but he couldn't identify anything that looked like a launcher. As he made his way aft, a flash lit up the horizon, showing the silhouette of a ship. Seconds later, a deep boom made his chest vibrate. The explosion was followed by barrage of others that illuminated the clouds from below. The American ships, and possibly planes, were attacking.

Adrenaline surged into his bloodstream and he took off in a sprint. An instant later he was sliding on his chest. He stood and rubbed his chin, which might have been bleeding but couldn't tell in the dim light. He continued at a controlled pace, slipping about every third step but maintaining his balance.

He had no idea what the U.S. Navy had planned to get him off of the ship. His first thoughts were that they'd try by helicopter since they'd arranged the rendezvous at the helipad. That would be a tough mission, he thought, and he didn't want anyone to risk their lives for him.   He understood the reason for the preemptive strike – there was an imminent threat. But his life was inconsequential. In fact, the world might be better off without him – he was the reason for the confrontation. If he died, and they followed with destroying the beacon, there'd be nothing left to fight about. But the smell of burning diesel and the sight of the two ships tugging the carrier told him that was a false sentiment. He – *one man* – had just destroyed an aircraft carrier. Every major country in the world would seek to make more like him.

Maybe the *final solution* was to enter the beacon and solve its riddle.

~ 9 ~

Wednesday, 10 June (2:01 p.m. EST)

McHenry already knew what the words were going to be.

"It's a hit," Finley said, and then added, "with secondary explosions."

McHenry's heart tightened. "Get us out of here," he ordered over his communicator. "Ready countermeasures and reload forward torpedoes." He turned to Finley. "Mark the next closest target."

Finley nodded, his face more solemn than McHenry had ever seen it. It was a tough thing for a man to do, end another's life. McHenry had done it before, and he'd hoped to never have to do it again. But that wasn't how it was going to be. Now there were over 100 more souls on their way to crush depth, never to be recovered.

"Fish in the water!" Finley yelled.

An image of sinking into a watery grave of his own flashed in McHenry's head. "Bearing?"

"Wait!" Finley exclaimed. "An explosion."

McHenry knew there were friendlies in the area – 2 American subs and 1 British. He hoped they were the ones doing the shooting.

"Lost track of one of the Chinese fast-attacks," Finley said.

It was an immediate relief, but they weren't out of the woods yet.

Finley concentrated on the computer monitor, and after 20 seconds, he said, "All clear."

The *North Dakota's* mission was to seek out and destroy the Chinese boomer. That being accomplished, they were to leave the cleanup to the other subs and get to the rendezvous point: the *Stennis*.

~ 10 ~

Wednesday, 10 June (2:06 p.m. EST)

The wind picked up pace and changed direction. Will caught motion in his peripheral vision and looked up to see a helicopter hovering in silence above the landing pad.

He moved as quickly as he could towards the black aircraft, but halted when he realized the burnt debris littered the helipad, making it unusable. The chopper would have to land somewhere else. There was no other suitable place nearby: he'd have to get back to the flight deck.

He started to wave to the helicopter when a rope ladder dropped from its underbelly to the deck, near the helipad. He got to it as quickly as he could, grabbed the highest rung he could reach, and hoisted himself up to get a foot in a lower rung. He struggled as the lower part of the rope ladder flopped under his feet, but he managed to hook the arch of his right foot in the lowest loop. The helicopter lifted him slowly from the deck.

When he was about 30 feet above the deck, a deafening blast of sound and searing light spewed from beneath the helicopter's nose and startled him, nearly making him fall. It was firing its heavy machine guns.

He looked back over his shoulder: dozens of Chinese military personnel skated around on the deck, firing weapons at the helicopter. Many of the sailors fell on the icy surface as they moved about, making their shots inaccurate, but bullets still whizzed through the air by his head and clanked against the armor of the helicopter.

The helicopter ascended, pulling him higher and out over the water. Short bursts from the chopper's guns above him created flames that left white afterglow images on his retinas. Bullets sprayed in more heavily from the carrier deck, filling the space all around him, and striking the helicopter. The huge Gatlin gun weapon he'd disabled on the way out erupted into flames.

A bullet whizzed by his ear, making it pop. Then everything

seemed to freeze in time. It was still over 100 feet away, but a bullet was on course to hit him. Before he knew what happened, the bullet missed its mark, and the man on the other end of the trajectory, the one who had fired the shot, was ablaze and rolling on the deck. He was screaming.

A fraction of a second later, the scene froze again. Two more bullets were on target: one to his back, the other to his thigh. An instant later, two more burning men shrieked and rolled on the deck. Their shots had been deflected.

He secured his grip on the ladder and adjusted his footing. Time stopped again: four more bullets on target. The relentless onslaught angered him beyond his threshold of control. He screamed in rage and seemed to black out for an instant. When he recovered he couldn't believe his eyes. The deck was strewn with rolling and flailing bodies ablaze. For an instant, all of the gunfire stopped. Although he knew the image would be burned into his mind, it was the screaming of the 53 men that would haunt him. How he knew that number, he didn't know.

The firing commenced.

Without warning, his body shifted sharply, making his foot slip out of the ladder and his right hand release its grip. A bullet had cut one of the vertical links of the rope ladder four rungs above his right hand.

His left hand now supported his full weight, and he spun in tight circles as the ladder twisted in the wind. His left wrist wrenched painfully as he struggled to keep his grip and flailed with his right hand to get a hold of the ladder. His hand was slipping.

A man yelled at him from above to hang on. It was the last thing he heard before he plunged into cold and utter darkness.

It was as if he'd hit a wall when he slammed into water. After the shock of the splash, his ears recorded only bubbling static. The water was so cold it was as if death itself had engulfed him. It was a feeling he'd experienced before, and he knew his body would be useless in seconds. He was already too deep: even if he got to the surface, his hands would be too sluggish to grip the ladder – if they were even able to get it close to him. He relaxed.

His thoughts slowed, and full-color images of his life passed into

335

the forefront of his mind: swimming with the family at the lake as a kid, Little League, Christmas when he got his first bike, fishing with his grandfather, the smell of grass on the football field, soccer in summer afternoons, bailing hay, dinner with the family, his high school girlfriend, graduating college, Denise … He was tempted to sleep but, as everything seemed to shut down, one thought remained: *his life had a purpose*. Even though he had no idea what it was, there was something he was supposed to do. And he was close to it somehow – he could feel it.

He had one last chance. With every synapse of mental capacity he had left, he relived the most painful things he'd experienced in his life. *All of them*: physical, psychological, emotional … sadness for the things he had missed, and for those that would be stolen from him if he died now. The next thing he knew, he was out of his body and above the waves.

He descended into the water and found his sleeping body. He grasped it somehow – as if he were picking up a baby bird from the grass – and pulled it upward. He brought it through the surface and out of the waves. The helicopter was still directly above him, as if no time had passed since he'd fallen. His sprawling body moved upward as if it were rising out of the depths of hell.

In what seemed like no more than a second, he'd taken his body from 20 feet beneath the icy waves to 100 feet above the surface. He brought it to the underbelly of the helicopter and shoved it through the open door on the side. The soldier manning the rope latter shrieked as Will's body slammed onto the floor of the cabin. Will recombined and then rolled on the floor and curled into a ball, shivering uncontrollably.

"What the f …" the soldier yelled. "I saw him fall into the water. How did you …"

The onset of hypothermia forbade Will's mouth to form words, not that he could've explained what had happened.

The helicopter ascended, rolled left, and headed for the open sea.

~ 11 ~
Wednesday, 10 June (2:48 p.m. EST)

Will's head bobbed sideways and bounced off the cabin floor as the helicopter landed on the deck of the USS *Stennis*. Lying sideways and curled in a ball, he welcomed the hands that helped him to his feet and unraveled his sluggish limbs from the thermal blanket in which the crew of chopper had wrapped him. A group of sailors met him as he stepped off the aircraft, and two grabbed him by the arms and helped him along. He recognized someone waiting in a wheelchair near the door, and was happy to see her.

Denise stood and grabbed his arm as he approached. "Why are you all wet?" she asked.

"Fell in," he said, barely getting his lips to move.

"What – into the water?" she asked, her face distorted in disbelief.

He nodded.

"Into the sea?"

"Yes," he said again, barely getting it out.

"How did you – "

Before she could finish asking the question he couldn't answer, medics peeled her from his arm and pulled him through a doorway and into narrow corridor. A tall man in his early fifties approached him.

"Captain Grimes," the man said and stuck out his hand. "Glad you made it, Dr. Thompson.

Will managed to nod and weakly shake his hand. "Thanks."

"Let's get you into dry clothes and fed. We'll meet in an hour," Grimes said and nodded to a female doctor who hooked Will's arm with her own and led him away. Five minutes later he was in a piping-hot shower trying to come to terms with what had happened over the past 24 hours. He'd disabled an aircraft carrier. He'd killed people. Many people. He'd also saved himself from certain death. He wasn't convinced that any of it had really happened: someone watching the events would have witnessed over 50 men spontaneously ignite into flames, and a body emerge from the depths of the icy sea and ascend into the sky. What he'd done had violated the laws of physics, among other things.

He reflected on what had happened while the cold water was leaching his soul from his body. His life had passed through his mind – all of the important scenes had flickered in front of his eyes like an old movie reel. But it wasn't a reminder – he hadn't forgotten any of those things. The purpose was to get them out of the way – they were hiding something that dwelled beneath. Something bad had happened to him that didn't fit into his current existence. And there was something for the future: he had a purpose. But he couldn't formulate the thoughts into words or images. They were *feelings*.

A half hour later he was in dry, comfortable clothes and eating a hot bowl of beef stew. He hadn't realized how hungry he was until he took the first few bites. The nourishment seemed to release tension and sooth his nerves. He could hardly keep his eyes open, but knew that he'd have little time to sleep.

"How do you like your new Navy clothes?" a woman said from behind him.

He stood and turned just as Denise rolled in and gave him a hug. Jonathan followed behind her, and Will almost didn't recognize him in the blue Navy garb.

Denise released him, and he shook hands with Jonathan.

"Heard you had a close call on the way here," Jonathan said.

Will nodded. "Slipped into the water. I was lucky to get out."

Jonathan gave him a sideways look indicating that it required further explanation, but didn't push it.

"Better eat well and get some coffee," Jonathan said, nodding to the bowl on the table. "Things are moving quickly, and you have a lot of catching up to do."

Denise sat at Will's right, and Jonathan directly across from him. He was too hungry to ask questions, so he just listened as Jonathan spoke. For the next 20 minutes he learned how Jonathan and Denise had gotten involved and how they'd lost the Chinese operatives in Chicago with the help of the Israelis. It was the story of how Chinese agents had caught up with them at Mar del Plata that angered him most. He wished Denise and Jonathan had stayed out of it.

Will got up and set his tray on a cafeteria-style conveyor, and then took Jonathan's advice and got a cup of coffee. As he walked back, he noticed that two others had joined their table: a dark-haired man, thin build, forties, and a woman who could have been the man's twin, but with red hair and dark-rimmed glasses. Both wore the Navy-issued clothing.

As Will approached the table, all eyes were on him. He remained standing.

"This is Daniel and Sylvia," Jonathan said. "I'd give you last names, but I don't know them."

Will nodded to the newcomers. "CIA," he said and watched their flushed responses. Direct hit, he thought.

"Daniel Parsons," the man said and walked around the table, hand extended. "I trust you, Dr. Thompson. Please, try to trust me."

The woman was next. "Sylva Barnes," she said and shook his hand. "There's a third, Horace, but he's been ill."

"Horace is an older man," Daniel explained. "He's also the most valuable intelligence resource we have."

Will nodded solemnly. "What are you planning?"

"That's what we wanted to discuss," Daniel replied and stood. "Captain Grimes is waiting in the ready room."

Will pushed Denise's wheelchair, and they lagged behind the rest of the group as they made the walk. When the others turned a corner ahead of them, Denise stopped the chair and stood, favoring the injured leg. She grabbed Will's arm with one hand and the side of his neck with the other. She pulled his head down and kissed him on the lips.

"I'm glad you're here," she said, looking into his eyes. "I'm glad you're okay."

They stared into each other's eyes until a voice rang out.

"Keep up," Jonathan said, sticking his head around the corner.

Will smiled as Denise settled back into her chair.

"We'll continue this later," she said, blushing.

"How long are you in that thing?"

"I get rid of the chair tomorrow morning," she said in a tone of defiance and with a serious look in her eye. "The wounds are small – only fragments – but they want to make sure I don't start bleeding again. I can walk now if I need to."

Will laughed.

"I can," she said.

"I know," he responded, still chuckling. There would be no arguing with her.

He rolled her around the corner and arrived at their destination a minute later.

They entered the room, and Will took a seat opposite Captain Grimes, who sat at the head of the rectangular table. Denise, and then Jonathan, sat to his right, and Daniel and Sylvia to his left.

Grimes started. "We need to get you up to speed quickly," he said. "We're going to rendezvous with the *North Dakota* in 30 minutes."

"The *North Dakota*?" Will asked.

"A submarine," Daniel added.

Will nodded. He knew where this was going.

"You're aware of the beacon?" Grimes asked.

"Aware," Will replied. "That's all."

"Then you know as much as we do," Daniel said. "I could give you the full rundown, but I think we should go over what you are going to do."

"We're under time pressure?" Will asked.

"Yes," Grimes said. "We just attacked the Chinese fleet. We might be going to war." Grimes' forehead crinkled, furrowing his brow. "We have taken a big gamble. The Chinese know we have you, and they know our next step. If they're going to attack, it will be soon. We have to move."

Will was confused. Why take a risk for a complete unknown? "Up to this point, the beacon has only made noise," he said, directing his words at Daniel and Sylvia in addition to Captain Grimes. "What are you not telling us?"

Grimes shook his head and nodded to Daniel.

"There's not enough time," Daniel said. "We've explained everything to Jonathan and Denise, and we'll share it with you when you get back."

Will looked over to Denise and Jonathan.

Denise grabbed his hand and looked into his eyes. "You have to trust us, Will."

Jonathan nodded in agreement.

"Okay," Will said and turned to Daniel. "What you want me to do?"

~ 12 ~
Wednesday, 10 June (7:13 p.m. EST)

This was it, Will thought. He hoped that there was a purpose for all of it – the humiliation, loss, and pain he'd experienced in the past two years. And also for the people who had lost their lives along the way – including those he'd killed.

It was his second time on a submarine. The first was during a visit to the Chicago Museum of Science and Industry as a kid. That one was a German U-boat. Based on what he'd seen of the *North Dakota*, modern submarines had come a long way.

Captain McHenry arranged a private quarters for him and they were in position near the beacon within an hour. It was odd to him how people could act as if they knew what was happening, and how to proceed, even though they clearly did not. Maybe that was what leadership was about. He didn't know what to expect, and he certainly didn't know what to do. All he knew was that it was time.

He separated and passed into a room of sailors staring at computer monitors. He then penetrated the hardened steel of the hull and emerged into cold darkness. Now in the water, the image of the submarine was clear in his perception even though there was no light. To the right, perhaps 1,000 yards off, was the silhouette of another.

The depth of the head of the beacon was greater than any distance he'd separated before. On his way down, the cold currents seemed to flow through him, and he noticed how they changed direction as he approached the sphere. He examined the beacon's surface; it was smooth, off-white, and flawless.

341

Time was limited – he was already exhausted – so he had to push on. He pressed into the surface of the sphere but met strong resistance. It was as if he was still in a rigid state – the form that he assumed to interact with the physical world. He concentrated on assuming the non-interacting, softened state and tried again. It was as if he were pushing his way through a thick wall of stiff gelatin and getting stuck somewhere in the middle. He struggled through more than a meter and emerged in the interior of the sphere.

It was empty – no water, but he sensed air. A soft white illumination soothed him and a sensation of comfort engulfed him. It was a feeling he'd never before experienced. It was as if his body, now a great distance away, no longer tugged on him. His "separation fatigue" was no longer worsening. He wondered if it was what death felt like and, just for an instant, worried that might actually *be* dead. The feeling was soon displaced by curiosity.

The sphere was much larger than it seemed from the outside, perhaps the volume of a high school basketball gymnasium. A white pedestal extended vertically from the direction of the beacon's stem and terminated at the center of the sphere. Although the contrast was subtle, the light inside the sphere seemed to focus on the end of the pedestal.

He descended to the pedestal. It was of the same texture, and composed of the same material, as the shell of the beacon. Its top surface was flat, horizontal, and circular, with a diameter of about a meter. Mounted to a pivot at its center was a black lever, a half-meter in length, which resembled the hand of a clock. The lever was thick at the pivot, maybe four inches wide, but tapered to less than an inch at the end. The tip pointed to an open, black circle, about the size of a silver dollar. If the open circle were located at the ten o'clock position, then at the two-o'clock position was a solid black circle. A thin arc connected the two, suggesting the lever could be turned from the empty circle to the solid one.

What was he supposed to do? What would be the consequence of turning the lever? It could be a booby trap – a bomb, or nuclear device. He frantically searched the entire sphere, including the pedestal and the location from where it emerged. There were no crevices, scratches, or imperfections of any kind. It was as if the entire beacon were cut from a single piece of material. It seemed that the sole purpose of the structure was to house the switch.

Being an experimental physicist, it was against his nature to flip switches without knowing their functions. Such behavior often resulted in smoking electronics, and costing a great deal of money and time. Nonetheless, he knew he had to turn the lever. There might never be another chance. His conversation with an old physics professor came to him once again: *if it were possible, humans would eventually do it, even if they destroyed themselves in the process.* The professor was right.

He grasped the lever and pulled it in the clockwise direction. It didn't budge.

Surprised, since in other instances he'd even been able to tear through steel with little effort, he grasped the switch again and turned with all of his might. It moved a few millimeters. He pulled again – it moved a few more degrees along the arc. Again, and again. The final turn spanned a few centimeters and aligned the end of the lever with the solid circle.

The pedestal immediately lowered away from him, slowly at first, then faster. He quickly realized that the ceiling of the sphere was moving towards him. *The entire beacon was descending.* He had to get out.

He moved to the ceiling, softened his state so that he could pass through the beacon's shell, and pressed upward. The material caused significant resistance and, as he emerged from the outer surface, cold water rushed upward and through him. The beacon was dragging him downward. Struggling, he completely freed himself from sphere, but not before it had dragged him another 100 meters below the *North Dakota*. The connection with his body was weaker than it had ever been.

As he ascended, he looked back just as beacon lowered into the seabed. As its spherical head pressed into the floor, sand and rock fell around it, filling in the void it had created. When everything settled, the area was indistinguishable from the rest of the ocean floor.

Will returned to his body. He opened his eyes and looked into the face of a medic who held a stethoscope to his chest.

"You okay?" the young man asked.

343

Will closed his eyes.

"Sit up," the medic said and shook him. "You've been out for two hours."

Will sat up and opened his eyes. "Anything happen here?" he asked.

A voiced boomed in from the doorway. "The beacon retracted into the floor," Captain McHenry said, out of breath. "Nothing else, as far as we can tell."

Will had expected something more, although he had no idea what.

"Did you get inside?" McHenry asked.

Will nodded. "Yes."

"What was there – what did you do?"

"It was an empty sphere except for a lever – *a switch*," Will explained. "I pulled it."

"What?" McHenry asked. "That's why it retracted?"

"I think so," Will replied.

McHenry turned to the medic. "Is he all right?"

The medic responded with a nod. "He's exhausted. Heart rate is high."

"Let him rest," McHenry said and turned to Will. "We'll surface and deliver you to the *Stennis* in about an hour."

McHenry and the medic left.

Will laid back, put his head on a pillow, and closed his eyes. As he fought through fits of nausea, he pondered what had just happened. He'd separated his soul from his body and actuated a device that seemed to be from a source beyond humanity.

Two years ago, he'd been living the life of a professor, concerned with menial tasks like grading exams and cutting the lawn at his small house. And then, without warning, he'd been plunged into a darkness he could never have imagined: the Red Box. The experience had liberated him from the confines of the physical world, and his perception of his own existence had fundamentally changed.

But the fundamental questions that constantly churned in the back of his mind nagged now more than ever. *What was his purpose? Why did he exist?*

Perhaps now an answer would reveal itself.

CHAPTER XV

~ 1 ~

Thursday, 11 June (7:55 a.m. EST – Weddell Sea)

As he showered, Will contemplated the events of the previous 48 hours. The memory of the men burning and screaming on the deck of the Chinese carrier haunted him. Thoughts of the future were foreshadowed by the possible consequences of pulling the switch in the beacon. What had he done? What had he become?

As he walked to meet the others, he tried to distract himself from the anxiety. He appreciated the stark differences between the USS *Stennis* and the Chinese carrier: the former was cleaner, more modern, and larger. It was also operable. The aroma of the food coming from the mess hall was intoxicating. He got in line and loaded a mountain of scrambled eggs, bacon, and potatoes onto his plate.

He sat on a bench next to a large, rectangular table. Everyone else was already there. Denise, now promoted to crutches, sat to his right, and Jonathan to his left. Daniel and Sylvia were sitting directly across from them, along with someone he didn't recognize. The gaunt man was probably in his nineties, and looked morbidly ill.

"My name is Horace Leatherby," the man said to Will. "It's nice to finally meet you. I regret not being able to see you before your encounter with the beacon."

"Pleasure to meet you," Will said and shook his hand. "I hope you're feeling better."

Horace shrugged. "I think I've improved."

"You actually saw the inside the sphere?" Daniel interrupted, eyes wide.

Will looked at the small man, took a bite of food, and nodded: no verbal response.

Daniel looked to Jonathan.

346

"Will, these people have been studying this thing from the beginning," Jonathan said, nodding towards Daniel's side of the table. "Daniel started investigating Red Wraith months ago."

"And what have you learned about Red Wraith, exactly?" Will asked.

"That you were its only success," Sylvia answered before Daniel could respond. "You're able to separate, a fact confirmed by your actuating the beacon."

Will took a bite of bacon, chewed slowly, and stared at her.

"You disabled the aircraft carrier," Sylvia added.

"It turns out that the predecessor to Red Wraith, the Nazis' Red Falcon project, involved more than just developing separation abilities," Daniel said. "I'd think you'd want to know the reason for it, considering all of the horror you've been through."

Will made eye contact with Daniel. "A reason? If it's something other than making monsters to wage war, I'd like to know." He was starting to think *he* was a monster.

"It was about the beacon from the very beginning," Daniel responded.

"Explain," Will said.

Over the next two hours, and a full carafe of coffee between them, Will learned the most disturbing and fascinating things: a strange message on a stone discovered in the pyramids of Egypt, Hitler's secret base, and the beacon. It was a message on the stone that had inspired Red Falcon and Red Wraith. And the ultimate objective of Red Falcon – a concept that eluded the creators of Red Wraith – was to get inside the beacon and flip that switch.

Will became more amenable to the idea of cooperating, and explained the details of what he'd seen and done inside the beacon. His report was short since there wasn't much to explain: an empty sphere and a switch. "I turned the switch and the beacon retracted into the sea bed, nearly dragging me along with it. That's all. The question now is whether something else has happened of which we're unaware."

Daniel nodded. "It might have initiated something."

"Like a war with China," Will said.

"Don't think so," Sylvia argued. "Thackett informed us that the Chinese are standing down. The President threatened major retaliation if they attacked. Besides, it's too late. We've already actuated the beacon. The world didn't end, and we haven't acquired some new, devastating power."

"The perplexing thing is that the Chinese, and probably the Russians, knew more about Red Wraith and the Beacon than we did – until recently, that is," Daniel explained. "We were just lucky to happen across the tunnel and the Nazi base, and to secure the waters around beacon, before anyone else did."

"The Chinese knew about it because there were leaks. Big ones. And the main contractor involved in Red Wraith, Syncorp, moved its operations to China," Will said and looked to Jonathan. "Hopefully the names I gave you will help to finally dismantle this thing."

Jonathan nodded. "We have people working on it already."

Will shook his head. "In the end, the Nazis organized the torture of thousands of people because of a cryptic message they found on an artifact?"

"Their interpretation of the White Stone could be the sole reason for the Holocaust," Daniel said.

Will flinched. "The Holocaust?"

"And possibly the cause of World War Two," Sylvia added. "Hitler was a fanatic about the occult and religion. When the Nazis discovered the White Stone in the early 1930's, Hitler became obsessed. It instigated the founding of a new Nazi institute by Heinrich Himmler in 1935, called *Ahnenerbe*, meaning 'inherited from the forefathers.' The purpose of this new institute was to research the archaeological and cultural history of the Aryan race. They searched for things like the Holy Grail and the Holy Spear, thinking they had some powers of divine origin, similar to the White Stone."

"Researchers from the Ahnenerbe Institute had deciphered parts of the outer rings," Horace explained, "giving the location of the beacon, and told them what to look for – or *listen* for, in this case. They sent a vessel –"

" – the *Schwabenland*," Daniel interjected.

"Yes," Horace said, "the official mission of which was to explore new whaling waters, but the real mission was to locate the beacon."

"They found it, of course," Daniel said. "Hitler was emboldened – this was before the war – and they looked for a place to build a hidden base to conceal their prolonged presence in the area."

"They found the ideal location," Sylvia added and looked to Will. "You should have seen it."

"Hitler must've believed he'd had an advantage, prompting him to start the war prematurely," Daniel continued. "He thought the beacon was a source of great power – power they'd have in time to win the war. It was a gamble he lost."

"The problem was that things didn't go well in the separation experiments," Sylvia explained. "The infamous Dr. Josef Mengele was tasked with the initial experiments. He failed, and then concluded they needed to intensify their experiments."

"Hence, the concentration camps – the Holocaust," Will said, shaking his head. "And for what? The remote chance that the beacon would give him the world?"

"You know it's not over, right?" Daniel asked.

Will made eye contact with Daniel and then looked into his empty coffee cup. "Yes," he said and looked back to Daniel's eyes. Will twisted in his seat. "That thing was beyond our technology and had a purpose beyond making noise." He readjusted himself again and scratched the back of his neck near the hairline. Of course it had a purpose.

"Even the material of which it is composed is beyond our understanding," Daniel said. "It can only mean one thing."

"Extraterrestrial technology," Jonathan said.

"Or a supernatural origin," Sylvia added quietly.

Will could tell she was uncomfortable suggesting such a thing. He understood. As a scientist, he'd have to conclude that neither choice – extraterrestrial or supernatural sources – would be likely. Given only the two options, however, his science background would make him choose the former. But he had more information than anyone else: he had experienced the supernatural world – in the separated state, and in his encounters in the Red Box. His mind was completely open as to the source of the beacon, what it meant, and what was to come.

"The question now is *when is something going to happen?*" Daniel added.

After a few seconds of silence, Jonathan asked, "How long are we going to wait here – I mean, on this ship?"

Daniel looked down at the table, trying to formulate an answer. "Don't know," he said, finally. "They want us to wait here for a while – *all* of us."

"For how long?" Will asked.

Daniel shook his head. "They didn't say."

"Who are *they*?" Jonathan asked.

"The CIA director, Naval Command, the President," Daniel replied. "You'll all be safer on the ship anyway. Back on land you might be abducted, or worse."

"I have business – " Jonathan said.

"You'll have full communication privileges. You can conduct your business from the ship," Daniel assured him. "But we have more pressing things. We have to study the materials we extracted from the base. I thought you all would want to help, including you, Will."

Jonathan and Denise both confirmed that they were eager to get started.

Will was intrigued. It was more than solving a puzzle, or exploring an unknown history. It was learning *his* history. "I'm okay with staying for a while," he said and looked to Denise. He was more than okay with it. He felt more comfortable now, on the ship, than he'd had in a long time. It was about the safest place on the planet – assuming the Chinese wouldn't attack. He didn't have to worry about being followed, and he was around friends who had taken great risks for him.

In addition to his overt anxiety, an underlying tension was sprouting and growing. There'd be a response to his pulling the switch – he *felt* it. And he needed to learn as much as he could before that happened. "When do we start?" he asked.

"You have a lot of background to catch up on," Sylvia said. She fidgeted with her hands and turned to Daniel. "Let's get to the files and bring them up to speed."

Her excitement propagated among the others.

They stood from the table, and serviced their food trays on the way out of the mess hall. Will followed behind and Denise fell back with him.

"I'm glad you're here," she said and leaned forward on her crutches. She grabbed his hand for an instant and let it go.

"Me too."

~ 2 ~
Friday, 12 June (2:43 p.m. EST)

Will sat at a large table in a room stacked with boxes and crates filled with books, files, and artifacts taken from the Nazi base. The smell of old books and light perfume brought back memories of college, studying physics in the stacks of the library with his girlfriend.

Daniel and Sylvia left to check on Horace. His condition was gradually deteriorating.

Denise sat across the table from Will and read files through black-framed glasses.

In a just over a day he'd gotten up to speed on Red Falcon's history and the Nazi base in Antarctica. His quick learning was thanks to Daniel's work; he'd compiled all of the important information into a detailed report. At first he thought it would be dry, factual reading. But it wasn't. The subject material was either too interesting or too disturbing to be boring.

Although it sickened him, he found the development of Red Falcon fascinating. Red Wraith had only picked up on the separation aspect of the research. They'd missed the White Stone, the secret base, and, most importantly, the beacon. That the Americans had missed the true

351

objective was a testament to the Nazis' ability to keep a secret. In the end, World War II, the Holocaust, the Nazi obsession with the occult and historic artifacts, and ODESSA, an acronym that stood for the organization of former SS members – were all connected to Red Falcon. They may even have occurred *because* of Red Falcon and, therefore, the beacon was the underlying cause of all of it. It was a dark, concealed thread of history that might never have been revealed had the beacon remained silent.

Only a few of the highest-ranking Nazis were fully vested in Red Falcon. The short list included Adolf Hitler, Hermann Göring, Joseph Goebbels, Heinrich Himmler, Wilhelm Canaris of German intelligence, and, of course, Dr. Josef Mengele – the monster responsible for the "hands-on" work. There were others who had participated in various arms of the project – the concentration camps, for instance – but they were oblivious to the full picture.

Will was surprised to learn that the allies had been aware of ODESSA well before the war had ended. The network was set up by the German SS to facilitate the escape of upper-echelon Nazis to, among other places, South America. However, even though they'd known about ODESSA, the allies seemed to have no idea about the Antarctic base. It was clear that Mengele had used the ODESSA rat path to escape to Argentina, and then to the base. He'd been sighted later in other South American countries until he'd finally died in Brazil in 1979, well after he'd carried out his hideous work and the base had been abandoned.

Denise sighed loudly, slapped a file on the table, and took a drink from her mug. She looked up and her dark eyes met Will's. "Can I ask you something?" she said.

"Shoot."

She hesitated, started to speak, and then stopped again.

"You want to know if I can really do it – separate," he said before she could speak. He knew that if it wasn't the specific question she hand in mind, it was in her mind somewhere. He'd wanted her to ask him about it.

"I do," she admitted. "But if you don't feel comfortable – "

"If I can't feel comfortable with you, then who? Why didn't you ask me long ago – right after I got out of the Red Box?" he asked and put down the file he'd been reading. He leaned forward and put his elbows on the table.

"I didn't want to pry – embarrass you."

He understood, and even appreciated the courtesy even though it implied disbelief. "The answer is yes, I can separate."

She nodded in a way that seemed that the answer didn't satisfy her.

"You need evidence," he said. "What do you want me to do?"

"What do you mean?"

"I can separate right now and prove it to you."

"No, you don't have to."

"Okay," he said and shrugged. He picked up the file and feigned reading. He knew if the roles were reversed that he'd want proof. He felt her eyes on him as he waited.

"What could you do?" she asked after a full minute of silence.

He slapped the file back on the table. He didn't want to do anything that might frighten her. "How about this," he said. "Write something on a piece of paper and hold it so I can't see it. You can't fold it or anything – that won't work. If you can see it, I can see it."

She looked at him with skepticism. "Okay," she said as she grabbed her notebook from the table and put it on her lap, completely out of his view, and wrote something on it.

"Ready?" he asked.

She nodded.

He sat back in his chair and relaxed, concentrated, and separated. He rose out of his body, above the table, and curled over to her side, read the words, and returned.

He opened his eyes, straightened up his body, and looked into her eyes.

"Well?" she asked.

"Who is *Carmen Davis*?" he asked.

Her expression evolved quickly from surprise to fear. "An alias I use sometimes," she replied.

"You're not going to freak out on me now, are you?"

She squinted her eyes. "That wasn't a trick of some sort, was it?"

He was ready for the reaction – the same he'd have under the circumstances. "I need to do something more drastic," he said. "What can I do to convince you?"

"Move something," she said.

He grabbed a book from the right side of the table and set it in front of her. "That's it?"   "Very funny. You know what I mean."

He closed his eyes and separated. He lifted the book about two feet and let it drop. He returned to his body as it hit the table with a thud.

Denise leaned away from the table. A tear rolled down her cheek.

He reached across and grabbed her hand. "Hey," he said softly. "I thought you knew what all of this was about." It was a statement and a question.

She nodded. "I know ... I heard about it," she explained. "It's different when you see it happening in front of you." She laughed and wiped a tear from her cheek with her free hand.

"The world is a different place now with that experience – actually seeing it – isn't it?" he asked.

"What do you mean?"

"Knowing what we're capable of," he said. It was something he'd thought about often. "I don't think it's a bad thing – to know. It's a new facet of our existence."

"What's it like?"

"Being separated?"

She nodded.

He had to think. It was something he'd never had to put into words.

"Is it like a dream?"

"No – not like my dreams anyway," he replied. "Mine are foggy, smeared. When I'm separated, it's the opposite; extreme clarity – details beyond imagination. Like when I look at the stars, I see everything as if I'm looking through a high-powered telescope. And the more I focus, the more I see. But it's so much more than that. It's as if the center of my consciousness – all of my senses – can move about without restriction."

"And you can move things," Denise said.

He nodded. "Yes – interact with them, or pass through them. I needed to do both to get inside the beacon and turn the switch."

"Do it again," she said, "the book."

"Why?"

"I want to see something."

He shrugged. "Okay."

He separated and lifted the book, but this time Denise grabbed it and tried to pull it down with one hand. He pulled a little harder, and she responded by grabbing it with both hands. He pulled a little harder and her arms stretched upward, straining. He was about to ease his tug when motion to his right caught his attention. There was something there – like a shadow, partially concealed behind the stacks of boxes and crates.

Will moved toward the crates, releasing the book, which slapped hard on the table. Denise said something, but he paid no attention. He moved to a stack on the far wall and peered around one corner. There it was, between the crates and the wall, crouching. It was dark, and had human-like features. It looked at him, and he felt as if its eyes were those of death itself. It jerked with claw-like hands to see if he'd flinch. It was trying to determine if he could see it.

Will remained still, but it suddenly lurched at him like a cornered cat.

The amorphous face then formed into the most hideous thing Will had ever seen – misshapen features, jagged fangs, large black eyes that seemed to be nothing but holes. And then it hissed; Will thought he could smell its rotten breath. The thing let out a ghastly screech and charged at him.

Will fled to the ceiling to avoid the advance. It chased him through the walls and down through the floor. An instant later, he was back in his body with the sensation of falling.

He hit the floor hard, his head just skimming the wall behind him. He'd fallen backwards in his chair. He stood up and Denise stared at him from across the table with a bewildered expression.

"What happened?" she asked.

355

"What the hell is in there?" he said, pointing at the stacks. He stood and moved to the crates. Denise followed.

"What is it?" she asked, shaken.

He opened boxes and then set them aside so that he could get to the next one on the stack. After he'd searched a half-dozen of them, Denise grabbed his shirtsleeve.

"What are you looking for?"

"They brought more back from the base than just files and books," Will said. "There's something else."

Denise nodded. "Yes, they brought the White Stone, a map, and … oh my God …"

She moved boxes around until she isolated two wooden crates, one larger and flat, about the size of small, square coffee table. The other was smaller, about the size of a microwave oven. "This must be it," she said, pointing to the smaller one.

Will's nerves tingled. He sensed the presence of thing that had chased him. He knew what it was – he'd seen one before, in the Red Box. It was a wraith. He dragged the crate out from the stacks. "What is this?"

Now pale with fright, she said in a shaky voice, "How could you have known that that was there?"

He grabbed her arm. "What is it, Denise?"

She shook her head in disbelief. "Daniel and Sylvia told us about it …" she stopped mid-sentence.

"Denise, please," he said softly and released her arm.

"It's an urn," she said. "A cremated body."

"Whose?" he asked.

She took a deep breath and looked him in the eyes. "Those are the ashes of Adolf Hitler."

~ 3 ~

Friday, 12 June (4:00 p.m. EST)

Daniel and Sylvia met Will and Denise in the mess hall. They sat at a table in the corner.

"Where's Jonathan?" Will asked Denise.

"In his quarters," she answered. "He's been inundated with phone calls – Foundation business."

"How's Horace?" Will asked.

Daniel and Sylvia glanced at each other. Sylvia answered. "Not well."

"Do they know what's wrong?" Denise asked.

Daniel shook his head. "His condition is worsening."

Will was concerned for the man, but his mind badgered him with other things. "How do you know those are Hitler's ashes are in the urn?" he asked Daniel.

"Keep it down," Daniel responded, cringing. "We don't need the whole world to know." He removed a bag of tea from his cup, squeezed out the last bit of water between his finger and a spoon, and put it on a plate. "His name was etched on the urn, and Mengele mentioned it in his notebooks."

"Whether or not they're his," Will said, "something's attached to them."

"What do you mean?" Daniel asked.

"The owner of those ashes came with them," Will said.

Sylvia swallowed hard. "I knew there was something about the urn – "

"Are you saying you can see ghosts?" Daniel asked.

Will couldn't tell if Daniel was scoffing or genuinely surprised. "I wouldn't call it a ghost," he said. "I'd call it a wraith, or a soul. And yes, I saw one when I was in the Red Box."

Daniel shifted in his seat. "I'm still not clear on what separation is exactly," he said.

"I'm not either," Will said. "But other than moving through walls and interacting with the physical world, I can see other … *entities* … when I'm separated."

Everyone remained silent.

"It was of a man who'd died in a nearby room – the one I saw in the Red Box," Will continued. "It was angry. It was a wraith."

"Hence the name, Red Wraith," Sylvia said.

"And I just saw one back in that room," Will said. "If those are Hitler's ashes in that urn, then I can only conclude that – "

"You just saw Hitler's ghost – uh, *soul*," Sylvia finished his statement.

"The Nazis had a side project," Daniel explained. "They tried to reincarnate Hitler by providing a soulless body for him to occupy."

"It was Hitler's planned escape out of Germany," Will offered. "He shoots himself, the body gets cremated, they take the ashes away – Hitler's soul hanging on tightly – and they try to free up another body for him to possess."

"It's beyond science fiction – it's *horror*," Daniel said. "And I'd think you were bat-shit crazy for even suggesting it if I didn't know what else has been going on."

"I felt ill at the base when I was near the urn," Sylvia said. "Was I sensing his presence?"

Will shrugged. "Could be," he said.

"We could dump his ashes overboard," Sylvia said.

Daniel shook his head. "No."

"Let's at least get it out of the room," Sylvia said. "Let the captain put it somewhere else."

"No," Will said, shaking his head. "Maybe I could talk to it." He'd never spoken while separated, but he could try.

After an awkward silence, Daniel finally spoke. "What could we learn?"

Will shrugged. "If the Nazis knew anything of importance, Hitler would have known," he said. "*Would* know," he corrected himself.

Jonathan joined them. He looked disheveled. "Sorry, I've been on the phone for hours," he said. He sat next to Denise who quickly brought him up to speed.

Jonathan seemed strangely unfazed by the information.

"Okay," Jonathan said in the tone of a professor posing a question to one of his classes, "suppose you really can talk to Hitler. Would you trust what he tells you?"

"Even lies reveal things," Daniel said.

Will thought it made sense to explore all facets of the problem. That he might communicate with the most evil human in history was surreal. And he had many questions – the answers to which were sought by the entire world. But he wouldn't have time. He had to find out what he'd done, and what was coming next.

Will stood. "I'm going back to communicate with whatever is connected to those ashes."

"Do you think that's a good idea?" Daniel asked. "If it really is Hitler – "

"I think *not* doing it would be a wasted opportunity," Will said. "We're running out of time."

Denise stood. "I'm going with you."

"No," Will said, left the mess hall, and headed for the file room.

Denise's crutches scuffed behind him, and he stopped and faced her.

"Do you think you should do this?" she asked with hard eyes. "Shouldn't this be a team decision?"

"There's no time," he replied. "Keep moving." He started walking again, Denise clanking along with him.

"Wait!" she yelled, and grabbed his arm tightly and tugged.

He turned.

"What's going on?" she asked, holding eye contact.

"I don't know," he replied. "But it's starting."

"What?" she asked. "*What* is starting?"

"*I don't know*," he replied, frustrated. "Now let's go. *Please.*"

She stared in his eyes for few seconds, and then let go of his arm.

He led the way to the file room, cleared off a part of the table, and retrieved the crate from behind the stack of boxes. It was a wooden box assembled with screws.

"Shit," he said under his breath.

"I'll find a screwdriver," she said.

She headed for the door, but Will grabbed her arm. "No time," he said and sat down in a chair near the crate. He closed his eyes and separated.

~ 4 ~

Friday, 12 June (4:43 p.m. EST)

Denise stood at the head of the table with Will seated at her right. His eyes revealed just a sliver of white between his eyelids. The crate, a foot in height and width, and two feet long, rested on the table a little more than arm's length from him.

The crate spontaneously shifted a few inches, and then creaked in strain. One of the boards cracked in half, and another ripped out from the rest of the structure like a match being torn from a matchbook. Two more ripped away, bending the screws fastening them to the base.

Will turned and looked at her, and seemed to acknowledge something in her face.

"You look mortified," he said, and smiled a little. "You wanted proof – "

"Did you see him?"

He pulled the remaining splinters of wood from the lid of the crate with his hands. "No, but he's here."

The open crate revealed molded packing foam, which he pulled out, exposing a metal box. He extracted the box and put on the table. He cleared away the debris and what remained of the crate and returned to the metal box. He actuated two slide buttons, releasing the lid with a click. He flipped open the lid, revealing the top of the porcelain urn. The vessel was in a leather sheath that was secured by leather straps. The urn was suspended in the center of the box's pillow-like interior.

She recognized the aged odor diffusing through the air, much like the smell of an old leather boot.

He removed the vessel and set in on the table.

"Look at the inscription," she said, turning the urn so that he could see the etching. It read: *Adolf Hitler, 20 April 1889 – 30 April 1945.*

~ 5 ~

Friday, 12 June (4:52 p.m. EST)

Will had known about the inscription, but still felt dazed seeing the words with his own eyes. If true, the remains of the world's most infamous villain were contained inside. But they were just ashes – carbon, calcium, and other elements that had no significance. He was more interested in what came along with them.

Without removing the leather straps that secured the vessel, he unbuckled one of the four wire clips that held the lid of the urn to the body.

Denise grabbed his hand. "What are you doing?"

"Looking," he said.

She released his hand and he unbuckled the other three clips and pulled on the lid. It was jammed with a hard crust that had formed over the tightly fitting piece, but he worked it free.

He and Denise bumped heads trying to look inside. Will won out and saw just what he'd expected. He moved to the side so that Denise could get a look. It was about two-thirds full – a little more than a pint of debris. He shook it gently, and tiny bits of bone surfaced.

He replaced the lid and clipped it. "There are remains in there, but it proves nothing," he said. "Now, you should leave."

"Why?"

"I don't know what's going to happen."

"Can he hurt me?"

"I don't think so," he replied. He was fairly certain that that was the case, but there were a lot of things he didn't know.

"Then I'm staying," she said, which looked to be her final answer.

"If things start flying around, get the hell out."

361

She nodded.

He'd felt something watching them ever since they'd entered room. He sat in a chair in front of the urn, closed his eyes, and separated.

The instant he left his body he spotted an imposing presence hovering over Denise. It was the dark, wraith-like entity he'd seen earlier, its filament-like tether connected to the urn. It seemed that it hadn't noticed that Will had separated.

It turned towards Will's body and mutated into something with human-like features. Its head got close to his chest and its appendages felt around – near Will's head and chest area. Its hands formed into long, deformed claws, and grasped something on Will's body and tugged hard.

Will sensed the tugging – a discomfort, but not pain. It was more like a tingling of nerves, like hitting the funny bone; only this sensation manifested itself in his chest, neck, and head. The thing struggled and yanked, and finally grunted in frustration before giving up and moving to Denise.

After searching her from top to bottom, it moved above the urn and looked around. It finally noticed Will perched in a corner of the ceiling.

The wraith formed into a hideous beast and rushed him. Will didn't budge, confident that there was nothing that it could do to him. It slammed into him, but he felt nothing more than a slight bump, shifting his position almost unperceptively. The wraith back up and charged again. Same result.

The enraged entity coiled up again, but before it could explode towards him, Will said, "Who are you?" His voice sounded odd – like how he sounded in recordings.

The wraith stopped, repositioned itself just above the urn, and straightened into a poorly resolved figure that Will recognized. It remained silent.

"Are you Adolf Hitler?" Will asked.

After a few seconds with no response, Will moved to a position above his body and faced the being.

"I command you to leave your body," the wraith said in a thick

German accent.

Will now understood what it was trying to do when it tugged at his chest: it was trying to pull out his soul.

"I have questions for you," Will said, ignoring the command.

The thing responded with a screech and surged towards him.

Will didn't flinch.

It returned to its position above the urn with an expression of rage frozen on its face.

"I will not answer your questions," it said. "I command you to die."

"You're not getting my body," Will said. "And if you don't answer my questions, we will dump your ashes into the sea."

The wraith looked down at the urn.

"We have the White Stone," Will said.

It seemed to contemplate Will's statement for a few seconds. "What is the time?" it asked.

"What do you mean?"

"The year. What is the year?"

Will told him.

"The years have passed like minutes and millennia," the wraith said. "The orb will have disappeared by now. The White Stone is useless."

"The orb – you mean the object on the seabed that was sending out a signal?"

"The drum," Hitler said. "It will have retracted into the sea floor by now."

"Why do you say that?"

"Its pulse rate was decreasing. When it finally stopped, it was to retract, not to resurface for a century. It should have been gone for a half a century by now."

"It has reemerged," Will said.

The wraith considered Will's words for a few seconds, and then asked, "What is the beat frequency?" It seemed show excitement in its amorphous facial expression.

"It has already retracted again."

363

The wraith coiled and groaned in disappointment.

"What were we supposed to do?" Will asked.

"Get inside it."

"Suppose we did," Will said.

"Did you?"

Will remained silent.

"I *knew* it," Hitler said. "You did. I felt it. Was it a button? A lever?"

"A lever – a switch," Will replied.

"You activated it?"

"Yes."

The expression of the wraith transformed from that of anxious interest to elation. "You fools!" The wraith spewed out a grating wail. He quelled his hideous cackle and added, "And you don't even realize what you have done."

Will felt as cold as ice. "Tell me!"

"The reason for my entire existence was to accomplish what you have done," Hitler said. "All that I've done – *everything!* – was in preparation for the orb. To activate that switch."

"What does it do?" Will pleaded. "Tell me!"

Hitler ignored the question and resumed cackling. "It is satisfying to know that my work carried on well after my physical existence in this world had ended. I should have known that I only had to plant the seed. Humanity is inherently greedy, power hungry, ruthless, and, most importantly, curious," he said. "Curiosity killed the cat." Hitler screeched in laughter.

"What's going to happen?"

Hitler shook his head in defiance.

"We'll dump your ashes – "

"Do it!" Hitler said. "I am free now. No reason to remain in this ugly existence – this limbo. Do what you will with my ashes." It cackled again and then seemed to stare at Will and study him. "You seem familiar to me. Who are you?"

Will remained silent for a few seconds – he didn't know how to answer the question. "I'm what you were trying to create, but failed," he finally replied.

"No, I have seen you before," Hitler said.

"That's impossible," Will said, confused.

The wraith seemed to sever its tie to the ashes and looked upward, and then looked back to Will and spoke. "You have deciphered the stone?"

"The three outer rings."

"You will find the deciphered inscriptions of the inner circles in the book by Schwinger. But it doesn't matter – the next stage will come irrespective of what you do or do not know. You have no control," it said, and then darted through the ceiling. Hitler was gone.

Will went back to his body and opened his eyes.

Denise looked at him expectantly. "Well?"

Will remained silent.

"What's wrong?" she asked.

He stood, put the urn back in the metal box, and placed it in the foam-padded crate.

"Will?"

"We need to get everyone together," he said, reaching for the door. "Right away."

Denise pushed her hip against the door, keeping it closed.

"What happened?" she asked sternly and put her hand on his shoulder. "Are you okay?"

"I think we're in trouble," he said.

"The ship?"

"No," he said, closing his eyes slowly. "The world."

~ 6 ~
Friday, 12 June (7:22 p.m. EST)

Captain McHenry sat in the mess room of the *North Dakota* and looked over an armament supplies request. The morale of his crew was

365

high after their mission to the Nazi base, but the mood had been tempered after taking down the Chinese sub. After the beacon descended into the sea floor two days ago, the mood electrified again.

McHenry's orders were to patrol the area for foreign subs and abnormalities. There was still potential for a Chinese counterattack, but it was waning. The *North Dakota* had been running quiet since the beacon had disappeared, except on two occasions where they'd sneaked up on Russian subs and pinged them – blasting them with active sonar to chase them away.

The Chinese had limped away from the area with their disabled carrier after they'd airlifted their task force from inland Antarctica. They hadn't found the base. The weather was getting wicked as winter was setting in, forcing the Russians to give up their search as well, but their subs still probed near the mouth of the tunnel. Active sonar arrays had been deployed all around the tunnel entrance, making it impossible for anything to get near it without being detected, and two U.S. subs patrolled the area at all times.

He had a feeling that the peace and quiet would be short-lived, and his impression was soon substantiated.

His first officer, Diggs, walked in and scanned the area. McHenry waved him over.

"Sir, we're hearing a signal," Diggs said.

"A sub?"

"No," Diggs replied. "Something more like the beacon, and in that same location."

McHenry put his papers in a folder and stood. "Same type of signal?"

"Not quite," Diggs explained, "broad frequency spectrum like the first, but it repeats at about 100 hertz – a much higher frequency than the first one."

The question was whether to investigate, or surface and report to his superiors. He decided on the former; once they'd verified the location, they'd go to radio depth and transmit a full report.

McHenry instructed Diggs to get close enough to the new object to get images. There seemed to be no other subs in the area, but this would attract them again. It was likely that the fleet already knew it was there – they were listening intently 10 kilometers north. The *North Dakota* was closer – less than 2 kilometers away.

They moved in quietly. The object was identical to the first, but was positioned at a much shallower depth. At 200 meters, the *North Dakota* could get close enough to take pictures without a using a deep-sea vessel like the ill-fated *Little Dakota*.

The crew collected high-resolution images and video, as well as sonar images of the object and the surrounding seabed. They ascended to radio depth and transmitted the encoded data to the *Stennis* with a message that the *North Dakota* would return to communication depth in an hour.

McHenry gave the order to dive and move northwest. They'd wait quietly until it was time to get new orders.

He made his way back to the mess room with Diggs. The faces of the crew had changed: their eyes again showed excitement and fear.

McHenry surmised that the appearance of the new beacon had to be a *response* to their previous action: deactivating the first beacon set something into motion. *What did it mean?* The reactive behavior made him nervous. Perhaps they should have left first one alone. But he knew they couldn't have done that – their adversaries wouldn't let them. Someone would have fooled with it, eventually.

~ 7 ~

Friday, 12 June (8:17 p.m. EST)

Will had been used to crowded classrooms as a physics professor, but it seemed like a lifetime since he'd last spoken to a group. Packed into the small room was Captain Grimes, a handful of officers, Denise and Jonathan, Daniel and Sylvia, and an ancient languages expert who had recently arrived to assist in deciphering the White Stone. Their eyes were all on Will.

367

"I don't know the best way to start this conversation, so I'll just spill it." Will said, "We have – *I* have – initiated a chain of events when I pulled the switch in the beacon."

"What do you mean by *chain*?" Daniel said. "The only thing that has happened so far is that the beacon retracted into the seabed."

"I don't know," Will responded. He struggled for words.

"Just tell them, Will," Denise blurted and then addressed the others. "He spoke with the thing connected to the urn."

They all looked to Will.

"Hitler's urn," Daniel said.

Will nodded.

"And this … thing … told you what's coming next?" Captain Grimes asked in a tone that was rife with skepticism.

"Not exactly *what* is going to happen," Will replied, "but that something *will* happen, and that it's going to be bad."

"What was this thing, and how does it know what's going to happen?" Grimes prodded.

"The better question is *who* was it," Denise said.

"Okay then," Grimes said, "*who* was it?"

"It was Adolf Hitler," Will replied.

Gasps filled the air.

"That's preposterous," Grimes said.

Will had had about enough of the skepticism. "Do you believe that separation is possible?" he asked Grimes.

Grimes's face went blank and he cleared his throat. "Well, to be honest – "

"Then how did he flip the switch inside the beacon?" Sylvia asked.

"I don't know," Grimes replied. "I'm sorry, but I'm not going for all of this hocus pocus stuff. It was a coincidence, or we had disturbed it enough to trigger some reaction."

Even though Will was used to people not believing him, it was becoming increasingly insulting. It implied that he was crazy, or lying. The government had taken him through hell to get him to transform, and now no one even believed he possessed the abilities they'd set out to give him.

368

Denise believed him, but she had seen it with her own eyes. None of the others had, except perhaps on video. But videos could be altered, faked.

Denise looked at him with desperation. "Just show them," she pleaded. "We need to get past this."

The room was silent. He didn't want to do it, but Denise had put him on the spot. If he didn't do something now it would cast doubt into their minds, and that might complicate things when the time came to respond to something in the future.

"What do I have to do to prove it?" Will asked, looking first to Captain Grimes and then to the others.

"What *can* you do?" Grimes asked.

"I can pass through matter, manipulate objects, among other things."

"Okay," Grimes said as he pushed a large plastic mug into the center of the table. "Move this cup."

Grimes' request conjured a flashback in Will's mind. It was a test that the head of the Red Wraith program had tried to force him to do: he'd commanded Will to tip over a bottle while he was confined to the Exoskeleton. He'd had to kill that man in the end. Remnants of that same rage now welled up inside him.

He closed his eyes and separated. He went to a position just above the mug and smashed it down with a powerful strike. Coffee and plastic exploded on the people around the table. He went back to his body just in time to catch some of the backsplash.

When he opened his eyes, everyone was wiping their faces and clothes, and it was clear that Grimes had taken the brunt of it. He regretted splashing Denise and Jonathan, but he was going for effect. Denise had a smile on her face. Everyone else looked confused and frightened.

One of the officers made a run for the closed door. Will instinctively separated and met the man just as he pulled it open it, and slammed it closed so hard that it cracked like the report of a firearm, inducing many of the observers to jump.

"Will, let him go!" Denise yelled.

He released the door and the officer, now frantic, opened it and ran out.

He recombined with his body and opened his eyes to see pale, wide-eyed faces, including Denise's. The wooden table was cracked and splintered in the area where the cup had been destroyed.

"Sorry," he said. "I wanted the demonstration to be convincing." He looked to Grimes. "Was that enough?" The question was not intended to be sarcastic.

Grimes nodded, his face still dripping with coffee.

"Now," Will continued, "with that behind us, let me explain what I know. Hitler was attached to his ashes. It was him."

He looked around at the severely attentive eyes, especially those of Grimes. The others seemed to be in mild shock, but were listening intently.

"What did he say?" Denise asked. "You were separated for almost twenty minutes in there."

Will had no idea that that much time had passed. "First, he tried to break the tether that connects my soul and body – he wanted to take over."

"Like a possession?" Grimes asked.

"I suppose so, yes," Will answered. "When that failed, he ordered me to get out – to die. He became very frustrated. That's when I talked to him. I told him he'd better answer my questions or we'd throw his ashes into the sea. That seemed to have some effect. I then asked him about the beacon. He said the purpose of his existence – every vile thing he'd done while on this planet – was to get inside the 'orb,' as he called it."

"To do what?" Daniel asked.

"Flip the switch and start some chain of events," Will answered.

"Which is what?" Grimes asked.

Will shook his head. "I don't know," he replied. "But it couldn't be good considering that Hitler wanted it to happen. He said it no longer mattered if we decipher the remaining rings of the stone – it's too late. He was elated."

Grimes looked anxious. "We've been in the area for a long time, and Naval Command is on the verge of giving us new deployment orders," he said and stood. He brushed a few shards of wet plastic from his shirt.

"It's only been two days since the beacon disappeared," Sylvia argued.

Grimes nodded. "After I get cleaned up, I'll make a request to remain in the area. In the meantime, you should get back to deciphering the White Stone inscription. Maybe we can get an idea of what's coming."

"That's another thing," Will said, recalling the last thing Hitler said before disappearing. "The translations of the White Stone inscriptions are in the book by Schwinger. Sound familiar to any of you?"

No one responded.

"Maybe it's in the books we took back from the base," Daniel said. "But we could have left it behind – there were thousands."

"How many did you bring back?" Will asked.

Daniel shrugged. "Maybe 100, but they were only the ones on the table in the library or in the vault – nothing stored on the shelves.

"If it's important enough to go back, we will," Captain Grimes said and then left the room. The other officers and the languages professor followed.

"That was quite a demonstration," Jonathan said, and shook his head. "I wasn't ready for that."

Daniel looked at Will with wide eyes. "I was skeptical at a subconscious level," he admitted. "No longer."

"Me too," Sylvia added.

Will sat forward with his elbows on the table. "When I said I felt something was coming, I meant it was imminent," Will said and stood. "Where are the books?"

"Follow me," Daniel said.

"I need to put on a clean shirt," Jonathan said.

So did Sylvia.

They agreed to meet in the research room in 20 minutes, and Will walked to his quarters. His chest seemed to tighten more and more as time moved forward. He was wrong to say that something "was imminent." He didn't want to frighten everyone. *It was already here.*

~ 8 ~
Friday, 12 June (8:37 p.m. EST)

Will went to his quarters and donned a clean jumpsuit and a USS *Stennis* baseball cap. He was pleased with his treatment by the captain and crew; wearing a uniform devoid of rank seemed to command more respect than an officer.

It would be a hopeless task to translate the remaining rings of the White Stone in time to influence what was coming – if that were even possible. Their only hope was to find the translations in the book by Schwinger.

As much as he tried to put it out of his mind, the fact remained that Adolf Hitler himself had claimed his sole objective was to flip the switch in the beacon. Will's nerves electrified with worry. Had he awakened everything that had been put to sleep in World War Two? So many people had died to thwart the Nazis' quest to take over the world. But he now thought Hitler wanted something different. Was there more to it than ruling the world? Did he want to destroy it? If so, Will felt as though he'd carried on their work for them. Would he be ultimately responsible for finishing the job? Time would tell.

He sighed and shook his head. Again, if he hadn't turned the lever, someone else would have. Separation research like that carried out in the Red Wraith project had already proliferated, as demonstrated by Cho. Destroying Syncorp, and anyone else attempting to emulate it, was a hopeless endeavor. It was like trying to stop the development of nuclear weapons. The difference was that Red Wraith research was easier than getting nukes; it didn't require rare materials like weapons-grade uranium or plutonium. It didn't take much to torture people. It might take a century, but eventually they'd create someone else with separation abilities. Someone would eventually enter the beacon and pull that switch.

He headed in the direction of the of the research room, but was cut off by Captain Grimes's first officer just a few steps out of the mess hall.

"The captain needs you right away," the officer said. "There's been a development."

Will followed the sailor to the ready room. Everyone was there, and all had concerned expressions. Denise seemed the most nervous, fidgeting with her hands.

"We picked up a signal an hour ago from a location near that of the first beacon," Grimes said. "We got verification from the *North Dakota*, with images."

Grimes opened a laptop and turned it toward the others. The images were identical to those of the first beacon. It seemed strange: he'd expected more than just another beacon.

"This one seems physically identical to the first," Grimes explained, "but there are some differences."

"Such as?" Denise asked.

"First, it's not exactly in the same location, but close – within a kilometer," Grimes said. "Second, it's located closer to the surface – at a depth of 200 meters."

"A sub can reach it?" Daniel asked.

Grimes nodded. "Finally, the frequency of the signal is about 100 beats per second."

"A hundred hertz," Will said. "The first one beat at just one beat per second?"

"Slightly more," Daniel said.

"There's something odd about this signal, however," Grimes added. "The frequency decreases by about one cycle every 10 minutes," Grimes replied. "It started at 101.7 beats per second when we first discovered it about an hour ago. It's now down to 95.1 Hertz."

"It's a countdown," Will blurted. "The wraith – Hitler – mentioned it. The Nazis knew that the first one was counting down. He said that it was supposed to retract into the seabed when the frequency reached one beat per second."

"But they'd had years to work," Denise said. "At this rate, we only have 950 minutes – less than 16 hours."

"What happens after 16 hours?" Grimes asked.

"Maybe we lose an opportunity – it sinks back into the seabed not to reappear for a century," Will speculated. "Or maybe something else …"

Recognition and urgency filled Daniel's eyes, and he looked to Grimes.

Grimes seemed to understand. "What do you propose?" he asked.

Will knew what they needed to do. "Bring me to it," he said.

Grimes nodded. "I'll summon the *North Dakota*," he said. "We'll get you there. But I must ask, if there is another switch, what are you going to do?"

"I don't know," Will replied.

"It won't be the same as the first," Daniel said.

Will agreed. What would be the point?

Will accepted the fact that, whatever he might find, it came down to him, and him alone, to make a decision on behalf of the rest of the world.

CHAPTER XVI

~ 1 ~

Saturday, 13 June (12:40 a.m. EST – Weddell Sea)

Will hadn't noticed the locker room smell his first time aboard the *North Dakota*. Having fallen in the icy sea hours before had probably distracted him.

Sylvia and Daniel stayed aboard the *Stennis* and, with the help of their expert from Stanford, were attempting to decipher the White Stone, or find the book by Schwinger. Despite Will's protests, Jonathan and Denise accompanied him on the *North Dakota*.

A sailor brought them to a ready room where Captain McHenry and his first officer, Diggs, were waiting. They went through some of the details of timing and positioning. Five minutes later, they were in the navigation room watching the distance close between them and the beacon.

As the *North Dakota* took position, Will was taken to an empty quarters. It was a small room with bunks on each side. He sat on one of the bottom bunks with his feet on the floor. He leaned forward, set his elbows on his knees, and put his hands over his face and rubbed his eyes. Denise sat on the bed directly across from him, her feet nearly touching his.

"I'm worried," she said, and touched his forearm. "What do you think this is? Aliens? God? What?"

Will looked at her and could only shake his head. If extraterrestrials were the source of the beacons, then mankind may soon have proof of intelligent life beyond Earth. Such a discovery would have been mindboggling to him just a year ago. But the idea was no longer so astonishing, and he thought that the truth would be more profound. Even extraterrestrials were confined to the physical world – at least that's how most people envisioned them. But *he* was evidence of existence outside of the physical world – an existence connected to humanity and, possibly, to something beyond it. Did it imply the existence of a superior being? Reincarnation? The possibilities were endless, and extraterrestrial life was insignificant in comparison.

"It's deeper than extraterrestrials," he said. "At least the way we think of them."

Denise flinched at a knock on the door.

"Yes?" Will said.

"We're in position," a sailor said and poked his head in the small room. "Ms. Walker, please come with me."

Denise stood, and then bent down and kissed Will on the cheek. "If I had to choose anyone to do this, it would be you," she said, and then walked out and closed the door.

~ 2 ~

Saturday, 13 June (1:17 a.m. EST)

Will was face up on the lower bunk with his head resting on a stiff pillow. Taped to the bottom of the bed above were pictures of a sailor's family – a smiling woman that seemed too young to have children. Her red hair was tied in a tight ponytail and she held a little blonde girl, maybe two or three years old. He knew the crew were away from their families for six months at a time and, by the nature of their job, put themselves in harm's way. He hoped that whatever was going to happen – whatever he was about to do – didn't jeopardize their safe return.

He closed his eyes and separated. He passed downward and to the starboard side of the *North Dakota*, through the floor and into the ballast tanks. Finally, he slipped through the hardened-steel hull and into the water. Cold currents flowed through him, a sensation that was both pleasing and uncomfortable. The orb emitted a tone that, at below 100 hertz, was ominously deep, as if it were growling. At less than 50 meters away, the sound was so intense that he felt it in the water around him.

He approached and touched the surface of the sphere, which was

376

vibrating. It was physically identical to the first beacon, but something was different. It felt dark, like an ancient ruin with a sinister history.

He softened his physical state and dragged himself through the shell and into its large, spherical void. The beating ceased, and the tug from his body was gone.

Illuminated in bright white light at the geometric center of the sphere was a circular platform. It was perched atop a tapered stem that protruded from the bottom. The rest of the void was as dark as sackcloth.

The platform was at least 20 feet in diameter, and looked to be composed of the same material as the beacon. On its smooth surface were two chairs and a white, circular table. Seated across the table from each other were two human-like beings – naked and hairless. They sat a meter apart, motionless and silent, staring blankly at each other with their hands flat on the table.

Will was moving closer when he sensed motion to his right. He darted to the opposite side of the sphere and looked into the blackness, in the direction of the motion.

A faint image, not unlike the wraiths he'd seen before, emerged from the shadows. This one seemed to take a human form, but the features were subtle, and he wasn't sure whether he was imagining them – like one's mind recognizes objects in puffy, white clouds in a summer sky.

"Why don't we settle into a physical presence and talk," the wraith said in a deep, grating voice that Will found unsettling.

"I don't understand," Will replied, almost startled by his own voice.

The wraith took a position just above the table. "Come," it said.

Will approached the table. He was close to the wraith now – so close that he thought he sensed heat radiating from its location.

"Take the empty body below you," the wraith said and pointed to one of the humanoid beings.

Will was confused. "What do you mean?"

"The body below you is vacant," the wraith explained. "It is pristine – it has never been occupied by a soul. Enter it."

Will froze. *Occupy another body.* Thoughts of demonic possession

377

entered his mind.

The wraith descended and entered the body below it, the eyes of which suddenly changed from those of a dead fish to those reflecting self-awareness, and life. The arms moved, and then it spoke. "Please," it said in a physical, epicene voice, and gestured with its hands to the body directly across from it.

Will moved slowly. As he entered the other body from the top, a warm sensation engulfed him and then seemed to pull him in. It was different from what he'd felt when he'd entered the CP inmate's body to pinch an artery. In that case it had been as if something were trying to repel him. The present situation was like falling into a tub of warm mud.

He opened his eyes and found himself looking into the face of the being across from him. The first thing he noticed was that his vision was perfect – much better than in his own body. He held his hands in front of him and examined them, turning them back and forth and squeezing them into fists and releasing. He couldn't believe what was happening: he was *someone else*. With the palm of his right hand, he pressed on his thigh, the one with the broken femur. There was no pain – it wasn't *his* body. In fact, he felt unusually comfortable – no pain of any kind. He wondered how much discomfort he'd lived with on a day-to-day basis: his leg, lower back, feet, neck, sinuses, knees … how much pain had he gotten used to?

"Who are you?" the being asked.

"I'm William Thompson," Will responded. "Who are you?"

The being stared at him.

After an awkward silence, Will asked, "Why am I here?"

"All that is relevant is that I am here," the being said.

"Why are you here?"

"You have reached maturity."

"Me?"

"Your kind."

"My kind?"

"Humanity."

Will's mind reeled. The words *existential implications* came to him – something Daniel had said to him. For an instant he panicked. "Will

I be able to get back to my body?" he blurted.

"Yes," the being replied and seemed to look deep into his eyes. "You do not yet understand that you can control time."

Will had no idea what he meant and looked back in bewilderment.

"You cannot go *backward* in time, but you can operate so quickly that time effectively stands still in the physical world. That is what we are doing now. Your physical brain can only think at a finite speed – it takes a minimum amount of time to process a single thought. It is physically limited. No such limitations exist when you are outside your body."

Will recalled the pistons in the engines on the Chinese carrier: they had slowed when he concentrated on grasping them. Perhaps he was moving, and perceiving, so quickly that they only seemed to have slowed. "But we're in physical bodies now," Will said.

"We are inside the sphere," the being said. "Time is essentially standing still on the outside."

"Who are you?" Will asked

"It is not *who* I am that matters. It is *what*."

"*What* are you?"

"I am the Inquisitor and Judge."

Will didn't like where the conversations was heading. "Judge of what?" he asked.

"Your world."

Will's chest tightened.

"I am here because I have been summoned," the Judge continued. "The probe was actuated three days ago."

"You mean the first beacon – a *probe*?" Will asked.

"Was it you who had actuated it?"

Will nodded.

"This action has confirmed that your world has come of age," the Judge said.

"Come of age?"

"Passed into a new phase of existence," the Judge explained. "The probe can only be accessed in the evanescent state, where the consciousness extends itself beyond the confines of the physical body. *You* have accomplished this. You turned the lever."

Regret flooded Will's mind. *Why had he pulled the switch?*

"Accessing and actuating the probe required an advanced level of development," the Judge continued. "First, you – your kind – had to discover and decipher the disk to obtain the location of the probe. Then you had to travel to that location of the planet – a place that is highly inaccessible. That had required you to exceed a threshold of technological development."

The bottom of the Southern Ocean was certainly an inaccessible place, Will thought.

"While discovering the probe requires a certain level of intellectual growth," the Judge explained, "you cannot access its interior unless you have developed an evanescent existence."

"And what happens now?" Will asked.

"Evaluation. Judgment."

Judgment? It implied a punishment – a sentence. "What are the ramifications?" Will asked.

"There are *existential consequences.*"

Daniel's words echoed again in Will's mind. "Our *existence* is at stake?"

The Judge nodded.

"On what is this judgment based?" Will's mind flooded with numerous negative images of himself, and even more of human history. His stomach churned.

"It depends on your answer to *one* question," the Judge said, keeping steady eye contact.

"One question?" Will scoffed. "How can the future of the world depend on one man's answer to *one* question?"

"It is a very revealing question," the Judge replied.

"What if your judgment is negative – what will happen?"

"A chain of events will be initiated to renew your world," the Judge responded.

"Renew?"

"Wiped clean, followed by a new genesis."

"Humanity will be wiped out."

The Judge nodded.

"And if we pass your test?"

"You will receive further enlightenment."

"To what end?" Will asked.

"Immortality."

Will was taken aback. What did that mean?

The Judge seemed to read his expression and his silence. "It is complicated," the Judge said. "But you are seeing a crude aspect of it right here – in that body you are occupying. If it were able to exit this sphere, it could be claimed by any free soul in the same manner as you are occupying it right now."

Will thought of the Nazis' plan to reincarnate Hitler. It seemed their conjecture was not as absurd as it appeared.

"But immortality reaches beyond the physical world," the Judge continued. "Even souls can be destroyed before they are cast."

"Cast?"

"Made a permanent part of existence. This is the true immortality."

"Our souls are not cast?" Will asked.

The Judge shook his head.

"What happened to those who have died – where are they?"

"They lie in wait," the Judge replied. "Their existence depends on the outcome of this inquiry."

Will felt like he was being crushed. Why was he put into this position? Why him? It then occurred to him: *why not him*? He was as guilty as those who had created him. He'd killed many.

"The idea of judgment should not surprise you," the Judge said. "All humans have an innate sense of immortality, death, and judgment. It is manifest in religion – a collective guilt and fear of judgment. But you also have hope – hope that there is something beyond this existence. Both your fear, and hope, are justified."

Will didn't feel any hope. "What if I refuse to answer your question?"

"It would result in a negative judgment."

Will wanted to flee back to the *North Dakota*. He regretted bringing things to this point, but he quickly rejected culpability. He'd been forced into it from the beginning. He did not acquire the ability to separate – to access the evanescent state – by his own will. It seemed to him that humanity had finally meddled with something that would lead to its destruction. He'd always thought that, if it were to happen, it would've been thermonuclear war, or some technology-gone-wrong, that would destroy the world. Humanity would eventually have done everything within its reach, most of which was driven by power, greed or, more benignly, curiosity. Either way, someone would eventually have occupied the chair in which he currently sat.

"Ask your question," Will said.

The Judge nodded and looked into his eyes. "You are here only because you have acquired the ability to transform into the evanescent state. There are only two ways to attain this ability."

Goose bumps formed on Will's arms. The Judge seemed to notice.

"The first way is through enlightenment," the Judge explained. "It is nurtured through the development of the intellect over generations. It is a progressive process accomplished through an environmental stimulation of evolution. In this case, the evolution occurs in both the intellect and consciousness, the latter of which you refer to as the soul."

The situation was looking bleak. "And the second way?" Will asked. He was pretty sure he already knew the answer. The face across from him became grave.

"The opposite of enlightenment," the Judge replied. "A single being is made to suffer so greatly that its consciousness wants to escape the physical world, but is somehow constrained."

"Torture," Will said.

The Judge nodded slowly, keeping eye contact. "I am here because you summoned me," he said. "Now the question becomes, how did *you* get here?"

Will's thoughts scrambled in his mind. The answer to the judge's question was unequivocal, but he couldn't answer – not with the truth. He remained silent.

The Judge reached across the table with both hands and grabbed both of Will's. "Torture, or enlightenment?"

Will's thoughts bounced back and forth between revealing the truth and lying. How should he answer? He knew it would take little effort to uncover the truth if he were to lie.

He then wondered if the Judge already knew the answer. It was obvious to anyone who looked that the world was no bastion of enlightenment. It was the opposite – it was a crucible of war, torture, disease, immorality, greed, and indifference to life. These things practically *defined* the world. If it were only he who was to be judged, Will would admit his every transgression. But he wouldn't condemn the world with his own words. It was not his place.

"You don't need me to answer that question," Will said. "Look for yourself."

The Judge let go of Will's hands and leaned back, never breaking eye contact. "The answer must come from admission, not observation," the being said.

"Why?"

The Judge remained silent.

Will's mind whirred. "Are you not able to observe? Are you confined to this object?"

"Judgment can only come from your testimony," the Judge responded.

"I will not answer your question."

After a long silence, the Judge said, "If you answer, you will be spared."

"What do you mean?"

"You will not suffer the regeneration," the Judge said. "Your soul will be cast."

"What about everyone else?"

The Judge shook his head. "Only you."

Will was insulted. He imagined an eternity of guilt. "No!"

"I can destroy you right now."

"I don't care," Will said. "You will not condemn the world on my words."

The being leaned forwards and its eyes darkened. "Very well," he said and leaned back. "You are free to go." He waved his hand as if to tell Will to leave.

Something was wrong.

Will exited the body.

The Judge, still occupying the other body, said, "Please, wait for a moment."

Will kept his position above the table as the Judge separated. However, instead of coming up to meet him, the wraith entered the body that Will had just exited. *What the hell was it doing?*

The face came to life, and then distorted in an expression of recognition, and then anger. After a short time the Judge said, "This body was pristine. By entering it, you imprinted upon it – all of your memories. And now, not only do I know everything that you know – I have *experienced* it. I know the answer to the question."

The being exited the body.

"Admit what happened to you," it screamed. "Say it!"

"No!" Will yelled back.

"Then you will be destroyed."

"What gives you the right to condemn us?" Will shot back.

"You have destroyed yourselves," the being replied. "Your intellectual development is stagnant. Your morality has been nonexistent from the beginning. You are still bound to your dirty planet, and will annihilate yourselves in your own filth – greed, war, and ignorance."

"Not everyone is guilty," Will said.

"You have all come from the same tainted origin," the Judge said. "Judgment has been made."

The being morphed into something that resembled a demon – more hideous than the wraiths Will had seen before.

But Will had no fear. He was ready to fight. He *wanted* to fight. Then a thought entered his mind out of nowhere.

He rushed towards the first body the Judge had occupied, and *entered it.*

~ 3 ~
Unknown Time

The body was identical to the one Will had first occupied. The difference was that his memory seemed to change – he began to remember things he knew he hadn't actually experienced. His consciousness became overwhelmed with information that surged so quickly he had no sense of what was happening around him. It was like trying to catch a waterfall in a bucket. Images of things he'd never seen before – alien to him – flickered before his eyes. And there were emotions connected to the memories. Most of it was beyond his comprehension.

An instant later, he was looking down upon a headless, twitching body. He watched as the wraith decapitated the second one, its head rolling off of the pedestal and into the darkness at the bottom of the sphere. Both bodies slumped forward, spurting blood on the white table that quickly poured off the edge and onto the platform.

Will realized that he'd just experienced being killed, but his attention quickly turned back to the wraith.

"You are vile," Will said. "*Evil.*"

The wraith sneered. "I am everything you fear. I am the Judge. I am the *Destroyer.*"

Will sensed the pedestal ascending towards him. The sphere was moving upward. He darted to the wall to his right as the wraith screamed at him.

"Your world is dead!" it screeched. "Your filthy world is dead!"

~ 4 ~
Saturday, 13 June (1:21 a.m. EST)

385

It took Will a few seconds to recognize the dark eyes that stared down at him. They were Denise's. He didn't recall the trip back to his body.

"We just rolled violently and alarms sounded," Denise said. "I came to see if you were okay. What's happening?"

He figured the *North Dakota* was jostled by the turbulence from the beacon's ascent.

"Couldn't you separate?" she asked.

He was confused for a second, but then understood. "How long have I been gone?"

"Two, three minutes," she replied.

Jonathan burst into the room. "We're following the beacon to the surface," he said, out of breath.

Will didn't know if that was a good idea.

"Let's go," Jonathan said, waving them to follow him.

Minutes later they were standing in a crowd of more than a dozen sailors staring at a bank of monitors. They were displaying various views of the probe with night-vision cameras.

The orb was clearly visible, rising into the sky. Will estimated it was already 100 meters above the surface.

"What the hell is that thing?" Captain McHenry said. He looked to Will. "What did you do?"

Will shook his head. "I'll explain later," he said. *If there was a later,* he didn't add.

They watched as the probe kept growing, the part of the stem at the surface of the water thickening as it rose.

After 10 minutes he could hardly see its spherical head. It had to be more than a mile high, and its stem at the water's surface had widened to a diameter of more than 100 meters.

"It stopped," a man said from behind a computer consul. "It's at a height of two kilometers."

"My God," McHenry said.

Everyone else stared in silence, waiting for something to happen.

And then it did.

Everything went dark, except for intermittent sparks that illuminated the area like flash bulbs.

"What's happening?" McHenry yelled.

"E-M pulse, sir," a man yelled back.

Will knew exactly what that meant. An electromagnetic pulse was a high-energy surge of electromagnetic fields that could destroy electronics. It could be produced a few ways, one was by detonating a nuclear weapon.

"We're supposed to be shielded!" McHenry's voice blasted in the dark. "Was it a nuke?"

"Unknown," a voice answered. "All systems are down."

"Emergency power," McHenry bellowed over warning alarms that seemed to come from every direction.

Another surge of sparks lit the control room in a bluish-white tinge, and then it went to darkness again.

"Another E-M pulse," someone yelled.

"Dive! Dive! Dive!" McHenry screamed.

Will found an empty chair and sat in it. He separated and passed through the upper hull and into the night. The probe loomed in the moonlight. He searched the horizon for any hint of a nuclear blast but found nothing. The skies were perfectly clear.

He followed the *North Dakota* beneath the surface and returned to his body. Denise squatted down and huddled next to him, grasping his forearm.

"You okay?" he asked.

"I just don't want to be in the way of people moving in the dark," she explained.

Will knew she wasn't easily frightened, yet her hand trembled as she squeezed his arm.

"It wasn't a nuke," he said. "I just looked."

Will stood and talked loudly into the dark. "There was no nuclear explosion."

Another flurry of sparks illuminated the room.

"How do you know that?" McHenry asked in the dark.

"Just trust me, I know," Will replied, not revealing what he'd done in case the crew hadn't been informed of his abilities. The scoffs that emanated from various directions indicated he was probably right to keep his mouth shut.

McHenry asked questions in the dark about the damage. The *North Dakota* needed repairs, but it was going to be okay. And they were safer at their current depth – a 150 meters of salt water would shield them from the E-M pulses.

McHenry set in a new course for the rendezvous point with the *Stennis*. He walked over to Will. "I hope there's still a carrier group to meet."

Will nodded. So did he.

~ 5 ~
Saturday, 13 June (7:28 a.m. EST)

The crew of the *North Dakota* managed to make repairs and get them off emergency power. It rendezvoused with the carrier group four hours later. McHenry was then ordered go to Mar del Plata, and then on to an American base for thorough checkup.

Now back on the *Stennis*, Will followed Denise and Jonathan into the ready-room, where Captain Grimes, Daniel, and Sylvia were waiting. Grimes sat directly across from Will at the head of the table.

"Where's Horace?" Will asked.

"Sick bay," Sylvia replied.

By her expression Will sensed that Horace wasn't improving.

"We can't approach the probe with anything – aircraft or surface ships – and I'm not risking another sub," Grimes explained. "The electromagnetic signal is just too strong for our electronics to handle."

"How was the carrier group able to avoid damage?" Denise asked.

"We're a few miles away," Grimes answered, "and our systems are well shielded."

388

"Have you analyzed the signal?" Will asked.

Grimes nodded. "It's stronger than anything we've seen, save a nuclear E-M pulse. About every few minutes there's a blast at all frequencies – radio to microwave wavelengths. Between blasts, it continuously broadcasts an encoded signal at a few discrete frequencies. That's all we know – we can't decode it."

"Has it changed at all since it started?" Will asked, wondering if it was another countdown.

"No," Grimes replied. "Just keeps repeating the same broadcast."

The term *broadcast* gave Will a sick feeling. The first two probes sent out signals intended for people on earth – sound waves in water. This one was broadcasting radio waves to the entire universe. Earth would look like a lighthouse to anyone who could detect the signal.

Will described what had happened inside the probe, and his conversation with the being – the Judge. It seemed that everyone believed him – no skeptics this time. Their expressions and body language projected worry, except for those of Grimes, whose face became stern.

"I don't see what else you could have done," Jonathan said.

"The question is what's going to happen next," Grimes said. "And when."

Will turned to Daniel. "What about the White Stone inscription? Did you find the book?"

Daniel shook his head and sighed. "We didn't bring the book by Schwinger back with us," he said. "It must be on the shelves at the base."

"We'll have to go back," Will said.

"That's not an option," Grimes said. "The *North Dakota* is disabled, and we're not sending another sub through the tunnel."

"Too risky?" Will asked, annoyed. "Do you see what's going on here?"

Denise grabbed Will's hand. "We're going to try to decipher it ourselves," she said. "The languages expert is working on it. She says it won't be as difficult as it was in the 1940's – much more is known about ancient languages."

"Why does it matter?" Grimes asked. "We've already done our

part. We needed the information before all of this happened."

It was a valid point, Will thought. But they still needed the information. "While it's true that we've already triggered something, we don't know what we set into action. If we have to go back to the base to figure it out, it would be worth it." Will looked to the others. "Let's hope our expert can crack it."

Just then, a young sailor entered the room and whispered something in Grimes' ear.

Grimes stood. "Let's go."

"What is it?" Daniel asked.

"The beacon stopped its broadcast," Grimes said. "It's descending."

~ 6 ~

Saturday, 13 June (9:45 a.m. EST)

The Antarctic air froze the moisture in Will's nose as he stood on the deck of the *Stennis* and squinted toward the dark horizon. A hundred others shivered with him, including Denise, and looked in a direction that felt like west. The carrier group had kept its distance, maybe a mile, but the probe's shadowy image made it seem much closer.

It was shrinking fast. All of the surface ships had beamed floodlights in that direction so that, even at a mile in dark conditions, they could see and hear the white, churning water where the stem of the descending beacon met the surface. Everyone remained perfectly silent for the next 10 minutes, until the spherical head finally plunged beneath the cold waves with an explosive, final splash.

Denise hooked her right arm around Will's left. "My face is numb," she said and pressed her cheek against his shoulder. "What do we do now?"

"Wait," he replied, trying to hide his concern. "Maybe we'll go home now."

Denise nodded, and then tugged at his arm. "Come on, I'm freezing," she said.

Will nodded and followed her. He needed sleep, but knew it would elude him. He feared the memories that would invade his nightmares. Many of those memories weren't even his own.

~ 7 ~

Sunday, 14 June (7:08 a.m. EST)

Will woke up and rubbed his eyes. If he'd dreamt, he didn't remember it. For that he was grateful.

The digital clock taped to the bunk above him read the same time as when he'd first laid his head on the pillow. Twelve hours had passed. It was a restless sleep.

He got out of the rack and showered. His stomach grumbling, he went the mess hall. He made his way through the line and left with a large plate of food. He nibbled on bacon as he looked for a seat. He found Denise sitting alone at a table in a corner and joined her.

"You walked right past me on the way in," she said smiling.

"Sorry, starving," he said. "Where are the others?"

"In the research room," she replied. "The scholar from Stanford, Candice Schilling, is with them."

"Did she say how long it's going to take?" he asked.

She shrugged and shook her head.

"I still think they should go back to the base and collect everything," he said, shaking his head. "They might have missed something other than the book."

"I agree," she said. "What do you think is coming next?"

He shrugged. "Nothing good. The probe sent out a signal to start the process. It means that, whatever's coming, it's coming from the outside."

"Outside of earth?"

He nodded.

They ate in silence for a few minutes. Denise left the table and returned with a bagel. "Are you coming back to Chicago when we get back?" she asked.

He hadn't given much thought to going anywhere. "I have some things to finish up in Louisiana."

She narrowed her eyes. "Going after Syncorp?"

"I have to tie up some loose ends, that's all," he replied. He was going to destroy Syncorp, but first he'd collect every bit of information he could find. He was going to find out whether the computers that Adler had used to bait him really existed.

She nodded and pursed her lips. "Is it another woman?"

The question caught him off guard. "Sure," he said, and shook his head slowly and laughed. "With all that's happening, I had time to find a woman on the side."

"Can I come with you?"

It was something he hadn't considered. Under normal conditions, there was nothing he'd like more than to spend time with her. He nodded. "If we get back before the world is destroyed."

"I'd like to be able to laugh at that," she said.

"Don't you have Foundation work to get back to in Chicago?"

"At this point, the Foundation is no longer my first concern," she replied. "I don't even know if I could function – my mind would be elsewhere."

He knew it would be the same for him. Although the world seemed peaceful for the moment something could come at any time.

Will caught a glimpse of Jonathan entering the cafeteria with a large plastic mug. "Looks like we have company," he said, and nodded in Jonathan's direction.

Denise looked over her shoulder and then waved her hand to get Jonathan's attention.

Jonathan filled his mug with coffee and walked over. "You two going to join us?" he asked, standing at the head of the table. "With the help of our expert, they're making some headway."

"Anything new?" Will asked. "Or just confirmation of what has already happened?"

Jonathan shrugged. "Not sure," he admitted. "But it's interesting, and we have a week to kill as we sail back to civilization."

Will laughed. "You always need a puzzle, don't you?"

"Keeps the brain alive," Jonathan replied. "Let's go."

They followed Jonathan to the research room. Most of the crates had been moved out since the last time Will was there, including the one with the urn.

Daniel and Sylvia greeted them as they entered and, although he'd seen her before, they formally introduced him to Dr. Candice Schilling, the ancient languages expert. She was a short, heavy-set woman with long gray hair wrapped in a bun. Her thick glasses magnified her dark eyes. She looked at him in what seemed to be both awe and suspicion. She'd been there for Grimes' cup demonstration.

The White Stone was on a felt cloth in the middle of a table. Depressed into its smooth, off-white surface were five rings of black symbols. Each looked to be of a different type of script, and they got longer as they went towards the outer part of the disk – the outer ring being the longest by virtue of geometry.

He looked at the outermost ring and read it – just as if he knew the language in which it was written. "To find the probe, divide the angles in units of radians along latitude and longitude," he read aloud. "Zero longitude intersects the place where the stone was discovered, zero latitude at the equator. Follow the drum to the probe." He then read aloud the numbers locating its exact position.

Dr. Schilling glanced at her notes, and then back to Will. "That's very close," she said. "You've read the notebooks?"

Will shook his head. "It's not just *close*," he said. He'd never studied ancient languages, but he knew immediately how he was able to read the script. It was from the Judge's imprint. The knowledge of the scripts just came to him.

He examined the second circle. "The inner void is accessed in the evanescent state. Evanescence is achieved by transcending mind and body."

Dr. Schilling looked at him, surprised. "How did you get that last line?" she asked and looked to Sylvia. "Transcending could also be interpreted as suffering. Did you guys have that already?"

Sylvia, looking pale now, shook her head.

"No," Will said. "The word is *transcending*."

"How can you be sure?" Schilling asked, doubtingly.

"Third," Will continued. "Turn the switch to summon the Judge. In three days you will be called again. Enter the orb before it recedes and seals your fate."

"Where are you getting this from?" Dr. Schilling asked, her voice raised and she seemed flustered.

"Fourth," Will said. "Should you fail, your world will be destroyed and renewed. Judgment is imminent."

"How are you doing this, Will?" Denise asked, trying to get closer to him.

Will stuck out his arm and shook his head for her to stop. "Five," he said, and read the innermost ring. "If you should pass, the casting shall commence."

"What does it mean?" Denise asked no one in particular.

Schilling paged frantically through her notes. "What he's saying is consistent with the fragments I've deciphered, as well as those from the notebooks taken from the base."

Will explained what the Judge had told him about the casting of souls. When he was finished, they all stared at him, except for Sylvia who had been writing it all down.

"Looks like we're at the fourth ring – and will never experience the fifth," Will said.

"I don't understand how you are able to do this," Dr. Schilling said. "This needs to be verified."

"It's correct," Will said. "But I don't know what good it does us. We needed this information long before I accessed the probe. Now we're at the inner ring, and it's not meant for us. It's too late."

Daniel cleared his throat and stood. "Maybe we should have

394

stayed in the south," he said. "What if another one appears?"

Will doubted there would be another probe. They should instead be looking to the stars.

CHAPTER XVII

~ 1 ~

Friday, 19 June (3:17 p.m. CST – Baton Rouge)

Summer in Baton Rouge beat winter in Antarctica.

Having Denise around brightened Will's mood, even with the threat on the horizon. At times, everything that had happened concerning the probe seemed like a distant dream. Other times, his head pounded with anxiety, as if he were watching a nuclear bomb drop from the sky above a city.

The sun beat down on them as he and Denise walked across the courtyard of his apartment complex and passed by the pool.

"Looks like the FBI set you up well," she said, admiring the fountain pouring water from the hot tub to the cool, blue water of the pool.

"Yeah, and in more than one way," Will said, referring to Roy and Natalie Tate, and the leaks.

Denise sighed and shook her head. "Jonathan vetted the agents who will be helping us with this."

Jonathan and CIA Director Thackett had gotten the FBI to move on Syncorp. They'd already gotten the warrants, and the NSA had already tapped into all electronic communications. No more data was getting to China. More shipments had gone out, and were allowed to do so as to not draw alarm, but they were being tracked. They'd be stopped when the operation commenced.

Will knew there was a chance that Cho had warned Syncorp that they'd been discovered, and ordered his minions to destroy evidence. He also could have set up a dead man's switch – a protocol that would set certain events into action if he failed to check in. In this case, it would be a literal interpretation of the device – Cho having burned to death on the deck of the Chinese carrier. Will had warned the FBI to move quickly, yet they still dragged.

Jonathan was arriving at Baton Rouge airport that evening to help direct the sack on Syncorp. His official position was that of legal advisor, as was Denise's. Will, on the other hand, was still on the FBI payroll.

Their first objective was to collect all of Syncorp's information. He hoped they'd find new information regarding impending events, but knew it was unlikely. The alternative was to sit and wait, and he was no good at that, and neither were Jonathan and Denise.

His second objective, unbeknownst to anyone, was to destroy everything at Syncorp – every instrument, computer, and production device in the place, as well as any products they had in stock.

"Should we get Jonathan's room ready?" Denise asked.

"It's ready," he replied. Jonathan would stay with them in his apartment. There was a sofa bed in the office. "Let's take a walk and then hit the pool."

"Okay," Denise said. "Where are we going?"

Will grabbed her hand and led her around the pool and through the clubhouse to the front of the complex. They took a left on a sidewalk, went through a gate, and stepped onto the asphalt running track.

"Pretty hot," Denise said.

Will nodded. "The pool will feel good afterwards. I just wanted to show you the rest of this place. There's another pool on the other side of the complex, and even a putting green with sand trap."

"You golf?" she asked.

"Not much," he replied.

They took a bend to the left, went north about 75 yards, and then another bend to the west. After 50 yards, live oaks from the cemetery on their right shaded them from the sun. Will was about to say something when he was distracted by something to his right. He thought he saw movement in the vines of the cemetery fence. He stopped and looked.

"What?" Denise asked.

"Thought I saw something."

He listened for a few seconds and then continued walking. He was about to ask her a question when he again detected movement to his right. He stopped and took a step closer to the fence.

"What is it?" Denise asked.

Will shook his head. "I don't know," he said. "I feel like ... well ... like we're being watched."

"You're scaring me," Denise said. "That's just an old cemetery."

The feeling became stronger and stronger, and goose bumps broke out on his arms despite the heat.

He walked to a bench on the inside of the track and sat down, facing north, towards the graveyard. He patted the bench next to him and Denise took a seat to his left.

He closed his eyes.

"What are you doing?" she asked.

"I need to check this out," he said. "Don't let me fall over."

He lowered his sunglasses from the top of his head to his eyes and separated.

In an instant he was 10 feet above his body, looking down on the two of them on the bench. He ascended above the live oaks of the graveyard and went to the northwest corner. He descended slowly, and watched for movement around the fence.

As he dropped through the thick interleaved canopies of the trees, a dark epiphany overcame him as he realized what he saw before him.

Hundreds of wraith-like ghosts were staring out the long, wrought-iron fence, next to the track. They seemed to be watching him and Denise, sitting on the bench.

He approached them from behind. When he got within 20 yards, one turned and moved towards him – not in a threatening way. The rest quickly surrounded him from all directions, including from above. Although the wraiths were similar many respects, they were also distinctly different. Their luminous features changed with time, but most assumed a human-like appearance. They looked frightened.

He remained still as they examined him. A static sound seemed to build and he realized they were all talking. He couldn't tell what they were saying.

One of the ghosts came forward, and the hundreds of others backed away to give him room. It was of human form, but looked different than the others. Will didn't recognize the being, although it reminded him of the Judge.

"Do I know you?" Will asked.

"You should," the wraith said. "It wasn't that long ago."

He recognized the voice. "Landau?" Will asked.

"Yes."

Will thought he might be dreaming, or going insane. Ever since his first encounter with him in the Red Box, he was never certain whether Landau was real or just a voice in his head. "What are you doing here?"

"Completing my task," Landau said. "Why do you think you are here?"

Will couldn't answer the question.

"Did you ever figure out where you were on July 19th, 1952?" Landau asked.

Landau had asked him that question repeatedly while in the Red Box, and it often seeped into his thoughts whenever he had a moment to think. His answer was always the same. "No," he replied. "I hadn't been born yet." He was concerned with the future, not the past.

"Everything is how it is supposed to be," Landau said. "You are where you are supposed to be."

"I don't understand," Will said. "Why are all of these ... people ... here?"

"Judgment has been passed," Landau said. "They have returned to accept their sentence."

The crowd of wraiths grumbled in what Will perceived as a tone of anger and fear.

"What is your purpose?" Will asked. "Why are *you* here?"

"I am the Shepherd," Landau replied.

"I don't understand."

"I take freed souls to a place of rest," Landau explained. "And I bring them back when is time."

Landau ascended 100 feet into the air and Will followed. The others remained where they were.

"I can no longer help you," Landau said.

"Help me?" Will asked. "You didn't help me! You're the reason I can separate. You're the reason I pulled that switch!"

"You are their only hope."

"What hope?" Will asked. "We are doomed."

"There would have been someone else within three years," Landau said. "The orb would have been activated."

"Cho – the Chinese?"

"Yes."

"But we're taking down their program."

"It is too late."

"So what does it matter who pulled the switch?" Will asked. "The answer to the question would have been the same – sealing our own demise. "

"The judgment is justified," Landau said. "But is not a punishment at all. It is a demonstration of compassion."

"What?"

"Can you imagine what the world would be like if others had your powers?"

Will could only envision violence on a scale never seen before.

"If a species is allowed to continue once it has transformed, unless it occurred through enlightenment, it will consume itself," Landau said. "It is indisputable. I have witnessed it."

"When will it happen – the regeneration?" Will asked.

"I cannot say," Landau said. "But there is still something that can be done."

"What – how?"

"By not taking the Judge's offer to save yourself, you have won the possibility for a reprieve of sorts," Landau said. "I knew you wouldn't take the bribe. That's why I selected you."

"Why didn't you tell me before it happened?"

"It had to come from you," Landau replied. "And the Judge would have known – he took your memories. I also knew you would recognize the opportunity to acquire the Judge's memories."

"I remember nothing from that," Will said, although he knew

something had to be there after he'd read the White Stone.

"It might seem inaccessible, but it is in your mind."

"What do you mean a reprieve 'of sorts'?"

"You can still avert destruction," Landau said, "and replace it with individual judgment."

"What does that mean?"

"Your actions in the orb have opened this possibility," Landau explained. "It illustrates that there might be some worth saving in your world – worth an individual look, so to speak."

"What about my actions on the Chinese ship" Will said, "what does that illustrate? I've killed many."

"You, too, will be judged," Landau replied. "If you earn that privilege."

"How can individuals be judged? On what information – evidence?"

"The imprint of a soul tells all," Landau explained. "It reveals everything from context to intention for every instant of a soul's existence. The Judge will see everything, and make a verdict."

"I will fail."

"Perhaps," Landau said. "Perhaps not. But it is worth your effort – for those who do not deserve a blanket judgment."

"What do I need to do?" Will asked with great anxiety.

"I cannot say," Landau said. "But I truly hope you find the way."

With that, Landau shot into the sky like a shooting star.

Will went back to his body and awakened next to Denise.

"How long was I out?" he asked.

"A minute," she said. "You look spooked. What did you see?"

He stood. "Please, let's go," he said and glanced towards the cemetery. He felt them staring at him.

"What happened?"

"Later," he said. "Please, let's go."

He grabbed her hand and took her away with him.

~ 2 ~
Friday, 19 June (5:10 p.m. CST)

Will awakened from what was supposed to be a short nap. He'd apparently been more exhausted than he'd thought after his encounter in the cemetery. It was just after 5 p.m., and he assumed Denise was still in the exercise room. He put on his swimming trunks and headed for the pool.

Seeing Landau notwithstanding, at some level he'd known what he was going to find in the cemetery. Perhaps that intuition originated from the imprinted memory he'd stolen from the Judge. The Judge's memory seemed to come through in his dreams, which had become more bizarre than anything he'd ever experienced. In the latest one, he dreamt he'd been stranded in a desert and, when he looked to the sky, it was clear he wasn't on Earth. In another, he'd fallen out of an aircraft into the night, and landed in the water near a small island. Most had elements of panic and doom, feelings that wouldn't fade until he'd been awake for hours.

He grabbed a towel and made his way to the pool. He took a quick dive into the deep end, and floated on his back and paddled lightly with his eyes closed, letting the final sliver of the late afternoon sun saturate his vision through his eyelids. It was an escape, if only for a second, to a place where he had no worries.

A few minutes later, the snapping sound of flip-flops came from behind him and got louder. He looked up to see Denise heading his way from the clubhouse. She put her things on a chair, sat on the edge of the pool, and dangled her feet in the water.

"It's nice," she said. "How long have you been here?"

"Just got in," he replied. "Getting hungry?" He wanted to talk about what he'd seen in the cemetery, but decided to postpone that conversation until they'd picked up Jonathan from the airport.

"Starved, but let's relax for a few minutes," she said. "I want to try

402

out the pool and hot tub."

"How about the pool now, and the hot tub after dinner when it's a bit cooler?"

"Sounds great," she said and stood. She removed her shorts and shirt, revealing a green, one-piece swimsuit. She tied her dark hair into a tight ponytail, which hung to the middle of her back. She was thin and fit, and her smile completed the image.

She made eye contact with him. "What?" she asked.

"Brains *and* beauty," he said, and smiled.

She jumped in and met him in the deep end. She had to paddle to keep her head above water. "You're not too bad yourself," she replied, and put her hands around his neck.

He started to say something but she stopped his lips with her own. After a few seconds she stopped and smiled at him. "I wanted to do that long ago."

"Me too," he said. He'd thought about it a lot when he left Chicago, and had decided that her safety was more important that developing a relationship with her. But things had changed. For the most part, the immediate danger of Syncorp and foreign operatives had subsided. A more devastating threat loomed in the near future, but affected everyone equally. Their time together might be short, so he decided to make the best of it.

She put her legs around his waist, hugged his neck tightly, and pressed her cheek against his. "Time to pick up Jonathan," she said, letting go and swimming for the edge.

He grabbed her ankle before she could get away, and pulled her back.

She yelped.

He let her go, only to grab her ankle again.

"I can't touch bottom here!" she yelled, laughing.

He let her kick herself free and then followed her to the edge. They got out, dried off, and collected their things. They went up to the apartment, showered, changed, and headed to the airport.

Jonathan's flight was late, and it was almost 8 p.m. by the time they departed Baton Rouge airport and headed back to the city. All were famished, and Will's suggestion of Cajun food was met with unanimous agreement.

He took them to a popular restaurant, just a few doors down from the Bullfrog, the bar that had been frequented by the gang of former Compressed Punishment inmates. He still wondered what exactly had happened to those men, and he felt guilty that he'd likely contributed to their demise by turning them in to the FBI. Roy was probably the leak from that side, and he was satisfied that the traitor had gotten what he'd deserved, along with Natalie Tate. He was ashamed, however, that he'd been the one to carry it out.

Jonathan informed him that Cho had died on the deck of the Chinese carrier. Will already knew. It was a killing he found difficult to regret. The man who'd killed Adler, and who was likely responsible for the massacre of the CP men, was identified as Lenny Butrolsky, a notorious Syncorp thug and former KGB assassin. It was the same man Jonathan had shot in shoulder in a hospital in southern Illinois. The animal was nowhere to be found.

There was a 30 minute wait to get a table, so Will got drinks for the three of them. When he returned, Jonathan and Denise were chatting on an outdoor bench under a pergola, adjacent to the restaurant bar. He handed them their drinks and leaned against a railing next to Denise. The stars peeked out of the purple eastern sky, and the cool breeze was sweet with the spicy aromas of Cajun cuisine. He breathed in deeply and sighed. It seemed odd to be back in normal life after what they'd been through.

"Tell us what you saw in the cemetery," Denise said.

Jonathan raised an eyebrow and looked at Will.

"Something has changed," he said, glancing back and forth between the two of them. "It seems they've all come back."

"Who has come back?" Jonathan asked.

"The people buried there – everyone who has died," Will responded.

Denise's dark complexion turned pale. "The dead are returning?"

Will nodded. "Seems so. But I want to check out some other

places. Another cemetery. Think about how many billions of people have lived and died on earth."

"Why are they here?" Denise asked, visibly shaking now.

"Awaiting the outcome," Will said. "If we'd been judged positively, this would all be over. If I hadn't pulled that switch, this wouldn't be happening at all …"

"If it wasn't you, it would've been someone else – eventually," Jonathan said.

Will knew that to be true – according to Landau.

"Do you think the judgment would have been different 100 years from now?" Jonathan continued. "Maybe we'd be the souls coming back awaiting punishment, but it would be in the hands of someone else. I don't know about you, but I'd rather be around to do something about it."

"Your pocket sounds like it's vibrating," Denise said and pointed to Will's shirt.

He hadn't had a phone call in weeks, and had only been carrying the phone by habit – it was a burner phone. He hadn't given out the number to anyone except Natalie Tate, and she was dead. He looked at the number; it wasn't one he recognized but he knew the 202 area code – Washington, DC. He answered.

"Dr. Thompson?" a man said.

Will recognized the voice as that of Daniel Parsons.

"Daniel?" Will replied. His heart twisted in his chest. News was coming.

"We need you to come to DC immediately," Daniel said. "Tickets are waiting for you at Baton Rouge airport under your alias. You still have your alias passport?"

"Yes."

"Good," Daniel replied. "Your flight leaves in 90 minutes."

Will hung up and looked at the clock. His stomach burned with hunger. He'd explain everything Landau had told him to Denise and Jonathan as they ate.

~ 3 ~

Saturday, 20 June (1:22 a.m. EST – Washington)

Will met Daniel at the ground transportation area of Reagan International Airport around 1:30 a.m. They drove to a large, nondescript building in a business district outside of Alexandria, Virginia. Daniel hadn't given him any specific information during the 30 minute car ride.

After going through a maze of security like he'd never seen before, they arrived at large, comfortably furnished room a little after 2:15 a.m. Sylvia and a man Will recognized but couldn't place sat on leather furniture surrounding a coffee table.

"I'd like you to meet James Thackett, Director of CIA," Daniel said to Will.

Thackett stood and held out his hand. "William Thompson," he said. "It's a pleasure to meet you."

As they shook hands, Will wished he could say the same in return, but his distrust of the CIA superseded any niceties he could conjure. It had taken him a while to tolerate Sylvia and Daniel.

"Please, sit, pour yourself some coffee," Thackett said. "We have a lot to discuss." He turned to Daniel. "Get it started."

Daniel's eyes focused on Will, implying the others already knew what was coming. Sylvia looked sick – even more pale than usual – revealing the tone of what he was about to hear.

"We don't have many details," he began. "But we got a signal."

Will remained silent.

"Radio waves," Daniel explained. "The signal appears in the center of the AM band – it can be heard between 1140 and 1150 on AM radio around the world. The frequency of the amplitude modulation is around 1000 Hertz – highly pitched to our naked ears, but detectable."

"So it should be easy to locate," Will said. "Land based?"

Daniel and Sylvia glanced at each other.

Daniel continued. "Yes, I suppose it is."

Will looked back and forth between Sylvia and Daniel. Thackett looked into his coffee mug, waiting for Daniel to deliver the punch line.

"What?" Will asked. "What am I missing?"

"It's coming from Mars," Sylvia finally blurted out.

"Actually," Daniel added, "that's the origin of the *closest* one. We've detected three so far, the other two are from empty space – unknown sources – beyond the solar system."

It took Will a few seconds to process the statement. His mind went into overdrive following multiple threads of possible consequences. It all boiled down to one thing.

"Signaling us?" Will asked. "Or *someone else?*"

"We don't know," Daniel replied, shaking his head. "But we think it's another countdown – the frequency is shifting."

"How long do we have?" Will asked, worried about what he was going to hear next.

"A little more than four years," Sylvia said.

"And you're going to try to send someone there?" Will said.

Everyone was quiet, but kept their eyes on Will. Thackett finally broke the silence. "Possibly to the closest one – Mars."

Thackett's face still seemed distorted, and then Will understood. "You're going to send me."

Thackett nodded. "It's too early to tell, but yes."

"Can we even do that?" Will asked. "We don't even have a manned space program. We can't even get to the moon."

"We've already spoken with the President," Thackett said. "NASA is about to be the most highly funded agency of the U.S. government."

Will shook his head. "Is there enough time?" he asked. "It takes three to four months at best, and that's expending a lot of fuel."

"That's out of our area of expertise," Daniel said.

"NASA is working up a plan," Thackett added.

Daniel pulled out a laptop and started it. "A European Space Agency satellite currently orbiting Mars was able to locate the probe and take a picture." He tapped on the keyboard, set the computer on the coffee table, and turned it towards Will.

Will pulled it closer and looked at the reddish image. It was fuzzy, but recognizable. There was a white object that resembled a water tower protruding from the red surface, near one of the poles. He nodded and pushed the computer away. "Looks like the others," he said. If it were sending out a signal to initiate an event, or to attract something, it would have to be deactivated. And, based on the construction of the other probes, only *he* could do such a thing.

"We need to protect you," Daniel said. "Whatever we're able to accomplish regarding a Mars mission will be for naught if you're not the one going."

"And you're existence is not a secret," Sylvia added. "Any country that's suspicious of our motives, or wants to get there themselves, will try to acquire you."

Or kill me, Will thought.

"Not to mention the lunatics that will want to hold the entire world hostage," Thackett said. "Kidnap you and threaten to kill you unless they get what they want."

"And there are some that just want the world to end," Sylvia said. "They'll to want to kill you just to make sure it happens."

It was clear that they'd thought about it. "How do we proceed?" Will asked.

Thackett cleared his throat. "We're going to need you to stay with us from this point forward."

"With CIA?" Will asked. "You realize that they – *you* – are responsible for everything. You made me."

"We understand your problems with the CIA," Daniel interrupted.

"I wasn't the CIA director when Red Wraith was active," Thackett said in his defense. "I had no idea what was going on when I started here. You'll be with the Omniscient group, and answer only to me. I will personally be responsible for you."

"You'll eventually need astronaut training," Daniel added. "But that won't start until two years out, unless they need you for something specific."

"I want Denise Walker and Jonathan McDougal with me," Will said.

"You can have whatever you want," Thackett said. "We can't force them, but we'll make them a good offer."

"It might be hard to drag Jonathan away from the DNA Foundation," Sylvia added.

Will thought otherwise; Jonathan would be in with both feet. Too much was at stake, and he was there to witness the origin of it all. He'd see it through, as would Denise.

"Then I'm in," Will said. "What do I do now?"

"You can start by giving me your mobile phone," Thackett said, holding out his hand.

Will pulled it out of his pocket and handed it to him.

Thackett took it and removed the battery and the chip. He then reached in his own pocket and handed Will a flat black phone. "This is the most secure device we have," Thackett said. "Our numbers are programmed in, as are Denise's and Jonathan's."

An electronic beeping sound emanated from Will's right. He looked at Thackett, and then to Daniel and Sylvia. They all looked confused.

The door opened, and an old man walked in.

"What the hell?" Thackett said, obviously surprised. "Horace?"

Will remained seated as the others stood.

"Are you well?" Sylvia asked, concerned.

"No," Horace replied. "But I had to see him." The old man pointed at Will.

"How did you know we were here?" Thackett asked.

Horace ignored Thackett's question and approached Will. "It's all in your hands, lad," he said, his voice weak and trembling. He held out his hand to shake.

Will stood, walked to Horace, and gently grasped the man's hand.

Thackett asked again. "How did you know we were here, Horace?"

Horace answered Thackett's question, but looked at Will. "Landau told me," he said.

Will flinched and let go of Horace's hand. "You spoke with him?" It didn't make sense. Will wasn't able to communicate with Landau unless he separated. "How?"

"I'm 98," Horace replied. "I'm dying."

Will stared at him, confused.

"He is the Shepherd," Horace said.

Sylvia gasped in recognition of Horace's words.

Will recalled that Landau had referred to himself as "the Shepherd" in the cemetery.

"*Death is the shepherd of mankind,*" Horace said. "Does that phrase mean anything to you?"

"No," Will replied

Sylvia's face distorted. "It's written above the entrance to the torture facility at the Nazi base."

"No matter," Horace said. "I can't say more, and I'm on borrowed time."

"You're going to die?" Sylvia asked in a meek voice.

Horace nodded. "The reason I came," he said, looking to Will, "Landau wanted me to deliver a message to you, as payment for my extra few hours of life."

"Yes?" Will said. His eyes locked in on Horace's.

"Go to the Nazi base," Horace said. "You will find answers there – about yourself and, more importantly, about the things to come."

"There are thousands of books and files," Daniel said. "It will take years to go through it all."

Horace continued. "According to Landau, what you are doing now was your purpose from the beginning. You were there, at that base, on July 19th, 1952."

The words made Will dizzy. "What?" Will asked. "How? What was I doing there?"

"He didn't say," Horace replied. "But that date means something to you?"

"Yes," Will replied. "It means something."

"My name, *Horace*, means *timekeeper*," Horace said. "And I'm telling you now that the age is ending. I do not know what the new age will bring, but you, William, will determine the future." Horace coughed and wiped his mouth with a handkerchief. "I'd better be getting back," he said as he shook everyone's hands, said goodbye, and left. His journey was at an end.

Sylvia wiped a tear from her cheek. "Why did he ask you those questions?" she asked.

"I'll explain another time," Will replied. He looked to Thackett. "I need to sleep."

Thackett nodded. "I think you'll like what we've set up for you."

"Secure?" Will asked.

"Yes," Thackett replied, smiling. "We want you to stay in this building for the night. If you like it, you can stay for good."

At this point, Will didn't care if they gave him a cot in a bathroom under a train station. He knew he was exhausted when he could only hold one eyelid open. The right eye always closed first when he was tired. It was closed now.

Thackett led the way.

~ 4 ~

Saturday, 20 June (3:29 a.m. CST)

Will followed Thackett into a room that looked like the penthouse suite of an ultramodern hotel.

"The kitchen is stocked with some basics in case you're hungry," Thackett said. "I'll let you figure out where everything is. Please, don't leave this room tonight. It will trigger some security responses that we really don't want to deal with right now."

Will agreed and Thackett left.

The room was magnificent. It took up the entire southeastern corner of the floor, about thirty stories up. The two outside walls were floor to ceiling windows, and he admired the moonlight beaming in from the southwest, and the stars in the east.

He adjusted the brightness of the recessed ceiling lights, illuminating a large couch facing the south windows. He needed a shower and sleep, but instead he sat down and leaned back, spreading his arms to either side along the back of the couch. The stretch felt good, and he yawned deeply, staring blankly into the night.

Looking back, he realized that he'd spent most of his life looking for purpose. Once one eliminated all of the distractions, responsibilities, desires, and fears, all that was left was a question: *Why do we exist? What is our purpose? Where does it all lead?*

The answers to those questions were just over the horizon, as they'd been from the beginning, and as they might always be.

Will found the bed, closed his eyes, and dreamt.

TIMELINE

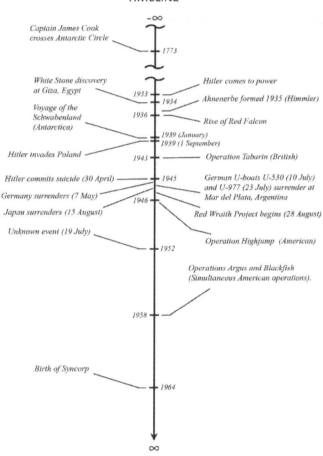

$-\infty$

Captain James Cook
crosses Antarctic Circle

1773

White Stone discovery
at Giza, Egypt

1933

Hitler comes to power

1934

Ahnenerbe formed 1935 (Himmler)

Voyage of the
Schwabenland
(Antarctica)

1936

Rise of Red Falcon

1939 (January)
1939 (1 September)

Hitler invades Poland

1943

Operation Tabarin (British)

Hitler commits suicide (30 April)

1945

German U-boats U-530 (10 July)
and U-977 (23 July) surrender at
Mar del Plata, Argentina

Germany surrenders (7 May)

1946

Japan surrenders (15 August)

Red Wraith Project begins (28 August)

Unknown event (19 July)

1952

Operation Highjump (American)

Operations Argus and Blackfish
(Simultaneous American operations).

1958

Birth of Syncorp

1964

∞

About the Author

Shane Stadler grew up in southern Wisconsin. After graduating from Beloit College (WI) in 1992, he earned a Ph.D. in experimental physics at Tulane University in 1998. He has since worked at numerous government research and defense laboratories, and is currently a professor of physics at Louisiana State University.

DARK HALL PRESS

Dark Hall seeks to promote a diverse body of quality works, advancing the tradition of Horror storytelling as well as providing exposure for up-and-coming writers.

Visit us online at

darkhallpress.com

Printed in Great Britain
by Amazon.co.uk, Ltd.,
Marston Gate.